CAPTURE

Also by Robert K. Tanenbaum

Fiction

Escape
Malice
Counterplay
Fury
Hoax
Resolved
Absolute Rage
Enemy Within
True Justice
Act of Revenge
Reckless Endangerment
Irresistible Impulse
Falsely Accused
Corruption of Blood
Justice Denied
Material Witness
Reversible Error
Immoral Certainty
Depraved Indifference
No Lesser Plea

Nonfiction

The Piano Teacher: The True Story of a Psychotic Killer
Badge of the Assassin

ROBERT K. TANENBAUM

CAPTURE

POCKET BOOKS
New York London Toronto Sydney

Pocket Books
A Division of Simon & Schuster, Inc.
1230 Avenue of the Americas
New York, NY 10020

This book is a work of fiction. Names, characters, places, and incidents either are products of the author's imagination or are used fictitiously. Any resemblance to actual events or locales or persons, living or dead, is entirely coincidental.

First Pocket Books hardcover edition June 2009

For information about special discounts for bulk purchases, please contact Simon & Schuster Special Sales at 1-800-456-6798 or business@simonandschuster.com.

Manufactured in the United States of America

10 9 8 7 6 5 4 3 2 1

Library of Congress Cataloging-in-Publication Data

Tanenbaum, Robert.
Capture / Robert K. Tanenbaum.—1st Pocket Books hardcover ed.
p. cm.
ISBN: 978-1-4391-4860-0 (alk. paper)
1. Karp, Butch (Fictitious character)—Fiction. 2. Ciampi, Marlene (Fictitious character)—Fiction. 3. Public prosecutors—Fiction. 4. New York (N.Y.)—Fiction.
I. Title
PS3570.A52C37 2009
813'.54—dc22

2009001736

To those blessings in my life;
Patti, Rachael, Roger, and Billy;
and
To the loving Memory of
Reina Tanenbaum
My sister, truly an angel

ACKNOWLEDGMENTS

To my legendary mentors, District Attorney Frank S. Hogan and Henry Robbins, both of whom were larger in life than in their well-deserved and hard earned legends, everlasting gratitude and respect; to my special friends and brilliant tutors at the Manhattan DAO, Bob Lehner, Mel Glass, and John Keenan, three of the best who ever served and whose passion for justice was unequaled and uncompromising, my heartfelt appreciation, respect, and gratitude; to Professor Robert Cole and Professor Jesse Choper, who at Boalt Hall challenged, stimulated, and focused the passions of my mind to problem-solve and do justice; to Steve Jackson, an extraordinarily talented and gifted scrivener whose genius flows throughout the manuscript and whose contribution to it cannot be overstated, a dear friend for whom I have the utmost respect; to Louise Burke, my publisher, whose enthusiastic support, savvy, and encyclopedic smarts qualify her as my first pick in a game of three on three in the Ave. P park in Brooklyn; to Wendy Walker, my talented, highly skilled, and insightful editor, many thanks for all that you do; to my agents, Mike Hamilburg and Bob Diforio, who in exemplary fashion have always represented my best interests; and to Paul Ryan, who personified "American Exceptionalism" and mentored me in its finest virtues.

CAPTURE

PROLOGUE

Hilario "Harry" Gianneschi leaned on the concierge desk at the Poliziano Fiera Hotel in Tribeca and stared forlornly down the hallway toward the hotel bar, enviously listening to the laughter and pulsating music. It seemed like every few minutes he saw pretty, well-dressed young women—alone, in pairs, or in groups of three or four—enter the lobby and make their long-legged way to the lounge, disappearing, sadly, from his view.

He sighed. Instead of working, he would have much preferred to be cruising the bar himself, using his dark, Italian good looks, runner's body, and charming accent to bed one of the beauties. And continue his search for *"l'amore della mia vita,"* he whispered to himself.

Although happily playing the field at present, he hoped someday to find "the one" to marry—preferably wealthy. *And blessed with generous breasts and wide baby-maker hips. . . .* Il mio dio, per favore. . . . *My God, please, is that so much to ask?*

His smile faded into a frown. Of course, his new wife had to be an American, too. As a native of Florence, the twenty-four-year-old Gianneschi had arrived in the United States some five years earlier on a student visa. But he'd dropped out after his first semester at NYU, and his visa had long since expired. That made him an illegal alien and subject to deportation.

But what am I to do? Despite his mother's pleas, he had no desire to return to Italy. He liked America and Americans—their optimism and generosity of spirit. He'd been told before he came that New Yorkers were cold, that they wouldn't give him the time of day, that they would watch callously while robbers took everything he had, including his life. But that had proved to be a big lie. Yes, there were criminals and rude people, places one did not go on the island of Manhattan unless you had a death wish. But most New Yorkers seemed more than willing to help a newcomer. The people he talked to were curious about where he'd come from, particularly if they were of Italian extraction, and even asked what he wanted to do with his life. No one in Italy, except his family, gave a rat's ass about his aspirations.

Gianneschi hoped that by marrying an American someday, he would be allowed to remain in the country permanently, and legally. Then he might go back to college, perhaps to study hotel management. Maybe even become a citizen.

He wasn't in a hurry; if he was, he could have persuaded one of his sexual conquests to wed him. Even one of his married admirers would have been only too happy to keep him like an expensive pet. But as a romantic, he wanted to be in love with the woman he asked to be his wife—take her back to Italy to meet his mother and a million other relatives. Then they'd return to America, make lots and lots of babies, and lots and lots of money, and grow old sitting together on the porch of some house in the country, watching their grandchildren play soccer . . . *okay, maybe baseball.*

But until such a woman appeared, he was content to continue as he was. He liked his job as a concierge at what he considered the best hotel on the island. The Poliziano Fiera, named after the famous Poliziano Fiera in Milan, fit neatly into a small triangle of land at the intersection of the Avenue of the Americas and West Broadway. A trendy boutique hotel, it featured a private film screening room with plush seating, surround sound, and state-of-the-art projection. Hollywood glitterati were known to attend premieres at the screening room and then retire to the hotel's bar, the Well, afterward to mingle with the crowd. The Well was located in the atrium, surrounded by the rooms on the floors above, and often featured the latest hot DJ and release parties thrown by the record companies for their artists.

He'd been working at the hotel for two years and was a favorite with the management and guests for his encyclopedic knowledge of New York City's hot spots and dining. Especially well versed on where to go in Tribeca, he explained to visitors that the name was a condensation of "Triangle Below Canal," and that it referred to the pie-shaped neighborhood running from Canal Street south to Park Place and from the Hudson River east to Broadway. It had once been an industrial area dominated by warehouses, but over the past twenty years had undergone reconstructive surgery, yielding expensive loft apartments, trendy bars and restaurants, and hip, intimate hotels like the Poliziano Fiera.

Celebrity or tourist, he charmed them all with his bright, white smile and heartfelt "*Benvenuto indietro!* . . . Welcome back!" when they returned to the hotel. He enjoyed talking to people and helping them with their problems.

However, he thought with another sigh, *there's no one to talk to now*. Only the torture of listening to women's voices tinkling like crystal from the Well. *If only* . . . His fantasy was interrupted by the sudden, urgent flashing of a red light on his telephone. Apparently, the occupant of the penthouse was trying to get his attention.

Harry sighed again, only this time out of reluctance to answer the phone. Mr. F. Lloyd Maplethorpe could try even his legendary patience.

Maplethorpe was a famous Broadway producer of musical theater who'd lived in the penthouse for several years and threw the best parties in the hotel. His credits included hits in the seventies (*Jimi Hendrix: The Musical*), the eighties (*Ronald Reagan: The Musical*), and the nineties (*Bill Clinton: The Musical*). However, it had been ten years since his last hit, years that had witnessed several short runs and an unmitigated flop, *Saddam Hussein: The Musical*. According to the hotel staff gossips, the word on Broadway was that Maplethorpe was getting desperate. His financial backers were getting cold feet after a decade of only breaking even or losing money. One more show with a less than spectacular run, they said, and Maplethorpe was finished.

Gianneschi uncharacteristically thought that such an end to F. Lloyd Maplethorpe's career—and presumably, his stay in the Poliziano Fiera—was fitting. In the fantasy world of the theater, largely made up of self-important and self-absorbed people, Maplethorpe considered himself the most important and treated everyone else like garbage unless they had something he wanted. Or they were willing to prostrate themselves and fawn all over him, at which point they would be tolerated until he grew tired of them.

Maplethorpe was a skinny, odd-looking man in his midsixties and looked every day of it, with a thin, pallid face and waxy skin. His protruding eyes were a washed-out hazel color that he unfortunately emphasized with blue eyeliner. Someone in his entourage had talked him into also using rouge and dying his thinning hair a shade of burnt orange. His eccentricities were legendary in the theater crowd—from his insistence that he personally select each and every actor or actress for his shows, and then changing them on a whim in the middle of a production, to stomping onstage during rehearsals to show an actor "how it's done." He'd once even tried singing a part in one of his own productions until his financial backers told him it wasn't working and that he had to stop or they'd pull their funding. Of course, when he was successful, his little tantrums and interferences had been forgiven as the eccentricities of genius. But of late, the shine had gone off and exposed him as a petty little man who'd pretty much beat to death the idea of turning pop culture artists and headline pols into Broadway musicals.

Harry Gianneschi didn't like him—not because of his appearance or oddities, but because Maplethorpe was as two-faced as a lira in his treatment of the hotel staff. He'd gush all over "the help" if he was showing off, but treat them as if they didn't exist if it suited his mood. He insisted that the "filthy" maids who cleaned his apartment wear rubber surgical gloves at all times, paper booties over their shoes, and face masks, "so I don't have to breathe their germs." And he was constantly asking the staff for favors—such as sending them out to a store at midnight for a bottle of wine or a package of condoms.

He'd once demanded that Gianneschi procure cocaine. *"I'm*

sorry, sir," Gianneschi had replied. *"I would not even know where to look."*

"Oh, come now, a gorgeous little wop like you can't find any party dust?" Maplethorpe replied, smiling at the brunette teenagers, one male and one female, he had draped on either arm.

"No, sir." And if I did, he'd thought, *even if you agreed to appear naked in a Macy's window, I wouldn't get it for you.*

Maplethorpe had narrowed his eyes and turned his back as if Harry no longer existed. Since then, he'd been even cooler toward the concierge and hardly spoke to him unless it was to make some new demand.

Gianneschi had reported the cocaine request to the hotel's management to protect himself in case there was a sudden spate of complaints from the guest in the penthouse suite. He was happy to have as little contact as possible. There was something about the man that made his skin crawl, and he thought Maplethorpe's behavior in the privacy of his apartment probably went beyond merely eccentric.

Maplethorpe reminded him of a spider, with his odd, buggy eyes, his strange physical mannerisms—including sudden twitches, as if his skin itched—and fingers that worked constantly in front of his body as he talked. But as a night concierge, Gianneschi had seen the young women who entered the elevators behind his desk with Maplethorpe. They were always beautiful brunettes—proof, he often thought, that even a man as ugly as the producer could bed well above his station, so long as he had money and/or something else the women wanted.

Such as a role in a musical, Gianneschi thought as he watched the flashing light on the telephone console. New York City was teeming with young women who dreamed of making it as actresses on Broadway. Sometimes it seemed that every pretty waitress he met, or secretary in an office, or woman working behind a counter at Macy's, was really an actress waiting to be discovered. The sad truth, however, was that there weren't enough parts for those who truly did have talent, much less for those who'd once starred in a high school musical and believed their mothers' assurances that they had what it takes.

A tiny fraction ever set foot on the stage, except as part of a tour. Most of the rest were disappointed. The smart ones eventually realized that they weren't going to become stars and found some other line of work if they wanted to remain in New York City. Some even managed to stay near the theater by selling tickets or working behind the scenes. Or they returned home to Lafayette, Indiana; Portland, Oregon; or Muskogee, Oklahoma, got married, had children, and tried out for roles at their local community theater.

But some held on to their dreams until they became desperate. Desperate enough to turn to prostitution—though the prettiest dressed it up a bit by describing themselves as "escorts" who worked for private "gentlemen's clubs" and bragged about how much they could charge to let men use their bodies.

Or desperate enough to follow a disgusting creature like F. Lloyd Maplethorpe up to his suite, hoping that if they fulfilled his fantasies, he'd help them with theirs, Gianneschi thought as he reached for the telephone receiver.

Whatever Maplethorpe did to them in his penthouse didn't seem to trouble some of the women. They'd emerge from the elevator an hour or two later, reapplying their lipstick, straightening their skirts, their expressions smug. But others appeared disheveled, with tears running down their cheeks and frightened looks in their eyes. He'd inquire if they were all right. *"Is there anything I can do?"* But they'd shake their heads and hurry into the night, never to be seen again in the Poliziano Fiera.

Gianneschi wondered if this call had something to do with the woman who'd accompanied Maplethorpe into the hotel that night. She'd seemed a little older than most the producer liked, somewhere in her thirties, but she was a beautiful woman.

Maplethorpe was obviously drunk as he'd tottered toward the concierge desk, but the woman seemed sober. The young concierge thought her face looked familiar. Perhaps she was an actress and he'd seen her in the hotel or in a commercial, but he couldn't quite place her. She smiled and laughed whenever Maplethorpe said something, but her voice sounded strained when she replied to Gianneschi's welcome. *"Thank you, you're very kind."*

Gianneschi pressed the button to summon the elevator for the couple and stepped back. Maplethorpe ignored him as he laughed in his affected way—a staccato "hahahahahahahaha"—at something he'd told his date. As the concierge watched them get on the elevator, his brown eyes locked on to her green ones, which softened for a moment. He thought she looked resigned or bored. Then she shrugged and smiled, as if to say, "What's a girl to do?" The doors closed and she was gone.

An hour later, Gianneschi answered the telephone. "*Buona sera,* Mr. Maplethorpe. How may I be of service?"

At first there was no answer and Gianneschi wondered if they'd been disconnected. Then he heard labored breathing and a small sob.

"Mr. Maplethorpe, are you there?"

"Harry? Is that you?" the man gasped.

"*Sì,* Mr. Maplethorpe," Gianneschi said, preparing for whatever strange request was coming his way.

"Oh thank God. Someone I can trust. . . . Harry, I need you to come up here immediately!"

Gianneschi caught the rising tide of panic in Maplethorpe's voice. Maybe the man was having a heart attack. *Or perhaps a reaction to a Viagra and cocaine cocktail, the dirty old bastard.* "Is there anything wrong? Shall I call an ambulance?"

"No!" The producer nearly shrieked the word. Then he caught himself and continued in a clipped monotone. "Don't call anyone. Just come up here."

"Right away, sir." Gianneschi hung up the telephone and shrugged. At least there didn't seem to be a medical emergency.

On the ride up, he stood with his hands clasped behind his back, rocking on his heels as he wondered what sort of emergency he was about to confront. Maybe the woman had passed out. Or maybe she'd rejected Maplethorpe's advances and was threatening to beat him up.

Now, that I'd like to see, Gianneschi thought with a smile as the elevator door hissed open.

The smile vanished as he found himself looking across the hallway at F. Lloyd Maplethorpe. The producer was waiting for him in the open doorway of his suite dressed in a black-and-white polka-dotted smoking jacket, which fell open as he stretched his arms out to Gianneschi, revealing a thin, concave chest and an odd sort of leather pants that failed to cover his shrunken penis. He was holding a gun in his hand.

"Oh, Harry," the man cried, his eyes bulging with what looked like genuine fear. "I've been bad."

"Bad, Mr. Maplethorpe?"

"Yes, Harry, very bad." Maplethorpe glanced over his shoulder and then back at Gianneschi. "Oh please, tell her I didn't mean to do it."

Gianneschi tried to peer into the apartment but couldn't see much beyond the producer. "Do what, Mr. Maplethorpe?" Fear was starting to creep up his spine. Then he saw the small flecks of red on the producer's right hand and sleeve of his gown. "What did you do?" He wanted to shout at the man, but fought to keep his voice calm.

F. Lloyd Maplethorpe blinked at him, tears melting his eyeliner, which ran in blue rivulets down his cheeks. His lower lip trembled like that of a child. "Do? Why, I . . . I think I killed her."

"I think I killed her." What more did a jury need? Roger "Butch" Karp, the district attorney of New York County, shook his head as he walked in the door of the Third Avenue Synagogue, contemplating his own question. *Apparently, something we didn't give them, or didn't make clear enough.*

Approximately eight months after F. Lloyd Maplethorpe made that statement to an Italian concierge at a Tribeca hotel, a jury had been unable to decide if the Broadway producer had murdered a sometime-actress-slash-waitress named Gail Perez. Just hours earlier that Friday afternoon, Judge Michael Rosenmayer had called the attorneys into his courtroom in the Criminal Courts Building at 100 Centre Street to inform them that the jury was hung and he was declaring a mistrial.

Now we have to do it all over again, Karp thought gloomily as he entered a room where a dozen or so teenage boys and girls chatted and laughed. With the judge's decision coming late in the day, there'd been no time to dissect or digest what had gone wrong in the Maplethorpe trial. Karp had made the decision to send all the players from his office—the assistant district attorney who'd handled the case and Karp's closest advisors—home for the weekend to ruminate over the case and get back to him on Monday.

Then he'd had to hurry to get uptown to the synagogue where as a "Jewish community role model" he regularly conducted a discussion class for teens, including his twin sons, studying for their bar mitzvah and bat mitzvah rites of passage.

He'd been asked to participate in the program by the youth rabbi, Greg Romberg, who had been tragically murdered that past July in a suicide bombing at the synagogue. The killer had been a young Harlem-raised black man who bought into the demagoguery of his so-called spiritual advisor at his 124th Street mosque that Jews were to blame for the world's woes, including his own personal misfortunes, and that killing them was sanctioned by God.

Romberg's death and that of a half dozen others who had gathered that day to worship had shocked a city whose wounds from 9-11 remained raw. However, the bombing had the unintended positive consequence of alerting Karp and other authorities to the presence of a radical Islamic terrorist cell, and thereby helping them thwart an attack on the New York Stock Exchange that could have had much more tragic consequences. The idea that the terrorists' own lies had foiled their plotting reminded Karp of the old Yiddish saw "Man plans and God laughs."

The noise level of the class rose as Karp walked to the front of the room, as if when they spotted his six-foot-five presence they felt compelled to get a last word in before the new sheriff came to town. As Karp sat on the edge of the desk, facing the students, he raised his index finger to his lips and the class moved rapidly from din to hushed to silence.

That is, except one young man who continued what appeared to be a quiet but intense conversation with a pretty redheaded girl seated behind him. Not surprisingly, the young man, a square-jawed, handsome fellow with wavy black hair and smoldering Mediterranean looks was his son Isaac, also known as Zak.

"Um, Mr. Karp, is there something, perhaps, you'd care to share with the rest of the class?" the senior Karp asked.

Zak turned around in his chair, his dark eyes angry. "No, sir," he replied curtly.

"Elisa dumped him for the Winter Dance in December. She's going with Giancarlo instead," volunteered Crissy Zubrinski, a plump girl with a tiny upturned nose, who prided herself on being the class gossip.

"I never asked her in the first place," Zak retorted as the rest of the class tittered.

Karp felt for his elder (by a couple of minutes) son. Zak was definitely the more aggressive and self-confident of the twins—the better athlete and Joe Cool at school. But when it came to attracting the opposite sex, women of all ages melted at the sight of the other twin, Giancarlo, with his classic refined features, porcelain skin, and ringlets of dark hair that fell about his face like some painting of a Renaissance prince.

Zak was no slouch in the looks department and had plenty of female admirers, though they tended to like him more than he liked them; it was the girls like Elisa Robyn, a beauty with brains, who eluded him. It didn't hurt Giancarlo that he was perceived as the sensitive, artistic sort—he could play a half dozen musical instruments and recite Blake, Byron, and Keats at the drop of a hat. Side by side, Zak and Giancarlo were Ghiberti's sculpture *St. John the Baptist* and Michelangelo's *David;* both beautiful works of art, but the former just a bit rougher, less sophisticated than the latter.

Zak liked to put on a tough exterior, but behind the bluster was a sensitive soul who took rejection hard. There was nothing to say now that wouldn't cause Zak more embarrassment, and the best strategy was to move on quickly.

"Okay, gang, let's focus here," Karp said. "I wanted to talk today about a concept I call 'the Big Lie,' and how it pertains to some of the issues we've been discussing. Any ideas about what I mean by the Big Lie?"

"It's when you act as if you like someone but really you're just using them," Zak suggested sullenly. "Or maybe it's when your brother stabs you in the back."

Karp winced. Obviously, this was going to take some mediation between Zak and his twin, but now wasn't the time. "Well, I was thinking more in terms of the Big Lie as it pertains to larger topics, such as in trials or historical events." He looked around the room but there were no takers. "Okay, then let me get the ball rolling. When I'm talking about the Big Lie conceptually, I mean people who create and present a false or delusional belief as reality, generally for nefarious, or bad, purposes. People who create the Big Lie claim that it has significant importance, when in reality it's just a mere illusion and doesn't really exist."

"Do you have an example?" asked Joey Simon, a severely nearsighted youth with a narrow, serious face. He was the only student in the class who felt compelled to take notes on the discussions even though there were no tests.

"Sure, I see it all the time in my line of work," Karp responded. "It's actually quite common for defense attorneys to blame the victim of a crime. A young woman gets raped because, according to the defense, she wore the wrong clothing, or was in the wrong place, or waited too long to say no. Or someone shoots and kills another person because the victim made them angry, or insulted them. In a more general sense, in which we think of society as the victim of criminal acts, then the Big Lie is used to blame society for the perpetrator's actions—he blames racism, or an impoverished childhood, or the lack of a male role model."

Karp thought of his friend the baker, Moishe Sobelman, a Holocaust survivor, and the faded purple tattooed numbers on his arm. "Or, we've talked about people who say that the Holocaust never happened—that six million Jews, and another six million others, weren't murdered by the Nazis and that the Jews made it all up. And in one of our future discussions, I thought we might examine how the Big Lie is at the root of many horrors like pogroms and the Holocaust, and how the Big Lie came to exist that the Jews killed Jesus and therefore have deserved whatever evil has befallen them over the last two thousand years."

"But if it's a lie, why would anyone believe it?" Elisa asked.

"Because they're good at lying," Zak muttered.

"That's right, Zak, they are good, indeed very good, at lying," Karp replied. "And that's a good question, Elisa. My theory is that the Big Lie is so outrageous, so 'out there' that people think, 'Well, they couldn't have made *all* of that up. You'd have to be crazy to say something like that if it wasn't at least partly true.' So some begin to accept at least the basic premise of the lie, if not all the details. Now something that is all entirely false is perceived as partly true—maybe even enough to cast doubt on the real truth."

"But if the Big Lie is so enormous that people believe at least some of it, how do you deal with it?" Giancarlo asked.

Karp stuck his hands in his pockets and cocked his head to the side. *"I think I killed her."* "With the truth, the simple, unvarnished truth."

1

A HOWL OF FEMALE LAUGHTER REVERBERATED DOWN THE hallway of the loft to where Butch Karp sat at the kitchen table trying to accomplish the gastronomical feat of eating breakfast and reading the Saturday *New York Times* without upsetting his stomach. He was losing the battle, too, as he labored through yet another editorial posing as a news story on the front page, under the headline:

JURY HANGS IN MAPLETHORPE MURDER TRIAL

More laughter interrupted his reading further. He looked up, his gold-flecked gray eyes narrowing as he wondered what it might be about. Zak and Giancarlo were already off to Central Park to play football with their friends, and his daughter, Lucy, was . . . *Hmmm, who knows where Lucy is these days . . . just "away" according to her voice mail.*

So something else was tickling his wife's fancy this morning. Another gale of mirth preceded Marlene Ciampi into the main area of the loft, which included a spacious living room, a kitchen, a library, and a foyer on an open floor plan. She followed close behind, holding up what appeared to be a letter.

"Look what I found going through those old papers," she chortled.

"Nude photographs from our wedding night?" Karp asked with a wink.

"Now *that* would be funny." Marlene smiled. "Especially because I was too drunk to remember it."

"All you need to know is that you said I was the best ever."

"Yeah, so you've told me. A regular Secretariat. But nah, this is real *and* it's hilarious." She laughed again and shook the letter at him.

Marlene had been fixing up the "den," which is what they were calling Lucy's former bedroom now that she'd more or less permanently relocated to New Mexico and parts unknown. His wife had decided that the space could be better used as a home office and that they didn't need to keep renting a storage unit in Newark for old papers and forgotten memorabilia. So a dozen boxes at a time, she was bringing the flotsam and jetsam of their lives to the loft and going through it "to get rid of anything we don't need."

When she started, Karp had made the mistake of saying he thought it might be a good idea so that someday they could "downsize" now that Lucy was gone and the boys were close to entering high school followed, presumably, by their leaving for college. But that had only earned him an icy stare from his wife, who had apparently not been thinking in terms of becoming an empty-nester in a few years. *"We'll always need a big enough place they can come home to,"* she'd replied, as if instructing a not-so-bright pupil. *"I'm even going to put a daybed in the 'office' so that Lucy will have a place to sleep. I'm not pushing our children out of their home, just cleaning house a bit and making some work space."*

Having been dressed down for practically kicking their children to the streets, he'd been careful about what he said after that regarding her task and was happy to see her smiling now.

"So what's so funny about a piece of paper?" He stood up from his chair and walked over to his wife, who held it away from him. At six feet five, he towered over her so that she had to look up, her dark brown eyes twinkling and her cupid's-bow lips twisted into a smirk that said "The joke's on you, buddy boy."

That was okay with him as long as it made Marlene happy. She was looking good these days. Not that he ever thought she was unattractive. Since the day they met as young assistant district attorneys for New York County, he'd been drawn to her classic Italian features, the petite but curvy body, and the way her soft, molasses-colored curls framed her face. Not even when she lost an eye opening a letter bomb intended for him, way back when they were first dating, had he thought differently.

However, the past few years had been rough on her and the rest of the family. After leaving the DAO, Marlene tossed aside her lawyer's shingle and gave the private sector a shot as a gumshoe for hire. Fate, karma, circumstances—whatever you wanted to call it—had taken her down a road in which she found herself dispensing vigilante justice on behalf of abused women, and then again when her family was attacked—a not uncommon experience. All of her behavior could be justified in an "eye for an eye" way, but she'd found herself caught up in a web of violence that she couldn't seem to extricate herself from. And it had taken its toll on her physically and emotionally, and on their marriage. As the district attorney for the County of New York and a man who believed in "the system," for all of its failings and imperfections, he opposed vigilante justice on principle. That his wife was in the middle of it had strained their relationship to the breaking point.

But they managed, he thought. He'd watched her making focaccia the other night, kneading the dough, lost in her own thoughts. She'd looked up and caught him gazing at her, then smiled and went back to her bread.

Lately, she just seemed . . . *What's the word I'm looking for . . . satisfied? . . . Yes, she seems satisfied.*

And yet, it had only been a few weeks since she had almost single-handedly stopped a terrorist attack on the New York Stock Exchange. If the terrorists had succeeded, the nation's economy could have collapsed, ruining lives and throwing the country into pandemonium. She'd killed several men to prevent it from happening, but it would have been hard to argue that every drop of blood wasn't justified. Still, there was the added trauma of nearly dying with her daughter . . . and the old bugaboo about people she loved getting caught up in the violence that hovered around her.

Of course, Karp worried that some new incident would push her back down the stairs of mental health. She'd get a taste of some act of violence and like an alcoholic who'd been on the wagon for many years and then tries "just a sip," she'd be hooked again. So he'd watched for some sign of distress—a warning that the old addiction was kicking in again. But after she'd taken a few days to hang out with their friend John Jojola in the New Mexican desert, she'd seemed to bounce back to her new normal as devoted wife and mother.

Maybe it's been too easy, he thought, but then chided himself for doubting that she was coming to peace with who she was and her role in the world. Her present mischievousness seemed genuine enough. He smiled and held out his hand for the letter. "Come on, give it up, gorgeous."

"Hmph, well, if you're going to say nice things like that, you will spoil all my fun," she said, pretending to pout. "Anyway, I was going through a box with some of your old law school papers and found this . . . I guess you could call it a letter of recommendation, from Robert H. Cole."

"My torts professor?" At the mention of his old Boalt Hall law professor at UC Berkeley, Karp smiled. He recalled many a fine classroom debate with Cole; he'd realized only after the fact that the professor was using those debates to push his headstrong and occasionally overly emotional pupil to perfect his use of reason and logic in order to win the argument.

"Good old Bob Cole . . . what a mentor that guy was for me," Karp said. "He was a master at the art of logic and persuasion. I learned more about how to problem solve from him as anybody before or since, except maybe Garrahy."

"Well, the man certainly had you pegged." Marlene giggled. "The letter's addressed to Francis Garrahy."

Karp perked up. New York District Attorney Garrahy was already a legend by the time Karp arrived as a snot-nosed, wet-behind-the-ears assistant district attorney out to save the world by locking up all the bad guys. The old man had seen something in him, a raw, hardworking Jewish kid from Brooklyn who aspired to a career in the Homicide Bureau, and he'd taken him under his wing.

The DAO required applicants to have three letters of recommendation, so Karp had asked Cole for such a letter and was glad he'd kept a copy of it. "So if you're not going to let me read it, what's it say?"

"'Mr. Karp is an able and intelligent man," Marlene began lightly. "He is highly motivated toward law and public service, and well trained. He is competent and fully qualified for excellent service in any law office.'"

"That's what had you laughing like a lunatic? Have you been hitting the cooking sherry again?"

Marlene stuck her tongue out at him. "I'm getting to it if you'll allow me to continue. 'He has had a remarkable career of extracurricular activities, which testify to his energy, well-roundedness and complexity of interests, a principled devotion to public service, and his ability to do a great deal of work successfully. In college he was a star varsity basketball player . . .'"

Karp winced. His promising basketball career had ended with a blown-out knee that had required major reconstructive surgery and finished any thoughts he'd entertained of playing pro ball.

"' . . . and a major student leader on a campus of over 25,000 students.'"

"I still don't see what's so humorous. If you ask me, it's a rather dry recitation of these extraordinary facts as they pertained to me." Karp grinned with a raised eyebrow and an "I gotcha" wink.

Marlene rolled her eyes. "Yeah, Saint Butch. Anyway, what I was laughing about was what Cole wrote in the last paragraph. 'He is a forthright, strong-willed, outspoken man, and his combination of aggressiveness and determination has no doubt made him controversial at times and has occasionally annoyed people.'"

Karp's wife, his darling companion, his one and only, burst out laughing and had to wipe the tears from her eyes before she could speak again. "Boy, this guy Cole was a master at the understatement. 'Has occasionally annoyed people.' Oh, that's rich!"

"Yeah, well speaking of annoying . . . is that it?"

"No, he goes on, 'Moreover, his manner is not entirely suave. . . .' He sure got you right, baby boy," Marlene chortled.

"Give me that," Karp growled, snatching the document from

her hands. He read silently for a moment before smiling and reading aloud: "'Yet, I would consider these attributes as more desirable than not. They suggest a kind of earthy ability to understand ordinary people and a willingness to see even the unpopular jobs through to the end. I recommend him to you without hesitation.' I suppose you were going to leave that out?"

"I was getting to it," Marlene replied, grabbing the letter back. "Give me that . . . I'm going to have it framed."

"Simple minds, simple pleasures," he suggested.

"Uh, I wouldn't talk, big boy. If I remember correctly, simple pleasures were about all you had on that extraordinary mind of yours last night."

"I beg your pardon? I am a very emotionally complex man with a great variety of needs and am quite capable of multitasking."

"Don't I know it, Romeo."

Karp grabbed for his Juliet, who deftly avoided his grasp. "What's next week look like for you?" she asked. "The usual Monday morning meeting, I assume."

"Yeah, but I have two others before that," he said.

"Your mistress and who else?"

"She couldn't fit me in . . . so to speak," he replied, which caused his wife to make a gagging sound. "So instead, I'm going by Moishe's shop. The old geezers in the Breakfast Club are looking for a new place to meet now that the Kitchenette moved, so I was going to introduce them to Moishe and Il Buon Pane."

"I should have known. You've been mumbling about cherry cheese coffeecake in your sleep. . . . So what's the other meeting?"

Karp held up a hand. "Guilty as charged on the coffee cake." Then he frowned and tapped the front page of the *Times*. "After that I'm sitting down with Tommy Mac to talk about where to go now with the Maplethorpe case."

Marlene nodded. Tommy "Mac" McKean was a longtime friend at the DAO who'd recently been made chief of the Homicide Bureau by her husband. "I still can't believe the jury hung and that scumbag's walking around town like he's been vindicated. I read that 'news story.' It said he's even going ahead with his new show, *Putin:*

The Musical, if you can believe that. And how poor Maplethorpe has been persecuted because he was trying to help out some nutcase who offed herself in his living room. . . . You're going to retry him, aren't you?"

"Without a doubt, kiddo," Karp replied. "We'll be asking Judge Rosenmayer to put us on the calendar for a new trial forthwith. But we'd better figure out where we went wrong, or the next time the jury just might acquit."

"How's Stewbie taking it?"

Karp thought about the question. Stewart "Stewbie" Reed was the assistant district attorney who had tried F. Lloyd Maplethorpe for the murder of Gail Perez. Stewbie was one of the most experienced and professional prosecutors in the Homicide Bureau. He'd won and lost cases before, but this one had been different—with all the publicity and scandal surrounding a famous Broadway producer, and up against a legendary defense attorney. There were a lot of pitfalls in such a case, and one of them was to get caught up in the hype and allow one's ego to get involved. A hung jury could mean a loss in Reed's confidence and the objectivity necessary to retry the case.

"That's one of the things I want to talk to Tommy Mac about," he replied. "I haven't said anything about it to Stewbie, except that no one was blaming him. But he's probably taking it pretty hard. It's been what . . . seven, eight months since Maplethorpe's arrest? He put a lot of time and energy into the case."

"And if I know Stewbie, a lot of his soul, too," Marlene added. She had once been the chief of the DAO Sex Crimes Bureau and had known Stewart Reed for many years, even working with him on several homicide cases that also involved sexual assaults. "He's a good man, Butch."

Karp nodded. "Yeah, I know, and a great prosecutor. He probably just needs a pep talk, and an extra set of eyes to help him plug any holes. Then he'll be good to go again."

"That's my guy," Marlene replied, and blew him a kiss as she turned to go back to the office. "So where are you off to now?"

"Thought I'd catch the train to Central Park and watch the boys.

Maybe treat them to a hot pastrami and corned beef at the Carnegie Deli on the way back."

"Sounds nice. Do try to avoid annoying anyone if you can help it."

Karp laughed. "If I don't know that I'm doing it, how can I help it?"

2

The large gray rat crept along in the dark, its nose twitching and whiskers spread like an antenna, alert for signs of danger. It padded around a puddle that oozed from the wall of a long since abandoned subway tunnel—sealed off from the main system decades earlier and forgotten—and stopped.

Cautiously, it approached a man sitting on the ground with his back against a wall. The rat was hungry and hoping to steal in for a bite, if the opportunity presented itself. The man did not move, even when the rat scampered across his outstretched legs in an exploratory dash. It circled back and hesitated, listening to the man's shallow breathing, sniffing suspiciously. Then it sprang forward, leaping onto the man's chest and sinking its long yellow incisors into his cheek, ripping off a piece of flesh.

The man woke at the sharp pain, and feeling the weight of the nearly two-pound rodent clinging to his chest, he screamed and shook his head violently. He tried to reach for his attacker but his hands were manacled and chained above his head. All he could do was screech and twist violently.

Surprised by the reaction, the rat jumped back and prepared to flee. However, it quickly realized that it was in no danger from the man. It hissed and was preparing to leap at him again when it was blinded by a sudden bright light. Confused, the rat froze in place and never saw the stick that broke its neck and crushed its skull.

"Oooh, lookie here, Jeremy, a fat Gotham City rabbit for the pot tonight," a short, dark shadow standing behind the flashlight beam chortled, holding the dead animal up by its tail in the light for his companion to see.

"Right on, Paulito. Nothin' like a bit of fresh meat," his tall, skinny companion agreed, turning his own flashlight onto his friend, a dwarf with a bulbous nose and thick, stumpy arms and legs.

"I 'spose that's what our dinner was thinking when he jumped on our friend Amir, here," the dwarf said, laughing.

The two men turned their flashlights onto the prisoner, noting the small trickle of blood running down his cheek. The man turned his head from the painful stab of the lights and flinched as the dwarf moved toward him. But the little man brought a large set of keys from a pants pocket and used one to open the lock that bound the chains.

"Come on, asshole, Father David wants to talk," the dwarf growled, grabbing the man by his elbow.

Amir al-Sistani groaned as he was helped to his feet. He then stood docilely as the two men fastened a rope around his neck and, giving it a light tug, led him into the darkness.

After his capture in an underground tunnel as he left the New York Stock Exchange building, believing that his plot to destroy the American economy was well under way, al-Sistani thought of little other than how to escape these wretches and their insane leader, David Grale. He dreamed of making his way back to the world of sunlight. Back to where he was known to his devoted followers as "the Sheik," and had hundreds of millions of dollars in Swiss bank accounts to buy every luxury, even as he plotted a radical Islamic takeover of the world with himself as the leader, the caliph.

On the fourth day of his captivity, he'd even managed to break free from his guards, Jeremy and Paulito, as they were escorting him to Grale for another interrogation. He'd fled blindly down a tunnel in the pitch black with no idea if he was running toward sunlight or deeper into the bowels of the city above.

Stopping at one point to catch his breath, he heard his captors laughing back in the direction he'd come from and calling for him to return. *"Better come back before the others find you . . . or then you'll be sorry."*

However, he'd splashed on for a few more feet through foul-smelling water, recoiling as his hand reached for a wall to steady himself and came away dripping with slime. Forcing himself to move forward, he finally had to stop at what appeared to be an intersection of two tunnels. He was trying to decide which way to go when he heard strange voices screeching and gibbering from the tunnel on the left; they sounded some distance away, but close enough to send shivers down his spine. Realizing then the futility of his efforts, and frightened of these "others," he stopped and waited for Jeremy and Paulito to catch him and bring him back to Grale.

"Well, I hope you have that out of your system," Grale had said with a chuckle, glancing at his grinning followers. *"It can be quite dangerous to wander alone in my kingdom. You might lose your way and starve to death in some dark pit—or perhaps meet one of the former 'pet' alligators you may have heard have made their home here . . . and that's no urban myth, I can assure you."* He laughed with his men, but his face had then turned grim as he added, *"Or you might meet others who live here—not like my fine friends, but* shayteen, *to use the Muslim expression, demons who look like men. And let me warn you, they would not be too squeamish to see what a well-fed terrorist tastes like."*

Grale lived with dozens of his followers in a surprisingly large cavern about the size of a university gymnasium. Within the cave's confines and some other nearby tunnels and openings, the inhabitants had created small "apartments" carved into the walls or, like Grale's, built from pieces of wood, bricks, and cinder blocks they'd gathered from the world above.

Scavenging seemed to be the inhabitants' main occupation as they came and went like ants foraging for the winter—leaving with nothing but the ragged clothes they wore but always returning with some useful item, whether it was a piece of food or of corrugated tin. al-Sistani had been surprised that these homeless beggars had electricity to dimly light and heat—via glowing space heaters—their filthy hole in the ground. Then it dawned on him that they must be tapping into the energy source for the subway trains that could be heard rumbling beyond the walls surrounding the underground encampment.

Grale had pointed to Jeremy and Paulito. *"These good men I've asked to watch over you are, in fact, your protectors as much as they are your guards. The others generally avoid the parts of my kingdom we patrol. But you never know when hunger will drive them to take chances, and with winter approaching they will be even more ravenous than usual."* al-Sistani realized then that he'd been allowed to escape as a lesson.

Al-Sistani originally believed that Grale had to be some agent of the Great Satan in Washington, D.C., part of a secret U.S. antiterrorism agency that was holding him incommunicado to keep him out of the American court system, where he would have been afforded a lawyer and rights. When he learned that wasn't the case, he'd offered Grale millions of dollars in gold for his freedom. But the lunatic just sneered at his offer. *"What use will I have for gold in the Kingdom of God?"*

Only then did he realize that Grale was simply insane. A religious zealot who saw himself as a modern-day Crusader, battling the forces of evil—in his case, Islam—as he waited with his followers, who addressed him as "Father," for the Apocalypse. So he'd pretended to be persuaded by Grale's counterarguments. He claimed to have seen the error of his ways and wanted to convert to Grale's version of Christianity—a sort of mystic Catholicism built around the concept that Armageddon was fast approaching.

He felt no shame or sin in pretending to convert to Christianity. According to the imams in the radical madrasah of Saudi Arabia, strict fundamentalist schools, the Muslim concept of *al-Taqiyya* allowed believers to lie and deceive if it was for the good of Islam and the conquest of the non-Muslim world. In fact, the imams insisted that Allah blessed such deceptions.

But Grale, whose glittering, intense eyes seemed to see into his mind, merely laughed. *"I find your 'conversion' insincere and, therefore, as a servant of Christ, I reject it as false,"* he'd said, smirking. *"Consider yourself a condemned man for crimes—committed and intended—against humanity. Your life is forfeit, but should you wish to prolong it, you will tell me everything you know about the plans of your evil brethren."*

At first, al-Sistani had refused to divulge anything. He'd expected to be tortured—as that's what he would have done—but was surprised that Grale did not physically abuse him. However, the rats and the wet darkness—and the gibbering voices that sometimes seemed too close as he sat chained against a wall—eventually proved too much. He decided that Allah wanted him to stay alive with his mind intact. And that meant feeding Grale tidbits of information.

Of course, he'd betrayed organizations and other terrorists with whom he had the least connection. The names and addresses of certain rogue members of the Irish Republican Army. Plans for suicide bombings in Muslim countries that he considered inconsequential to his grander plans to establish a Muslim caliphate.

He'd been prepared to go on with further betrayals, but after the first hour, Grale's eyes had clouded over and he'd gripped his head with both hands and moaned. *"Get him out of here,"* he'd screamed, waving a hand at al-Sistani.

As he was hustled out of the cavern, al-Sistani wondered if he might outlast his captor. He'd seen Grale coughing up blood—*probably tubercular,* he thought—and the man had so little flesh between his skin and bones that he looked almost skeletal.

After the interrupted session, a week had passed with no more contact with Grale. He'd asked Paulito why, but the dwarf just shrugged. "He's in one of his moods. Believe me, you don't want to talk to him when he's like this. Not unless you want to feel his knife. When he's like this, he hunts the others above and below the streets, including some of them you told him about."

Imagining the gaunt, spectral figure rising from the shadows, his knife raised, al-Sistani had shuddered. *Better them than me, however.*

Many days had passed since that conversation, or at least what he believed were many days—in the darkness it was impossible to tell exactly how long. Then the rat had attacked him and Jeremy and Paulito appeared to bring him back to Grale.

As they entered the cavern, the people there stopped what they were doing to watch him walk past. Many were disfigured and cripples; they were missing teeth and sometimes arms or legs. Quite a number were obviously mad as they muttered to themselves, twitched, hopped about, and looked at him with confused, frightened, or angry eyes. Their unwashed bodies and foul breath made him nauseous.

Most of them appeared to be men, though some were so disgustingly buried beneath stained rags and dirty faces it was impossible to determine their sex. However, there were some women, and even children and teenagers. In his eyes, they were a loathsome, scabrous people—the end product of decadent Western civilization and proof that all it needed was a push into oblivion from true believers such as himself.

He thought of them as human garbage, unwanted even by their fellow Americans. But they seemed to see themselves as a community of equals; their pathetic shows of affection for one another, and the way those who appeared more or less mentally and physically competent took care of those who weren't, disgusted him.

Grale's hovel was at a far end of the cavern in a cave dug into the wall at the back of some sort of raised cement platform that al-Sistani guessed had once been part of the subway system. Usually, the madman sat on the platform in front of his shack in an ancient, overstuffed leather chair, watching over his flock. He dressed in a cowled monk's robe that shadowed his gaunt face so that the hollows beneath his dark and feverish eyes were accented against the nearly luminescent quality of his skin.

As they approached, he saw that the madman held a chain leash attached to a leather collar that was fastened around the neck of a naked and prostrate man.

Grale yanked on the leash, forcing the prisoner to raise his filthy head. Shocked, al-Sistani found himself looking at Azahari Mujahid, sometimes called Tatay, a *mujahedid* holy warrior. He was from the Philippines and was noted for his spectacular bombings of infidel targets throughout his home country and Indonesia. He'd been brought to New York to assist with al-Sistani's plan to destroy the American economy.

So that's at least part of why my brilliant plan failed, al-Sistani thought. Somehow Tatay had been discovered and captured before he could complete his mission with Nadya Malovo. *Is there nothing this bloodthirsty maniac doesn't have his hand in?*

"I see you recognize my dog," Grale snarled. "But no, I would not treat a dog so. However, a mass murderer of innocent men, women, and children? A demon who shows no mercy to those who had never harmed him? Yes and yes again, a thousand times yes. So now he pays a penance on earth before he goes to meet his maker and then into the everlasting torment. But only after I have wrung everything he knows from him. We are near that point, aren't we, dog?"

Tatay looked from Grale to al-Sistani, and then the mujahedeen, bomb-maker extraordinaire, slayer of infidels, threw back his head and started to howl.

Grale laughed, a harsh sound with no joy in it, and yanked on the chain to stop him. Then he leaned forward and fixed al-Sistani, his eyes burning with some mad internal fire. "My dog, here, tells me that there was another plan—something that would be set into motion should your plan fail. Tell me about it."

"I don't know what he's talking about," al-Sistani mumbled.

"Well, then one of you is lying!" Grale bellowed as he jumped up from his chair, lifting Tatay to his knees. With his free hand he pulled his wicked curved knife from the folds of his robe and before anyone could react, he drew the blade across the terrorist's throat.

Hot blood had spurted from the platform and struck the horrified al-Sistani in the face and chest. He opened his mouth to scream but nothing came out except a high-pitched whistling.

Grale let go of the leash and Tatay's body fell back to the ground where it twitched as the man bled out. "You'd do well to remember Proverbs 12:22, 'Lying lips are an abomination to the Lord.' I will give you one more chance to tell me the truth. Tell me what you know of this plan or join my dog in hell!"

Al-Sistani tried to think of a way out. "In the name of Allah the most merciful, I tell you I don't know," he pleaded.

Grale nodded and suddenly Jeremy grabbed al-Sistani's hair and pulled his head back. The dwarf, Paulito, stepped in front; a long knife had appeared in his stubby hand, the tip of which was pressed into the prisoner's throat.

"Then there's no reason for you to live," Grale said.

Hardly able to breathe, al-Sistani felt the warm rush of urine down his leg. "I'll tell you," he cried out. "The tunnel . . . they plan to blow up a tunnel!"

"Which one!"

"I don't know. By Allah, I swear this is true. They did not tell me!"

Grale hesitated and al-Sistani felt the knife pull back from his neck ever so slightly. "When?"

"I don't know," al-Sistani said. "Before the end of the year."

"And what is your part in it?"

"Nothing," al-Sistani cried. "My plan was to attack the New York Stock Exchange."

"You're lying to me again," Grale hissed. "If you have nothing to do with it, why are your friends so anxious to have you back that they will pay millions of dollars, and have even risked exposing themselves to find you?"

Al-Sistani felt the knife pinch into his skin. "Money! They need my money to pay for it!"

"They? Who are they? The Sons of Man? They certainly don't need your money."

It didn't surprise al-Sistani that his captor knew about the secretive, powerful group of American business, political, and military leaders who plotted to take over the U.S. government while conspiring with him to set the scene for the coup by throwing the U.S. economy into chaos. Unsure of how much Grale already knew, he'd decided to tell part of the truth. "They want to make it look like the Iranians did it and cause a war! The war will allow them to gain power."

Grale looked hard at him, then leaned forward and sniffed. "Again, you're lying to me. I can smell it . . . the fear. Is it really worth dying for? Now tell me . . . last chance . . . who is behind this plot? Or join your friend." With that he bowled the head of Tatay across the platform, from which it fell and rolled to the captive's knees.

Al-Sistani screamed and tried to move away but was pinioned by Jeremy and Paulito. "It is the Sons of Man, but a faction that disagrees with their leadership council and needs my money. They also need the help of my followers."

"What faction? Name them." Grale leaped off the platform and leaned close so that only he could hear his prisoner. "Tell me," he whispered. "Who is their leader?"

"I don't know," al-Sistani whimpered quietly. "I've only heard rumors."

"No more wasting my time, tell me about these rumors!"

Al-Sistani looked up and into Grale's glittering eyes, saw the madness, and knew that there would be no more second chances to tell the truth. "His name is . . ."

Grale sat back in his chair with a strange, excited look on his face. "As it is written in Revelation, 'Then another horse came out, a fiery red one. Its rider was given power to take peace from the earth and to make men slay each other. To him was given a large sword.' Perhaps the end of time is here at last!"

3

THE PRETTY RED-HAIRED COCKTAIL WAITRESS IN THE TIGHT, low-cut dress sized up the two "customers" trying to look both inconspicuous and older at a table in the back of the Well lounge in the Poliziano Fiera Hotel.

Fourteen, maybe fifteen, she thought to herself as she walked over. The lounge was hopping—the famous Broadway producer, Mr. F. Lloyd Maplethorpe, was throwing one of his preproduction cast parties—and the boys had probably hoped to avoid getting noticed in the crowd. They studiously avoided looking in her direction, staring off instead in the direction of the DJ booth, nodding their heads to the music.

They were both good-looking teens, she noted as she approached. *Five years older and I might have thought about robbing those cradles.* One of them looked like he'd stepped out of some Renaissance painting of a young prince—which, as an art student at NYU, she could appreciate—with his porcelain skin, ringlets of dark hair, and refined features. He glanced at her as she stopped in front of their table before looking quickly away. *Whoa,* she thought, *this one's going to be breaking a lot of hearts someday*.

The other boy was a beauty, too, but in a more rugged, masculine way. He had an olive cast to his skin, thick, dark eyebrows beneath short black hair, and a shadow that promised to be a heavy beard someday. When he looked up at her, she thought her knees might buckle. *Pull yourself together, he's a kid!*

With an effort, the waitress scowled and placed a hand on her hip. "So what's up, *boys*?"

The more rugged of the two looked at her and flashed his pearly whites. "A Corona with lime," he replied, and turned away as if he'd suddenly found something interesting in the potted palm next to him.

The waitress fought to keep a smile off her face. The kid apparently thought that talking in a baritone would improve his chances of landing a beer.

The other boy smiled sweetly. "Just a Coke . . ." He glanced at his companion, who glared at him, and corrected his order. "A rum and Coke, that is."

"Uh-huh . . . can I see some ID, please?" She held out her hand as the two boys exchanged glances and then reached into their back pockets and pulled out their wallets. They each handed her a driver's license.

The waitress held the licenses up in the light. "Okay . . . let's see, Mr. Bob Smith of 1234 Mickey Lane, Mount Vernon, New York, and Mr. Roy Jones of 2468 Mouse Street, Newark, New Jersey, it says here that you're twenty-three and twenty-five years old . . ."

"I'll be twenty-four in March . . ." the pretty one said helpfully.

The waitress squinted at the boys. "I need you to wait here," she said. "We're now required to run the licenses of all new customers through a computer with the National Security Administration. Doing our part to combat terrorism, you know. I'll be right back."

The boys looked quickly at each other, the alarm spreading across their faces like a grass fire. They stood and reached for their licenses.

"That's okay, it won't be necessary," said the pretty one.

"We just remembered that we have another pressing engagement," added the other.

The waitress kept the cards out of their reach. "Nonsense," she purred. "This will only take a moment and then I'll get those drinks right to you. I'm sure your other engagement can wait." She leaned over the table as though to wipe something, which she knew gave the boys a good view of her cleavage.

The pretty one blushed and looked down at the table. The other didn't take his eyes off her chest, but managed to stammer, "That's very nice of you, but we're already late to meet our breasts . . . I mean our guests . . . at another bar. So if you could just give us back our licenses . . ."

"Sorry, hot stuff, but I'm keeping these," the waitress said, standing up. "And I don't want to see you back in here until you're twenty-one."

As the disappointed boys started to gather their coats to leave, a commotion broke out at the entrance of the lounge. The waitress turned toward the sound and squealed as a young Latino man entered the room with a beautiful Latina on his arm. "Oh my God, it's—"

"Boom!" shouted the second of the boys. "He's our friend!"

The waitress rolled her eyes. "You two never stop, do you?" she said.

The boys didn't have to answer. Instead, Alejandro "Boom" Garcia looked in their direction and sauntered over with a wide Cheshire cat smile. "Zak . . . G-man . . . Zak . . . wassup, dawgs?" Proudly aware of the looks of astonishment on the faces of the waitress as well as the other patrons in the lounge, the boys embraced their short, barrel-chested friend.

Giancarlo and Isaac Karp had met Garcia, a former gang leader of the notorious Inca Boyz from Spanish Harlem, several years earlier when he was still just an aspiring hip-hop artist trying to break out of the gang life. He'd actually helped their dad bring down the infamous sociopath Andrew Kane, and had since signed a major recording deal and moved to Los Angeles to pursue his musical career.

"So how'd my homies hear about this little shindig?" Garcia asked as they all sat down at the table.

"Read about it in the *Village Voice*," Giancarlo replied. "It said there was going to be a cast party and that there was a rumor you might perform because Carmina's in the cast." He looked over at the strikingly beautiful young woman sitting next to Garcia.

Carmina Salinas had long, wavy dark hair, large jade-colored eyes, and full red lips that exposed perfect white teeth when she smiled at Giancarlo and laughed. "A very small role," she said, then shrugged. "But who knows? It could be the start of something big."

"So are you going to rap tonight?" Zak asked Garcia.

"Stick around, bro, I just might spit out a few lines," the rapper replied. He looked around the lounge and then back at the twins. "So where's your mom and dad?"

The twins looked sheepish. "They're not here."

"They were trying to order drinks with fake IDs when you came in," the waitress said.

Garcia closed his eyes and slapped a hand to his forehead. "Oh, shit," he exclaimed. "You guys sneaking around again? Man, you're gonna get me in trouble with your old man. He's gonna get some cop to write me up on some traffic beef, then lock me up and throw away the key. Where's he think you're at?"

"The movies," the boys answered. "He'll never know."

Garcia shook his round, shaved head. "Well, you sit tight and don't get into no trouble, though I know with the two of you that's like asking dogs not to sniff each other's butts," he said with a grin. "I promised Carmina that I'd do this thing for her group, but I can't stay long. I got another appointment, after I take you home first."

"Ah, come on," Zak complained. "We don't have to be home until eleven. You were out raising all kinds of hell when you were our age."

"We read about it in your biography, *Boom: A Gangster's Life in Spanish Harlem,*" Giancarlo added.

"If that's all you got out of that book, then you missed the message," Garcia replied, his voice now serious. "I was close to your age when I got locked up in juvie for shooting a man. I'm lucky he lived. And I'm lucky that I'm not rotting away in Attica. Besides, if your dad don't put me away, your mom will kill me if something happens to you because you came to one of my shows at a bar."

"Okay, okay, we get it," Zak said, then smiled sweetly up at the waitress. "Now, could we get those drinks?"

She smiled back. "Yeah, sure, what was it you ordered? A couple of Cokes?"

Zak looked disappointed, but Giancarlo seemed relieved and said, "Sure, Cokes will be fine."

The waitress turned and left. A minute later, there was another sudden buzz of voices in the direction of the hotel elevators, followed by the grand appearance of a thin, sallow-faced man in a peach-colored three-piece suit with matching fedora. Aware of the whispers and the looks from his backers, some of whom, according to the gossips, were connected with the mob and not happy with him, F. Lloyd Maplethorpe surrounded himself with bodyguards and sycophants—an odd collection of freaks who dwelled on the edges of the theater scene and lived essentially to flatter and entertain their master. In return, he allowed them to bask in his glory and attend the parties so that he would appear to be popular and liked. They swirled around him now as he made his way through the crowd and from table to table like a king among the peasants.

"Carmina! My darling girl," Maplethorpe said in his high-pitched nasally voice when he spotted them. He walked over and grabbed each side of Carmina's face with his white-gloved hands and kissed her on both cheeks.

The man turned to his followers. "My friends, allow me to present the lovely Miss Carmina Salinas . . . one of the next stars of Broadway," he announced with a grand flourish of his hand toward the subject of his praise, who smiled and blushed. "I will just have to find the perfect role. Then, under my personal tutelage, she may well become the next Idina Menzel."

"*Gracias*, Mr. Maplethorpe," Carmina replied. "I'm just happy to be part of this show." She turned to Garcia. "This is my friend, Alejandro 'Boom' Garcia, and these two young men are—"

"Boom Garcia!" the producer shouted, cutting off further introductions. "Oh my God, I was *soooooo* hoping you would attend. I am simply thrilled, thrilled, I tell you, that you've joined our little party tonight. . . . I may look a bit eighties this evening, but I really do like hip-hop. . . . It's so gritty and real; it makes me feel like I almost know what it's like to live in the ghetto. You really must sign my copy of your CD, *Spanish Harlem Soliloquy*."

"I'd be happy to," Garcia replied without much enthusiasm.

"Excellent! Isn't that excellent?" Maplethorpe shouted to his circle of admirers.

"Excellent!" they shouted back.

"Do I understand that you may sing for us tonight?" Maplethorpe asked.

Garcia looked surprised. "I don't think you could describe what I do as singing, but I told Carmina that I'd rap a little from the new CD."

"Oh, goodie," Maplethorpe replied, clapping his hands together like a child promised an ice cream cone. "And I insist that after this little soiree is over, the two of you join us upstairs in my suite for a little private party." He leaned forward and whispered, though in a stage voice loud enough for all to hear. "It could get quite wild . . . anything goes, you know."

Garcia shook his head. "I'm sorry, but maybe another time. I have to be somewhere else at ten."

Maplethorpe looked like he'd just been told that his favorite cat had died. He turned around in a circle, looking from one sympathetic face to another, all of whom then cast their baleful eyes on Garcia.

"You're breaking my heart," Maplethorpe whined. "Are you sure? Well, it must be some very important music business." He sighed heavily and turned to Carmina. "And what about you, my dear, surely you're not going to leave your castmates so early?"

Carmina looked at Garcia, whose face remained expressionless. "Well, I came with Alejandro."

"But you heard him, he has business to attend to . . . so you should stay." Maplethorpe looked at Garcia. "We'll make sure she gets home safely. I'll have the concierge arrange for my limo to drop her anywhere she wants to go."

Garcia looked at Carmina and shook his head. "I'll take her home."

Carmina's eyes flashed with anger. "I don't need you to answer for me," she said before turning to the producer. "Sure, I'll stay. It would be nice to get to know the people I'll be working with for a long time."

"That's the spirit," Maplethorpe gushed. "Yes, a long, long time . . .

a glorious hit show. Who knows what could happen down the road. We'll certainly want to take it on the road, and those roles will be opening up. . . . Now that it's settled, I must away to greet my other guests. Ta-ta!"

With that, Maplethorpe glided off followed by his retinue. When he was out of earshot, Garcia turned to Carmina. "I don't think leaving you with that dude is a good idea."

"You're not 'leaving me' with him. It's a party . . . and a chance for me to make a good impression. What's with the attitude?"

"Attitude?" Garcia scowled, his dark eyes bright. "Are you forgetting that last week the dude was on trial for blowin' some poor woman's brains all over that little penthouse you want to party in?"

"He was innocent. She committed suicide. That's why he's not in prison."

Garcia shook his head. "You got it wrong, *chica*. Jury couldn't decide one way or the other. It don't mean he's innocent."

Carmina's nostrils flared as she hissed. "I ain't stupid. But I think the cops are the ones who got it wrong. How could he make something like that up? I mean, Mr. Maplethorpe could fuck—" She stopped when Garcia nodded at the twins, who were listening with fascination. She bit her lip. "'Scuse me, amigos, 'Jandro seems to think that you've never heard the word 'fuck' before."

"Plenty of times," Zak replied quickly. "Don't mind us."

Carmina laughed. "As I was saying, Mr. Maplethorpe could have sexual relations with a different girl every night without having to put a gun in their mouths. Some girls will do anything to get a part. So it doesn't make sense that he would shoot someone over sex. I feel sorry for Miss Perez, I really do. She was from the hood, and I met her once; she was a nice lady. But maybe she was hoping he would give her a big part in the show, and when it didn't happen, she decided she'd had enough. I mean when your dreams are gone, what do you have left? Especially if you're getting a little older and your looks are starting to go."

Garcia was unconvinced. "I saw the way he was checking you out. Dude wants in your pants, 'Mina."

The young woman shrugged. "Maybe," she agreed, then laughed at his expression. "But he ain't going to get there." She reached over and patted his cheek. "Come on, 'Jandro, you've known me since we was kids growin' up on the streets together. If I was going to lose my self-respect, I would have done it a long time ago back when I was hangin' with you losers in the Inca Boyz. But the only thing I lost back then was my virginity to a certain hot-blooded gangbanger named Boom." She leaned over and kissed him on the mouth. "But I never, ever lost my self-respect."

"Wow," sighed Giancarlo. "That was better than a movie."

"Frickin' hot is what that was, you dork," Zak pointed out.

"Oh, like you're some Don Juan," his brother replied.

"I don't know any Don Juan."

"You're an idiot."

"I'm an idiot? You can't even remember to stick with the plan—order a drink like you've actually done it before. 'I'll have a Coke . . . and maybe some milk, too, please.' We could have got away with it if you weren't such a geek."

"Yeah, and whose idea was it to make such ridiculous licenses? Mickey Lane and Mouse Street? Bob Smith and Roy Jones? My, how imaginative."

"Yeah, well, you wouldn't even go to Ivan's to get them. Maybe if you had, I wouldn't have had to come up with something on the spot."

"Yeah, great, if Dad knew you were going to a convicted forger for fake IDs . . ."

"The only way he'd find out is if you told him . . ."

The twins stopped arguing when a spotlight suddenly illuminated their table and Maplethorpe climbed up on the dais next to the DJ booth. Grabbing a microphone, the producer shouted, "Welcome! Welcome! Dear, dear friends and the wonderful cast of *Putin: The Musical*!"

A roar of approval went up from the crowd, encouraging Maplethorpe to go on. "Yes, yes, even in this horribly trying time in my life . . ."

The crowd groaned sympathetically. Someone yelled, "It's that bastard Karp's fault. Karp's a Nazi!"

Garcia looked over at the twins and grinned. "Maybe I should tell them who's here," he chuckled. "You'd never make it past the door."

"You wouldn't dare!" the boys replied, glancing around nervously.

"Got any money?" Garcia replied with an evil laugh.

Maplethorpe held up his hands, and the crowd grew quiet again. "Thank you, my dearest friends, for your support and your kind words—especially those aimed at my tormentor, Herr Karp," he said with a laugh, and was joined by the crowd. "But drink up . . . it's on me. I just wanted to introduce a special guest who has graciously joined us to help celebrate our new adventure. Please welcome, Mr. Alejandro Garcia, aka *Booooooom!*"

Those in the crowd still sitting jumped to their feet and with the others cheered as Garcia waved his hand and stood. He walked quickly to the dais and, after briefly conferring with the DJ, began freestyle rapping.

Thirty minutes later, Garcia bowed to the gyrating crowd and handed the microphone back to the DJ. It took him another five minutes to reach the table where the twins sat with Carmina. He plopped down, wiping the sweat from his head with a napkin.

"Don't touch me, you're all sweaty and disgusting," Carmina complained. "You been out there in SoCal eatin' like a pig . . . no wonder you're sweatin' like one. You need to come back to the SH for some home cookin'."

"Do I hear somebody begging me to take her back?" Garcia replied, looking at the twins as if surprised.

"Ain't nobody beggin' nobody for nothin', fool," Carmina retorted. "You had your chance to make something happen with this señorita and you fucked it up. And don't you come sniffing around later tonight when you get done with whatever mysterious business is so important you can't stay for this party. Ain't nobody lookin' for you to come back to Harlem neither."

"We'd like it if he did," Giancarlo said innocently.

Carmina smiled and patted his hand. "That's 'cause he's got you bamboozled, like he used to bamboozle me. But believe me, I'm doing you a favor if I can get him to keep his dimpled ass in L.A."

Garcia put an arm around Giancarlo and pulled him away from Carmina. "Don't you listen to the Wicked Witch of Spanish Harlem. She'll cast a spell . . . her grandmother was into voodoo down in

Puerto Rico, and it rubbed off on her." He looked at his watch and quickly downed his glass of water. "*Vámonos, muchachos*, time to split. I'll drop you off at your folks' on my way uptown."

Garcia leaned over and kissed Carmina. "I still don't like this."

"Go on," she replied. "I can take care of myself. Hell, I had years of practice fending you off before I let you into the promised land."

Garcia laughed. "More like weeks. But speaking of the promised land, you sure I can't come sniffing around later?"

"You can sniff all you want," Carmina said with a shrug, "but it might get you a cap in your ass. Take your chances, lover boy . . . or not."

4

Stepping out of the SoHo loft building Monday morning, Karp was surprised by the crisp bite of the air and shivered. It was a clear day, but the October sun had yet to warm the bones of Crosby Street. Its old paving stones and brick buildings were bathed in shadows, and the chilly air that had blown in the previous night from the East River lingered in the narrow confines.

Still, once he'd pulled his peacoat a little closer and adjusted to the nip, Karp breathed in deeply, savoring the day's freshness. *Gotham City's best in autumn*, he thought. The ripe smell of the city that permeated July and August, and even warm Septembers, dissipated on the breezes that blew more frequently and cooler in the fall. He thought he could even detect salt air on the wind.

In the parks, the oaks, elms, maples, lindens, and hundreds of others he couldn't name but enjoyed just the same were putting on their annual color pageant. A stroll through Central Park was like walking inside a sunset, surrounded by splashes of reds, oranges, purples, yellows.

On Saturday, he'd watched his twin boys playing football on the fallen leaves and thought, *Life truly does not get any better than this . . . a perfect day—well, almost*. When they had lunch afterward at the Carnegie Deli on Seventh Avenue and Fifty-fourth Street, nobody was talking about the Yankees. *No World Series this year, those bum underachievers.*

October just wasn't quite right if the Bronx Bombers weren't still in the race. Karp sighed. Looking up at the robin's-egg-blue skies above the buildings, he regretted that he wasn't walking the half dozen blocks south to work at 100 Centre Street, the New York Criminal Courts Building. It was bound to be much warmer in the sun, and he would have enjoyed the stroll. Who knew how long this Indian summer would last before winter descended? But Moishe's place was more than a mile, too far to walk and get back to the office on time.

Karp trotted down the two steps from the building's front door to the sidewalk and almost ran into a tall, unkempt man wearing a tattered green army field jacket and carrying a plastic milk crate, who came barreling around the corner from Grand Avenue.

"Why, Mr. Karp, an unexpected pleasure meeting you here this morning," the man said, casually brushing his tangled mat of gray hair back from his face.

"Why, I live here, Mr. Treacher," Karp replied. "But I'm sure you know that. We've spoken on this very spot on other occasions."

"We have?" Edward Treacher's watery blue eyes rolled wildly in their sockets as if searching the interior of his cranium for some memory of these alleged earlier meetings. Then he smiled sheepishly. "Well, I have to admit, the late sixties were not kind to my long-term memory. I can scarcely recite my Chaucer anymore. Let's see, 'In April the sweet showers fall, and pierce the drought of March to the root, and all' . . . ummmm . . . 'The veins are bathed in liquor of such power, as brings about the engendering of the flower . . . ' How's that?"

"I wouldn't know. I forgot *The Canterbury Tales* a long time ago, if I ever really knew them, and I didn't indulge in mind-altering substances," Karp replied.

Treacher was about to respond when he was interrupted by a shout from across the street. "Everything okay, Mr. Karp?"

Turning toward the sound of the voice, Karp saw the police detective getting out of the dark blue Lincoln Continental parked across Crosby. He didn't like the fuss or expense of having a driver-slash-bodyguard, or using the armored sedan with gas costing more than four dollars a gallon. But Clay Fulton, his old friend and the detective in charge of his security detail, insisted in the wake of the NYSE attack.

"We still haven't caught everybody responsible," the burly black man had pointed out just the day before. *"Nadya Malovo's out there somewhere. And so are the Sons of Man, who are probably getting a little irritated with your constant interference with their plots. The car's there, use it, or I'll have to drive over every morning to pick you up myself."*

Karp waved to the sedan driver. "It's okay, Detective, I'll be just a minute." He turned back to his visitor.

Filthy and odiferous, Edward Treacher was a regular around the Criminal Courts Building and Soho, though he'd been known to drift as far as Columbia University on the north end of the island and down to Battery Park on the south. According to old-timers in the area, he'd once been a respected professor of religious studies at New York City University, but had started experimenting with LSD during the Summer of Love and one day went on a trip from which he'd never quite returned. He'd walked away from his job at the university and had been living on the streets, or institutionalized at various public mental health hospitals, ever since.

Now he made his living preaching from the Bible on street corners while standing on his milk crate, hoping tourists would throw something in his collection box. Or that aggravated shopkeepers or residents would pay him to move on.

"Good for you . . . just say no to drugs," Treacher said, nodding sagely. "That's what I tell kids. 'Just say no, or you'll end up a burned-out old wreck like Professor Treacher.' Not that I'd take it back. Oh no, not everyone gets to hold a conversation with God for thirty years. All up here, of course." He pointed to his shaggy head, then abruptly changed the subject. "A lovely day, wouldn't you say, Mr. Karp?"

"Yes, Mr. Treacher, a fine autumn day." Karp liked the "burned-out old wreck." The man actually hid a quick wit, a well-educated mind, and a kind heart behind all the dirt. He suspected that

Treacher and some of the other street denizens who hung around the Criminal Courts Building were connected to David Grale, the madman vigilante who lived beneath the city in its tunnels and caves with some of his followers. At least Treacher and his brethren seemed to be able to communicate with him and seemed to serve as his eyes and ears aboveground.

His feelings toward Grale were more mixed. He'd met him many years before, when the younger man was just a Catholic layperson working in a soup kitchen for the homeless. Or actually, he'd been introduced to Grale by his daughter, Lucy, a young teen volunteering at the kitchen when she developed a crush on the darkly handsome social worker. Only later had they discovered that while Grale served soup during the day, by night he murdered men who'd been preying on the homeless. He claimed that the men he killed were actually demons inhabiting the bodies of men.

"Ah, yes. Autumn. A fine time to spread the Good Word," Treacher said as he placed his crate on the ground and stepped up onto it. He then shouted so the few passersby walking past on Grand Avenue jumped a bit. "Verily I say, '*While the earth remaineth, seedtime and harvest, and cold and heat, and summer and winter, and day and night shall not cease!*' That's Genesis 8:22, folks. Be kind and support my ministry. You, too, may turn a wretched life—mine—around for Jesus."

Karp had covered his ears when Treacher shouted and now asked, "What's with the shouting, if you don't mind me asking? It's pretty quiet around here this morning, and I think you gave me a concussion."

"Sorry about that," Treacher replied with a grin. "But it's part of the show. The rubes want fire and brimstone . . . even in sweet little passages like that one. You show me a street preacher who doesn't shout out the Good Book's message, and I'll show you a hungry man."

"I understand. Just next time, perhaps a little warning."

"Will do. So how's the family?"

"Fine. Marlene's painting some these days. And the twins are back in school and complaining about homework."

"Ah, yes, the drudgery of homework," Treacher sighed. "I do remember that. Ridiculous way to teach; good for memorizing trivia, but does nothing to develop the mind."

"Nevertheless, getting it done may affect whether they get into college."

"Yes, indeed. So where's our dear Lucy? I haven't seen her around in a bit."

Karp started to answer, then stopped. He didn't really know where she was and for some reason he didn't want Treacher or anybody else to know either. Grale took a particular interest in Lucy, and while so far it had all been to her benefit, it was also troubling.

"She's living out of state these days," he said.

"Ah, yes, New Mexico, wasn't it?" Treacher replied.

"Yes, New Mexico." Karp hadn't meant to sound so short. He considered Treacher a harmless street person who'd once even testified for him in a murder case. The man on trial was a dirty cop, and it had taken courage and integrity to come forward. Whatever damage he'd done to his brain cells in the past, Treacher's short-term memory had been dead on, and the cop was convicted.

"Are you expecting her back for a visit anytime soon? I'd love to have a chat with her. She's always so interesting and quite helpful with my Latin and Greek."

See, the old man just wants to speak in foreign tongues. Lucy was a language savant—she was apparently up to nearly eighty, if one included dialects of some root languages. He shook his head. "No. Nothing planned. Maybe over the holidays."

"The holidays?" Treacher frowned. "That's a long ways off. Must be tough, not seeing her more often and all."

"Yeah," Karp agreed. "But I guess they all leave the nest sometime." The question raised one of his own. "So what do you hear from David Grale these days?"

Treacher frowned and shrugged. "Nothing much. In one of his moods, I understand."

The question seemed to bother the street preacher and he got down from his crate, picked it up, and turned to walk away. "Well, I must away. Places to go, people to see, you know. Cheerio!"

Watching him disappear around the corner, Karp shuddered as if the breeze had crept beneath his coat, only this was a sudden chill of premonition. Pulling his coat even tighter, he turned to walk across the street to the waiting car, wondering what else he couldn't see.

5

Halfway around the world from where Butch Karp chatted with Edward Treacher, and about twelve hours ahead in time, Nadya Malovo gazed indifferently out of the passenger-side window of the Soviet-era troop transport as it bounced along a rutted dirt road in the Caucasus Mountains of Dagestan. *Wretched country*, she thought, not bothering to hide the look of distaste on her face as the truck slowed to make its way around a small horse-drawn cart. *Peasants, horseshit, barren mountains, and backward, illiterate Muslims everywhere I look.*

Although Dagestan was officially a Russian Federation Republic on the eastern border of Chechnya, Muslim insurgents controlled the rugged terrain outside its cities and major towns. The men she was riding with, as well as those in the transports ahead and behind, were Muslim, but not Dagestanis. They were foreign fighters, mostly Arabs, aligned with al-Qaeda and hoping to create an Islamic state in Dagestan. They knew her as Ajmaani and believed that she, too, was dedicated to the establishment of a caliphate, a one-world order based on a strict interpretation of Shari'a, or Islamic law as interpreted by the radical mullahs. Dagestan was to be one of the stepping stones to world domination by a single leader, the caliph.

As Ajmaani, she was a legend, the leader behind a Chechen

Muslim takeover in 2004 of a Beslan school in which several hundred people were murdered, including nearly two hundred children. She smiled at the memory.

Since then she continued to make a name for herself among the mujahedeen with attacks on civilian targets in Russia. And then her employers had asked her to branch out. Some of the men with her in the truck were aware that she'd been involved with the attack on the Pope at St. Patrick's Cathedral in New York City, and more recently, the effort to destroy the "Great Satan" by the destruction of the New York Stock Exchange.

Both missions had failed in their ultimate goals, but not completely. The psychological effect of the attacks was almost as important as whether they had succeeded. *Especially to the Sons of Man*, she thought.

Just like her Russian bosses, the American power-group was using the bogeyman of fanatical Islamic terrorists to prime the public into accepting a takeover of the government by highly placed men in politics, the military, law, and business. They were already on the precipice; now all that was needed was one last nudge and frightened Americans would abdicate their precious rights in favor of safety.

A former KGB agent, Malovo had found a more lucrative calling after the fall of the Soviet Union working for a confederacy of mob bosses, corrupt politicians, and former military officers. Then the shared aims and strategies of her employers and the Sons of Man brought her into contact with the latter, especially a former SOM council member named Andrew Kane, a man she detested personally but admired for his ruthless pursuit of power.

Malovo's musings were interrupted when the driver failed to avoid a pothole, causing her to hit her head on the roof of the truck. "Наблюдайте вне, вы идиот!" she cursed. The man apologized profusely, wiping beads of sweat from his brow and glancing nervously at his passenger.

Most of the men in the truck usually saw women as nothing more than chattel. Certainly not mujahedeen, holy warriors. Yes, the occasional, usually dimwitted female could be persuaded to wear a martyr's vest beneath her robes and blow herself up at a police checkpoint. But even then they were controlled and used by men as nothing more than a means to an end.

However, none of the men would have dared put Ajmaani in that class. She was a beautiful woman, somewhere in her mid- to late forties—as an orphan, even she wasn't exactly sure—with short blond hair and azure blue eyes set wide apart above her high cheekbones, courtesy of her Slavic ancestors. She purposely dressed in what she knew these conservative religious men would consider inappropriate, provocative clothing—form-fitting pants and blouses that she would leave partly unbuttoned to draw their attention to her breasts. She enjoyed the anger, and lust, she saw on their faces, knowing they were too afraid to say what they were thinking.

They were all aware of her penchant for summarily executing anyone who irritated her or got in her way. All of them had known men who enjoyed killing—some were those men—but no one they'd ever met reveled in death quite the way she did. She'd been known to kill—usually with her knife but willing to use whatever was available—men for what she called insubordination, which was anything she said it was. Even the toughest of them had been bled like sheep on a holy day.

They feared her even more than they respected her. And that's exactly what she wanted. *A fearful man hesitates before striking, which is long enough to kill him. A man who respects you will wait for the right moment, and then strike without thinking.*

Malovo was getting tired of the company of such men. She'd never believed in any social movements. Lectures from her political teachers at public school in Moscow about revolution and freeing the masses from the yoke of capitalism had left her cold.

Fortunately, her old KGB instructors were practical men who used ideology only as a tool to control others. They didn't care what she believed in, only that she was smart, vicious, and obeyed orders without question. She wasn't motivated by ideas, she was driven by lust—for power, for money, for death and dominion over others, and occasionally, for other women. Because of this she was in Dagestan, preparing one more time to risk her life.

Malovo sighed, though she was careful to turn away from the driver so that he did not notice. She was tired. Not of the killing;

she still found satisfaction in that. But of risking her own life, the only thing in the world she deemed precious. There had been several near misses of late, and deep in her gut there was a feeling that time was running out.

If the attack on the stock exchange had gone down as planned, she would have been officially retired, traveling the world, living off the millions in gold that would have been deposited on her behalf. *No paper transfers. Paper money would have been worthless with the U.S. and world economies crashing. But gold, gold was always a girl's best friend.*

Unfortunately, the plan had failed. Thanks, in part, to Ivgeny Karchovski, her former lover and now mortal enemy.

The assassin's reverie ended abruptly when the driver started honking the horn. Looking ahead, she saw that the convoy she was in was barely crawling around an obstruction. A horse-drawn wagon piled high with hay was partly blocking the road, one of its wheels having fallen off and rolled into a ditch.

As the truck drew close to the cart, the farmer turned away to berate his horse, which still pulled at its traces and rolled its eyes wildly. The farmer was a tall, stooped man dressed in the local peasant garb, as was his stout wife, who in the conservative style of the countryside had covered her head and most of her face with a shawl.

Malovo couldn't see the man's face, not that she particularly cared, but for a moment her eyes locked with the other woman's. The gold-flecked gray eyes had a Slavic cast to them, not unusual in that part of the world, which had seen a multitude of invaders, from Greeks and Huns to Mongols and Russians.

They exchanged a look for only a moment, and she'd seen nothing in the other woman's eyes except a dim curiosity. Then the woman turned away and started yelling at her husband in Avar, one of the three main languages of Dagestan. Malovo only knew a few words of Avar but gathered that the woman was comparing him to the rear end of their horse.

What a life, she thought, sneering. *Married at puberty to be a brood sow for some Neolithic caveman. She probably squats in the field to deliver the next generation of subhumans. Someday all such worthless people—the peasants, the Muslim fanatics, the beggars and cripples—will be eliminated or enslaved.*

While the plan to destroy the U.S. economy was brilliant in concept, and would've been devastating if it had worked—the American public would have had no choice but to turn to strong men willing to take control during a time of crisis—it was too complicated. Too much reliance on one domino crashing into another, tumbling into a pattern leading to a disaster.

Malovo much preferred more direct action. Which was why she thought Operation Flashfire, a plan set in motion by the failure of the stock exchange attack, was much more likely to succeed. Not that it was a simple strategy—there were timetables and a certain amount of reliance on the abilities of her coconspirators—but overall there were many fewer, interrelated steps.

However, there was one major glitch. The presence of Amir al-Sistani, the despicable little toad who insisted he be called the Sheik, was integral to both plans, which had come as a surprise. Without anyone's knowledge within the Sons of Man, or her current employer, he'd set up a rescue operation in the event he was apprehended by U.S. authorities if the stock exchange attack failed.

For the second plan to be implemented, his required presence had ensured that maximum efforts would be taken to secure his release from U.S. custody, which wouldn't have proved too difficult to accomplish. The Sons of Man were a powerful organization with tentacles running throughout the U.S. political, legal, military, and business worlds; reasons would have been found to turn him over to another government for "prosecution" that would never occur. Or something would go wrong with the U.S. case against him, forcing it to be thrown out on some technicality and requiring his deportation to a friendly country.

However, for all of his cunning, Amir al-Sistani had not counted on falling into the hands of a madman who answered to no government. Malovo's eyes narrowed as she thought about David Grale. Her spies told her that Grale was keeping al-Sistani prisoner, stalling the implementation of Operation Flashfire. The meeting she was driving to in an obscure village in the Caucasus Mountains was an attempt by her employer to get around his absence.

The convoy swung around a bend in the road, and she saw what she presumed was the village, a collection of a couple dozen mud-walled and thatch-roofed houses set on both sides of the road at the bottom of a hill. She noted the lack of locals, who she presumed had fled, were in hiding, or lying in mass graves. The only people she saw were armed men on patrol, or standing idly by, breaking off their conversations as the trucks entered the village.

The convoy stopped in front of the largest of the houses, the dust hardly settling before several of the men she would be talking to walked out of the doorway. *Idiots,* she thought, *better to remain in the building and wait for me rather than come out into the open unnecessarily.*

She scanned the surrounding hillsides, noting the distant figures of armed men standing sentinel. Everything appeared to be reasonably safe, but she still waited until her cadre of bodyguards from the other trucks had surrounded her vehicle to shield her from sight. Only then did she open the door and step out.

Two miles back along the road, the stout peasant woman complained to her "husband," but in Russian, not Avar, which he did not speak. "Oh my God, I'm sweating like a pig in all of these clothes," Lucy Karp said.

Ivgeny Karchovski stood rubbing his back, which ached from stooping over in the posture of an overworked farmer. Six feet four, he usually stood straight as one of the local fir trees. "Don't complain, *dorogaya moya*, people see what they expect to see," he replied as he removed the horse from its harness. "Even someone as perceptive as Nadya saw only two stupid peasants, a bent old man and 'fat' older woman." He hesitated. "That was her, wasn't it? I glanced when they first approached but couldn't let her see my face."

"How nice! You called me 'my dear,' Uncle Iv." Lucy smiled. "*Dorogaya moya* has a nice sound to it. But yeah, it was her. For a moment, I was afraid that she recognized me even though she's only seen me twice, briefly, and this time I had my face covered."

Ivgeny grimaced. "I didn't like Jaxon sending you on this mission. I know Nadya—unfortunately all too well and better than anyone, and I know how dangerous she can be. She has a sixth sense about danger; it's how she's lived this long."

"Yeah, well, all I can say is your taste in women is questionable." Lucy wrinkled her nose and shook her head. "Besides, someone who knew the local language and wouldn't be a dead giveaway had to come. You don't know Avar or Lezgi, and your Russian pretty much pegs you as raised in and around Moscow, not Dagestan. And none of the others are any better at the language. Besides, I'm a covert operative employed by the government of the United States and a certain amount of risk comes with the job—though if I'm caught, my story is that I'm an interpreter for a United Nations fact-finding team who has lost her way."

"Uncle Iv? How impudent the young are becoming," Karchovski replied. He studied the young woman in front of him with admiration. Her gift for languages was astounding. Even the men who worked for his family's "import-export" business in Dagestan swore that her Avar and Lezgi—ethnic languages of the region and spoken worldwide by perhaps a million people—were that of a native speaker. Several times on this mission her ability to speak the local dialect had saved them from suspicion; Russian was spoken in Dagestan, but Russians were not popular.

Yet, he was still uncomfortable with exposing her to danger. She was, in fact, a relative—not a niece but a cousin, the daughter of his first cousin Roger Karp, the district attorney of New York.

"My taste in women? Nadya was as beautiful as she was dangerous when she was young . . . a very stimulating combination to a lonely army officer fighting the mujahedeen in Afghanistan. And she was good at hiding the corruption in her soul."

"The corruption in her soul? You Russians are so poetic," Lucy scoffed, rolling her eyes. "I think a better description might be 'hiding her sociopathic tendencies.' But enough about your past conquests of dangerously ill women, isn't it time to tell the boys that she's on the way?"

Ivgeny held up a small electronic device. "I already have," he replied. "As soon as you confirmed it was the . . . target." He gave the horse a whack on the rump to send it trotting off down the road. "Let's go."

The pair left the disabled cart in the road and walked across the field to the barn of an abandoned farm. Inside, they changed quickly out of the peasant garb and into the Westernized clothing of city dwellers out for a drive in the country.

Lucy opened the door of the barn further, looking up toward a distant hill. "Good hunting, my darling," she whispered. "And be safe." She turned as Ivgeny wheeled a Ural 750 motorcycle with sidecar out of one of the stalls in the back.

Karchovski pulled on an old-fashioned leather helmet, swung his long leg over the motorcycle, and started the engine. He revved the engine and grinned. "So, I look like James Dean, no?"

"Uh, no," Lucy replied. "More like Boris Karloff in leather. Besides, who said you get to drive?"

"Such impudence! And like hell I would put my life in the hands of such a *бёнок* Now have a seat, it's time to leave."

Lucy laughed and got in the sidecar, pulling on her own helmet as Karchovski put the motorcycle in gear and roared out of the barn. At the road they stopped and looked in the direction Malovo's truck had gone, then Karchovski turned the other direction and raced off up the road.

6

As the premonition of an unseen threat faded for the moment, Karp motioned for the detective to remain in the sedan and walked around to the front passenger side. "Good morning, Detective Neary," he said as he opened the door and got in next to the driver.

"Morning, sir," Detective Al Neary replied without a lot of enthusiasm.

"What's new?" Karp asked, noting a crumpled copy of the sports section from the *New York Post* lying on the seat between them.

"You mean, other than the Knicks still suck, the Jets are playing like horseshit, and the Rangers are goin' nowhere but down the toilet?" the young man replied in his thick New York Irish accent, then shrugged. "Not much."

"Pretty much the same with the Yankees," Karp commiserated.

"I'd thank you to never mention those bums in this vehicle again," Neary replied. "After that meltdown in September . . . and to that bunch of stiffs from Boston . . . Jesus H. Christ on a stick! 'Scuse my language, but I've sworn off baseball."

"But aren't you the guy who named your kids after Yankee players?"

"Yeah, Lou Gehrig Neary, Joe DiMaggio Neary, and Micki

Mantle Neary. . . . Micki's a girl, so me and the wife spelled it with two *i*'s instead of an e-y."

"I'm sure she'll appreciate the gesture someday."

"It was that or name her Babe Ruth Neary. But I didn't want a bunch of guys runnin' around her high school callin' my little girl Babe. I mighta had to shoot one of 'em."

"Well, then I'm glad you chose Micki with two *i*'s. Our caseload at the DAO can't handle another cop brutality trial."

The short green-eyed detective laughed. "Yeah, and I wouldn't do so well in the joint. So where to, chief?"

Karp turned toward the younger man and wiggled his eyebrows. "How'd you like a piece of the best cherry cheese coffee cake in the world?"

The detective put the Lincoln into Drive and lurched away from the curb. "Got to be Il Buon Pane at Third and Twenty-ninth."

Karp was impressed. "You're right. But how'd you know?"

Neary looked at him like he was nuts. "You're askin' a cop how he knows where to find pastry and a good, hot cuppa joe?"

"Yeah, okay, I'd expect nothing less from my NYPD guardians," Karp conceded. "But it's a small place so I didn't think anybody else had heard of it."

"Well, actually, you're probably right, unless you live in the neighborhood or someone turned you on to the place," Neary admitted. "But I used to walk that beat when I was first comin' up on the force, and Moishe's one of those old-school guys who still believes in free coffee and a snack for the cops. Makes the bad guys think twice about hittin' a place that's popular with New York's finest. Go ahead, rob the banks. Kidnap the women. Beat the crap out of each other. But never, ever roll a place where cops get free eats. Not if you want to keep your ass out of Riker's Island."

"Then Il Buon Pane it is," Karp chuckled. "And make it snappy. I'm starting to drool all over one of my favorite Father's Day ties."

Ten minutes later, Neary had successfully battled morning rush hour and let Karp out in front of the little bakery.

"Sure you don't want to come in?" Karp asked.

"Nah, I'm going to stick with the car," the detective answered. "My luck the frickin' city street department would come along and tow it just out of spite. But if you'd send out a piece of the cherry cheese coffee cake and a cuppa, I'd be much obliged. I might even stick around and give you a ride to the office. . . . On second thought, make it a piece of the blueberry cheese coffee cake. I've heard blueberries are good for you."

"Yeah, blueberry cheese coffee cake has got to be healthy. I'll make sure you get a piece. But after that you don't have to wait, I'll be about thirty minutes and I can catch a cab . . ."

"Take your time, I ain't going nowhere. Clay would have my ass. Besides, I want to reread the story about last night's Knicks game so that I can get my blood pressure to spike again. . . . Those dumb-ass wastes of space . . ."

Karp got out of the car and stood there for a moment looking at the bakery, its big windows filled with every sort of delicacy, from many-tiered wedding cakes to pastries to loaves of breads. A vent above the window, apparently leading directly back to the ovens, poured a delicious aroma over the sidewalk that chased away any thoughts of a cold winter.

It never ceased to amaze him that a place like Il Buon Pane—a two-story, redbrick affair probably built sometime around the beginning of the twentieth century—could still exist on a busy intersection in the heart of Manhattan. Although lease prices had fallen after 9-11 and the subsequent exodus to supposedly safer havens on the other side of the East and Hudson rivers, it seemed incredible that an old neighborhood bakery could pay the rent and support its owners and their employees.

Then again, there was always a steady stream of customers going into the shop. Some appeared to have been arrested by the bouquet of fresh bread and drifted into the store as if sleepwalking; others swung open the door with obvious joy written all over their faces, like soldiers home from a war.

Karp knew how they all felt. His stomach growled at the thought of a warm, dark rye right out of the oven, slathered in Pennsylvania apple butter. Or the German chocolate cake so rich that a simple taste was ecstasy, though who could stop at anything less than a full piece? And yet all these delights were trumped by Moishe's cherry cheese coffee cake—sensually warm, oozing cherries and cream cheese, and big enough to feed a family of four.

Glancing up, Karp noted the Star of David in the window of the apartment above the store. Moishe and his wife, Goldie, lived above the bakery, a quiet Jewish couple who kept Shabbat by closing on Fridays late afternoon and Saturdays and attended the Third Avenue Synagogue near Central Park.

He'd met them one day several months earlier when Marlene's father, Mariano, who had been recently diagnosed with senior dementia, left his home in Queens, took a subway, and then walked the rest of the way to the bakery. Il Buon Pane had once been owned by a boyhood friend from Italy, and in Mariano's confused state, he thought his friend still owned it. But Mariano's friend had died many years before after selling the bakery to Moishe and Goldie, who had immigrated to the United States after World War II. Moishe had worked for the owner for many years and took over when he retired.

It turned out that Moishe had been in the synagogue when the suicide bomber attacked. He'd been one of the lucky ones who'd survived with nothing more than bruises and cuts. But then, he was a born survivor, having lived through the horrors of the German death camp at Sobibor during World War II.

Detective Neary could still be heard cursing his hometown teams in the car when Karp opened the door to Il Buon Pane. He grinned when he saw the small elderly man with the big ears, which seemed to be the only thing preventing his baker's cap from sliding down over his face. Moishe was turned away from him, smiling at a customer as he took one of her hands in both of his and thanked her for visiting his shop.

The customer, a young woman, looked up at Karp, a beatific smile on her face, as if she'd just had a word with the Pope. She opened the bakery bag she clutched and bent her head to sniff the contents. "Strudel," she murmured as she turned and headed for the back of the shop.

"Butch!" the old man shouted as he turned and saw him. He wiped his flour-coated hands on his apron and came out from behind the counter with both arms extended. "It is so good to see you, my friend. . . . Such a thing to be able to say that the district attorney of New York is my friend! What a great country! Shalom!"

A half dozen customers turned to watch curiously as the gnomish little baker embraced the giant man in the off-the-rack dark blue suit. The special attention embarrassed Karp a little, but Moishe was so open and unaffected that Karp clapped the little man on the back and gave him a squeeze. "Good to see you, too, my friend," he said, looking around behind the counter and toward the doorway leading to the ovens. "Where's Goldie?"

At the mention of his wife's name, Moishe turned somber. "She's upstairs in bed," he said quietly. "Today is the anniversary of the day the Germans rounded up her family in Amsterdam and shipped them off to Auschwitz. It still troubles her that of them all—her parents, two brothers, and her older sister—only she survived. Every year it's the same; she shuts herself in the dark and wants to be alone with her memories."

Karp nodded. "I understand. I'm sorry if this wasn't a good day to invite my friends to visit your shop."

Moishe brightened. "Nonsense. This is my Goldie's day to grieve. But she would not want all the world to cry with her. That's not Goldie. No . . . today is a good day and some of your friends are here already. . . . I am looking forward to a few moments to listen in on the conversations of great men!"

"I think that you'll more than hold your own in these conversations," Karp said, "that's why I asked them to come here. They're always interested in meeting other agile minds."

"Well, then I hope a genius comes in for a Danish, because otherwise they may be sorely disappointed." Moishe laughed as he led the way toward the back of the shop. "You haven't seen our new sitting room. The electronics store next door went belly up and there was no one to take the lease. So the landlord—an old friend and customer—agreed to lease it to me for a percentage of the profits, which is a good deal for both of us."

Karp was surprised to discover that a doorway had been built between the old bakery and the space next door on Twenty-ninth Street. He'd been dropped off on Third Avenue and he hadn't noticed that the space had been converted into a tastefully decorated sitting room with tall tables surrounded by bar stools, and couches with coffee tables.

Quite a few people were already in the back, enjoying their treats. Some were gathered in small groups that buzzed with earnest conversations. Elsewhere, young couples drank their coffees and looked dreamily into each other's eyes or laughed about some private joke. Others sat alone, working on computers.

"We have wireless," Moishe explained. "As you can see, it helps with business."

"You've got Starbucks beat, hands down."

Moishe looked troubled. "Do you think it's too corporate? Too impersonal? I agonized over whether to ban computers. Cell phones aren't allowed. This should be a place to be alone with your thoughts, or with someone else who is also here, not a disembodied voice."

Karp shook his head. "Not at all. I think it's very smart, and I think it's going to be a great success." He noticed the young woman from the front sitting with her eyes closed and the same smile on her lips as she slowly chewed a piece of her strudel.

The little man's blue eyes brightened above his prodigious nose. "Ah, good, I was worried that you'd think I sold out to the Man." He pointed. "And there are your friends."

Karp looked where he was pointing to a group of older men sitting around a circular wooden table at the very back of the room. Several of them were already waving, trying to get his attention. He walked quickly over. "I see the Sons of Liberty Breakfast Club and Girl-Watching Society has already convened."

"Ah, the prodigal son has arrived," a thin, distinguished man with long gray hair tied back in a ponytail and mutton-chop sideburns said as he stood and held out his hand.

"Your Honor," Karp replied, taking the man's hand. Although he looked like an aging hippy from the Village, Frank Plaut had once been one of the most respected federal judges with the Second Circuit Court of Appeals and a professor of law at Columbia University.

Karp turned toward the others. In all, seven men sat at the table.

Besides Frank Plaut, there was a former Marine who fought at Iwo Jima, Saul Silverstein, Father Jim Sunderland, top defense attorney Murray Epstein, the poet Geoffrey Gilbert, former U.S. attorney for the southern district Dennis Hall, and a retired editor of the *New York Post*, Bill Florence.

The men referred to their group as the Sons of Liberty Breakfast Club and Girl-Watching Society. They were a self-described group of "old codgers whose wives chase us out of the apartment once a week" to meet over breakfast and debate politics, the law, art, foreign affairs, and anything else that interested them.

When Karp arrived, he found Father Sunderland talking about the Maplethorpe case. "The prosecution presented its case, and he seems guilty. But then the defense called all those experts and suddenly I wasn't so sure anymore."

"It was the old spaghetti defense," former federal prosecutor Dennis Hall said.

"Spaghetti defense?" Moishe asked, having just wandered over.

"Yeah, throw it all against the wall and see what sticks," Hall explained. "Just how many 'expert witnesses' did the defense call, Butch, a dozen?"

"Something like that," Karp agreed, sitting down. The others knew that as a rule he didn't comment much about ongoing cases. He trusted these men, but someone might innocently let something slip in the wrong company, and it'd be in the newspapers by morning. He didn't believe in trying his cases in the court of public opinion, nor did he want something he said to be used by a defense attorney.

"It's ridiculous," Hall complained.

"Au contraire," replied Epstein, who as a former defense attorney was Hall's counterpart in these philosophical legal debates. "The defendant has the right to produce any and all evidence that might throw doubt on what the prosecution alleges, or demonstrate his innocence. It's up to the state to prove its case and counter the defense experts if it can. That's our system of justice."

"The spaghetti defense has nothing to do with justice or the search for the truth," Hall retorted. "It has everything to do with trying to befuddle the jury. Defense attorneys hope that if they throw enough nonsense in the air, Susie Housewife, Joe Plumber, Bernie Businessman, and Miguel Mechanic on the jury will be too confused to convict their client beyond a reasonable doubt."

"Ah, but the so-called search for the truth is the role of the district attorney," Epstein pointed out. "The role of the defense attorney is to zealously represent his client and force the state to prove its case."

"Which means the state has to call its own dozen witnesses to match up against the defense's hired guns."

"Why?" All eyes turned to Karp, who then rephrased his question. "Why does the state have to match the defense experts?"

Hall and Epstein both shrugged. "If for no other reason, juries expect it these days," Epstein said. "They've all been watching *CSI* and *Forensic Files*. They think that both sides are supposed to call experts to battle it out."

Karp nodded as if something had just occurred to him, but instead of saying anything, he turned to Moishe. "So Moishe, what do you think about this debate over expert testimony?"

Moishe waved his hand. "I'm just a baker. What do I know of these things?"

"Humor me," Karp replied. "We have these august attorneys—two of the best in the business—who say that the prosecution and the defense ought to call as many experts as they deem necessary and then let the jury sort out who's telling the truth."

The little baker thought for a moment. "Well, in baking—and, I have found, in life—usually less is more. Too much sugar and the flavor is lost in the sweetness. Too much fruit and you can't taste the pastry. If something is good, don't mess it up by adding to it. . . . Maybe it is the same in the courtroom. Sometimes it compounds a lie to repeat it, even if it's to counter the lie. It is like these people who claim that the Holocaust never occurred. They have a thousand small lies that they claim proves their point. These lies add up to the one big lie. A lie so big that even good people begin to wonder if there is at least some truth to it."

"So you're saying too many experts cloud the picture?" Hall said, shooting his friend and adversary Epstein a smile.

"In a way," Moishe agreed. "The one big lie is like a giant raging beast and throwing small rocks can't bring it down; they only give it substance—otherwise, why throw?"

"So how do you bring down the one big lie?" Karp asked, intrigued by how the turn in conversation mirrored his discussion in the Jewish role model classes just a few nights before.

Moishe held up his arm and pulled down on the sleeve, revealing the number tattooed there by his former captors. "The truth."

Karp shook his head and clapped his friend on the shoulder. "From the mouths of bakers . . ."

"Hear, hear," Bill Florence cheered, pulling a silver flask from the interior pocket of his suit coat. "Moishe, if you don't mind, we sometimes enjoy a little spice with our coffees."

"Ah, men after my own heart," Moishe replied, holding out his cup. "I've found that it helps me with my kneading."

7

LYING ON A HILLSIDE ALMOST THREE MILES AWAY FROM where his girlfriend was climbing into a motorcycle sidecar, Ned Blanchett peered down the scope of his .50 caliber Barrett M107 at the trucks arriving at the edge of the village below. Otherwise, he moved as little as possible, relying on his Ghillie camouflage suit to blend into the gray-green rocks and brown grasses surrounding him.

What the hell am I doing here? he wondered, resting his cheek against the LRSR, or long-range sniper rifle. A few minutes earlier, as he waited for the signal from Ivgeny Karchovski, he'd allowed his thoughts to wander back to the days only a few years distant when he was just a simple ranch hand in New Mexico. If he hadn't decided to go dancing at the Sagebrush Inn south of Taos that night, he might never have met Lucy Karp and her mother, Marlene Ciampi. But he had, and life had never been as simple, or safe, again.

Not that he had any regrets about the path his fate had taken. A shy young man more comfortable with horses than women, he'd figured he might never meet a woman to settle down with. But he'd fallen in love with Lucy and to his surprise, she with him. The flip side of that was he found himself thrust into the violent and bizarre world of the Karp-Ciampi clan, battling murderers, terrorists, and other psychos.

At the same time, he'd come to accept that without her, he would have lived out his life on the range and never gotten involved in a world that seemed so out of kilter with the natural beauty of his surroundings. After the terrorists attacked the World Trade Center on September 11, 2001, he'd been outraged but also felt impotent to do anything about it. Now here he was, a member of a secret agency headed by "former" FBI special agent S. P. "Espey" Jaxon, preparing to assassinate a terrorist.

When Jaxon first approached him about signing on, the agent explained that he needed team members who were "below the radar." No one from other government agencies, except for a few trusted men he'd brought in with him from the FBI. He said it was because he wanted people who didn't have federal personnel files on them. But there was also the implicit message that the Sons of Man, who'd been his particular target, had their tentacles in law enforcement agencies from the Department of Homeland Security to the FBI to the CIA.

According to the official story, Jaxon and his men left the bureau to work for a private security firm and hefty salary increases. Blanchett assumed that given such a short list of people who could be trusted, the existence of their small force was known to very few people, though Jaxon seemed to be able to summon extensive resources.

Those resources had apparently determined that the Sons of Man were up to more mischief and that once again Nadya Malovo was central to the action. Apparently, no one had been able to determine exactly what the threat would be, so it was decided that killing Malovo might at least throw their plans into disarray. It wasn't quite the same as cutting the head off the snake to kill the body—that would have to wait until Jaxon was ready to go after the SOM leadership—more like pulling its fangs.

By ripping open her heart with a .50 caliber bullet, he thought. The now familiar twinge of guilt rippled across Blanchett's mind as he contemplated shooting a woman, even one as evil as Nadya Malovo, from nearly a mile away. As he was raised in the Old West, steeped in its myths of fair play and face-to-face confrontations, this smacked to him of an ambush—something normally attributed to "the bad guys."

Shortly after joining Jaxon's "company," Blanchett had been spirited off to a training facility on the West Coast where he and others were put through a course, which they were told was similar to what it took to qualify for the Navy SEALs. Only this was more secret. He and his comrades were prohibited from talking freely. They were allowed to discuss harmless, general topics—like baseball and women—but they weren't supposed to share information about which agencies they belonged to, who they worked with, or anything that might identify them or their missions.

Out of nearly two dozen men and women who started the training, only he and a half dozen others completed it. Along the way, a tough but skinny young cowboy had been transformed into a tough, muscular man with broad shoulders, narrow hips, and a steady aim that could put a bullet into a five-inch circle from a half mile away.

After completing the course, he'd been whisked off to sniper school at yet another undisclosed location in the South. Jaxon had taken note of Blanchett's native ability with guns—both the .45 caliber Peacemaker he used for quick-draw and pistol shooting contests, and the Winchester rifle he carried on the range. Years of shooting both from horseback had trained his eyes and reflexes to snap off an accurate shot at the precise right moment even on the move.

Of course, all that shooting had been in fun or boredom, or to deal with the occasional predator, like mountain lions and coyotes. Then he'd met Lucy and he'd been called upon to shoot a man for the first time in her defense, and others later as he became embroiled in the perpetual violence surrounding her family. But those killings had come in the heat of battle when faced by other armed men, and it was kill or be killed.

Not lying here like a snake in the grass, he thought. He wiped his eyes and forced himself to recall the conversation he'd had with the Special Forces sergeant who'd been his instructor at sniper school when he'd brought up his concerns. The sergeant, a tall black man who never seemed to blink, had looked thoughtful, as if it was the first time he'd run into this issue.

"How do most people die in a war?" he asked at last.

Blanchett had shrugged. *"Bullets . . . bombs."*

"Yeah, bullets, bombs, Army cooking and syphilis," the sergeant said, *"but what I meant was, do they die up close and personal—hand to hand, gunfight at the OK Corral? Or do they die because some motherfucker whose face they've never seen sent some shit their way that takes their poor, unfortunate asses out of here?"*

"Uh . . . if you mean from a distance, I guess that would be right," Blanchett said.

"Damn straight. Not since the days of rocks and, I guess, swords and clubs have we done most of our killing eye to eye. In fact, most military innovation has been a trend to kill from greater and greater distances because one, it's safer, and two, it has a hell of a demoralizing effect on the enemy."

Blanchett's lips twisted. *"I get your drift. But it still don't feel right."*

Again the sergeant was silent for a moment before he spoke. *"Nothing wrong with that feeling. The Bible says 'Thou shalt not kill' and that ain't something you should ever feel good about ignoring. But sometimes killing evil motherfuckers is necessary, especially if by letting them live, you endanger innocent people you could have saved . . . or the men and women you serve with and who are counting on you to protect them from the enemy."*

The sergeant clapped him on the shoulder and held on. *"Tell you what, cowboy, I've done three tours in Afghanistan and Iraq and there was several times when the joker shooting at me was close enough and good enough that they nearly made it count. And tell you what: I much preferred killing their buddies from a safe distance with a .50 cal M107. I don't like it, but I think to myself, 'What if I don't take the shot and a week later he takes over a jet and flies it into a civilian office building, or I hesitate to blow his brains all over the yard and before I can come to my senses, the son of a bitch murders an innocent hostage?' That's what I think about when I contemplate pulling that trigger."*

Half a world away from the woods where that conversation took place, Blanchett looked back down the scope as the trucks pulled up in front of the house Ivgeny's men had pointed out as the likely meeting place. The men were hard-faced Dagestani who apparently worked for the Karchovski family business. Ivgeny had introduced them as men he'd served with in Afghanistan—including two Muslims—and their sons.

Jaxon had described the Karchovski business as smuggling black-market goods into Russia and the surrounding area—from vehicles to liquor to designer clothing—and then turning around and smuggling immigrants into the United States. In answer to Blanchett's unasked question, the agent shrugged and said, *"I know . . . feds and Russian mob bosses make strange bedfellows, but sometimes the enemy of my enemy truly is a great friend."*

Yeah, aren't we an odd band of desperados, Blanchett thought. *A former commie army officer turned gangster, a ranch hand from New Mexico, smugglers, FBI agents . . . and a female linguist from New York City.*

Blanchett furrowed his brow as he thought about Lucy and the danger she was in. When she told him that she, too, was joining Jaxon's squad, he'd been vehemently opposed. But she'd responded with the fiery spirit that had first attracted him to the gangly young woman from back east.

"Don't tell me what to do, Ned Blanchett," she'd responded, her hands on her hips, which he would have found endearing except that she was spitting mad.

"It's too dangerous," he tried to reason.

"You mean it's too dangerous for a girl. But it's just as dangerous for you, or more so, because I'm sure Uncle Espey will try to keep me out of the action when he can. I don't know why you think you're any better at this sort of thing than I am."

"It's just something I feel like I've got to do for my country."

"Our country," she'd corrected him. *"I'm just as patriotic as you are. Now get over yourself and accept that I'm in just as deep as you are."*

That had pretty much been the end of the discussion. He'd had to give in, if for no other reason than she stopped listening to his reasons.

"Target should be exiting the vehicle any moment," said a voice next to him. "Distance 1623 Mike. No breeze."

Oh yeah, I forgot, Blanchett thought as he made a minor adjustment on the scope. *We also got an Indian and a Vietnamese gangster on our side.* His spotter lying next to him with binoculars trained on the village was John Jojola, the former chief of police for the Taos Indian Pueblo and a former guerrilla fighter with the army during the Vietnam War. He, too, had been caught up in the Karp-Ciampi family tornado, which was fine with Blanchett because even in his fifties, Jojola was a good man to have in a scrap, and as a spotter for the sniper team.

When Jaxon first went over the mission while they were on a jet winging across the Mediterranean, Blanchett had asked why they weren't using a Predator unmanned drone armed with a missile to take out Malovo.

"Good question," Jaxon answered. *"But there are several reasons. One, we want to be sure we get her, not just blow up a building; we may never get this sort of intelligence and catch her off guard again. Two, the State Department doesn't want to get into it with the Russians about taking military action in airspace they consider theirs, even if the locals don't. And three, we don't know who all is going to be present at this meeting, and again, the State Department is concerned that a missile strike might cause collateral damage we don't intend."*

"In other words, somebody we might want on our side someday could die," Jojola scoffed. *"One day they're terrorists, the next day they're freedom fighters."*

"Exactly," Jaxon agreed. *"It's unfortunate that politics get in the way of simply doing what's right or what's safer. The State Department wants deniability, and it boils down to making sure Malovo is the target, which Ivgeny and Lucy will confirm, and that we do our best to limit other casualties."*

After entering Dagestan, they'd been escorted by men working for Karchovski and spent several days reconnoitering the countryside and working out the details of their plan.

"How's security?" Blanchett asked. He could sense Jojola looking carefully around. An hour earlier, with the light fading, Karchovski's men had crept into position, and at a signal, they cut the throats of the sentinels stationed closest to where Blanchett and Jojola would set up. Karchovski's men immediately assumed the lookouts' positions so that no one in the village would raise the alarm. Blanchett and Jojola would be counting on the men to cover their escape as well.

"Good," Jojola replied in a low voice. He picked up a camera and trained the lens on the village below. "Two men have exited the house to greet our friend. Got a couple good face shots. But she's still in the truck, like she's waiting for something . . ."

Blanchett tensed, wondering if they'd been discovered. Would the men below start charging up the hill while Malovo escaped? He decided that if the trucks started to move, he'd chance a blind shot at the passenger side of the second vehicle, which Karchovski had signaled was the one with his former lover aboard. It wasn't a great option. The M170 fired a round that would go through a reinforced concrete wall, but he'd still be shooting at a target he couldn't see.

"There we go," Jojola whispered, "she was waiting on the bodyguards. . . . She's all yours."

Blanchett fixed the crosshairs on the passenger side of the second truck. He had hoped for a clear shot at his target's chest, which was a more sure thing than her head. A head was smaller, and sometimes moved out of sync with the body. But Malovo's guards had moved so close to the truck that he knew his only clear view would be her head.

The door opened and he saw blond hair begin to emerge. He began to slowly let his breath out and ever so gently increased the pressure on the M170 trigger as he waited for his target to stand upright. But instead, Malovo surprised him by stooping as she got out of the car so that he couldn't see her through her human shield. The group then hurried for the open door of the building, followed by the men who'd come out to greet her.

"Should I take the shot?" he whispered.

"Negative. We're only going to get one chance. Let's see if we can't get a better target when she leaves. She may feel safer when it's dark. If not, we'll take the best shot available then."

* * *

Nadya Malovo didn't relax until she was well inside the house. Granted, if the Americans knew where she was, they might attempt to kill her with a drone or a cruise missile. But she'd weighed the odds and—without knowing that her hunters had reached the same decision—concluded that the United States would not risk an international incident just to kill her.

She didn't like putting her life in the control of men she had not personally trained. But the local mullah had a fierce reputation fighting jihad against her countrymen in Afghanistan and the Americans in Iraq. At least he had some experience and battle-tested men.

One of the men who'd walked out of the building on her arrival now pointed to a table on which there were several laptop computers open and running. He was a small man with distinctly Arabic features, which followed, since he was a Saudi. "*Salaam, assalamu alaikum,*" he said in formal greeting. "Please, have a seat."

"*Salaam,*" Malovo replied curtly, then remembered that she was here in part to cultivate this man's goodwill. "*Assalamu alaikum wa rahmatullahi wa barakatuh.*" She turned to another of her hosts, a tall, thin black man, and repeated the greeting.

"*Salaam,*" the man replied with a small bow. He smiled tentatively and added in English, "I apologize, but I don't speak Arabic."

Malovo nodded. She'd noted the British accent that identified him as a native of one of that nation's former Caribbean colonies.

"All Muslims should learn Arabic so that they may read the Qur'an as it was intended," the first man sniffed arrogantly. "Soon enough, all peoples will be required to speak Arabic, and to learn the Qu'ran. *Inshallah.*" He smiled condescendingly at the black man. "That means 'God willing.'"

The black man's eyes narrowed. "I know what it means," he hissed.

Malovo had heard enough. She did not have time, or patience, for their spat. *How these people believe they can rule the world when they cannot be in the same room without quarreling is a mystery,* she thought. *But for now my employers need them.*

"Since that glorious day is not yet here, we will speak English," she said, and looked from one man to the other with a smile on her face but murder in her eyes.

The Arab bowed his head. He knew her reputation and decided that perhaps he had dangerously overstepped. “But of course,” he replied. “I did not mean to offend, only a suggestion so that my brother, Omar, might want to learn to read the words of the Prophet in his own language.”

“The words of the Prophet translate in any language to the truth,” Omar grumbled. “But no offense was taken, Ali.”

“Then we will speak no more of it,” Malovo said. It was a command, not a suggestion.

The men nodded and they all sat down at the laptops. “I’ve prepared a PowerPoint presentation on Operation Flashfire,” Ali said.

Malovo frowned. “You do realize that much of what the Americans have learned about the great jihad has been from computers they’ve seized. They’re good at recovering even material that was thought to have been destroyed.”

Ali’s smile disappeared. “I am aware that others have made that mistake. However, I assure you that only one copy of this presentation will exist when we leave here and that is on a computer far from this place. The hard drives have been programmed so that after we turn off these computers, they will self-destruct when someone attempts to turn them on again.”

Malovo nodded. “Then let’s see what you have gone through such trouble to prepare.”

A half hour later, the three conspirators closed the three laptops. “Your computers have now been rendered worthless,” Ali noted as he closed his and placed it carefully in a case. “Are there any questions?”

“It is a good plan and all appears to be in order as previously discussed,” Malovo replied. “My question is: Are you both prepared to go forward on schedule?”

Omar spoke first. “We are ready.” He and Malovo looked at Ali.

The little man shrugged and looked apologetic. “We are ready, too,” he said. “But you know that there is an unresolved piece of this puzzle. Nothing can be done until the Sheik has been returned to us.”

Amir al-Sistani, curse your duplicity, Malovo thought. “We have been trying to locate the Sheik and effect his . . . release. But so far we have met only resistance."

Ali shook his head. "This is not acceptable. We cannot proceed unless he personally allows it."

Malovo stared malevolently at the man. "We understand that was part of the original arrangement. But this contingency was not part of the Sheik's otherwise brilliant concept." *The idiot.* "Perhaps we did not make it clear that we are willing to pay a bonus for the plan to go forward, even if we cannot produce Mr. al-Sistani."

Ali made a face as if what he had to say pained him. But in truth, he was enjoying having the upper hand over so formidable a woman. "You and your employer have made it abundantly clear that cost is no object. However, even if we wanted to go forward under such conditions, we could not, as the Sheik has powerful friends in my government who would not betray him."

"But we are not even sure that he is alive," Malovo pointed out. "Should jihad be held back because of one man?"

"Depends on the man." Ali shrugged. "What do your spies tell you?"

"That he lives," she replied honestly. "But that was two weeks ago. He is in the hands of a madman, and who knows his fate since then."

"Madman or government agent? I find it hard to believe that a homeless beggar was able to thwart the Sheik's attack on the stock exchange."

"We have considered the possibility," Malovo conceded. "But if he works for the government, no one we know—and we have highly placed sources in all security agencies—is aware of it."

"Well, it is not our problem," Ali replied. "It is your problem. Deliver the Sheik or we cannot proceed. Bring him safely back to us, and we guarantee that your schedule will be met and the operation will go forward. Is that not right, Omar?"

The black man nodded. "As God wills."

Malovo wanted nothing so much as to dig her thumbs into their eyeballs. *But that won't make you rich,* she cautioned herself. "Very well, I'll report that everything is ready, except for arranging the return of Amir al-Sistani."

Ali smiled and nodded. "*Allahu akbar*. God is great!"

"Indeed," Malovo replied. "*Allahu akbar*! Now, it is time to leave. You will hear from us soon."

At the doorway, Malovo hesitated and looked outside. The sun had set, and while it would not be absolutely dark for another hour, it would have to do. She did not like to stay in one place very long. At a signal, her bodyguards surrounded her and her two coconspirators and they walked out the door.

As she circled around to the passenger side of the truck, Malovo glanced up at the tall hill. Something wasn't right. Her well-honed instinct for self-preservation caused her to dart suddenly forward just as a large angry insect zipped past her head. She heard a sound behind her like a melon split open with a hammer and then from the other direction the report of a large-caliber rifle.

Malovo glanced back and saw Ali lying on the ground, the top of his head missing. *Sniper!* Her mind screamed with the warning as she dropped to the ground and crawled to get under the truck. She looked up just as one of her bodyguards was knocked off his feet as a bullet passed through his chest in a gout of blood.

"Attack, attack!" she screamed, pointing in the direction of the rifle's report. "Up there."

Unsure of what they were attacking or in which direction to go, the bodyguards began firing in a variety of directions up at the hills. Two more of her men fell as high-velocity antipersonnel rounds punched cantaloupe-size holes in their chests. Now others were shooting down at them from where their sentinels had been.

However, these were battle-hardened men who quickly organized and began to direct their fire toward the unseen enemy on the hill. Two heavy machine guns were quickly set up and began raking the hillside, while other men began charging toward the enemy position with their assault rifles and rocket-propelled grenades.

With the firefight raging, Malovo felt the moment had come to make her escape. She jumped up and opened the door of the truck. The bewildered and frightened driver sat in his seat with his hands gripping the steering wheel. "Drive, you idiot," she screamed.

The men she'd arrived with saw what was happening and ran for their trucks as the local men continued the fight. The trucks lurched forward and circled to leave the village the way they'd entered.

The driver's-side window of the truck Malovo was in disappeared along with the front of the driver's neck. He clasped his throat with both hands and looked at his passenger as if hoping she would know what he should do next. Her response was to lean over and open his door, and then shove him out as she slid into his seat. She stomped on the gas pedal and the truck roared down the road.

"Let's go, Ned," Jojola yelled as slugs from a machine gun stung the ground above their heads.

"Dammit, I missed her!" Blanchett swore. He sighted down through the scope—now operating on night-vision settings—and fired at the fleeing truck below with no noticeable affect.

"Couldn't be helped, she ducked at just the wrong moment," Jojola replied. "One of those other jokers took it instead."

"I don't even know who he was. Maybe he's one of those guys the State Department was worried about."

"Fuck that," Jojola replied. "He wasn't here collecting for the March of Dimes. He's a bad guy and so are the rest of those assholes you nailed. But a bunch more of them are heading this way. We've got to move."

A rocket-propelled grenade struck the slope twenty-five yards away, showering them with debris. The two men jumped up and began running over the top of the hill as Ivgeny's men on the other hillsides gave covering fire.

Out of sight, they paused a minute to catch their breath. "I can't believe I missed," Blanchett moaned.

Jojola turned and grabbed him by the shoulders. "Ned, forget it," he said. "I've missed plenty of easier shots. You can't account for the target doing something unexpected. Besides, Ivgeny has a little surprise waiting. She's in a panic and heading right for him."

As if to accent Jojola's prediction, a muffled explosion echoed over the hills in the direction Malovo had fled. The Indian smiled and patted Blanchett on the back. "I think that was a good sign," he said. "Now let's get going again. We've got to cover five klicks and we don't have a whole lot of time to do it."

Watching from a different hilltop two miles away, Ivgeny Karchovski and Lucy Karp stood for a moment looking at the burning wreck of a troop transport. A few seconds earlier, the trucks had come hurtling around the bend, fleeing the village. Assuming that Malovo would again be in the middle truck, Karchovski had allowed the first truck to pass the disabled cart and then detonated the IED buried beneath the hay when the second truck drew next to it. The explosion had blown the heavy transport off the ground and flipped it over. None of the occupants had escaped the ensuing flames.

After the explosion, the first transport had not even slowed down and was now heading toward them. The third stood idling on the road as if afraid to pass the same spot.

"Do you think she's dead?" Lucy asked. When she wasn't answered right away, she glanced over at her companion and was surprised to see what appeared to be a look of sadness on his craggy face. "Ivgeny?"

The mob boss looked down at Lucy as if she'd interrupted his dream. Then he gazed off in the direction of the village. "I heard Ned get two shots off before the others started shooting," he said. "I hope he was successful. If not"—Karchovski stopped and looked at the burning truck—"no one survived that."

Lucy glanced again at the tall man next to her, who looked so much like her father. In some ways they were such polar opposites—lawman and outlaw—but there were many more similarities, including integrity, honor, and, surprisingly, sensitivity.

"Ivgeny, I'm sorry."

Karchovski faced her and reached out to pat her cheek. "Don't be," he replied. "Whatever feelings I might have once had, they died a long time before this night."

Without saying anything else, he turned and walked to the motorcycle and started it. He patted the sidecar. "Come, beloved cousin, your prince awaits."

8

An hour after entering Il Buon Pane, Butch Karp regretfully turned down the offer of a second piece of cherry cheese coffee cake and joined Detective Neary in the Lincoln.

"One hundred Centre?" the detective asked.

"Yes, master, back to the salt mine."

The detective chuckled. "I thought you was one of those guys who loves to work . . . burning the midnight oil all the time. Sees the kids on the weekend."

Karp knew that the detective was kidding, but the comment struck home. He tried to be a good family man. With the kids he'd always made time to help with homework, attend school functions and sports events. He'd never been afraid to show his affection with Lucy and the boys, or felt he had to prove that he loved them by enforcing the rules he wanted them to live by. He was even teaching a role model class for the twins' bar mitzvah courses.

And Karp more than loved his wife, he adored her. She was the most interesting person he'd ever met. She knew him better than he knew himself, and knew what to say and do at the right time. Their connection went beyond finishing each other's sentences to knowing what the other was thinking. Combine that with the fact that after nearly thirty years of marriage they still made love like wolverines, and he figured he'd found his soul mate.

Yet he knew that his family shared him with another love. Like one of those men whose duplicitous lifestyle with two wives and two families in two different cities. Only his other "family" was his job, and more often than not, it got the best part of him. It sapped his energy and his emotional bank. He'd come home after a fourteen-hour day or a seventy-hour week bushed and ready for a little quiet reading and then bed. Too often on weekends, if he wasn't in the office preparing for trial, he was perusing evidence binders at the kitchen table, or otherwise giving off vibes that he wanted to be left alone. Of course, that would just make him feel guilty, for as much as he may have deserved a little downtime for himself, it would be at the cost of his time with the kids or with Marlene.

Yet it was more than just being a workaholic. The job itself was hazardous to himself and to his family.

Being a prosecutor could be a dangerous job in any jurisdiction. The world was filled with angry misfits and career criminals who might take offense to the notion of being held accountable for their crimes. But there was no denying that being the district attorney of New York—home to eight million people, a significant percentage of them criminals, including gangsters of every nationality—might increase the odds of an attack.

Yet taking even the sheer size and demographics of his jurisdiction into account, the amount of violence he and his family were subjected to went beyond the pale for other district attorneys as far as he could tell. Trying to look at it objectively and come up with an explanation why this would be, he reasoned that New York City had become a symbolic target for terrorists and criminal masterminds. Therefore, its law enforcement agencies, including the DAO, were simply on the front lines of a war the rest of the country wasn't experiencing. *Yet.*

"Maybe," Marlene had said one night shortly after the attack on the stock exchange, *"they see you as a symbol, too—a face and a name they can visualize as the threat to their plans, or a human being who represents a way of life they want to destroy."*

As far as Karp was concerned, he was just doing his job, enforcing the laws of the State of New York. Nothing personal about it. If the DAO couldn't prove its case, then he didn't care if it was Osama bin Laden himself, he wouldn't let the case go forward.

Lucy argued that the seemingly constant maelstrom of violence surrounding the family wasn't as simple as he was trying to make it out to be—a hazard of the job. Some of the violence that had been directed at him, and his family, had nothing to do with the DAO and was too extreme just for coincidence. *"There's a reason why our family is in the center of all this,"* she'd argued. *"Like it or not, believe in God or not, call it fate or karma, but we're* supposed *to be involved. I believe that David Grale is right. The world is headed for a final confrontation between good and evil, a battle, as they say, of biblical proportions."*

"So you're basing this upcoming Armageddon on the prognostications of Grale, the Avenging Angel of Gotham City?" he'd asked. *"And that we have been drafted into the Army of God without so much as a by-your-leave?"*

"Something like that," Lucy had said, sticking her tongue out. Since childhood, she'd been preoccupied with the spiritual side, especially her mother's Roman Catholic heritage, though Marlene was, at most, a Christmas and Easter Mass Catholic. Lucy, on the other hand, had even considered becoming a nun and claimed that she received "visits" from a fifteenth-century martyr named St. Teresa of Avila who offered wise advice and comfort.

Karp considered these manifestations to be psychological. His daughter even admitted that the saint appeared in times of stress and danger. But whereas she believed in a supernatural cause, he thought it was her mind's way of functioning at a higher level when under pressure, a sort of survival mechanism having more to do with her adrenal gland than with guardian angels.

There were times when Karp considered whether he should walk away from the DAO. Move to someplace safe and warm, like Beverly Hills, where he could teach law, and enjoy more quality time with his wife and the boys. But he stayed because he loved what he did, knew he was good at it and that it was important. He didn't see evil in the supernatural sense that Lucy did, but he knew it existed in the hearts and minds of some people and that he had a responsibility to help combat them.

"Uh, sorry, I didn't mean nuttin' by that last comment," Neary said, glancing over at Karp with a worried look on his face. "It was a stupid joke. And hey, thanks for gettin' me that piece of coffee cake. It was even better than I remembered."

"Don't worry about it, Al," Karp replied. "I know you were only yanking my chain. You just hit a little closer to home than I probably care to admit; maybe I need a wakeup call."

The detective smiled and nodded. "Happy to be of service. Next stop, the salt mine."

They drove the rest of the way to Centre Street in silence, each lost in his own thoughts. Neary with the pitiful performance of his beloved Yankees. Karp rewinding *The People vs. F. Lloyd Maplethorpe* in his mind. Lying in bed the night before, going over what he knew of the case, he'd wished that he'd been more involved with the actual trial strategy.

Karp had no problem with Reed being assigned to the Maplethorpe case. Stewbie was one of the most senior prosecutors in the Homicide Bureau and an excellent choice. And it wasn't like he'd been on his own. His trial strategy had received the critical vetting by the bureau chiefs and other select assistant district attorneys who met every Monday morning to review important cases. It was an intensive process in which the ADA presented his case, as well as demonstrated that he had anticipated the tactics a defense attorney might use. Then they all tried to pick it apart.

Yet, you missed something, Karp thought, then shook his head.

In the tradition of other celebrity murder cases, Maplethorpe had hired a dream team of famous attorneys, headed by Guymore G. Leonard. Tall, tan, and handsome as a movie star (and in fact he had appeared in several cameo roles in films produced or directed by former clients), Leonard was known for his fringed leather coats, cowboy hats, ostrich-leather boots, and his flair for the dramatic in and out of the courtroom. A darling of the media, he could always be expected to toss out a great quote, and seemed to regard gag orders handed down by judges as a personal attack on his constitutional right of self-promotion. He lived on a ranch in Montana, and only rarely took on cases—preferring to rake in the proceeds from books, lectures, and consulting—unless they were the sort to place him firmly in the spotlight, as well as pay his outrageous fees.

Leonard was assisted by two other attorneys, Mark Hayvaert, a short, pugnacious man who looked and acted like a bad-tempered bulldog, and Jeremiah Hyslop, a Harvard law paper-pusher whose main purpose was to flood the court and prosecution team with motions and demands, which of course had to be answered. The purpose was, of course, to distract, delay, and keep the prosecution team responding to each trivial motion instead of focusing on trial preparation.

Leonard and his colleagues were attended by a large retinue of legal assistants, private investigators, and forensic experts, including psychologists, psychiatrists, sociologists—all with their individual area of expertise—and blood-splatter and ballistics experts. There was even a professor of linguistics whose sole purpose had been to throw doubt on one of the prosecution's star witnesses, Harry Gianneschi. The professor had testified that Gianneschi had "misinterpreted" Maplethorpe's comment "I think I killed her."

Against this formidable army, Reed had been assisted by a young assistant district attorney only recently assigned to the Homicide Bureau. Her main function was to keep track of testimony and witnesses, and to know where to get her hands on documents and evidence.

Still, it should have been enough, Karp thought as Neary turned right on Canal and headed into Chinatown. It was a simple case, and boatloads of spurious motions and superfluous experts didn't change that fact. *Sometimes less is more.*

Karp didn't make a habit of second-guessing his assistant district attorneys. He believed in his mentor Garrahy's maxim: Pick good people, train them well, put them through their paces at the Monday meetings, and then let them do their jobs.

Neary swung around the block so that they were heading north on Centre Street as they pulled up to the Criminal Courts Building on the right. "Out in front or the Franklin Street side?" the detective asked.

"Out front would be great," Karp replied. Sometimes he took the private elevator from the Franklin Street entrance of the courts building, an entrance used only by judges and other authorized court personnel, to an anteroom next to his eighth-floor office, which he could enter without even passing his receptionist. It was handy for arriving unseen, but usually he liked to enter the building the same way everybody else did, through the front door on Centre Street. It sort of got his head in the game. But the detective wouldn't have understood, so he just explained, "I want to pick up a copy of the *Times*."

"What for? Parakeet cage needs a new liner?" Neary replied with a snort. "Planning on going to the Fulton Fish Market and bringing home a little something in the sports pages for supper?"

Karp laughed. "Actually, I like the crossword puzzle," he said truthfully. Word puzzles and watching movies were a habit he'd picked up from his mother.

Neary pulled over to the curb in front of the Criminal Courts Building next to a dark green newsstand. "Thanks, Al," Karp said, getting out. "Oh, and I think I'll walk home tonight."

"Clay ain't gonna like that."

"I'll break the news to him as gently as I can. But consider yourself off the hook."

"Thanks, Mr. Karp, I wouldn't mind getting home to the old lady while she's still awake."

There's that twinge again. "I understand," Karp said, closing the door and turning toward the newsstand just as the vendor greeted him.

"Good morning . . . m-m-motherfucker shitface . . . Butch. What will it be today? The . . . crap crap craaaaap . . . *New York* . . . oh oh nice tits . . . *Times*?"

Karp grimaced as shocked tourists on the sidewalk looked from the vendor to him and back, as if he'd encouraged the profanity.

There was only one man on the planet as far as he knew who sold newspapers, or anything else, with an accompanying stream of obscenities. However, Dirty Warren, the smiling vendor gazing at him through thick, smudged glasses, had an excuse for his over-the-top verbiage. The little man suffered from Tourette's syndrome, a misfiring of some of his brain's circuits that caused facial tics, body twinges, and outbursts of inappropriate language that fell like pornographic commas into the middle of his sentences.

At least that's his excuse for most of it, Karp thought as he walked up to the stand. There were times when the skinny little man with the Pinocchio-shaped and perpetually drippy nose got angry or agitated, and then the cursing seemed a bit more deliberate. In fact, he'd once asked Dirty Warren, an apt nickname given his words and hygiene, if that was the case.

The newspaper vendor had looked genuinely shocked and without so much as cracking a smile replied, *"I don't . . . oh boy oh boy, kiss my ass dickweed . . . cuss."*

Ever since, Karp had wondered if Dirty Warren was trying to be funny that day or if he really didn't realize what his affliction sounded like. He did know that there was a lot more going on beneath the filthy orange stocking cap that Dirty Warren wore no matter what the weather than appearances and mannerisms had initially indicated when they first met.

Dirty Warren was peering at him innocently, his watery blue eyes magnified behind the glasses. "Good morning, Warren," Karp replied. "Sure, a copy of the *Times*, please."

"Thanks. Hey, I got one for you . . . whoop whoop butthole . . . this morning," Dirty Warren said.

"Go ahead, give it your best shot," Karp replied. He and Dirty Warren had been playing a game of movie trivia ever since they'd met years ago, with the newspaper vendor asking questions and Karp answering. So far the score was Karp, approximately a million, and Dirty Warren, zero.

"Who played David Filby in the . . . hoo hooo . . . 1960 version of *The Time Machine*?"

"I hope you didn't stay up all night thinking of that one. The answer is Alan Young."

"Okay . . . anus sphincter . . . smart guy, who played Filby's son, James?"

Karp rolled his eyes. "Boy, I hope you've got more game than this the next time you bring it. The son, James Filby, was also played by Alan Young. And even though modern remakes are supposed to be off-limits for our little contest, you might be interested to know that Young also appeared in the 2002 version of *The Time Machine*. What was his role?"

Dirty Warren's unshaved jaw dropped. He wasn't used to fielding questions himself. "I don't . . . shit vagina . . . know."

"He's the florist. Geez, I think you owe me a free newspaper or something."

"Fuck you, Karp!"

"Warren, I thought you didn't cuss."

"Twat penis balls!" Dirty Warren yelled, and started hopping up and down on one foot, his face contorting under a tsunami of muscle spasms. Only with great effort did he calm himself. "Aw, I knew you'd get that one. I was just seeing if I could catch you . . . oh boy oh boy whoop whoop monkey asses . . . in a senior moment."

"Senior!" Karp snorted, then grinned at the vendor, who grinned back.

"Yeah, old as the hills and . . . whoa lick my scrotum ass-banger . . . twice as dusty, as my dad used to say."

"Well, if I'm going to be insulted, and you've got nothing better than softball trivia questions, I think I'll leave," Karp said with a wink, and turned to go. But prompted by the movie—with its underground-living, evil Morlocks—he was reminded to ask the vendor, "Any word from David?"

Dirty Warren scratched beneath the stocking cap. "Nothing . . . except that he's in one of his moods." The little man peered around the side of his newsstand as if watching for spies. "But I'll tell you this. There's been some other folks . . . fuck me naked . . . asking around about our dark friend. They're offering big money for any information about him or that piece of terrorist shit . . . shit shit oh my God shit . . . he's entertaining. And these folks with the money ain't nice like you and me . . . asswipe motherfucking pig . . . not by a long shot."

Karp scowled. "Do me a favor, if any of these folks come around again, give me a call," he said. He reached into his coat pocket and pulled out his wallet, which he opened to find a business card. "My office and cell are on this. I'll trust you to be discreet."

Dirty Warren gingerly took the card, as if he was being handed an ancient and fragile document. He tore the top half off that had Karp's name, leaving just the phone numbers on the bottom. "There. Even if I'm cut into a million pieces and the bad guys . . . holy shit whooo boy . . . get this, they won't know whose phone number is on it."

"Good thinking, Warren. Give me a call if you see or hear anything to do with al-Sistani or David."

Dirty Warren looked troubled. "Well, I'll call if those folks come around again. But I don't discuss David's business . . . fuck your sister screw me . . . even with you. For starters, he'd probably slit me from appetite to asshole . . . asshole asshole . . . if I did."

Karp nodded. "Wouldn't want that to happen, but if you do speak to him, or can get word to him, ask David to contact me, please."

The newspaper vendor gave a little salute. "Will do, Governor, though even you don't want to . . . suck me dildo . . . see him when he's in one of his moods. When he's like that, he's not the David Grale we all know and love."

"I understand. Well, off to the salt mines," Karp said.

"Yeah? Speaking of salt mines, what was the only movie ever blacklisted in America?"

"Another easy one, but a great trivia question and an important film. *Salt of the Earth,* blacklisted in 1954 at the height of the Red Scare."

Dirty Warren clapped his hands. "Figured you'd know that one. It was based on a true story about a . . . screw my ass . . . strike at a zinc mine in New Mexico by Mexican-American workers trying to get the same wages as Anglo workers. Just making the movie . . . bitch bastard sack of shit . . . was enough to get the actors, director, and producers branded as communists; some of them were even deported and never allowed back into the United States. It was a big lie, of course—accuse all those people of being communists just to get out of paying them more. But people were afraid of communists, so the big lie worked, and the movie was banned for a long time."

"I know it well, Warren," Karp replied. "It became a famous First Amendment case and went all the way to the U.S. Supreme Court, where the movie guys won, but many years later, after it was too late." He waved. "Got to run. It's been fun."

"Yeah . . . hemorrhoids hooker blow me . . . I'll get you yet."

As Karp turned back again to the looming gray mass of the Criminal Courts Building, he bumped into and nearly knocked over an old beggar. The man had been lurching along the sidewalk, hunched over in a ratty old sweatshirt with the hood pulled nearly down to his chin.

Karp reached out and caught the man before he fell, and for a brief moment caught a glimpse of his face. The man appeared to have some disfiguring disease that had destroyed the skin of much of his face, so that his two startling blue eyes stared out of a puckered mass of red and purple.

"Watch it," the beggar snarled, yanking his arm out of Karp's grasp and pulling the hood further down.

"Sorry," Karp replied, but the man was already shuffling away from him.

Karp was nearly to the front door of the building when with a sinking feeling he realized what had just happened. The sudden bump, the tug on his coat—he knew without knowing that he'd just been pickpocketed.

He reached up to the inside of his coat pocket expecting to discover that his wallet was missing, but instead he found that something had been added. A plain white envelope, folded over. He tore off the end and removed the contents—a single note card on which written in pencil were these words: "In Casa Blanca plans are made that have to do with the art of war. One can be a house, the other is usually not an art. But when you look at both what do you see? And so does the deadly connection between the two sides."

A riddle? Karp walked back out toward the sidewalk and looked in the direction the beggar had gone, but the man was no longer in sight, swallowed up by the sea of pedestrians. He glanced over at the newsstand, where the vendor was trying to sell a tour guide to a couple of older tourists. "This here magazine is the best in the city for finding Dylan Thomas's old hangouts . . . whoo boy whoo boy poop nipples . . . including the White Horse Tavern . . . nice ass bitch . . . and the Chelsea Hotel. Hey, where you going? Don't you . . . fuck me clit . . . want the magazine? . . . Shit!"

Karp shook his head and headed into the building. *Only Monday and it already feels like a long week.*

9

As the nondescript sedan approached the small port-of-entry post at the U.S.-Canadian border, its female passenger placed her gloved hand inside her purse and felt for the gun. A full moon glimmered off the first snow of the season, casting dark shadows beneath the forest of pines that lined either side of the two-lane road. The same incandescence illuminated the small border crossing post, but otherwise there were no lights on in the building or any other sign of human activity.

The lack of border security did not surprise Nadya Malovo, who released her grip on the weapon and relaxed back in her seat. She was well aware that while the United States and Canada shared more than five thousand miles of border—compared to the United States and Mexico, which shared nineteen hundred—there were fewer than a thousand U.S. Border Patrol agents in the north, while there were twelve thousand in the south.

There were also hundreds of small ports-of-entry along the U.S.-Canadian border used by the locals on a daily basis with little impediment to their travels. Malovo shook her head as she reflected that only six or so years after the attack on the World Trade Center, the U.S. Border Patrol still dedicated more of its resources to catching illegal immigrants crossing the border to work than to preventing more terrorist attacks.

There wasn't a terrorist in the world who didn't know it was easier to slip across the northern border than the one in the south. Rural border checkpoints like the one they now glided past even posted their daytime hours and weren't manned overnight. It didn't take a lot of sleuthing, either, to discover such details thanks to congressional hearings about border security, which were duly reported by the press; all any terrorist had to do was search the Internet.

Waiting to cross into the United States several weeks after the attempted assassination in Dagestan, Malovo had read an article about how investigators working for the U.S. General Accounting Office had carried a duffel bag containing what would have appeared to be components for a nuclear bomb across the U.S.-Canadian border without being stopped or questioned. She'd filed that interesting possibility away for the future, while wondering how a nation as powerful as the United States could be stupid enough to advertise how to carry out successful attacks.

Nadya's driver was a young white American convert to Islam who volunteered that he was the son of two wealthy corporate lawyers in Buffalo, New York. As he recounted in boring detail, he'd run away from home as a teen "with no purpose" until wandering into a downtown mosque where he'd been recruited by the imam. The man was a radical Wahabte who advocated the ultimate world domination by strict Islamic rule and had convinced him of the justice of Islam's fight with evil America.

The young man had grown his beard, a patchy effort, as Allah commanded, and after months of listening to increasingly violent rhetoric from the imam, he had been filled with a desire to strike a blow against "the enemies of God." It was somewhat disappointing that instead of some attack, his first mission was to escort a "very important person" through a border crossing he'd become familiar with as a boy traveling to Canada with his father to fish. *Perhaps after this I will be allowed to become a martyr*, he thought as he drove, and his mind turned to fantasies of dying in a blaze of glory. *Inshallah*.

Of course Malovo could not have cared less about the young

man's story or his religious zeal, which like any new convert he talked about incessantly. In fact, she wanted to tell him to shut up, but for now it suited her purposes to come off as a submissive and not overly bright female. She waited until they'd driven several miles beyond the border crossing, all without seeing another vehicle, and then turned to her companion and, as if embarrassed, said, "I need to . . . um, how do you say, piss? No?"

The young man glanced over at her and nodded. When he'd picked her up at a truck stop in Canada, he'd been dumbstruck by her looks and barely submerged sensuality, which was compounded by a sexy accent. He was troubled by his sinful thoughts, but not enough to stop him from checking out her breasts jiggling beneath her sweater whenever he thought she was looking out the window.

"Uh, that's right," he said. "But there won't be a rest stop for another twenty miles."

Malovo squirmed a little in her seat. "I am sorry, but I cannot wait so long," she whimpered. "Perhaps there is a side road and I can"—she paused to giggle shyly—"piss in woods?"

The young man smiled. "There's no one around. I can just pull over here." He started to slow the car but Malovo touched his arm.

"No, please," she said. "I don't want to be by the road if border patrol comes. Is there no place where I cannot be seen from highway? You could be my guard."

A fantasy of what might happen if he was standing next to the woman when she dropped her pants materialized in the young man's mind. And as if reading his thoughts, Malovo gave him a tiny smile and added, "I don't care if you want to watch. You are cute, *mal'chik*."

The small logging road that appeared a quarter mile later couldn't have come too soon for the young man, who swerved off the highway onto the snow-covered track. He was going to stop but Malovo urged him on a little farther "for privacy, please."

At last she was satisfied and told him to pull over. She got out of the car and began to take down her pants, which her driver took as a signal to open his door and hop out of his seat. Not wanting to miss anything, he hurried around the back of the car. However, the smile on his face disappeared as he found himself staring down the barrel of the pistol in the woman's hand.

"What's wrong?" he squeaked.

"Nothing," Malovo said with a shrug. "It's just the . . . what is the expression? . . . 'end of the road' for you. But I give you chance . . . you may run if you want."

Something in the woman's eyes told the young man that there was no debating the issue. He turned and took off into the woods, slipping on the snow as he tried to gain traction. "No, please!" he screamed. "In the name of Allah the merciful!"

Malovo laughed at his frightened pleading; she preferred a chase when there was time for it. Trotting easily after the young man, she wanted him to feel fear as he dodged from one shadow beneath the trees to the next. When they were well into the woods, she lifted the gun and sighted along the barrel, waiting for him to appear again in the moonlight. When he did, she pulled the trigger. The bullet caught the young man in the small of the back, severing his spinal cord. His legs stopped working and he crumpled onto the snow, crying out in pain and terror.

Malovo walked up to her prey, amused by his attempts to crawl away from her. She stepped around in front of him so that he stopped and rolled over on his back. *Sort of like a puppy,* she thought. "You really are pathetic."

"I helped you," the young man cried. "In the name of Allah, why are you doing this?"

Malovo paused and tilted her head to the side, as if the question hadn't occurred to her. Then she shrugged. "Because I enjoy it," she replied, and shot him in the face.

The dying man gurgled as blood flowed into his throat. She was pleased to see in his eyes that he was still aware of what was happening. "*Do svidaniya, mal'chik,*" she said, and pulled the trigger one last time.

Finished, Malovo squatted to relieve herself, idly watching the young man's fingers twitch as his brain sent out its last electrical signals. Then she stood and turned the body over and took her victim's wallet from his pants pocket. *Twenty-six dollars?* she thought as she pocketed the money. *Hardly worth the effort.*

However, robbery was not her motive. The fewer people who could identify her or help her enemies trace her movements, the better. With any luck, the body wouldn't be discovered for months, if ever. But just in case, she wanted to make it more difficult to identify him and trace him back to the mosque in Buffalo. No one would miss the young man, probably not even his estranged parents. And the imam, an immigrant from Saudi Arabia, had been happy to provide a white American for the mission rather than one of his own.

Malovo walked back to the car and got into the driver's seat. She drove forward until finding a wide spot in the road to turn around. Rolling past where her driver had stopped, she noted with satisfaction that only a few footprints in the snow could be seen from the road. Nothing to cause a passerby to become suspicious and follow them to her victim. A few minutes later, she was back on the highway, headed south for New York City.

Six hours later, with the sky turning gray with a hint of pink in the east, Malovo abandoned the car in the long-term parking lot at the airport in Newark. Because she'd worn driving gloves from the truck stop, she didn't have to worry about wiping down the car's interior for her fingerprints. And by the time the young man's body and prints were matched to the car, she would be long gone from the United States.

Malovo caught the shuttle from the lot to the terminal and then stood at the curb until a taxi pulled up. The cabdriver was a "believer" from Somali who, if questioned, would say that he picked up a "man from Chicago" and dropped him off in Queens. The mileage would add up close enough to their destination in Brooklyn Heights.

As they'd passed over the Brooklyn Bridge from Manhattan, Malovo had looked south in the direction of Brighton Beach. *Ivgeny, my love, have you returned from your vacation in the Caucasus? When this is over, perhaps I will pay you a visit before I leave.*

Immediately following the assassination attempt, she had jumped to the conclusion that her former Russian employers had arranged it. Retribution for working "freelance" to the highest bidder. Or it could have been Dagestani, or even Chechen, nationalists who resented her part in turning their quest for independence into another battleground for Islamic extremists.

The more she thought about it, the more she was convinced that her former lover was involved. Uninhibited by political interference from the outside, the Russians could have called in a massive strike from the military instead of a covert action. And the commando precision of the attempt seemed too professional for the nationalists, who would have come in with guns blazing or simply relied on the roadside bomb.

Yet Ivgeny was certainly capable of carrying out the attempt, especially if it was true that he was working with the Americans. Only a reflexive move, at the moment the bullet left the rifle, had saved her life. Otherwise, she would have been the corpse instead of the Saudi Arabian. And the secondary plan—the bomb hidden in the hay cart—had the old guerrilla fighter Ivgeny's imprint all over it. If one didn't work, another would.

However, again luck had been on her side. Fleeing the village, she'd passed the truck in front. She wasn't thinking of the possibility of an attack from another direction, only escaping the village and the man on the hill who'd hunted her like a deer in the forest. She'd lived because she had uncharacteristically panicked and pushed ahead of the lead vehicle. But Ivgeny, or whichever of his men had detonated the bomb, thought she was still in the second truck and allowed her truck to pass, and thus she was beyond the blast.

Someday I will settle this between us, she thought as she noted Governors Island in the distance.

A few minutes later, the taxi pulled up to a brownstone mansion on Pierrepont Place in Brooklyn Heights. Wearing a knit hat and sunglasses, Malovo stepped from the car, and though she was uneasy over being seen at that early hour, the only witnesses were a few solitary joggers out for a run on the Brooklyn Heights Promenade.

Walking up to the gated door, Malovo noted the security cameras strategically placed so that no one could approach the front or sides of the house without being seen. She assumed that the back entrance was covered as well, and knew that the man who currently resided in the mansion would have an emergency exit should his enemies discover his lair.

Pressing the buzzer outside the gate, Malovo shuddered. She recognized that certain men were dangerous, like New York District Attorney Karp, who seemed to find a way to thwart her at every turn, and the madman David Grale. But she feared only two, Ivgeny Karchovski and the man she was about see.

He, too, had once been her lover—if that's how one described such a relationship. Unlike with Ivgeny, where physical attraction and other emotions she preferred to deny combined so that she had enjoyed being in his arms, this other man's attentions had been forced upon her by her former Russian bosses, who'd hoped her charms would give them leverage over him. But he'd used her like the cheapest Moscow whore. He did not make love, he raped.

Malovo let out a deep breath and collected herself. Theirs was now a strictly business relationship, and she would never have to allow his advances again. She still feared him—he was even more cold-blooded and cruel than she—but she knew better than to show it, as he would use it to his advantage.

"Yes?" replied a voice from the speaker next to the button.

"I'm here to see Mr. Erik," she said.

"Your name?"

"Christine Day."

"Your business?"

Malovo fought to keep the impatience out of her voice. *This silly password game is for amateurs. He already knows that it's me.* But she answered dutifully. "I'm looking for the Angel of Music."

There was a buzz and a click as the lock on the gate opened. She pulled the heavy steel gate aside and reached for the front doorknob just as another click indicated that it, too, was unlocked. She turned the knob and walked into the expansive foyer. A tall, muscular man stood up from a chair at the base of a circular stairway and walked toward her. His gun was holstered beneath his arm. She also observed other men with automatic rifles watching her from other parts of the room and at the top of the staircase.

She noted that all the men were white and mostly cut from the same Anglo-Saxon or Germanic cloth. *He doesn't trust the Muslims any more than I do,* she thought. *Just cannon fodder to help him accomplish his plans.*

The guard took her purse and searched it. He pulled the handgun from inside and stuck it in the waistband of his belt.

"I'll want that back," she said.

The man looked her in the eyes and smirked. "When he says you can have a gun, you can have a gun."

Malovo let the man's insolence pass. But when he got down on a knee and began patting her down with too much time and attention on her crotch, she growled. "Touch me there again and you will regret it."

The man looked up at her and snorted. "I'll touch where I want." He started to move his hand back up her leg, but his exploration ended when she shifted and drove her other knee into his temple with all of her strength. There was a sickening crunch and the man collapsed, but before he even hit the floor she'd snaked his handgun from its holster and pointed it at the man at the top of the stairs.

"Stop!"

The shouted command saved the guard's life, and probably Malovo's, as the other men in the room held their fire, too. She lowered her gun and looked at the man who had appeared next to the man at the top of the stairs. Tilting her head toward the man lying unconscious on the ground, she snarled, "Your men are undisciplined, *Mr. Erik.*"

The man shrugged. "Yes, perhaps, but loyal so long as their paychecks arrive on time." He leaned over the rail and spoke to one of the other guards. "Check on Bronson and see if he's alive or dead. Either way, take him to my boat and dump him in the Atlantic. And let that be a lesson to all of you that you have one purpose only—protecting me—anything else will get you killed."

The other guards swallowed hard and nodded. One went over to the fallen man and toed him in the ribs, eliciting a groan.

"Make sure you tie him to an anchor or something," Erik said. "I don't want him floating ashore anytime soon." He nodded his head at Malovo. "Now, if you're through playing the femme fatale, join me in the library, I'll be there in a minute." With that he turned and walked away.

Malovo entered the second-floor library, which like its owner was cold and dark—the floors, desk, and walls of black granite, with black leather furniture, all accented with stainless steel. Three tall, dark-tinted windows framed in steel allowed in just enough light for her to see her employer as he joined her.

As usual, he was well dressed in an Armani suit despite the early hour. But where he had once been tall, blue-eyed, blond, and handsome, he now hunched over as though from stomach pain and leaned on a heavy cane with a silver head. He still had his blond hair, but beneath it he wore a silver mask covering his face so that only his intense Aqua Velva eyes could be seen.

Malovo had once seen what was under the mask and had no desire to look on that hideous mess again. But the mind behind the mask and the horror was as sharp, and glitteringly vicious, as ever, and she was counting on it to make her rich.

Erik crossed the room to the windows and motioned her over. "Quite a view, isn't it," he said when she was standing next to him.

She had to admit that it was a striking scene. Almost straight across was the entire south end of Manhattan Island, with the ragged skyline of the Financial District up to the Brooklyn Bridge; farther south in the harbor the Statue of Liberty raised her torch.

Erik turned and walked stiffly to the chair behind the desk. Sitting down, he indicated she should do the same. "Sorry to hear about the unfortunate incident while on your travels," he said. The man's voice—once that of an eloquent rising star on the political scene—now had a lisp as a result of the deformity beneath the mask.

"A curious way to describe an attempt to blow my head off," Malovo replied. "Perhaps you would not have been heartbroken if it had succeeded?"

"Au contraire, my dear Nadya," Erik chuckled. "Your death would have been a serious setback to my plans."

"I'm touched by your concern," Malovo replied dryly.

Erik shrugged. "No need to pretend we like each other in the least. Back in the day you weren't even a good fuck; then again, I didn't care whether you were or weren't, it was just to relieve stress. However, the bad fortune I was talking about was the capture of of that little raghead from Saudi Arabia. Any hope we had of moving forward without al-Sistani a free man remains remote."

"So then the plan is off?" Malovo felt her stomach knotting. At this rate, she would never be rich and safe; and someday soon she would move a split second too late and she would die.

"No, it has only become more imperative that I arrange for the release of al-Sistani."

"Do you know how to find him?"

"Roughly. As you know he's with Grale, and I have a spy who might be able to lead a small force to free him. But it would be risky—these scum who follow Grale know the tunnels and sewers as well as the rats, and they'll fight if Grale tells them to."

"Have you tried to buy his freedom?"

Erik snorted. "Yes, I sent an emissary with an offer of one million dollars."

"What happened?"

"He was found in Central Park the next morning . . . well, everything except his head."

"How do you know al-Sistani hasn't told them about the plan?"

"My spy says that so far he has given them only false information about the target, though he has named my former compatriots with the Sons of Man."

"So if you're not going to attack Grale, what do you plan to do?"

"My spy tells me that there is someone even more important to Grale than al-Sistani. Someone he would do anything, give anything, to be with as his madness grows."

"Are you sure it is not feigned?" Malovo asked. "Before he died, Ali, the Saudi, said he thought that Grale works for the U.S. government. That he's part of a secret antiterrorism agency and this whole madman routine is just a ruse."

Erik laughed and leaned forward. "Bullshit. You forget that Grale and I go back quite some time, and according to the old adage, 'It takes one to know one,' and I know that he's quite insane. He lives beneath the city with a ragtag band of beggars, drunks, whores, and invalids who see him as some sort of messiah leading them down the road to Armageddon. That's why money means nothing to him. But apparently the king of the underworld would like a queen."

"And who is she?"

The man behind the mask giggled. "Oh, you're going to love this . . ."

When Malovo heard the name, it dawned on her that she also now knew the identity of the fat peasant woman she saw in Dagestan. "Then, perhaps you would be interested to know who was involved in the plot to kill me."

An hour later, Erik returned to the little anteroom off the library, where he lit a match and sucked on the end of a pipe he'd recently filled with opium. It seemed to be the only thing that stopped the pain in his stomach and his face.

10

"So what do you think? Did he screw the pooch?" As he spoke, Ray Guma didn't look up from the fat cigar he rolled between his right index finger and thumb. He couldn't light the Belicoso—even if Karp had allowed him—because the good citizens of New York City had passed a law prohibiting smoking in any building. And today it was making him more irritable than usual.

Karp shook his head. "No, not really. I've spent a couple of weeks reading over the transcripts and going through the evidence for the Maplethorpe trial and for the most part, I think Stewbie did his usual solid job. If anything—and maybe this was a reaction to the media frenzy—he might have tried to do too much."

"How do you mean?" Tommy Mac leaned forward in the leather chair he was sitting in next to Guma. They were both sitting in front of Karp's desk, and Tommy Mac looked like he was about to jump to his feet and object.

Ready to defend his guy . . . good, Karp thought. He liked to see that his new Homicide Bureau chief thought of the team first. Some guys might have tried to sell a subordinate down the river if his performance reflected poorly on their decision making. But Tommy Mac, wasn't the sort. Giving the Maplethorpe case to Reed had been one of his first major decisions, and he'd stuck by his man.

And Karp was fine with both men. *That's not the point of this meeting,* he thought. They were all sitting in his office on the eighth floor of the Criminal Courts Building. It was an office once occupied by his mentor, Garrahy, and he'd pretty much kept it the way the old man left it, even restoring the few things his predecessor had changed. The room had an old library feel to it, a quiet shadowy office with mid-twentieth-century light fixtures and dark wood paneling that covered three of the walls, while the fourth wall was dedicated to shelves of books from floor to ceiling.

Green-shaded lamps on tall brass stands supplemented the ancient overheads; a shorter version of the lamps sat on Karp's desk. A large wooden world atlas sat next to an overstuffed leather reading couch in a corner next to the bookshelf on which the fourth man in the room, Karp's special assistant, Gilbert Murrow, sat quietly listening.

Further muting the room, heavy green drapes hung around the windows overlooking Centre Street. They and the matching green carpet still smelled faintly of old cigar smoke and possibly a splash or two of a spilled scotch and water, another legacy of what Guma called "the good old days." Though a nonsmoker, Karp actually liked the olfactory reminder of the past.

More and more recently, he'd found himself getting nostalgic for those early years. Born and raised in Brooklyn, he'd gone to law school with one goal, to work for the district attorney of New York County. Now when alone in the office, his thoughts sometimes drifted to conversations or even the occasional stern lecture from the old man. Both had made Professor Cole's "controversial" and "annoying" law student a better prosecutor and a better human being.

Karp noticed Guma's raised eyebrows at McKean's challenge. They had contrasting styles on the field and in the courtroom. Guma was the tough, combative inner-city kid from New Jersey who'd learned his game on the hardscrabble sandlots. Everything he did—from his batting stance to his throwing motion—was his own unique version, which worked because he was also a natural athlete. McKean, on the other hand, had been raised in the suburbs north of Manhattan, and had attended a football powerhouse, New

Rochelle High School, where he was coached by the legendary all-American Paul Ryan.

As prosecuting attorneys, both were competitive and good at what they did. But Guma, while intimately familiar with the facts of his cases, was more likely to ad-lib and—to continue with the baseball metaphor—swing for the fences if the defense left a change-up hanging over the plate. McKean was methodical, intense but without the theatrics. He came up with a game plan and stuck to it—content to plug away one play at a time, wearing down his opponents.

"What I mean, Tom, is that as I was looking over the transcripts again this past weekend," Karp replied, "I started wondering if maybe Stewbie fell into the trap of trying to box with these guys. They'd hit him with some nonsense—like this blood-splatter guy—and Stewbie had his own guy saying the complete opposite. They'd put a psychologist on the stand, and he'd put one on the stand. No wonder the jury was confused. But maybe he didn't have to stand there and take the hits while trying to counterpunch. He could have just stayed back, and they'd have never laid a glove on him. To cast this another way, the defense case was an illusion, but seems to me that Stewbie made it real by responding to every little bit of their bullshit."

Karp waited to see if McKean was going to jump down his throat in defense of Reed. But he just looked thoughtful, and then replied, "You may be right. I was getting a sense of that, too, but thought it was easy for me to criticize after the fact. You want to take him off the case?"

Pursing his lips, Karp shook his head. "No. We've all done it. Felt like we had to stand toe-to-toe and trade jabs when it wasn't necessary. We might have even gotten away with it once or twice. But Stewbie ran into a double whammy with a celebrity defendant and a high-octane defense team that makes its living with smoke and mirrors. I want him to go at it again, only this time—with all of us working to really keep it focused—I'm betting he'll get off the ropes and knock 'em out."

"Good," McKean said, looking relieved. "I was hoping you'd say that. Stewbie's a hell of a prosecutor. If he's got a fault, and I don't know that this is one, it's that he cares too much. He's been taking this pretty hard, so it'll be good for him to get back in the ring and settle this."

Guma scowled as he stuck the cigar in his mouth.

"What's up, Guma?" Karp asked. "You disagree?"

"Nah, I've only glanced at some of the expert-witness testimony, and I'd have to agree with you," Guma replied. "But all these boxing metaphors make me want to fight someone, and thinking about this Maplethorpe asshole really ticks me off. Apparently his new show is a big success; the press is fawning all over him and the audiences stand up and applaud when he appears onstage after the performances, like he's won the Nobel Prize."

Karp looked over at his friend. He, Guma, McKean, and for that matter Marlene and their other old chum, V. T. Newbury, had all started at the DAO about the same time. "Goom," as Ray was more or less affectionately known, had been a cocky, muscular son of Italian immigrants, a self-ordained ladies' man who reveled in his nickname, the Italian Stallion. However, a bout with cancer several years ago had changed him, at least physically. His body was now frail and depleted, his once dark, wavy hair had turned white almost overnight, and his olive complexion had faded to pale and translucent. But his mind was still sharp, and if he was more reflective and mellow these days, his dark eyes still smoldered when confronted by an injustice.

"Since when have you cared what the public thinks?" Karp said with a smile.

"I don't," Guma groused. "If they want to support that freak—I mean look at him, the guy looks like a bug-eyed vampire—that's their business. I just hate the way he and his buddies in the press are rubbing it in our faces. I can't wait till we nail his ass and send him off to Attica, where he can direct the annual inmate Christmas pageant."

Karp and the others laughed. But over in the corner of the room, Gilbert Murrow cleared his throat in the way only he could do when he wanted to interject something he knew no one wanted to hear. As the keeper of Karp's schedule, as well as his spokesman and office manager, one of his tasks was to keep track of the political side of things, since his boss hated that aspect of his job. "I don't have to tell you gentlemen how the second trial is being spun in the press by Maplethorpe's lawyers."

"I care even less about the press than I do the theater crowd," Guma growled.

"I second Goom's feelings," Karp said, "but I guess you're referring to the editorial in this morning's *Times*."

"Right." Murrow nodded. "According to the fish wrap, it's a vendetta—that essentially the deadlocked jury was a repudiation of our case. And that the only reason we're pursuing it is because the district attorney of New York's got an ego and sees a chance to make a midterm splash and get lots of publicity by taking down a celebrity."

"Even though we're not the ones trying our case in the media," Guma pointed out.

"So much for the gag order," McKean snorted.

"But how do I respond to that?" Murrow complained.

"We don't," Karp replied, "except in the courtroom, with the evidence, and then we let the jury decide . . . not the public and not the press."

Murrow sighed and slumped back on the couch. A short, pear-shaped man who favored vests, bow ties, and John Lennon–esque wire-rimmed glasses, he was not an imposing figure. But he looked after Karp's interests like a pit bull, and was often frustrated that his boss refused to respond even a little when defense attorneys made their cases in the newspapers.

"You seem a little uptight, Gil," Guma teased, "must not be getting any action."

Murrow turned red, but then shrugged. "Well, Ariadne *is* out of town."

"I was right," Guma said. "Gilbert's gonads are a bit stressed. She stepping out on you?"

Murrow stiffened. He was aware of a brief affair between Guma and his girlfriend, Ariadne Stupenagel, an encounter she said she regretted and blamed on too much booze and Guma's persistence. But even Murrow had been surprised when for the first time in her hedonistic life, Ariadne had apparently fallen in love and settled down with him. "As a matter of fact, Guma, she's in Trinidad working on a story about Islamic militancy in the Caribbean."

"The Caribbean?" Guma looked surprised. "I thought the islands were more into Rastafarianism and Santeria, smoking ganja and cutting the heads off chickens. Maybe a little voodoo thrown in."

"Mr. Sensitivity as always," Karp interjected. "But I also didn't know there was Islamic extremism in the Caribbean."

"Apparently so," Murrow said. "In some places, like Trinidad, there are not just a lot of Muslims but it's actually a hotbed for terrorism. So Ariadne's trying to interview some of the leaders who led a bloody coup to take over the government and establish an Islamic state twenty years ago. Apparently, the movement is picking up steam again."

"Wow," Guma said. "I have to admit that girl of yours has got some big *cojones* if she's just going to walk up to these fanatics, especially the way she dresses, and stick a tape recorder in their faces and start asking questions."

A worried look crossed Murrow's round face. Ariadne was impossible to miss even in a crowd. She was nearly six feet tall, which made her almost six inches taller than he was; a bottle blond who liked plenty of makeup and tight-fitting, colorful clothes that showed off her ample curves and mile-long legs. But she was not just a pretty face with too much lipstick. She'd interviewed, and apparently slept with, some of the most famous—and in some cases dangerous—men in the world, including Fidel Castro in his early years. When it came to getting a story, she was fearless and that often got her into trouble.

"I can't say I'm thrilled she took the assignment," Murrow admitted. "She may be a cat with nine lives, but I think she's used a bunch of those up already."

"Well, Ariadne knows how to take care of herself . . ."

Karp's attempt to reassure his aide was interrupted by a buzz from his intercom followed by the supercilious voice of Karp's receptionist, Darla Milquetost. "Mr. Reed to see you."

"Send him in, thank you, Darla," Karp replied, and sat back in his chair.

The door opened and a handsome, well-dressed man in his early forties started to enter the room, but hesitated before continuing when he saw who was there. "Gosh, all the heavy hitters," Stewart Reed said with a smile, though his voice sounded tense. "Should I have brought a blindfold and cigarette?"

"Unfortunately, you can no longer smoke in New York City," Guma groused as he chewed on the end of his cigar. "The tobacco Nazis have seen to that."

Karp rolled his eyes as he pointed to an empty chair next to McKean. "No need for either, Stewbie. Have a seat. We're just talking about the Maplethorpe retrial."

Reed froze as he was starting to sit. "You replacing me?" He blinked hard and bit his lip.

Karp was surprised by the reaction. *He really is taking this hard. Better defuse this right away.* "Nonsense," he replied. "It's been your case from the beginning, and it will still be yours when this is all over."

Reed swallowed hard and nodded, taking his seat. "Thanks. But I would have understood, sometimes a fresh set of eyes and—"

Karp held up a hand to cut him off. "Again, it's your case, and you handle it the way you believe is best, but I agree that a fresh set of eyes might help. That's why I asked Guma, Tom, and Gilbert to sit in on this . . . and one more . . . wherever he is." He leaned forward and touched a button on the intercom. "Darla, has Mr. Katz arrived yet?"

"No, but I hear him out in the hall . . . apparently saying his good-byes to Miss Bond," Mrs. Milquetost sniffed.

Karp feigned a look of shock at his receptionist's tone. Darla Milquetost was a prim and proper widow in her midfifties, and she no doubt did not approve of office fraternization. And because she treated Assistant District Attorney Kenny Katz like a son, Karp assumed that her displeasure was directed at the young woman involved.

"Ah, well, then send him in as soon as he can tear himself away from Sondra," Karp said. He turned to look at Reed, who was contemplating his immaculate fingernails as they waited.

Stewbie Reed was widely considered to be the best male dresser in the DAO, especially now that the independently wealthy V. T.

Newbury had moved on to private practice with his uncle in the family firm of Newbury, Newbury and White.

Reed was not independently wealthy, but judging by the look of him, he was one of the few assistant district attorneys in the DAO who spent a hefty percentage of his paycheck on haberdashery. Most male ADAs stuck with the bar mitzvah–blue coat and slacks straight off the rack, but Reed's suits were tailor-made and expensive. He never seemed to have a wrinkle on him or, for that matter, a hair out of place on his neatly barbered head.

Karp had once asked him how he managed to get from the apartment near Washington Square in the Village, where Reed lived, to Centre Street without scuffing his always immaculate shoes. Stewbie smiled and allowed that he left a half dozen pairs of dress shoes in the office and wore running shoes to get back and forth. *"I have other dress shoes at home for going out."*

There was a knock at the door, which immediately opened to reveal Kenny Katz. The twenty-eight-year-old ADA was sort of the anti-Stewbie, at least in appearance. He was perpetually rumpled and Karp had once seen him use a Magic Marker to disguise a scuff mark on one of his shoes before going into court. A crooked grin, long sideburns, and curly brown hair that he wore in what Karp called a Jewfro made him look more like a left-wing college radical from the sixties than a prosecutor. But he was a classic case of looks being deceiving.

Katz walked with a slight limp he'd earned the hard way. Following the attack on the World Trade Center in September 2001, he'd quit law school at Columbia and enlisted in the army, serving with the elite Rangers in Afghanistan and Iraq, where he'd been awarded the Bronze and Silver stars for valor, as well as a Purple Heart. After his discharge, he'd returned to law school for the sole purpose, like Karp before him, of joining the New York DAO.

Karp chuckled to himself as Katz sauntered into the room, thinking that some people probably found his young protégé annoying, much like Professor Cole had said was the case with him. And yes, the kid—as Karp thought of Katz—could come off as cocky, but that belied a genuine steadiness and humility; he never boasted or even talked about his military service or his medals, and it wouldn't have surprised Karp if he was the only one in the DAO who knew about them.

"Ah, Mr. Katz," Karp said, looking at his watch, "kind of you to join us."

Katz blushed. "I was, uh, discussing certain legal strategies with Miss Bond."

"Such as the best time for a rendezvous in the file room?" Guma inquired. "Been there, done that."

Katz grinned and turned red. But it was Karp who spoke. "Uh, no need to reply to Mr. Guma's ancient recollections of conquests real and imagined. His mind hasn't been out of the gutter since puberty."

Guma laughed. "I resemble that."

"You don't just resemble it, you're the spitting image," Karp shot back.

The banter went back and forth for a little longer, but then they stopped talking and all eyes turned to Karp. "Well, I asked everybody here to discuss what's next with the Maplethorpe case, which is coming up at the end of the month, and get your thoughts together on . . ." He was going to say "what went wrong" but caught himself; this wasn't about finding fault and he wanted Reed to know that. "On why you think the jury hung and what we can do to plug any holes, or anything we might have missed the first time."

He sensed Reed tensing at the comment and hurried to add, "However, I want to start by saying, I've been over the transcripts—including most of the pretrial hearings—and Stewbie, no one can fault your handling of the case. No one knows for sure why this jury hung. It could have been as simple as one Broadway aficionado who slipped through the cracks at voir dire, maybe even lied for the purpose of getting on this jury to save Maplethorpe."

Reed's lips twitched into a brief smile and he nodded. "Thanks. But it still feels like someone tore my heart out. I keep going over the trial in my head, trying to figure out where I lost the jury."

"Have you come up with anything?" McKean asked. "I'm with Butch here in that while we may need to alter our game plan a bit, I think you did a hell of a job."

Reed shrugged. "Nothing I can put a finger on. I thought my expert witnesses were pretty damn good, but maybe theirs were just more believable. I've been over my summation a dozen times, and I think I could have been better there, too."

"Maybe you're overthinking this thing," Guma suggested.

"What do you mean?" Reed asked. He smiled but his voice was defensive again.

"Just that maybe less would be more."

"I thought preparation was supposed to be the hallmark of this office?" Reed's jaw had tightened and his eyes glistened.

Guma looked up at the ceiling. "Look, Stewbie, I'm not trying to second-guess you . . ."

"Well, it certainly sounds like it . . ."

"I'm just trying to raise the possibility that maybe between all these experts, the jury got confused. And maybe this case was as simple as saying 'This scumbag stuck a gun in that poor woman's mouth and pulled the trigger.' That's all."

"If it was that easy, you should have tried the case. I obviously fucked it up."

Karp cleared his throat. This was not going the way he intended. He'd never heard Reed use the F-bomb and if he got his back too far up, he wasn't going to be receptive to suggestions about how to proceed. "Okay, gentlemen, this isn't getting us anywhere. I don't disagree with Guma in some respects, but at the same time, Stewbie handled the case the way 99.9 percent of the prosecutors in this country, including those in this room, would have. But the old tried and true didn't work this time around, so maybe it's time for us to think a little bit outside the box."

Guma and Reed had each started to say something but shut their mouths, and Karp used the moment to ask a question about one of the pretrial hearings. "I was reading the transcript from a motions hearing," he said, "and at some point, Maplethorpe seemed to go ballistic, but the record stopped. What was that about?"

Reed relaxed and nodded. "It was the oddest thing. That was a hearing when they were still considering an insanity defense. Maplethorpe's lead mouthpiece, Guy Leonard, was introducing some psychologist's interview with Maplethorpe when he said something about Maplethorpe's mother. That she'd left him as a child, and Leonard wanted to introduce a photograph of Maplethorpe and his mother when he was maybe five or six. Suddenly, Maplethorpe jumped up out of his chair and started shouting, *'Objection! Objection!'*"

"Which is when the judge struck it from the record," Karp noted.

"Yeah, but the best was still to come," Reed said with a laugh. "Maplethorpe was practically frothing at the mouth, and at his own lawyer no less. Leonard, who'd been standing near the witness stand, came over to calm him down, but Maplethorpe threw a pitcher of water at him."

"You're kidding me," Guma said. "I would have loved to have seen that."

"It was pretty amusing . . . Leonard's there with this big water spot on his trousers—and that pitcher wasn't light, it must have hurt. And the whole time, Maplethorpe is screaming, *'You leave my mother out of this!'* They had to restrain him and take him out of the court."

"You get a chance to explore that during the trial?" McKean asked.

Reed shook his head. "Unfortunately no. They didn't end up going for an insanity defense, and they didn't bring up any childhood issues, so there was no way to go there. I still have a copy of the photograph in the file, he's all dressed up like a little cowboy . . . in fact, I'm working on something one of our witnesses—that Italian guy, Hilario Gianneschi—said that may actually be related."

"How so?" Karp asked.

"I'd rather not say at the moment," Reed replied. "It's just a wild thought . . . something the guy told the cops about what Maplethorpe was wearing, but he said it in Italian. I told Leonard that I might want to enter the photograph as a prosecution exhibit, but not what for yet."

"You speak *paisan*?" Guma asked.

"A beginner," Reed said. "I've always wanted to visit Rome, so I'm going next summer with my sister and I've been taking lessons."

Karp nodded. "Well, let me know if anything pans out. In the meantime, let's all take one last look at the transcripts and meet again same time next week. When's the next court date and what, if anything, is scheduled?"

"A hearing next week over more drummed-up nonsense. Otherwise, I'm just going over my opening and summation, and reviewing the witness testimony to see if I can spot any weaknesses with their experts or mine."

"Okay," Karp replied, looking at his watch. "Sorry, guys, I have another meeting. But I wanted to get to the final item and that is that I'm asking Kenny Katz to sit second chair with Stewbie on the retrial."

Karp caught the quick, hard look Reed shot in Kenny's direction. Katz also reacted by dropping his jaw; this was news to him, too.

"I don't need any more help," Reed replied. "Miss Brinkerhoff did fine."

"I don't think you do, either," Karp replied evenly. Reed's voice was getting angry, but he was not going to turn this into a confrontation if he could help it.

"Then I guess the purpose would be to have someone keep tabs on me—make sure I don't fuck up again?" Reed asked. "Or maybe Kenny should do the summation."

Katz squirmed uncomfortably in his seat at the sarcasm. No prosecutor worth his salt willingly gave up giving the closing summation in a murder trial. It would be like throwing a no-hitter through eight innings and having the manager yank you in the ninth because you walked someone.

"Not at all," Karp replied. "As a matter of fact, I don't expect him to do much more than sit there and observe a pro at work. It's up to you to use him, or not, however you see fit. Do I think we can make improvements on how we go forward with this case? Yes. But my main reason is that this is an unusual case with a lot of nuances, and while you and I might not see another like it before we retire, he might and the experience would be invaluable."

Karp was telling the truth. One of his "failings" as a district attorney, at least in his own opinion, was that he hadn't done enough to bring along the next generation of assistant district attorneys.

The top echelon at the DAO, with guys like McKean, Guma, and Reed—*and don't forget V.T.*—was one of the best in the country. But Garrahy had always emphasized what the longtime Yankee fan called "the farm system"—identifying the best prospects among the young assistant DAs and pairing them up with the best veterans. It was the reason that Karp had taken Katz under his wing. *But we need to do a lot more of that.*

Reed didn't respond to Karp's explanation except with a curt nod. He didn't speak for the rest of the meeting, and then left as quickly as he could get away. Katz followed on his heels.

Guma held his cigar up as if inspecting it for holes. "That went well," he said.

"He'll be okay," McKean replied. "He's taking everything a little personally. But he's a pro and he'll come around once he's had a chance to chew on it."

Karp nodded. "That's why I didn't want to announce that Kenny is second chair at the staff meeting. I don't want to embarrass Stewbie. The rest of the staff can find out on their own the old-fashioned way . . . office gossip."

Guma laughed. "Darla Milquetost, you mean."

Karp chuckled as the others stood and left the office. The door had just shut on the last of them when Milquetost buzzed him. "You have a call . . . from Giancarlo."

11

"*You have a call . . . from Giancarlo.*" Karp was surprised. His family rarely called him at work. He looked at his watch, almost quitting time, and Marlene had warned him to be home promptly. Lucy and her boyfriend, Ned, had been in town for the past week, but Ned was leaving tonight and Marlene was whipping up one of her special spaghetti dinners. He picked up the telephone and pressed the Line button, expecting to be asked his ETA. "Yeah, G, what's up?"

"Have you figured it out, Mr. Karp?" The voice was young, but it was not his son.

"Who is this?"

"Andy."

"Andy who?"

"It doesn't matter," the boy replied. "Have you figured it out yet?"

"Figured what out?"

"'In Casa Blanca plans are made that have to do with the art of war. One can be a house, the other is usually not an art. But when you look at both what do you see? And so does the deadly connection between the two sides.' It's a riddle. I love riddles."

Karp looked down at the folded envelope that was still lying on his desk. "What about it? You mean *Casablanca* the movie?"

"That's for me to know and you to find out. Can't you see it?"

"Not yet, why don't you give me another hint? Was that your dad who put the note in my pocket?"

The phone was silent and Karp thought he'd lost the connection. But then the boy sighed and said, "It's the worst that could happen."

"What is, Andy? Are you trying to tell me about someone getting hurt?"

"That's for me to know and you to find out."

"Well, sorry, Andy, but I don't have time for games . . ."

"This isn't a game, Mr. Karp. Ask Lucy about Dagestan."

"How do you know Lucy?"

"We're old friends."

"What about Dagestan?"

"Just ask. Then you'll know I'm not just playing games. I got to go, see ya later, alligator."

Karp hung up and then walked over to the couch where Murrow had been sitting and picked up the *Times* that was lying on one of the cushions. He was looking for a short article in the international news section that he'd glanced at before the meeting.

Here it is, he thought, and reread the story citing a Russian news agency that blamed Islamic terrorists for the murder of a Saudi Arabian shipping executive in—drum roll, please—Dagestan. Apparently, Ali Ashoor, whose company operated refrigeration ships for transporting food and other items needing cold storage, had been in the country to negotiate a contract for shipping milk "when his party was ambushed while traveling through the Caucasus Mountains." The Russian Army was said to be in pursuit of the Islamic "bandits and criminals responsible for his murder."

The date of the incident coincided with a trip abroad Lucy had taken. In fact, she and Ned were visiting her family home on Crosby Street on their way back to New Mexico from wherever it was. She avoided talking about where they'd been and he and Marlene had known better than to press.

He'd had to admit to himself that there was a lot he didn't know about his daughter's involvement with Espey. Sometimes he and

Marlene didn't hear from her for a week or more, but up to that point, they'd chosen to think it was because there was no telephone or cell phone service at the ranch cabin where she lived with Ned. Only when they drove into Taos could she call.

Still, it was hard to imagine his daughter connected to the assassination of a reputed businessman in a country he'd never heard of. But as he thought about what Andy had said, the picture was pretty clear. His daughter was a spook involved in a deadly, high-stakes game of kill or be killed with terrorists.

Karp was still mulling over the telephone call when his next visitors arrived in his office. However, they didn't enter through the usual means, past his receptionist, but walked in from the anteroom, where they'd just stepped off his private elevator from the Franklin Street entrance.

He pushed the button on the intercom. "Darla, please hold all my calls, and I'm not to be disturbed until I let you know."

"Of course, Mr. Karp."

Karp swiveled his chair toward the visitors and stood up to greet them. "Espey, good to see you," he said, shaking his hand before turning to the other man to shake his. "And V.T., it's been too long."

"I concur," Vinson Talcott Newbury replied. "I can't wait to be finished with this and get back to prosecuting criminals instead of acting like one."

"Me, too," Karp agreed. "It's tough to find experienced prosecutors who'll work for peanuts."

Newbury had laughed, his perfect white teeth contrasting with the perfect tennis-tanned face. Approximately the same age as Karp, V.T. had thinning blond hair, but he still looked like he belonged in a martini commercial—the extraordinarily handsome Anglo-Saxon man in the bow tie and tuxedo charming the beautiful woman in the low-cut black evening dress. He was the quintessential New England blueblood—sophisticated, cultured, educated, urbane, and wealthy.

The blue blood came from his mother's side, but his father was no slouch, either. Vincent Newbury had been one of the partners in his family's white-shoe law firm of Newbury, Newbury and White—one of the biggest and most prestigious in New York City.

At least until his own brother murdered him, Karp thought.

Dean Newbury thought he'd gotten away with killing his brother, who'd been a good, principled man whose father and whose brother never trusted him with the family's darker secrets. And so far, Dean Newbury was right.

It was part of the reason that V.T. had concocted the scheme, with Karp's reluctant agreement, of pretending that V.T., after a violent mugging—all for show but real enough to have landed him in the hospital—had decided to quit the thankless job of ADA and take up his place at the family firm. The hope was V.T. might uncover the evidence needed to prosecute Uncle Dean for his father's murder, and also expose the family's other business with the Sons of Man and their plan to create a fascist U.S. government.

"How'd you get away from Uncle Dean?" Karp had asked as the three men sat down.

"I needed to file some motions on a civil case," V.T. replied. "But I have to be careful. If you remember, you and I supposedly don't like each other anymore, so there'd be no reason for me to stop by and chitchat."

They all knew that while Dean Newbury seemed to be opening up more to his nephew, he still had not brought him entirely into the fold. "I don't know that he entirely trusts my about-face from dedicated public servant to power-mad Nazi," V.T. joked. "He'll talk about plans in a general sense, but no names or details. If I hint that I'm on board with his philosophy, he keeps reciting the Sons of Man mantra in Manx, '*Myr shegin dy ve, bee eh,*' or in English, 'What must be, will be,' whatever that means in this context."

"Well, be careful," Karp said. "I wasn't a big fan of this undercover-prosecutor operation in the first place. You're making light of it, but your uncle and his pals play for keeps."

"I'm taking it nice and easy," V.T. assured him. "I say the right things, things that a new convert to the program might say, but I don't ask questions or try to join anything. And if the old geezer doesn't completely trust me yet, he does seem to be relaxing his guard around me."

"V.T. has passed on several tips that have panned out," Jaxon volunteered. "Including the names of some of the men he believes belong to the SOM council. A who's who of U.S. politicians, businessmen, attorneys, judges, military officers and even movie stars. And recently a pretty significant piece of intelligence about Nadya Malovo."

"Yeah? So," Karp had responded, turning to Jaxon, "want to tell me about Dagestan?"

Jaxon and V.T. raised their eyebrows and looked at each other. "What makes you think I know anything about . . . what'd you say . . . Dagestan?" the agent asked.

Karp smiled. He and Jaxon went way back. The latter had once worked for the DAO until deciding he'd rather catch criminals than convict them. The former FBI special agent in charge of the New York district looked like a G-man with his pewter-gray crew cut, chiseled features, and steely gray eyes.

"Well, maybe it's nothing, but I thought you might be interested in a conversation I just had with a mysterious youngster named Andy," Karp replied. "He told me to ask Lucy about Dagestan."

Jaxon and Newbury exchanged another look. "Tell me about this conversation," Jaxon said.

After Karp recounted what he knew, Jaxon sat back in his seat and bit his lip before responding. "I'm not trying to be mysterious here, Butch," he said. "I'd trust you with my life and you know it. But this stuff is classified—even V.T., who provided some of the information I'm about to discuss, doesn't know what I did with that information. But more than that, the less you know about any of this, the better for all of us in case you ever get hauled in front of a congressional committee and told to spit it out. We're all aware that the public's right to know isn't always behind these congressional subpoenas. The Sons of Man have influence in Congress. We believe there are members, or at least sympathizers in the House and Senate; it would be very much like them to use one of these hearings to put you under oath to try to find out what you know about their plans."

"I understand," Karp replied. "So just tell me what you think I ought to know. If that's nothing, then that's the way the cookie crumbles."

"Well, this is one of those tips from V.T. that I was talking about," Jaxon said, turning to Newbury. "Go ahead and tell Butch how this came about."

V.T. shrugged. "It was just a case of good ol' Uncle Dean getting a little forgetful. We were chatting in his office about some unrelated lawsuit when he got up to use the restroom. It gave me a chance to glance at some of the papers on his desk, and I noticed a sticky note with a few words and numbers written in pencil. 'Malovo.' 'Makhachkala.' And what I presumed to be a date. I knew that Nadya is public enemy number one and passed the info onto Espey. That's about the extent of my involvement."

V.T. turned back to Jaxon, who took up the story. "Makhachkala is the capital of Dagestan. So I contacted our friend, Ivgeny Karchovski," the agent said, hesitating—he was one of a handful of people who knew Karp's familial relationship with the Karchovski mob boss—"who as I suspected has great contacts in Dagestan—apparently quite the smuggler's thoroughfare. His people were able to ascertain through their sources that there was going to be an important meeting in a little village in the mountains and that at least one of the participants would be the infamous Islamic terrorist Ajmaani, an alias for Nadya. We were able to get there first, take a look around, and set up a plan to—you didn't hear this from me—eliminate Nadya Malovo."

Karp noted the use of the word "eliminate" as a euphemism for assassinate. The fact that he would have welcomed the news of Malovo's death made him wonder if, like so many others, he'd developed a moral immunity to certain types of homicides. That he was becoming comfortable with the idea of committing an evil to prevent an even greater evil. *And isn't that like believing that the ends justify the means?* he wondered.

"Were you successful?"

Jaxon shook his head. "We thought we had her, but we missed. The woman has an uncanny ability to sense danger, as well as a great deal of luck."

"Better to be lucky than good, I guess," Newbury said.

"Perhaps," Jaxon said, "but if you're good enough, you don't have to rely on luck. Eventually, luck runs out, but good is something you can work at, even improve. Unfortunately, Nadya is both lucky and good. But someday one or the other won't be enough."

"What about this Andy?" Karp asked. "It would seem that you're compromised."

Jaxon rubbed his chin. "It definitely worries me. Outside of my people, all of whom I handpicked, you can count on two hands the number of people who are supposed to know about us and still have a few fingers left over."

"So you have a traitor?" Newbury asked.

Jaxon's face clouded over at the thought. "I don't know . . . I wouldn't have believed it . . . but somebody's talking or found out some other way."

"Ivgeny or his people?" Karp asked.

Jaxon gave him a funny look. "His people weren't told Lucy's real name, so it would have had to come directly from him. You believe he'd do that?"

Karp thought about his cousin. The man was a gangster, yet he had a code of honor as rigid as his own, and it wouldn't have allowed for Lucy's betrayal. "*Nyet,* as our friend would say," he replied.

Jaxon nodded. "I wouldn't, either."

"And does this Andy or whoever controls him qualify as a traitor, per se?" Newbury asked. "I mean, he's telling you—the district attorney of New York—that he's aware of a federal antiterrorism agency's actions in some far-flung country. Maybe he thinks he's a whistle-blower, like the Iran-Contra thing a few years back."

"We don't know who else he's telling," Jaxon pointed out.

"I guess that's true," Newbury said. "So what's with the word game? What does any of this have to do with the riddle?"

"I've been thinking about that, too," Karp replied. "The phrase 'In Casa Blanca plans are made that have to do with the art of war' would seem to be suggesting the White House and plans for war. However, it says that one 'can' be a house, which indicates that it isn't necessarily. So if the note meant *Casablanca* the movie, I wondered if maybe the German Nazis in the film were an oblique reference to the Sons of Man."

"How does the art of war fit in either scenario?" Newbury asked.

Karp shrugged. "I don't know. I know that's a book, but I don't know much about it."

"*The Art of War* was written in the sixth century B.C. by the Chinese military strategist Sun Tzu," Jaxon said. "It has thirteen chapters, each devoted to one aspect of warfare. Even now it's considered one of the most definitive works on military strategies and tactics ever written. But what it has to do in context with the rest of this, unless it's just meant to sound threatening, perhaps a plot against the White House for the war, I don't know. Your guess is as good as mine."

"'But when you look at both what do you see?' I take it he means when Butch looks at Casa Blanca and Art of War . . . the White House and a book?" V.T. asked.

"Or is there something significant about having to look at both of them in some sort of context together—that separately they don't mean anything?" Karp pointed out.

"And last but not least, 'And so does the deadly connection between the two sides,'" Jaxon said. "So when this deadly connection—which I'm taking to mean a person or maybe a group who operates between Islam and the West—looks at Casa Blanca and Art of War, they also will see what we would see? Which at the moment is nothing."

"I don't get it, either," Karp said. "But Andy, whoever he is, does seem to be trying to warn me. He said it would be 'the worst thing that could happen.'"

"And what would that be?" Jaxon asked.

"Wish I knew," Karp replied. "There's just something about the way he phrased the threat that bothers me. . . . I mean, what is the worst thing that could happen? Another terrorist attack with massive fatalities? The end of the world?"

"A death in the family?" Newbury ventured softly.

Karp grimaced. "On a personal level, that's certainly the worst. And something I worry about every day, especially with Lucy, now that you've lured her over to the world of spooks and assassins."

"Want me to fire her?" Jaxon replied.

"Yes . . . but no," Karp said with a sigh. "I want her safe, but I guess the parents of every soldier serving in Iraq and Afghanistan would prefer their children to be safe, too. She wants to serve her country, and this is how she is choosing to do it. It's not my call."

The rest of the meeting was spent catching Karp up on a curious conversation that V.T. had with his uncle regarding Amir al-Sistani. "As you know, the family firm represented Prince Esra bin Afraan al-Saud when he came to the United States on business, and that al-Sistani was essentially his business manager. But al-Sistani was using the prince, and his billions, to try to crash the stock market."

"And al-Sistani murdered him," Karp added.

"Right." Newbury nodded and continued. "And as we all know, al-Sistani was last seen being escorted into the deep, dark underworld by David Grale. Anyway, last week, dear old Uncle Dean came into my office and asked if I had any way of contacting Grale. He said, 'I know there's some connection between that madman and the DAO, and I just thought that perhaps you were aware of how to communicate with him.' I said I didn't know how to contact Grale, which was true, and Dean left. But I could tell he was disappointed. I asked him about it later, but he just said that people would pay dearly' to have al-Sistani in their control. He didn't say who or for what reason."

"But apparently these unknown people are either worried about what al-Sistani might say, which I wouldn't mind hearing myself," Jaxon said, "or they want him for something else."

"I understand he was pretty wealthy," Karp suggested.

Jaxon nodded. "And that could be all there is to it: these people want to ransom him so that the eternally grateful al-Sistani rewards them with riches. We've tried to find and freeze any and all accounts linked to al-Sistani, though the Saudi government has not been very cooperative in identifying them or closing the accounts that the prince may have had that al-Sistani had access to. Even if they did, we probably haven't located all of his funding and he may have quite a nest egg stashed away."

"I sense a 'but' coming," Karp said.

Jaxon laughed. "Yeah . . . but I don't know what that 'but' is. I wish Grale would cooperate and hand over al-Sistani. For a while, we were receiving pretty decent information from Grale—a lot of it through your contacts, Butch . . ."

"Dirty Warren, the Walking Booger, and Edward Treacher," Karp said. "Glad they were helpful."

"Very helpful . . . at least for a while," Jaxon replied. "But it's been quite some time since we heard from them. I don't suppose you've anything new to report?"

"I asked," Karp said, shaking his head. "But all I get is that Grale is in one of his moods, and apparently isn't talking to anybody."

"I don't get why he won't give up al-Sistani," Newbury said. "I thought we're all on the same side."

"Grale is on his own side," Karp replied. "It so happens that our mutual aims have meshed over the past couple of years. But I think if he thought that God's will was something that contradicted our efforts, he'd go with God."

"Maybe he doesn't trust us," Jaxon suggested.

"Could be," Karp agreed. "He's indicated before that he thinks the DAO, as well as federal law enforcement agencies, have been infiltrated by evil demons. The only people I know that he seems to trust completely are Marlene, and particularly Lucy."

"What about you?" Newbury asked.

"He knows that my office would prosecute him for homicide if he was caught," Karp replied. "I'd have no choice, except that I'd probably have to ask the state attorney general to appoint a special prosecutor to avoid any conflict of interest."

"Lucy wanted to try to find him herself. In fact, I had to order her to avoid contact or she'd have gone underground to look," Jaxon said. "We'd already sent a team in several weeks ago to look for Grale and al-Sistani. All they found were rats and a maze of tunnels and sewers. But the squad leader told me that he and his men felt they were being watched the whole time. It gave him, and I quote, 'the heebie-jeebies,' and this guy is a former SEAL. No way I was letting Lucy go in, especially by herself like she wanted."

"Well, thank God for that," Karp said. "Even if no one else bothered her, I don't like these reports about David Grale's mental health these days. I believe he's what we in the legal profession would call 'a danger to himself and others.'"

12

"MOM . . . DAD . . . DO YOU HAVE A MINUTE?"

Sitting on the couch in the loft, Karp looked up from his book, *The Tipping Point* by Malcolm Gladwell. Marlene, who had been resting her head on his lap and purring as he absently used his free hand to massage her dark curls, lifted herself onto an elbow.

Something in their daughter's voice elevated their parental alert system from yellow to orange. Even Gilgamesh, the big presa canario hound, lifted his mammoth head as his nose and nub of a tail twitched in anticipation.

Lucy had just walked into the living room with Ned from the bedroom/office down the hall. Both were blushing as they held hands, which seemed to be the only thing that kept the young cowboy from bolting out the door. Always shy, he looked nervous as hell compared to their daughter's beaming countenance.

"Sure, sweetheart, all the time in the world if it's for you," Karp replied, though he was getting a queasy feeling in the pit of his stomach.

"Good because we have something to tell you," Lucy began hesitantly.

"Oh God, you're pregnant!" Marlene groaned, sitting upright and scanning her daughter as if looking for some telltale sign of impending motherhood that she had somehow missed an hour earlier at dinner. Gilgamesh barked and ran to the door, hoping that someone had invited him out for a walk.

"Geez, Mom," Lucy replied, as if her mother had uttered the dumbest statement in the history of mankind. "But . . . well, actually, Ned has something to say first." She tugged her boyfriend, who was standing a little behind her, forward.

Blanchett's face had assumed the coloring of a maraschino cherry and he had to clear his throat several times before he managed to stammer, "I . . . uh . . . well, I meant to try to ask you this in private . . . man to man," he said, addressing Karp. "But . . . um . . . I have to leave tonight for a little while and there didn't seem to be any other opportunities . . ."

Man to man? What is this? Karp wondered, and then he understood. Theoretically he'd known that this day would come, but he was no more prepared for it than he was to hear that Ned was taking his daughter to Mars. He looked over at Marlene, whose face was undergoing a transformation from "very concerned" to "dawning realization" as a smile crept onto her lips and tears sprang to her eyes.

"That's okay, Ned," Marlene said for him. "You go right on ahead and tell us what's on your mind."

Ned looked at Marlene gratefully and nodded. "Thanks. I wanted to do this proper but looks like I'm just gonna have to shoot from the hip now. . . . I ain't much good at talking, so I'll just spit it out." He drew himself up to his full height. "Sir, Mr. Karp . . ."

"Butch," Marlene offered softly.

"Uh, yes, ma'am," the young man replied. "Anyway, Mr. Karp, sir, what I'm trying to say is that I'd like to ask for your daughter's . . ." He pointed with his free hand to Lucy as if there might be some confusion regarding whom he was talking about. "Um, hand in marriage." He stopped talking, though his pronounced Adam's apple continued to bob up and down in his throat, which he kept trying to clear.

Karp felt all eyes turn to him, even the dog's, and realized that his mouth was hanging open like a fish at Fulton's Fish Market. Marlene poked him in the ribs. "You've just been asked a question."

In all his years on the planet, Karp had never been at a loss for words except at the births of his three children: overcome with love for his wife and the tiny wrinkled babies she'd produced, he'd been speechless. He hadn't expected that this question would have the same effect, but the reality that the better part of Lucy's love would now be dedicated to another man hit him like a punch in the kidneys.

"Yeah, I know," he said huskily, trying to smile through his own tears. Marlene seemed to realize what was going through his head and leaned her head on his shoulder and rubbed his arm.

"It's okay, babe," she whispered. "She'll always be your little girl."

Karp nodded. "I take it you've already asked Lucy?" he croaked.

Ned glanced quickly at Lucy, a little confused. "Uh, well, yes, I have . . . sorry, I know that was putting the saddle on before the blanket, but I figured there wouldn't be much point asking you if she was just going to say no . . ."

Karp held up his hand. "You don't have to apologize. I asked Marlene before I dared approach her dad." He sighed as he looked at his daughter, noting again the changes in her.

Lucy had blossomed. Physically, she'd filled out with plenty of womanly curves—though muscular from living a ranch life with Ned; even the prominence of her Roman nose had receded as her face grew fuller. But more than the physical changes, he'd noted the maturation in her voice and eyes—as if the wise woman who'd always been inside had decided that it was time to show herself. He knew those eyes had witnessed more terrible things than any young woman in her twenties should have, and a certain amount of maturity could be expected from that. However, with Lucy it was more than unfortunate experience that made her the woman she was now, it was her determination to conquer her fears by confronting them head-on.

Especially since signing on with Espey, he thought. He respected her decision, but had a hard time accepting it when she announced that she was working in the lethal field of counterterrorism. He'd argued that there were a lot of other, less dangerous ways to contribute to her country. But she'd essentially told him to buzz off; it wasn't his decision to make.

Ned Blanchett had changed, too. He'd always had a wiry toughness about him, and when faced with danger—particularly in defense of Lucy—he'd reacted decisively and lethally. But he, too, had grown beyond the young man he'd been since joining Jaxon. Karp, who'd been a fan of Western movies since childhood, thought Blanchett epitomized that image of the heroic archetype. Strong. Silent. Brave. Loyal. And deadly when necessary.

"*Dad!*" Lucy shouted, stomping her foot for emphasis. "Aren't you going to say something?"

Karp blinked. He hadn't realized that he was taking a long time to answer. He looked at his daughter. "Did you accept?"

Lucy rolled her eyes. "Are you *trying* to be obtuse? Of course I accepted. I love Ned, and I want to be his wife more than I've wanted anything in my entire life. But he wanted to get your blessing . . . a silly chauvinistic practice, if you ask me, like a woman is some sort of commodity to be exchanged between consenting males . . . after all, I am quite capable of making my own—"

Her father held his hand up. "Nothing silly about it," he replied. "I appreciate the the gesture, Ned." He stood up and crossed the room with his hand outstretched. "Or should I call you son?"

Grinning and blushing even harder, Ned pumped his hand vigorously. "I'm so durned happy right now, you can call me a lowdown snake in the grass, if you want."

Then everybody was laughing and crying and hugging. The twins, who'd been in their room, came out to see what the commotion was all about and were soon immersed in the festivities with their new brother-in-law, while Gilgamesh pranced around the group barking with joy.

A few minutes later, with Marlene on the telephone telling her father the news and the twins wrestling with Ned, Lucy walked up to her father and laid her head on his chest. "I love you, Daddy."

Karp wrapped his arms around her, remembering the times he'd held her in the past. "I love you, too, Luce. I have from the moment the doctor handed you to me after you were born. Just remember what your mom said, you'll be Ned's wife, but you'll always be my little girl."

"Always, Daddy . . . always and forever."

The embrace lasted until they both became aware of Ned standing off to one side, his black Stetson in one hand. "Sorry to interrupt," he apologized. "But I need to skedaddle. Mr. Jaxon and some of the others are waiting for me back at the corral. We're leaving directly from there before sunup tomorrow."

"Where are you going?" Karp asked before realizing that he wasn't going to get much of an answer.

Ned smiled. "To talk to a man about a horse. Sorry, Mr. Karp, but I'm not allowed to say."

"No need to apologize. I forgot you're not just an old cowhand from the Rio Grande anymore."

"I still have an old Roy Rogers album with that song on it," Ned said, laughing. "Boy howdy, I used to love that show—saw all the reruns on the local Taos station when I was a kid."

"You're still a kid," Karp said, and shook his hand again. "Take care of yourself."

"I will," Ned replied, and turned to Lucy. "Walk me out?"

"With pleasure, you good-lookin' cowpoke, you."

"Shucks, ma'am, if'n I'd a-knowed that you was gonna lay it on with all that honey, I'd a-asked yew to marry me a long time ago," Ned replied, laying it on a bit thick himself. He set the Stetson on his head, took his Marlboro Man sheepskin-lined coat off the rack next to the front door, and shrugged it on.

"Come on, Gilgamesh," Lucy said to the dog, who was watching their every move and sprang up at the invitation. "Let's go for a walk. At least I'll have one big strong male to walk me around the block."

The couple and the dog left the apartment, got on the elevator, and rode it to the ground-level foyer, where Ned and Lucy looked up and waved at the security camera.

Upstairs, Karp was looking at the monitor near the door and waved back, although they couldn't see him. He continued to watch as they checked a different monitor in the foyer that was connected to a camera outside the entrance. Apparently there was no one suspicious lurking outside the building, so they left and disappeared around the corner onto Grand Avenue, where, Karp suspected, a car would be waiting for Blanchett.

As they left his sight, Karp felt a shadow cross his heart. *It's the worst that could happen.* Lucy and Ned may have matured into strong individuals, even ones capable of looking after themselves, but they were up against people who had no regard for human life. He let out a deep breath and turned away from the monitor. At least it didn't appear that Lucy would be going away on whatever mission Ned had declined to discuss.

The more immediate concern, of course, was that some unknown boy, and presumably whatever adult was telling him what to say, knew about Lucy's clandestine activities.

Therefore, whatever message Andy was trying to send with "Casa Blanca" and "art of war" needed to be taken seriously, Karp thought as he watched his daughter return from Grand Avenue and walk past the building with Gilgamesh.

Two hours later, he was lying in bed with Marlene discussing "Andy" and his own concerns for Lucy's safety when the telephone rang. His heart skipped a beat. . . . *No good news arrives at midnight,* he thought.

"Hello?" he answered. Karp sat straight up in bed. "Oh no," he groaned. "Yeah, Clay, I'll be waiting. Ten minutes." He hung up the telephone.

Taking in the stunned look on her husband's face, Marlene blinked hard and then dared to ask, "What happened?"

"Stewbie Reed is dead," Karp said as he slid out of bed and began to dress.

"Oh my God," Marlene cried. "How?"

Karp stopped and stood gazing out the window of their bedroom. "Apparently he hung himself."

"I can't believe it," Marlene said, getting up. "Why would he do something like that?"

When Butch didn't answer, Marlene guessed what he was thinking. "It wasn't your fault," she said.

"I don't know," Karp said. "Maybe I was too hard on him. Maybe assigning Katz to help on the case pushed him over the edge. I knew the case was eating at him and he blamed himself. Maybe I should have—"

"Butch, it was not your fault," Marlene said again. "Losing a case is not a reason to kill yourself; prosecutors lose cases. Stewbie has been around a long time, this wasn't his first hung jury. There had to be something else going on."

Karp's shoulders slumped. "Maybe. . . . Anyway, I need to go. Fulton's sending a car to take me over to Stewbie's apartment in the Village." He started to leave the room but hesitated in the doorway.

"Butch . . ."

"Yeah, I know, it wasn't my fault," he said as he walked out.

13

"**Here we are,**" **announced the cabdriver.** "**Two forty-**nine Forty-ninth . . . St. Malachy Chapel."

Marlene paid the fare and got out in front of the small gray Gothic church known as the actor's chapel. Built at the beginning of the twentieth century, St. Malachy had since the 1920s attracted actors, dancers, and musicians seeking refuge from the nearby Theater District. Just a couple of blocks west of the hustle and noise of Times Square, it had served as the setting for the funeral of Rudolph Valentino and the wedding of Douglas Fairbanks Jr. to Joan Crawford, and was certainly the only Catholic church in the world with chimes that played "There's No Business Like Show Business."

Although not as grand as St. Patrick's Cathedral or the massive St. John the Divine, it was one of Marlene's favorites and the current assignment of Father Mike Dugan, a Jesuit priest, another character who'd become embroiled in her family's unusual history. But she wasn't there to visit with him.

On the way over to the church, she'd asked her driver to turn west on Forty-seventh to take her past the Augusta Theater, where F. Lloyd Maplethorpe's latest hit, *Putin: The Musical,* was playing. At the little island created by the convergence of Broadway and

Seventh Avenue called Duffy Square, she'd noted the line of people waiting at the discount ticket office and wondered how many of them were hoping to get in to see *Putin*.

She'd glanced up at the marquee above her head bearing the name of Maplethorpe's hit production and her stomach turned. *I guess the Irish writer Brendan Behan was right when he wrote "There's no such thing as bad publicity except your own obituary,"* she thought. But it galled her that a craven coward like Maplethorpe would be enjoying such success a few weeks before his murder trial, while a good and decent man like Stewart Reed was lying on a cold steel table at the morgue.

Funeral services for Reed were still a week away. His sister was serving in the army in Iraq and had been granted a hardship leave to attend the services and care for their invalid mother, but she wouldn't arrive for several days.

Marlene felt guilty, but wished it could be over sooner. Devastated by Reed's suicide, her husband was obsessing over riddles sent to him by some mysterious little boy and his pickpocket father, convinced that there was a real threat and worried about the implications for Lucy. It didn't help that Ned was away on some secret mission and Lucy was leaving that night to return to New Mexico alone.

Knowing that it might be a while before she heard from her daughter, Marlene had planned to stay home all day with Lucy. But then she got a telephone call from Alejandro Garcia asking her to meet him at St. Malachy. Lucy had told her to go ahead. *"I have some errands to run before I leave. We'll have time to talk at dinner."*

Marlene and Butch had learned that the reformed gang leader turned rap star was back in the city when he'd shown up at the loft with the twins in tow a few weeks earlier. She'd been out walking Gilgamesh and was returning home when a limousine pulled up and the twins popped out with Garcia.

"'Sup, Marlene," Garcia had said, his round, boyish face lit up with his trademark grin.

"Alejandro, good to see you," she exclaimed, holding her arms out for a hug. *"I read that you were back in town. And here you are arriving in style . . . and with my boys."*

"Yeah, check it out, señora," Garcia said. *"I saw the boys walking home . . . I think they said from the movies . . . so I offered them a lift."*

Marlene caught the follow-my-lead look from Garcia to Zak and Giancarlo. *"That was kind of you,"* she said, giving her boys the eye. *"I can't wait to hear all about the movie."*

Zak had yawned. *"Boy, am I tired. I think I'm just going to go to bed. We'll tell you all about it tomorrow, Mom. Isn't that right, G?"*

"Absolutely," Giancarlo responded, barely able to stifle a yawn of his own. *"Really wore ourselves out playing football in the park."* The twins had hurried into the loft building.

Marlene had laughed. *"Guess that's what you'd call 'buying time' or 'by morning the old lady will probably forget.' I won't ask you to betray a confidence, but thanks for bringing them home."* She nodded up at where the lights were on in the loft. *"Come on up and say hi to Butch."*

"Are you loco?" Garcia laughed. *"A notorious gangster hanging with the Man in his crib?"*

"Quit it." Marlene laughed. *"We're all proud of you, including Butch. We have both of your CDs, and I think he knows all the words to the current big hit 'Spanish Harlem.' Or at least he does a pretty decent job of lip-syncing with the twins, and even busts a few moves when he thinks I'm not watching. Come on in, maybe we can get him to do it."*

Marlene was only exaggerating a little. She and Butch appreciated that unlike other rappers their boys sometimes listened to, Garcia avoided using profanity, never used "niggah" or any derivations thereof, and never felt like he had to refer to women as bitches or "hos." His lyrics still resonated with the anger and frustrations of the streets, but they were antiviolence and preached respect for one another. The twins had pointed out that he might have made more money if he'd sold out to gangsta rap or got more sexually explicit, but he'd stayed true to his beliefs in using his music as a constructive force.

"The Man bustin' moves? Uh, gracias, but no, I don't think I want to see that," Garcia said with a look of mock horror on his face. Then he smiled. *"But maybe some other time. I appreciate the offer. . . . Anyway, I need to cruise. I'm supposed to meet up with Father Mike, and I'm running late. I was at a cast party with an old girlfriend who has a part."*

"Really? Which show?"

"Putin: The Musical," Garcia said, and noted the sour look on Marlene's face. *"Yeah, I know, I know. I'm not wild about it either. But she's just trying to make it on Broadway and it's a job. She's also having a hard time believing that little punk-ass is a killer. Or she doesn't want to believe it."*

Alejandro had obviously been uncomfortable talking about Maplethorpe, so Marlene had patted him on the shoulder. *"I understand. Say hi to Father Mike,"* she said. *"I hope you're not going in for confession, he might be up all night listening to your laundry list of sins."*

Garcia laughed, but then a troubled look crossed his face. *"Unfortunately, it's nothing as simple as that. I don't know if you heard about it, but a couple of my old homeboys got shot up a couple weeks ago."*

"The Inca Boyz shooting in Central Park? Sure, I read about it in the newspaper," Marlene replied. *"The press speculating that it was some sort of turf war."*

"Well, for once they got it mostly right. Another gang is trying to muscle in on my old hood in the SH. They call themselves the Rolling 777s. They're Black Muslims."

"A Muslim street gang?"

Garcia nodded. *"Damn straight. I've been told that the triple Seven is a special number to Muslims, like triple Six is to devil worshippers. Word on the street is that they were associated with that mosque that was involved with that attack on the New York Stock Exchange. Until recently, they mostly stayed in the black part of Harlem, but according to my former homies the Inca Boyz, that's not true anymore."*

"So what's different about them?" Marlene asked. *"Aren't they just sort of a younger version of Nation of Islam?"*

"No, they're a lot more radicalized than that," Garcia replied. *"We hear they get their direction from overseas."*

"Al-Qaeda?"

Garcia shrugged. *"I don't know. But they do a lot of talking about jihad and that Islam is the only religion for brown people—black or Latino. I know they're a lot better organized and more militant than the average street gang like the Inca Boyz. We were mostly about protecting our hood and trying to make a little money. The Rolling 777s sell dope and whores and guns just like any other big gang—apparently it ain't against their religion if their customers ain't Muslim. But mostly what they're selling is radical Islam, and if you ain't buying, they can get nasty. My homeboys are mostly retired from the gangbanger life, but these shootings has got everybody riled up and lookin' for revenge. Father Mike asked me to come back and see if I can help him avoid a street war."*

That had been in early October and Marlene had not seen Garcia since. As she walked up to the carved wooden doors of St. Malachy, she wondered what he wanted.

When she got his call that afternoon, she figured it had something to do with the Inca Boyz and the Rolling 777s. But was surprised when he said he wanted her to "meet someone who might have something to say about the Maplethorpe case . . . if you can get her to talk about it."

Marlene had suggested that if this person was a witness or had information to provide regarding the case, it would be more appropriate for her to talk to a police detective or someone with the DAO. But Garcia had nixed that.

"I don't know that I can get her to talk even to you," he'd said. *"She sure as hell ain't ready to talk to the 5-0 or your old man. Maybe that's the next step, but she's heard me talk about you before and knows I trust you."*

Marlene was surprised to find the door of the church locked. She knocked and after a few moments heard a latch being turned. The door opened and she smiled at the sight of the rugged countenance of the gray-haired priest who stood there beaming at her.

"Marlene, my old friend! Come in out of the cold, child," Father

Mike Dugan insisted. She stepped over the threshold and into a bear hug from the former Notre Dame football star.

"It's good to see you, too, Father," Marlene replied, looking beyond him at the apparently empty chapel. "Is Alejandro here?"

"Not yet," he said. "But any minute."

About the same time that Marlene Ciampi went past the Augusta Theater, Alejandro Garcia greeted Carmina with a dozen roses as she left her dressing room. "For the most beautiful and talented actress, *muy bueno*."

Carmina rewarded him with a smile and a kiss. "Alejandro Garcia, are you trying to tell me you recognize your mistake when you walked out on me?"

"Oh no, never me, *chica*. If I remember right, you was the one who said she didn't want to be my girl."

"That was back when you was the Inca Boyz gang leader and headed nowhere fast," she replied. "Then you shot that punk in the ass, and they sent you to juvie. Next thing you know, you're a big-shot rapper and no room for me in your life."

"I don't remember no letters or visits at juvie," Garcia pointed out.

"I don't remember being invited," Carmina retorted, and then reached up and touched his face. "Doesn't matter, *mi amor*. We both had our own roads to follow."

"Maybe those roads don't always have to be in other directions," Garcia responded, taking her hand and raising it to his lips.

Carmina giggled and was about to answer when she looked over his shoulder and a cloud passed across her face. Garcia looked behind and saw F. Lloyd Maplethorpe, dressed in a crimson suit, approaching, accompanied by a large, heavily muscled man and, of course, followed by his gaggle of sycophants.

"Ah, the lovely Carmina," Maplethorpe squeaked in his Truman Capote–esque voice, "and Boom, what a pleasure to see you again. Did you catch the show? You did? Didn't you just love it? You know I've been thinking that perhaps after this I should do a hip-hop musical. Perhaps you'd write the score for me?"

"Sounds interesting," Garcia said without enthusiasm. He noticed that Carmina kept her eyes down even when Maplethorpe reached out and lifted her chin with his finger. He reacted instinctively to intervene, which caused the big man with Maplethorpe to step forward menacingly.

Maplethorpe caught the escalation in tension between his bodyguard and the young Latino and chuckled. "Now, now, Gregor. Mr. Garcia was only resenting my touching his girlfriend. He was playing out his role as protector, which is as it should be. Then again, he should know that Carmina and I have a special relationship that goes beyond the theater. Isn't that right, my dear?"

Carmina nodded but stepped back and away from his hand. "Yes, Mr. Maplethorpe, we're . . . friends."

"Excellent," Maplethorpe said, and clapped his hands as if Carmina had just performed her lines perfectly. "You do remember our little agreement, darling?"

"Yes, of course, Mr. Maplethorpe," Carmina responded. She looked at Garcia and saw the anger rising to the surface of his face. "Our business agreement."

Maplethorpe tilted his head and then smiled as if he was catching on to some hint. "Yes, indeed . . . our business agreement." He stepped forward and patted her on the top of her head. "There's a good girl. Now I really must be off. Boom, dear boy, you really must call my assistant the next time you're in town. We'll do lunch and talk about my idea."

With that, Maplethorpe suddenly turned and walked away, his retinue parting like the Red Sea before an iridescent Moses. The man named Gregor lingered a moment to stare at Garcia, his wide, scarred face and thick features contorted into a sneer.

However, although six inches shorter and forty pounds lighter, Garcia didn't blink or look in the least intimidated. "You got a problem?" he demanded.

"Alejandro! Please don't," Carmina said, placing a hand on his chest.

The big man smirked. "That's right, listen to girlfriend," he said in heavily accented English. "Safer that way."

"Fuck that, *pendejo,*" Garcia spat, but Carmina grabbed him by the arm and guided him away. The big man laughed and the young rapper started to turn back, but Carmina dug her nails into his skin.

"It's not worth it," she said.

"Okay, okay, get your claws out of my skin," Garcia said after they walked out of the building. He turned to face her. "Now are you going to tell me what's going on between you and that greasy little shit Maplethorpe? You've been acting like this since I left you at that party."

Carmina then shook her head. "It's nothing. A business arrangement."

"Sounds like something a Forty-second Street whore would say," Garcia replied.

Carmina's dark eyes flashed with anger. "That's easy for you to say, 'Jandro. You have your record deal, but I'm still trying to make it. Maybe all your money made you forget where we came from; maybe you should come back to the neighborhood more often and see what's going on. But maybe you're too good for us now."

Garcia's brow knitted and the muscles around his thick neck tensed, but then he relaxed and smiled. "You're right, *muchacha querida*. I've been gone too long. And I've made so many compromises with producers, it's a miracle my asshole doesn't hurt."

"So poetic." Carmina laughed. "But that's better, *hermano*. So are you going to buy me an expensive dinner now, Mr. Big Shot Recording Artist?"

"I suppose I owe you that," Garcia acknowledged. "But I want to stop by St. Malachy and say hello to Father Mike first."

"Good. I can use the walk to work up a big appetite. Champagne and lobster sounds *muy delicioso*."

"Aieee! *Pobre yo* . . . you have expensive tastes," Garcia complained with a grin. "You better marry a rich man!"

Carmina leaned forward and kissed him. "I intend to, *mi amor*, as soon as I'm a big star so that I can afford to take care of him in style."

Fifteen minutes later, Father Mike Dugan answered another knock at the chapel door and opened it to admit Alejandro and Carmina.

The former smiled when he saw Marlene. "Let me introduce you two fine-looking ladies. Marlene Ciampi, this is Carmina Salinas, the first girl who ever broke my heart. It is a wound I will keep forever."

Marlene smiled and held out her hand. "Good for you, Carmina. Sometimes a broken heart is the only thing that brings these macho idiots back to earth."

The younger woman laughed. "*Eso es verdad* . . . that's true. But he is lying. He had his chances, but he didn't want to be tied down. Then again, I thought he was going to end up behind prison walls or six feet under in the ground. Who was to know that they would pay him for stuff he used to do for free on a street corner?"

"This woman was created by the devil," Garcia said, shaking his head sadly. "She had no faith, but now I'm stylin' . . . I'm like Justin Timberlake, I brought sexy back Latino style."

"You brought macho posing back, you mean," Carmina teased.

Marlene watched the pair as they bantered back and forth. *They certainly make a beautiful couple,* she thought, *and it's obvious they're in love.* "So, Carmina, I hear you're in *Putin: The Musical*."

"She's practically the leading lady," Garcia boasted. "If they picked according to beauty and talent, she would be."

Carmina rolled her eyes and punched him on the arm. "As usual, he's lying through his teeth, trying to get laid . . . oh, sorry, Father."

"That will cost you an extra Hail Mary, my child."

"Tonight before I go to bed . . . alone," Carmina said, looking over at Garcia, who glanced up at the ceiling of the church as if he'd suddenly noticed something fascinating. "Anyway, Marlene, I have a few lines and a small solo in one of the songs about Iraq called 'Shock and Awe.' Mostly I'm in the chorus and the big group scenes."

"Wow, sounds like a lot," Marlene said, and then sighed. "I do love musical theater. If you can keep a secret, I'm a closet diva who sings in the shower, imagining that I'm Mary Martin's character in *South Pacific*."

"Who?" Alejandro and Carmina asked at the same time, and shrugged.

"Never mind, you're too young," Marlene sniffed. "So have you been in anything else I might know?"

"Probably not unless you're a fan of off- and off-off-Broadway," Carmina said. "But at least I've been working onstage, which is more than a lot of girls can say. Because of *Putin,* I'm not even an actress-slash anymore. At least while we're open."

"An actress-slash?" Marlene asked.

"Yeah, you know, ninety-five percent of the girls in this town who dream of being a star are actress-slashes. If you ask them what they do for a living, they're an actress-slash-waitress, or an actress-slash-secretary . . ."

"Know any actress-slash-hookers?" Garcia asked, dodging another punch aimed at his chest.

"They'd have to be an actress to be your lover, *poco pene,*" Carmina retorted.

Garcia turned to Marlene. "In case you need that translated, my dirty-talking friend just said I have a small penis, which I can assure you is not true."

"Too much information," Marlene replied.

"Especially in a house of God," Father Mike added, pointing up. "That will be ten Our Fathers."

"What! She gets one Hail Mary and I get ten Our Fathers, that's not fair," Garcia complained.

"She's also been to Mass within the last week," Father Mike replied. "And how many times have you been in the past year?"

"Uh, I plead the Fifth," Garcia replied.

"That only works in human courts," the priest said. "Not God's court."

Laughing, Carmina turned to Marlene. "So what do you do when you're not singing in the shower?"

"Well, I'm pretty lucky. I've got a bit of money put aside—"

"Don't let her fool you," Garcia interjected. "She's rich as the Pope."

"I doubt that," Marlene said. "But I'm pretty well off. I was part owner of a successful VIP security firm and sold my interest a few years ago. So now I paint a little, try to keep twin teenage boys out of mischief, and still do a little private investigation work from time to time. I used to be a prosecutor with the District Attorney's Office . . ."

Carmina's smile gave way to a frown and her eyes narrowed. "You're the wife of the district attorney." She glared at Garcia. "You tricked me, you *pendejo*!"

"I just think that maybe you should talk to her," Garcia tried to explain.

Marlene looked confused. "I'm sorry if this was a surprise, Carmina; I'm in the dark as much as you about why Alejandro asked me to come here."

Carmina whirled to face Father Mike. "What did you tell them?"

The priest held up his hand. "I did not reveal the secrets of the confessional, if that's what you mean, though you know where I stand on this. But so that I'm not a party to this outside of the confessional, I'm going to leave the three of you to hash it out. I do have to open the chapel again in a half hour, if you'd please keep that in mind."

"You don't have to leave, Father, I am," Carmina replied, and started to turn away from the group.

Alejandro reached out and grabbed her arm. "Please, Carmina, I'm sorry I surprised you, but I knew you wouldn't come if I told you Marlene would be here. She's not a cop and she doesn't work for the DA anymore. But I trust her and she can help."

"There's nothing to help," Carmina spat.

"No? It doesn't take a genius to know that something's been trippin' you out since the night I left you at the bar with Maplethorpe and took Zak and G-man home . . ." Realizing what he'd just said, Garcia winced and looked over at Marlene, whose jaw dropped.

"The twins were at a bar?" she asked.

"Sorry, they heard I was going to perform at this cast party," Garcia explained. "I didn't know they were going to be there, and we left as soon as I got done."

Marlene rolled her eyes. "Well, I'll be having a little talk with the boys later. But let's address where we're at right now. . . . Carmina, I'm sorry if Alejandro put you on the spot. If there's something you know that's connected to Mr. Maplethorpe's trial, then I'd urge you to get in touch with the proper authorities. Or I can just listen and maybe give you my thoughts without it going any further."

Carmina looked carefully at Marlene, but then bit her lip and shook her head. "I don't want to get involved."

"I understand that," Marlene replied. "Believe me, I've been involved in far too many of these things to wish them on anyone else. On the other hand, a woman is dead and a man will soon be on trial for killing her. They both deserve all the evidence to be heard and justice to be served. And if Maplethorpe is a sexual predator, you should know that sexual predators don't stop until they are caught and prevented from hurting anyone else."

"You have no idea what you're asking," Carmina replied. "If something happened that night—and I'm not saying that it did—if I testified against Mr. Maplethorpe, I would never work on a stage in this town again. I can hear the rumor mill now: 'She's just saying it because she didn't get the part she wanted.' I'd be just another girl everybody believes tried to jump-start her career from the casting couch and then complained when it didn't work. And they'd think I'd probably say something about the next producer or director if I didn't get what I wanted. Nobody, but nobody, would ever hire me."

"So you fucked him?" Garcia demanded to know.

"Screw you, 'Jandro," Carmina shot back. "No, I didn't fuck him, though maybe you should watch what you say when you walk into a church."

"Then what is it, 'Mina?" Garcia asked. "Anytime that freak comes around you can't even look him in the eye. And that's not like you."

"It doesn't matter," Carmina replied. "Nothing I could say would bring that woman back to life, and my dreams would be gone." She started again to walk out of the church.

"Carmina, wait!" Garcia yelled. "Let's forget about it and go to dinner."

"I'm not hungry anymore, 'Jandro," the young woman replied, and headed for the door.

Garcia turned to follow but stopped to apologize to Marlene. "I'm sorry. I guess I fu—messed that up."

"It's okay," Marlene replied. "You were trying to do the right thing. Now go catch your girl and make it up to her."

Across the street from St. Malachy Chapel, Gregor Capuchin watched as first the young woman and then the young man left the church. The young man quickly caught up to the girl and then they argued, though not loud enough that he could hear what they were saying. After a few minutes, however, they appeared to make up, kissed, and then walked off toward Times Square with his arm around her shoulders.

Lovers' spat, he mused, and started to turn away when he saw another woman leave the chapel. He had good eyes and there was something about her face that seemed familiar. He jogged across the street as she started to walk toward Broadway. "Excuse me, please, can you direct me to Radio City Music Hall?" he called after her.

The woman turned to face him in a way he recognized from his former military service as that of a trained fighter. But the woman relaxed as she presumably determined that he wasn't a threat, and judged from his foreign accent and request for directions that he was a confused tourist.

"Sure," she replied, and pointed east on Forty-ninth Street. "Go straight until you reach Sixth Avenue, which is also called Avenue of the Americas. Cross Sixth and turn left, then up a block. You can't miss it."

"Ah yes, thank you very much," Gregor said with a little bow.

"You're welcome," the woman replied, and resumed walking. Apparently, she wondered why he hadn't moved and turned back. "Did you understand?"

"*Da, da,*" Gregor replied. "I understand. Am waiting for wife. She is in hotel." He pointed across the street at a cheap older hotel.

"Well, enjoy your stay," the woman said, and walked off.

He watched her go as he pulled a cell phone out of his coat pocket and called his employer. "The girl just left with her boyfriend," he said. "But there was someone else."

"Who?" Maplethorpe asked.

"It took me a moment, but long time ago, when I was still working for Ivgeny Karchovski, he met with same woman in Brighton Beach," Gregor replied. "I was there and heard her name. Marlene Ciampi."

"The wife of the district attorney," Maplethorpe hissed.

Gregor noted the fear in his employer's voice. "Yes, that is her."

"What was she doing with a Russian gangster?" Maplethorpe asked.

The man shrugged. "How do I know? They did not ask me to join them at table. Perhaps they are lovers, I don't know. All I know is that she was in the church with the other two and that the door was locked. No one else has gone in or out of church, except old priest. What do you want me to do?"

There was a pause as Maplethorpe considered his options. "I can't trust that little bitch Carmina," he said at last. "I can't afford to have her testify against me."

"So again I ask, what do you want me to do?"

"I want you to take care of her," Maplethorpe replied.

"It'll cost double the last."

"What? That's outrageous! Why should it cost more?"

"Because the more I do, the greater the chance that I'll be caught."

"Well, just make sure you take care of this problem without it coming back on me," Maplethorpe said. "Make it look like an accident or something."

"You let me worry about that. We have deal?"

"Yes. When?"

"You let me worry about that, too."

"But soon? The trial is in three weeks. I don't need any more trouble."

"Perhaps you should have thought of that before."

"I've already heard that from my lawyer, thank you very much. Just take care of it."

"Okay, boss, no problem. Consider problem gone."

14

Amir al-Sistani was convinced that his health was slipping away with every hour that passed in the dark. Half naked beneath a thin blanket, he shivered and panicked as another rumbling, wheezing cough escaped his chattering lips. He recalled Grale's red-stained handkerchiefs and was convinced that he could taste blood in his mouth.

Kept in total darkness, except for the infrequent flashlight beams of his captors and the occasional interrogation in Grale's cavern, he was disoriented and had no sense for what day of the week it might be, or even what time of day. His memory seemed to come and go, and sometimes he had a hard time distinguishing between dreams and reality.

In fact, lately he'd been having hallucinations. Or at least that's what he thought they were, such as the most recent event in which he'd been dragged from his sleep by pale, hardly human creatures with big eyes and sharp teeth. They'd pawed at him as he screamed in terror and slipped into unconsciousness.

When he awoke, one of Grale's men sat next to him. The man was not one of his usual guards, but a stranger who stayed in the dark so that al-Sistani couldn't distinguish his facial features.

"That was close, friend," the man said. *"Damn Jeremy and Paulito. They were supposed to be guarding you."*

"What were those things?" al-Sistani cried out.

"The others? Why, unclean spirits . . . as in the Book of Mark 3:11, 'And unclean spirits, when they saw him, fell down before him, and cried' . . . only these weren't crying, they were looking for a meal. Lucky for you I showed up. But I have to go, perhaps we'll speak again soon. Don't tell anyone I was here."

The man left and was replaced a few minutes later by his usual guards. However, he'd visited several times since and seemed to want to help him. al-Sistani never saw the man but knew him by his odor, which was foul, and manner of speech, which was educated and lucid—at least compared to the rest of the rabble. His visitor brought him decent food, instead of the moldy bread and gruel he usually received, and even a wet cloth to wash his face.

"Why are you doing this?" al-Sistani had asked him the last time.

"The Good Book says, 'Ye have heard that it hath been said, Thou shalt love thy neighbor, and hate thine enemy. But I say unto you, Love your enemies, bless them that curse you, do good to them that hate you, and pray for them which spitefully use you, and persecute you.' That's Matthew 5:43–44, friend," the man whispered. He sidled closer until al-Sistani could feel his bushy beard against his face, and he felt faint as the man's horrible breath wafted over him. *"Besides, I wanted to ask you a question."*

"What question?"

The man hesitated, as if listening to something in the dark, then continued. *"Were you telling the truth about the gold?"*

"For my freedom?" al-Sistani replied, a glimmer of hope leaping into his mind. *"Yes, yes, of course! Get me out of here, and it's yours. More gold than in your wildest dreams!"*

The man didn't reply at first, but then patted him on the shoulder. *"I need to think a bit. After all, the Good Book says, 'The love of money is the root of all evil'—that's Timothy 6:10, by the way—not money itself. I don't love money, but I sure would love to live better than I currently do, and the Good Book doesn't say there's anything wrong with that. . . . We'll talk later."*

Al-Sistani had been buoyed by the hope that a traitor in Grale's camp might yet save him. But it had been several days since the man had last visited and he wondered if he had decided against helping him. Not that he planned paying the disgusting infidel with anything except death if he managed to escape, but the lies fit under *al-Taqiyya* and therefore were approved by Allah.

His despair turned to fear as he heard the shuffling of feet coming toward him in the dark. They might be the unclean souls, the *shayteen,* he thought, and trembled. But fear turned to excitement when he recognized the smell of his potential benefactor.

"I've been thinking about your offer," the man whispered. "It's tempting, but we'd never make it out of here. All the passages are watched. Nothing happens in this part of the city without Grale knowing."

Al-Sistani realized that the man was losing his nerve. "Is there something he desires?" he asked in a panic.

"He can't be bought, if that's what you're thinking," the visitor said. "He doesn't care about money or creature comforts."

"Surely there is something? No man is without desires."

The visitor was silent and al-Sistani could almost hear him thinking in the dark. "There is someone he is obsessed with," the man began slowly. "A young woman."

Al-Sistani saw his opening. "Of course, of course, what man doesn't desire a woman? You say it is one particular woman—not just any will do?"

"No, it's one," the man replied. "He broods about her. I think she's part of the reason for his black moods. I thought he was above all that, but apparently he's just another man with sins of the flesh on his mind. 'Lust not after her beauty in thine heart; neither let her take thee with her eyelids,' Proverbs 6:25."

Al-Sistani caught the tone of disgust in the man's voice and sought to exploit it. "The Qur'an says, 'Obey not him whose heart we have made heedless of Our remembrance, who followeth his own lust . . ."

"I see you're a man of God," the visitor replied. "That's a good thing. But even if he lusts after this woman, how does that help me help you?"

"My friends, the ones who can pay you, they might arrange to . . . exchange this young woman for me. Perhaps with your help this could be managed?"

"Grale would have my head if I was caught helping you, especially if she was involved."

"Then you must be very careful until I am safely traded for the girl. Then he'll be so intoxicated with lust, he won't care about you. And even if he did, you will have enough money to go anywhere you like, start a new life. He'll never find you from his little sewer hole."

"What if I said I want one million dollars deposited in gold, where I say."

"That is nothing to me. I will give you two million. It's nothing to me."

Suspicion crept into the visitor's voice. "How do I know you'll pay me after you're with your people?"

"I swear by Allah, may he take my soul. Ask anyone who knows, the Sheik always rewards loyalty and those who help him," al-Sistani replied.

"Not good enough," the man said. "I want something up front."

Al-Sistani thought quickly. "When you go to my friends, you will instruct them to give you . . . one hundred thousand dollars. Tell them I said it is for Operation Flashfire. When you have the money, you will assist them with locating and . . . capturing . . . this woman. When the arrangements for the exchange have been made, nine hundred thousand in gold will be deposited wherever you ask. The rest, when I am safe."

Again the man fell silent. If not for the smell of him, al-Sistani would have thought that he'd left. "Tell me how to contact your friends," he said at last. "I'll see what I can do."

"Allah be praised!" al-Sistani replied, and whispered the information. "Did you get that?" But there was no answer forthcoming from the dark.

Several days later, Lucy walked out into the living room of her parents' loft with two suitcases. "Well, it's time," she announced.

"You sure I can't give you a ride?" Marlene said. "It wouldn't be any trouble."

"No thanks, Mom," she replied. "Besides, I need to check in at the office before I leave, and even you aren't allowed in there."

"How about I walk you to the street? It's dark outside," Karp said.

"Nope," Lucy replied. "I called a cab and he'll be here any minute. It's also cold out and I wouldn't want those old bones catching a chill. And isn't it past your bedtime?"

"Hey, watch it with the geriatric slights," Karp replied with a laugh. He looked at his watch. "It's only eight thirty, I still got another half hour in me."

"I calls 'em as I see 'em," Lucy responded. "But really, I'm going to wait in the foyer until the cab arrives and then make a dash. Now come on, give me a hug, it could be a while before I get back here . . . and I've about given up getting you to come to New Mexico."

"One of these days, I promise," Karp said, and hugged his daughter.

"Deal," Lucy replied. "And again, I'm sorry about Mr. Reed. He was always such a nice man, and handsome—he dressed like a model."

"That was Stewbie," Karp agreed. "And thanks. He'll be missed at the office."

"What are you going to do about that case? The Broadway producer."

"The Maplethorpe case," Karp replied. "We have a hearing tomorrow. But I'm meeting first with Kenny Katz to talk about what to do. . . . Stewbie's services aren't for a few more days; his mother wanted to wait for his sister to get here."

Marlene wedged herself between the two to hug her daughter. "It's time for you to go or you'll miss your plane. Call when you get to Taos, even it it's going to be, what, early morning when you arrive? It's always tough reaching you at the ranch."

"Yeah, I know," Lucy said. "Though I have to admit I kind of like it. Peace and quiet. No pesky parents to tell me what to do."

Lucy started to leave but then turned and embraced her parents one more time. "If anything ever happens to me, I hope you both know how much I love you," she said, stifling a tiny sob as she stood back.

Marlene reached out for her daughter's arm. "Is everything all right?"

Lucy sniffled and nodded. "Yeah. I'm fine. I just miss Ned and was having a moment of homesickness for you guys, too."

"You're welcome to stay here until he gets back," Karp said. As usual, he felt at a loss when women were crying.

"Nah, I need to get back and check on the ranch, make sure the animals are okay," she replied. "And I love it there this time of year. The aspens are turning color and the high peaks have snow on them. I'm okay, I just had a moment there."

"I don't blame you for wanting to get back, sounds lovely," Marlene said. "Do let us know when our new soon-to-be son-in-law gets back safe and sound."

"I will," Lucy said more cheerily than she felt. She'd only heard once from Ned in the two weeks he'd been gone, and that was a short text message: I LOVE YOU, BACK SOON. *And gone again soon, too*, she thought, wondering when, if ever, the dream of the little house on the prairie, kids, and a quiet life would come to fruition. *Or are we stuck on this counterterrorism carousel the rest of our lives? Careful, don't jinx it!*

Riding in the elevator, she thought about her last conversation with Ned the night they announced their engagement. As the car from the agency had pulled up on Grand, she'd grabbed him by the lapels of his coat and kissed him hard on the lips.

"Like my dad said, take care of yourself, cowboy," she'd said, choking up. *"I don't want to be a widow before I'm even a bride. I couldn't live without you."*

Ned's smile had disappeared. *"Don't talk like that,"* he said. *"It's bad luck. You might jinx it."*

Lucy nodded and nuzzled into his chest. *"My bad. I forgot you're a superstitious hillbilly."*

"Hey, I'm not the one who talks to dead people."

"Teresa is not dead, she's a saint and so is alive and in the pres-

ence of Jesus. It's not the same as freaking out because a black cat crossed your path, or thinking that stepping on a crack is going to break your mother's back."

"Yeah? Well, how would you feel if you did step on a crack and your mom hurt her back? What then, smarty-pants? Answer me that."

"Well, okay, I won't say anything else that might 'jinx it,'" Lucy replied. *"Because if something did happen to you after that, I'd—"*

"Ah-ah," Ned said, covering his ears, *"don't say it!"*

Lucy laughed and kissed him again. *"All right, all right, lips are sealed against jinxes. I just wish I could go with you. It's not fair. I'm supposedly part of the team, but I'm always getting left behind."*

Ned brushed her hair from her cheek. *"Nobody says you're not part of the team. But the whole concept behind our group is the fewer, the better. Everything has to be below the radar, and the more people involved, the harder that is to pull off. If you don't have a specific job to do—like you did in Dagestan—then you don't go."*

Lucy put a finger to his lips. *"I hate it when you and Jaxon are right. Just be careful."*

"I'll be careful, plus I have Espey, John, and Tran with me."

"A bunch of old men."

"A pretty damned tough bunch of old men if you ask me. Hopefully, this time we'll catch her and put a stop to whatever she's up to. Then you and I can go back to the ranch for a while."

"How do you know Nadya's even down there?"

"We don't for sure. But Jaxon thinks it's a pretty good educated guess on someplace to look based on the guys who were at that meeting in Dagestan. Even if she's not, that's one of the places we may be able to pick up her tracks."

"Tracks? Like some sort of skunk?"

"Or a snake."

"Well, if you find her, don't bring her back alive."

Ned's eyes narrowed. He hadn't expected that kind of a statement from his fiancée. The girl he'd met was so gentle she'd cried when she hit a coyote after the animal darted in front of her truck at night and died. *"Damn, Lucy, we're getting a little bloodthirsty, aren't we?"*

"Maybe. Maybe all of this is turning us into the people we're after. But all I know is the longer that woman is alive, the longer no one I know and love is safe. Especially whoever might be trying to catch her. You'll be there trying to figure out how to get her back safe and sound for a trial, and she'll spend all of her time thinking about how to kill you. Just kill her, like you were going to do in Dagestan."

Ned looked deep in her eyes and then nodded. *"I get her in my sights again, and she's history."*

Lucy leaned up and kissed him again, only this time more softly. *"Good. Now here's your ride. Hurry back or I might have to start hanging out at the Sagebrush Inn lookin' for another cowpoke to give me a poke."*

"Yeah? And I hear some of the gals in the Caribbean are mighty friendly, too."

"Ned Blanchett! Don't you dare," Lucy warned, pushing him toward the car. *"I'll know if you do—women always know—and I'll make a steer out of you."*

"Wouldn't that be like cutting off your nose to spite your face? Except it won't be my nose that gets cut, or your face that is spited. But you just keep them knickers up where they belong, and I'll be home 'afore you know it."

"I'll try." Lucy laughed. "Adios, mi amor. Vaya con Dios."

"Y tú," he answered, and was gone.

In the foyer, Lucy watched the monitor until a yellow cab pulled over to the curb across the street. Waving one last time in case her parents were watching, she walked out the door.

As she stepped down to the sidewalk, Lucy realized with a start that someone was standing off to the side just out of the illumination of the streetlight. She hadn't seen anyone else on the monitor and tensed, only to relax when she recognized her visitor—a middle-aged woman dressed in a nun's habit from the fifteenth century.

"St. Teresa! I've been wondering where you've been," Lucy said, reverting to archaic Spanish. "I thought maybe I was just in danger too much of the time for you to keep up."

"I've been with you the whole time," the apparition replied.

"You've just been too preoccupied to notice. But you're in grave danger now, my child."

Lucy nodded. Now that she wasn't with her parents, she could admit it to herself. "I know, and I'm afraid."

"You could turn from this path," St. Teresa replied. "Let someone else bear this cross."

"No," Lucy said, shaking her head. "There's too much of that going on in the world already."

"Then go with God, child. I'll be with you when you need me most."

"Y tú," Lucy replied, and started to walk over to the cab, but it suddenly pulled away from the curb and disappeared around the corner on Grand Avenue. She jumped at the sound of a voice behind her.

"Ah, the lovely Lucy Karp," a man said. "The very epitome of 'Beauty is the mark God sets upon virtue.'"

Lucy laughed as she turned, recognizing the voice and the tall figure who owned it. "What now, Professor Treacher? Citing Emerson instead of the Bible?" She walked toward the street preacher who stood just outside the darker shadows of the alley.

"Ralph and I go back a long ways," Treacher said with a bow. "But, of course, the Bible has its own verses on beauty. 'Oh my beloved, you are as beautiful as the lovely town of Tirzah, yes as beautiful as Jerusalem!'"

"Hmmmm . . . Tirzah, eh?" Lucy replied. "I think I like Ralph Waldo's verse better. Oh, and by the way, friend, that's from Song of Solomon, chapter 6:4."

"Very good," Treacher replied.

Lucy looked Treacher over with surprise. "That's a nice-looking parka you have on tonight," she said. "Is it new?"

"Days old," Treacher said proudly. "Warm as bread fresh from the oven."

"And new boots?"

"Not more than a few miles on them," Treacher agreed.

"Well, you seem to be doing well these days."

The old man looked troubled for a moment, then replied, "Why, yes. Seems a rich uncle died and left me a bit of an inheritance."

"I see," Lucy said. "But why are you standing out here at night? It's freezing. If this 'inheritance' isn't quite enough, why don't you let me give you some money for a room tonight? I hear it's going to get bitter cold."

Treacher's ragged face softened and his eyes clouded over for a moment. Then he shook his head. "I'm afraid that tonight will be more bitter than most," he said softly. "I'm sorry, Lucy."

"Sorry?" Lucy's puzzled look turned to one of alarm when she noticed the dark sedan sitting in the alley behind Treacher. The doors of the car opened, though the lights inside stayed off.

"How could you?" she yelled, and turned to run, but the old man was ready. He reached out with a Taser stun gun, which he touched to the back of her neck. There was a momentary flash of blue, a slight buzzing, a muffled cry, and then she slumped into his waiting arms.

The other men stepped forward and quickly relieved Treacher of his unconscious victim. "We'll take her from here."

"She's not to be harmed," Treacher warned.

The leader of the men laughed. "What do you care, Judas? You have your thirty pieces of silver . . . or at least as much as you're going to get until, Allah willing, you complete your task."

"I care because Grale won't want his little prize damaged," Treacher growled, "or you may get your pal back in little quivering pieces."

The man spat on the ground. "Don't worry," he said. "Our instructions are to deliver her safe and unharmed. After that . . . it is not my responsibility what happens to the American whore."

"You've been warned," Treacher said. "Now let's talk about something important . . . my money."

15

"Mr. Karp, in the matter of *The People versus F. Lloyd Maplethorpe*, what are your wishes?"

Judge Michael Rosenmayer peered over at the prosecution table, where Karp and Kenny Katz sat quietly locked in an animated conversation. Lean and handsome, Rosenmayer had a physical appearance that matched his tough, no-nonsense reputation after nearly twenty-five years on the bench for the Supreme Court of New York—which is the trial court, unlike in most states, where the Supreme Court is the highest appellate venue.

Karp stood and, with a final glance toward Katz, said, "The People wish to go forward as scheduled."

Rosenmayer looked surprised. He was used to lawyers asking for delays on just about any pretext; rarely did they voluntarily forgo extra time, *especially* when they had a valid excuse. "Are you sure? Your office just lost the lead prosecutor in this case to an untimely death, and I am prepared to grant you additional time. And by the way, my sincere condolences; Mr. Reed was a fine lawyer who appeared before this court numerous times, and from everything else I've observed and heard about him, he was a good man, too. It's such a tragedy, and all I can add is that none of us know what demons another man may be dealing with."

"No we don't, Your Honor," Karp replied. "And I appreciate your offer and especially your kind words regarding Stewart Reed. He was, indeed, a good man and a skilled, conscientious public servant who will be sorely missed. However, the People are ready to proceed."

The judge's kind words about Reed had caught Karp emotionally unprepared and he'd choked up at the end as he recalled the last time he saw Stewbie Reed. Detective Murphy had taken him to the Waverly Place apartment building, where he climbed out of the car into the glare of red and blue flashing lights of a police cruiser, an unmarked detective's sedan, and an NYFD ambulance. Several camera flashes went off as he stepped to the curb; either someone had alerted the press, or a couple of locals were hoping to make a buck selling tragedy to the press.

Chief of the DAO detective squad Clay Fulton was standing at the front door and let him into the building and then led the way up three flights of stairs to Reed's apartment. The big former college middle linebacker stepped aside when they entered the apartment, and that's when Karp saw Reed. He was hanging by the neck from an overhead pipe above the hardwood floor of his apartment living room, his eyes protruding and his face blue.

Karp noted that Reed had decided to die in the same manner he lived, impeccably dressed—from his Brooks Brothers shirt, silk tie, and tailored suit to his Allen-Edmonds dress shoes. *"My God, I can't believe this. Has anybody notified his family?"* he'd asked, his voice catching as he looked up into Stewbie's lifeless eyes. *"I think his mother lived in Queens."*

"Maspeth . . . it's where he grew up," Fulton said. *"I sent a detective to her house to take her to the medical examiner's so she can identify the body. Someone from Victim's Assistance will meet them there and stay with her."*

"Thanks, Clay," Karp said as he tore his gaze from the dead man and looked around the apartment, a one-bedroom with a small living room and smaller kitchen. It was all tastefully decorated and immaculately kept, the hardwood floors perfectly polished to a golden sheen. He turned back to Fulton. *"Clay, I'd like you to handle this."*

The detective frowned as he gave Karp a questioning look. "*You know something I don't?*"

Karp had hesitated, but then shook his head. "*No. At least nothing I can put a finger on. It's probably just the shock; I never saw this coming. But we owe it to Stewbie to be thorough.*"

Fulton had been thorough and nothing had turned up amiss. But the image of Reed hanging from the pipe had continued to haunt Karp. Not so much the proximity of death—he'd certainly seen enough of that in his career—or even that this was the death of a friend and colleague. As he'd explained to Marlene, it was more like one of those what's-wrong-with-this-picture puzzles. Something was out of place, but even though he'd gone over it a hundred times in his mind, he couldn't say what it was. "The People are ready to proceed."

"Very well, Mr. Karp," Judge Rosenmayer said, and turned to the defense table, where Maplethorpe, dressed in a bright blue silk suit with oversize white-rimmed glasses, sat with his team of attorneys. "Mr. Leonard, do you have any problem with proceeding as scheduled?"

"Why, no, Your Honor," Guy Leonard replied in his booming baritone as he rose from his seat. He was one of the most famous defense attorneys in the country—just as tall as Karp, but leaner and tanned, as though he actually worked on the cattle ranch he owned near Bozeman, Montana. He favored Stetson hats to wear over his long gray shoulder-length hair, and cowboy boots, which, according to one fawning article in the *New York Times* at the beginning of the first Maplethorpe trial, set him back two thousand dollars a pair. He completed the image by wearing doeskin leather coats with fringes on the arms and turquoise-studded bolo ties. "I must confess that I expected my esteemed adversaries to request a continuance; however, I agree that it is time to put this matter to rest once and for all. The horror of how this beautiful young woman chose to end her life has been devastating for my client, who only wishes to move on from this tragedy for all parties and restore his good name."

Rosenmayer nodded and appeared ready to ignore the speech

and move on, but Leonard held up a hand. "I do have one request, and that is if we're to continue with this circus, who will be representing the District Attorney's Office? Will it be the young man attending to Mr. Karp today? I'm assuming he's capable of taking on a case of this importance."

Karp heard sniggers from the spectator section at the personal jab at Kenny Katz and glanced over at the defense table in time to see Maplethorpe cover a smile with his hand. The producer then half turned to look back at the adoring retinue that sat in the pews behind him.

Aware of the heat rising in his face, Karp smiled and kept his voice in check as he replied. "Mr. Katz, as well as every assistant district attorney in my office, is quite capable of handling this case, which by the way is no more or less important than any other case in which an innocent person is heinously murdered."

As he spoke, Karp looked again at Maplethorpe and was gratified to see him blush crimson at the suggestion that his was a run-of-the-mill trial, no more important than that of a common killer. "However, I will be representing the People with my esteemed associate Mr. Kenny Katz as cocounsel."

Raising his eyebrows in surprise, Leonard snorted theatrically and shook his head as he drummed his fingers on the defense table.

"Do you have an issue with that, Mr. Leonard?" Rosenmayer asked.

Leonard tilted his head and smiled as though he'd just been told an ironic joke. He gripped the lapels of his doeskin coat, rocked back on his heels, and chuckled. "No, no, Your Honor," he replied. "If my *esteemed* colleague, the *elected* district attorney, wants to turn this travesty into more of a media circus than it has already been, I suppose it's his right. But might I inquire as to what prompted this spectacular entry?"

Karp kept his eyes on the judge as he responded. "If there's been a 'media circus' surrounding this trial, counsel need only look in the mirror to see who has repeatedly disregarded Your Honor's prohibition regarding talking to the media about this case."

Leonard held his hands apart as if he had nothing to hide. "I do not seek out the press," he said in a wounded tone. "If anything, I have from time to time responded to questions that are put to me that unanswered would further sully my client's good name. The longer these lies linger in the public's mind, the greater the chance that they will poison the jury pool. Indeed, I believe that there have already been grave injustices along such lines. And what are the good citizens of New York to think when their *elected* district attorney takes it upon himself to prosecute a respected, *law-abiding*, until proven otherwise, member of the community."

"Not that it's any of Mr. Leonard's business," Karp retorted, "but the fact of the matter is that before the death of Mr. Reed, I undertook an extensive review of the case files and court transcripts from the first trial. I am the attorney in my office who is the most familiar with the facts, and my schedule at this time also allows me to undertake the case."

Leonard was about to respond, but this time it was the judge who held up his hand. "Save it, Mr. Leonard," he said, "I wouldn't want you to wear out that marvelous voice before the new jury gets to hear it. Now, is there any other official business that doesn't require an overabundance of rhetoric?"

"As a matter of fact," Leonard said, "I would like to know if the district attorney will be calling any additional expert witnesses who did not testify during the first trial? If so, we have not received any notification so that we might review their bona fides."

As though watching a slow, rather boring tennis match, the judge turned his head to look over at Karp, who responded, "We have no plans to call any additional witnesses. If we feel the need later, we will be sure to let counsel know in a timely manner."

Without waiting for Leonard to speak, Rosenmayer banged his gavel on the dais. "Very well," he said. "Jury selection begins in two weeks, which I will point out is the week before the Thanksgiving holiday week, when I plan for us to take Thursday and Friday off. If necessary, we will begin again the following Monday. Understood? Then court is adjourned in the matter of *The People versus F. Lloyd Maplethorpe*. . . . Oh, and once again, I ask that both sides, and their associates, refrain from making remarks to the press. I don't care if they insinuate that your client is the Antichrist, am I clear, Mr. Leonard?"

Leonard looked surprised by the question. "Why, of course, Your Honor. I shall endeavor to remain at arm's length from those—to paraphrase Spiro Agnew—nattering nabobs of negativism," he replied, turning his head so that only the spectator section could see him wink.

"Make sure you do, Mr. Leonard, or suffer the consequences," Rosenmayer said with a glower so stern that Leonard's smile dropped from his lips like a stone.

"Yes, Your Honor."

16

Dean Newbury leaned over and looked through the telescope across the East River at the island of Manhattan. He found it fascinating that he could see the faces of the pedestrians on the Brooklyn Bridge so clearly. *Unaware that they're being spied upon like protozoa under a microscope*, he thought, turning the telescope to take in the skyline. *It all really is quite a magnificent sight, too bad it may be necessary to destroy it.*

With the aid of the silver-knobbed cane he carried, the old man straightened up, wincing at the currents of pain that shot through his back. He glanced around the expensively furnished Brooklyn Heights mansion's library. *It's hell getting old.*

The door behind him clicked open and he turned in time to see Congressman Dent Crawford cross the room with his hand extended and a wide smile on his chubby, youthful face. "Dean Newbury, so good of you to drop by."

Newbury didn't bother to raise his own hand to shake. "Cut the bullshit, Crawford. Why did you feel it necessary to meet now?" He'd known Denton J. Crawford IV since his birth forty-three years earlier. The younger man was the son of a congressman from Vermont who'd followed in his father's footsteps, assuming his seat on the Hill and on the council of the Sons of Man after his father's death three years earlier.

Surprisingly, considering the Sons of Man's far-right leanings, the Crawfords were notable champions of the far left; but that was part of the plan. Infiltrate the opposition, make them appear radical and disconnected from the concerns of ordinary, middle-of-the-road Americans, and destroy any chance of a large, cohesive liberal alliance with the moderate majority when it came time for the Sons of Man to seize power.

Both of their families had occupied a seat on the council since the late 1700s, when the founders of SOM, a group of smugglers from the Isle of Man trying to escape the British Navy, came to the young United States of America to pursue their criminal enterprises, which laid the foundation for the current empire. The Newburys had always been among the top leadership of the council, but the Crawfords had never distinguished themselves. They were given their orders by the council on how to vote in Congress, and what radical left-wing ideas and groups to support.

The father was an idiot, Newbury thought, *and the son isn't much of an improvement. And yet . . .* Somehow young Dent Crawford had come up with a plan that might just accomplish what Newbury had been unable to do.

The younger man had first proposed his idea as an alternative to Newbury's strategy to cause a panic at the New York Stock Exchange—jeopardizing the nation's economy and setting the stage for a coup. Some members of the council, especially the younger members, worried that Newbury's idea was too complicated.

Only Newbury's preeminence on the council had swung the vote in favor of his plan. Still, enough of the others forced the council to accept Crawford's plan as a backup. Unfortunately, the stock exchange had not failed, and he was being forced by the decision of the council and his allegiance to the greater goals of SOM to swallow his pride and assist Crawford.

Now is the time to strike, Newbury thought, *or I'll find another way.* The country was ripe for change—an unpopular war, the major political parties mired in partisan sniping and gamesmanship, terrorism, and a flagging economy created the conditions, and the Sons of Man had never had so many well-placed men in positions of power and influence. He wanted only to live long enough to see it all come to fruition.

Always a pragmatic man, Newbury recognized that SOM was undergoing a changing of the guard. The Young Bastards, as Newbury and his generation of council members called Crawford and his cohorts, had been agitating over the past few years for a greater role in determining council policy. At first, they'd been ignored by older members of the council, but they'd gained support among the major and minor families that made up the core of SOM. The Young Bastards were rash and impatient; they had little sense of history or the careful planning that had for generations gone into preparing for SOM's final triumph.

Andrew Kane had been one of them and a perfect example of the pitfalls of allowing the young too much leeway. Outwardly a charming, successful lawyer and onetime candidate for New York City mayor, Kane was in fact a murderous, narcissistic sociopath, brilliant but doomed because of his ego and the interference of District Attorney Karp, as well as Karp's family, and the odd collection of friends who seemed to constantly show up in the proverbial nick of time.

When the council hesitated several years earlier to go forward with Kane's plan to kill the Pope while destroying St. Patrick's Cathedral, all of which would be blamed of course on Islamic terrorists, he'd gone ahead on his own. Now Kane apparently had been killed by David Grale, his plan foiled and his body carried away by the Hudson River.

Newbury had disliked Kane and didn't mourn his death. But the bigger concern had been that Kane's unilateral action had drawn attention to the Sons of Man before they were ready. It could have been a disaster, and the council had to act swiftly and decisively to put out the fires created by Kane that could have led authorities to SOM.

However, Newbury had at least respected Kane for his ruthlessness and cruel brilliance. He'd always thought of Crawford as a lightweight like his father. But then last spring, the younger man had suddenly emerged as a major player with a plan that, Newbury had to admit, might just work where his had failed.

Newbury was torn by that possibility. On one hand, the ascension of the Sons of Man to a position of global dominance depended on a strategy of creating social, political, and economic turmoil in the United States such that the population would forgo their precious freedoms in exchange for a protective, all-powerful fascist state. As a true believer, Newbury thought the Sons of Man were performing a "greater good" by saving the United States from being overrun by immigrants, its social values undermined by faggots, socialists, and liberals, and its rightful place in the world usurped by Third World and third-rate countries. He lamented that the United States was becoming a nation of "mud people"—the color of mud with a mud culture.

No longer a decent nation for the white race, Newbury thought. However much he hated to admit it, Crawford's plan might change that. If all went well, a devastating terrorist attack would be blamed on the Iranians—in part by "proof" that would be brought before the House Committee on Homeland Security, which Crawford chaired. The United States would retaliate, possibly with nuclear weapons, the entire Middle East would be engulfed in the flames of war, and chaos would rule at home, to which SOM's carefully placed men would bring order and security in exchange for ultimate power. Their associates in other parts of the world—Russia and Europe, in particular—would also seize power during this tumultuous time so that a new world order could be established with the Sons of Man on top, their allies underneath, and a watchful eye kept on China until the "Asia Question" could be addressed.

On the other hand, the congressman's success meant that the power on the council would most likely pass to a new generation who didn't respect those who'd patiently planned for so many years. "So your courier delivered the message that your people are prepared to go forward with the plan," Newbury said.

Crawford smiled and shrugged his round shoulders. "There will be a small delay in the date because of the incident in Dagestan—and by the way, we still have no good information on how our enemies nearly succeeded in killing our friend Ajmaani. Now that would have thrown a real wrench in the plan."

Newbury scowled. "Then I suggest you tighten security, or perhaps I can recommend someone with experience who may know something about it."

The younger man's eyes blazed for a moment at the insult, but he quickly smiled again. "It's not a problem. I was just noting that there will be a delay in Operation Flashfire, one of several days—unfortunately—and that might limit the collateral damage. Still, the numbers should be significant, in the thousands."

"I still don't like that part of your plan," Newbury said. "Too much carnage."

"Don't tell me you've developed a conscience in your old age?" Crawford smirked. "The Dean Newbury of even a decade ago wouldn't have minded throwing away a few thousand lives if it was for the greater good."

Look how the jackal gloats now that he thinks the lion has grown old, Newbury thought, *but he better keep a distance between us. I still have claws and teeth.*

"Conscience has nothing to do with it," he growled. "I think it's a tactical mistake. We want the American people afraid more than we want them angry. Think about how they responded to the attack on Pearl Harbor in 1941 and the attack on the World Trade Center in 2001. Ask the Japanese, the Taliban, and al-Qaeda about the wisdom of angering the American public. Too many deaths and that's how they'll respond. However, striking at their daily lives, making them worried about leaving their homes, or how they'll survive if 'Islamic fanatics' threaten to take over the world, and they'll be happy to let us take care of the problem for them. My plan would have accomplished that."

"But your plan failed," Crawford sniffed. "And many on the council, as well as the families, are not very happy with you. Your failure lost a lot of money. Billions."

"A drop in the bucket compared to our net worth," Newbury snarled.

"Perhaps, but they don't want any more such drops," Crawford retorted. "Maybe they think that you and your generation on the council are past your prime. We'll see how they respond when my plan succeeds and we are in control. *Myr shegin dy ve, bee eh,* right? What must be, will be."

Newbury's blood boiled but he held his temper. Now was not the time to tear the heart out of this jackal. "You have al-Sistani, then? The last we heard from you and your cohorts was that the plan could not go forward without him."

Crawford smiled. "Not quite yet. But we are making arrangements that should take care of that problem. A bit late, perhaps, but better than never."

"Might I ask what these arrangements are?" Newbury asked.

"I can do better than that," Crawford replied. He pressed a button on the desk and a television blinked on in the corner. "This is a live feed from a secret location. Have a look."

Scowling, Newbury turned and saw a young woman tied to a chair with a hood over her head. Crawford picked up a microphone from the desk and spoke into it. "Abu, we'd like to see our guest, please."

A dark-haired, dark-complected man appeared briefly on the monitor and pulled the hood off the woman. She blinked once, then her face grew angry. "Let me go, assholes, or you'll regret it."

Shocked, Newbury looked at Crawford. "You kidnapped Lucy Karp? Do you know what kind of manhunt this will cause?"

"No one even knows she's gone," Crawford replied. "We have spies around the Karp family, as well as among this piece-of-shit Grale's little band, and knew that she planned to travel back to her home in New Mexico, where apparently—can you imagine in this age of technology—there's no cell service. Last night her parents received a text message from her cell phone saying she landed safely, and then she'll be out of range. That will buy us days, even a week or two, without raising alarm, and then it will be too late. In fact, when her parents do learn she is missing, they'll be too distracted with her safety to interfere again with our plans. And then we have a little surprise for Karp . . . icing on the cake, if you will."

"So what has she got to do with al-Sistani?" Newbury asked.

"Apparently, our nemesis Grale has quite the thing for our little flower. We believe that he will hand the Sheik over to secure her for himself, or at least save her from us."

"A prisoner exchange?"

"Well, that's probably how Grale will view it," Crawford said. "But we like to think of Miss Lucy more as bait we're going to use to rid ourselves of this lunatic once and for all."

"Grale is a dangerous man to set traps for," Newbury warned. "He's a religious fanatic, and we all know how dangerous they can be. We certainly use enough of them ourselves."

"Let us worry about Grale," Crawford said. "But speaking of dangerous men, how's your nephew? Wouldn't it just be easier to kill him and not have to worry if he's truly a changed man?"

"To paraphrase you, I'll handle my family's business," Newbury spat. "If I think anyone is too dangerous, I know what to do—this old lion has been killing jackals for years."

For a moment, Crawford's eyes looked unsure, but then he let the threat slide. *The boss will deal with the "old lion" soon enough,* he thought. "Well, I'd invite you to stay for a late supper, but I'm sure you have better things to do, including your part in helping our plan succeed."

Newbury looked hard at the younger man, wondering again where he'd suddenly found a backbone. "Indeed," he replied. "We'll be ready, just make sure the council is kept apprised—through me—of your progress."

A few minutes after the old man left, Crawford stood at the big picture window looking through the telescope when he heard the other man enter. He knew who it was without looking by the thump of the cane on the floor. "So how'd I do?" he asked without turning.

"Well enough," came Erik's lisping reply. "What do you want? A medal for performing a simple task?"

Crawford knew better than to react angrily to the slight as he turned to look at the man with the silver mask for a face. "I don't think it was a good idea to kidnap Lucy Karp. What if her parents learn before we're ready? Karp could get the entire NYPD looking for her."

The masked man's eyes glittered. "I've thought of that. Indeed, I may use that to my advantage."

Crawford nodded and turned back to the skyline across the water. "Magnificent view," he said.

"Enjoy it now, because it's about to change," Erik sneered. "And Crawford?"

"Yes, sir?"

"The next time I want your opinion, I'll cut it out of you."

Across the river from where Crawford blanched at Erik's threat, Karp left the Criminal Courts Building and found Dirty Warren waiting for him. The little news vendor was hopping from foot to foot, his face twitching. "Holy shit, Karp . . . piss on your motherfucker . . . you work long hours."

"Hello, Warren," Karp replied. "You're out a bit late yourself."

"I wanted to . . . crap crap whoop shit . . . whoop . . . give you a message," Dirty Warren stammered as he wiped at a drip of snot on the end of his nose.

"Well, okay, what is it?" Karp asked, wondering what could have agitated his odd friend so much.

"Andre Previn was just seventeen years old and had just joined MGM's music department when he played the piano music for this 1947 film," Dirty Warren said.

Karp's jaw dropped. "You stood out here freezing to ask me movie trivia?" He rolled his eyes as if to suggest Dirty Warren was crazy, which he was.

"Just answer the . . . motherfucker . . . question, asswipe."

Karp looked sideways at Dirty Warren. *Was that the Tourette's or . . . ?* "It's not even a tough one," he said. "The answer is *It Happened in Brooklyn* starring Frank Sinatra, Peter Lawford, and Jimmy Durante, among others. If you're going to freeze to death just to try to catch me tired at the end of a long day, you're going to have to come up with something better than that."

Dirty Warren shrugged. "It wasn't my question . . . ooooh boy ooooh boy."

Karp smirked. "What's the matter? Got to bring in reinforcements?" He expected the little man to smile at the insult and retort, but instead Dirty Warren looked worried and mad.

"It was that guy who's been hanging around . . . suck tits . . . sometimes lately," Dirty Warren said. "He wears a big hoodie sweatshirt so nobody ever sees much of his face. I think he's crippled and deformed or something. Anyway, he must have heard us playing movie trivia the other day . . . lick me Martha whoop whoop . . . and this afternoon said to ask you that one."

The pickpocket, Karp thought as he looked around, hoping to see the man. *I'd love to ask him a little trivia myself.* "You could have asked me tomorrow," he said. "Why'd you wait?"

Dirty Warren looked around to make sure no one was listening. "I don't like the guy . . . bastards bitches bitches . . . he gives me the creeps," the news vendor said, staring intensely at Karp through his Coke-bottle glasses. "But I figured he was just another . . . ooooh boy boy oooooh boy shit cunt . . . insane street person. But then he said that he knew Lucy and my antennae went up. How'd he . . . shit piss oh boy oh boy . . . know her name? He made sure that I understood he was trying to pass on a warning in his riddle. He kept saying 'It's the worst that could happen.' That's just how he said it, 'the worst that could . . . oh fuck me naked scrotum . . . happen.' So I figured you better know sooner than . . . cocksucker sphincter . . . later."

At that moment, a blast of frigid air came whistling up from the concrete and steel canyons of the Financial District. Dirty Warren cried out at winter's early bite, pulled his thin coat around his skinny body, and started to scurry off but then stopped short. "Oh, and he said to tell you to think about the . . . motherfucking . . . view."

"The view?" Karp asked.

Dirty Warren shrugged. "Yeah, but don't ask me. My brain is frozen solid. Just think about the view, that's all he said. With that, he turned and disappeared down Franklin Street and into the darkening evening.

Karp shivered, but more from what he'd just heard than from the night air. He started to walk home while punching in a number he had for Jaxon. There was no answer, so he left a message. "We need to talk. And by the way, if Lucy contacts you, tell her to phone home."

17

The two American tourists sipped their beers and chatted at the open-air bar, seemingly oblivious to the crowds wandering the busy plaza on the other side of the street. Some who noticed them that evening, including several prostitutes, thought they might be gay. Otherwise, what were two tan, good-looking men—one middle-aged and the other in his early twenties—doing alone together when there were so many beautiful women available in Port of Spain, the capital city of Trinidad?

A more careful, or suspicious, observer, however, might have noted that one or the other was constantly keeping watch on a business advertised as Trinidad & Tobago Dairy Products, Inc., across the street on the other side of the plaza. It would have taken an even more alert pair of eyes to have registered the Asian businessman sitting on a park bench eating a hand-carved papaya, and the Indian-looking T-shirt vendor, as well as several local black men who also kept track of who entered and left the business.

Jaxon noted with satisfaction the placement of "Asian businessman" Tran Vinh Do, and John Jojola, the former chief of police for the Taos Indian Pueblo, as well as the members of the Trinidad national antiterrorism agency. But suddenly he ducked to hide his face behind Ned Blanchett, who had his back to the woman walking toward them who Jaxon had recognized.

"Shit," Jaxon exclaimed under his breath.

"What?" Blanchett replied, tensing for a fight.

"It's that reporter, Ariadne Stupenagel. She's coming this way."

Blanchett cringed. He knew the reporter would recognize him, too; she was one of his future mother-in-law's best friends, whom he'd met on several occasions. "Did she see you?"

"I don't know," Jaxon replied. "I turned and she was looking right at me." He chanced a peek around his partner and slumped. "She's making a beeline for us."

"What do we do?"

"Hope she knows how to take a hint," Jaxon growled. The agent stepped out in full view of the approaching journalist and looked straight at her. However, he continued talking to Blanchett and gave no sign that he recognized her.

Ariadne slowed her stride, then caught the hint and continued toward the two men. She sat on a stool next to Ned, but other than a flirtatious smile, she said nothing to indicate that she knew them. The bartender showed up quickly to take the drink order—a strong local rum called *babash* and pineapple—for the statuesque blond in the strapless sundress. He gave a slight nod toward the two men next to her and shook his head before leaving to fetch her drink.

"My, my, you never know who you might run into in the islands," she murmured while turning her head to watch the bartender walk away.

"Hello, Ariadne," Jaxon replied, though he kept his eyes on Ned. "Small world."

The conversation ended when the bartender returned with Ariadne's drink. He looked again from her to the two men and back again before shrugging and going on about his business.

"The bartender thinks you're gay and that I'm wasting my time," Ariadne said, taking a sip.

"What?" Blanchett scowled and threw a hard look toward the bartender.

"Don't worry about it, honey." Ariadne laughed. "It's a good cover. Usually spies and undercover agents are too macho to use it unless, of course, they really are gay. But you should go with it . . . everybody in Trinidad figures every white guy is either with the DEA, the FBI, Homeland Security, the NSA . . . or the Russians, or the Chinese, or the Venezuelans . . ."

"I wouldn't know anything about that," Jaxon said, turning toward her as if just starting a bar conversation. "We're just here on vacation."

"So you really are gay?"

"Hell, no," Blanchett sputtered indignantly before Jaxon patted him on the arm.

"Don't let her get your goat, cowboy." Jaxon chuckled. "Yep, just a couple of bachelors enjoying some beach time and cold beers."

"Yeah, and I'm here for the deep-sea fishing," Stupenagel replied. "My guess is that you're in lovely Port of Spain for the same reason everybody else is nervous about this place: Trinidad is the largest exporter of liquefied natural gas to the United States and a hotbed of radical Islamic activism. So, it's about the LNG, isn't it?"

"And what brings you to Trinidad?" Jaxon asked, ignoring her parry and chuckling as if she'd just told him a joke.

Ariadne smiled as she shrugged. "Same thing, except I'm going to write about how every spook down here and their government figures that sooner or later, crazy Islamic terrorists are going to hijack one of these LNG tankers, float it near a big population center, rupture the holding tank, and then ignite it. My sources tell me that the resulting fireball will melt steel and incinerate concrete—not to mention human beings—up to a mile away, and still have enough heat to leave second-degree burns on exposed skin two miles away. About as close to a nuclear explosion as a terrorist can dream, but without all that fuss with fission and smuggling weapons-grade plutonium in suitcases."

"Pretty tough to pull off in a U.S. port." Jaxon laughed as he signaled for two more beers. "LNG tankers have to provide ninety-six hours' notice of their approach, and the Coast Guard is all over these tankers as soon as they hit American waters. They're inspected and checked for explosives. Then they're escorted to the terminal facilities by a small navy and air force that includes tugs, helicopters, and armed Coast Guard cutters."

"Yeah, and there's no way a bunch of raghead terrorists with box cutters were going to hijack airliners and crash them into commercial and government buildings," Ariadne scoffed. "Some of those facilities in the States are close enough that hijackers could make a run at a waterfront population area. Hell, there's a floating facility at the mouth of the Long Island Sound. And it's a big ocean out there, even the Coast Guard can't be absolutely sure that a friendly captain is who he says he is."

"So are you learning anything new?" Jaxon asked, then laughed as if he'd told a joke and rubbed Ned's shoulders, causing the younger man to jump.

"Well, I think we have a right to be afraid," Ariadne said in a low voice. "There's something going on, but I haven't been able to find out exactly what it is. Twenty years ago, radical Islamic plotters staged a bloody coup, trying to take over the government of Trinidad and Tobago and turn it into an Islamic state. The coup was put down, but the main players—and a lot of new young recruits—have been rebuilding for another try ever since. The two major groups are Waajihatul Islaamiyyah, aka the Islamic Front, and Jamaat al Muslimeen, and the fact that they are back and worse than ever is not a good thing. Along with the goal of establishing an Islamic state in Trinidad, they've declared holy war against American and British interests in the Caribbean. Of the two, the Islamic Front is openly allied with Osama bin Laden and al-Qaeda. Islaamiyyah is tied to a terrorist organization by a similar name in Indonesia that was responsible for the bombing in Bali a few years ago.

"Jamaat might be the worst of the lot. After the coup, they basically turned into a bunch of Muslim thugs—more gangsters than religious fundamentalists, though they couch everything in the rhetoric of radical Islam. A few years ago, Trinidad ranked second worst behind Colombia for kidnappings—especially the wealthy and politicians—to make a buck. They also deal drugs and do murders for hire. But at their core, they're still committed to an Islamic state. Right now an American-born member of Jamaat, whose father immigrated to New York City from Trinidad, is on trial in Miami for attempting to buy arms—including AK-47s, grenade launchers, and antiaircraft missiles—through a Florida mosque. He intended to smuggle the weapons into Trinidad for another coup attempt."

Ariadne paused as two prostitutes, who'd suddenly wondered if they'd allowed an interloper to snag two potential clients in their territory, walked up. "Why are you talking to this white cow," one said, putting her arm around Ned, "when you could be having fun with us?"

Standing up, Stupenagel, who was several inches taller and outweighed the bigger of the prostitutes by fifteen pounds, growled, "Get your big ass out of here, sister, before I kick it up around your ears."

The woman's eyes narrowed, but she hadn't expected the hard-nosed reaction. She noted the muscles in the white woman's arms and decided she was not a soft American, nor could she afford to be arrested again. "Watch your back, bitch," the prostitute sneered, and sauntered off with a nod to her companion to follow. "If you two gentlemen want something with more spice, we'll be over here."

As she sat back down, Stupenagel saw the amused look on Jaxon's face. "Glad I was able to provide a little comic relief, Espey. Anyway, the minister for national security in Trinidad is smart and tough and knows what he's doing, and his antiterrorism squads are well trained and resourceful. So far they've kept the radicals in check. But everybody here knows, and I suspect you do, too, that all it takes is one slipup and thousands could die in an instant. . . . So, now that I've told you what I know, would you mind telling me what you're here for?"

"Vacation," Jaxon replied.

"Even off the record?"

"Even off the record."

"Well, then I guess you wouldn't be interested in a guy named Omar Abdullah?" Stupenagel caught the looks on the men's faces and chuckled. "Remind me to set up a poker game with the two of you when we get back, I'll own your pensions."

Jaxon laughed. "No doubt. So this guy . . . what'd you say his name was? Homer?"

"Omar, but I could tell by the looks on your faces that you already knew the name," Stupenagel said, "which means you've read his file and know that he's with Jamaat and committed to the cause. He's perfectly willing to die in a glorious fireball for Allah."

"So what's he have to do with Trinidad?" Jaxon asked.

"You mean other than the fact that he's here?" Ariadne glanced quickly at both faces and shook her head. "I wouldn't just own your pensions, I'd win your firstborn children . . . if I wanted them . . . which I don't. I have enough of a child in my darling Gilbert Murrow. How is my little Murry Wurry snuggle bunny, by the way?"

"I'll be sure to refer to him that way the next time I see him at the DAO," Jaxon replied with a laugh. "But the last time I spoke with him, he was missing you."

"Aaawww, I miss him, too," Stupenagel cooed. "He's going to be one worn-out lover boy after I get home."

"Uh, you were saying something about Homer being in Trinidad?" Jaxon said, changing the subject.

Stupenagel nodded. "Port of Spain to be exact. Or so I've heard from my sources; I haven't actually seen him yet."

"You know what he looks like?" Blanchett asked. "All I've seen are a bunch of fuzzy photographs."

"I certainly do." Stupenagel smiled. "After all, the Big O and I go way back."

"The Big O?" Jaxon's eyebrows shot up.

"That's what I used to call him back when we were . . . friends."

"Friends? You were friends with one of the world's most wanted terrorists?"

"Well, perhaps a bit more than just friends." Stupenagel giggled. "But back then you and the other American spooks were referring to guys like him as freedom fighters. I met him in Afghanistan in the early 1980s. He was fighting the Soviets as a foreign mujahedeen from Trinidad, and I was a young, horny reporter for the Associated Press stationed in Islamabad. I was interviewing him in the mountains and, what can I say, he swept me off my feet. . . . It was so romantic, sitting in his cave on the side of a cliff after making wild and scandalous love, watching Soviet helicopters searching the valley below . . ."

"You and Homer . . ." Blanchett said with a look of horror.

Stupenagel sighed. "Like I said, I was young and he was this gorgeous black hunk of Muslim machismo. Please, don't tell Gilbert. It was a long time ago, but my Murry is the jealous sort. Anyway, Omar's men didn't like him consorting with a fallen woman like me—they said it was for religious reasons, but personally, I think they were envious. I mean, I saw what some of their women looked like behind the hajib, and no wonder they're willing to blow themselves up. Anyway, Omar ignored them until the Soviets captured and tortured him; he escaped but he was a changed man, even more radicalized and violent. He told me I had to leave his camp, or he'd allow his men to stone me to death for 'being a whore,' which is just proof of the ridiculous double standard for women in the Muslim world."

"I take it you didn't stay in contact with Omar," Jaxon said.

"No, I'm allergic to rocks and being bludgeoned to death," Stupenagel replied. "And he just wasn't a pen-pal sort of guy. I did hear that he had joined up with the Taliban and was training in an al-Qaeda camp when the United States invaded, and that he ended up in Pakistan with the rest of the rats. But now he's back home and that worries me."

"So is tracking him the reason you're here?" Blanchett asked.

"No, I had no idea he was back in Trinidad until I got here and started nosing around," Stupenagel replied. "My editor got a note from someone suggesting a story about the link between LNG tankers and potential Islamic terrorism, and I lobbied for the job. Anyway, I was talking to the national security minister about a group of fundamentalist Islamic schools in Trinidad and Tobago that are suspected of recruiting and financing terrorists when he mentioned that one of the schools was in Omar's old hometown. I decided to visit my former lover's old haunts when I picked up a rumor about a famous local jihadi who had returned to his native land. No one I spoke to seemed to know why he was back, other than that if the prodigal native son was in town, then something big was going down."

"Anything else?"

"Hey, what's with the non quid pro quo interrogation? Are you at least going to pick up my bar tab?"

"Let me buy you a drink . . . or four," Jaxon offered.

Stupenagel smiled and signaled the bartender. "I'll have a double and these kind gentlemen have offered to pay."

The bartender looked surprised but shrugged and started making the drink. *Maybe these two are kinkier than I originally guessed,* he thought.

The reporter turned back to Jaxon. "A little bird told me to keep on eye on the Trinidad and Tobago Dairy Products, Inc., office across the plaza, which I was doing when I spotted you and your boyfriend . . ."

"I ain't his boyfriend," Blanchett bristled.

"Like I said, Ned, you might want to pretend," Stupenagel teased. "In fact, I'd suggest a small public display of affection would go a long ways . . ."

"Ain't no way I'm—"

"She's yanking your chain again," Jaxon interjected, rolling his eyes.

Stupenagel laughed. "Sorry, Ned, but it is funny to watch you turn the color of a ripe tomato. But seriously, remember that everybody is watching everybody else in this town. My sources tell me that Omar is supposed to show tonight."

"You sure?" Jaxon said, leaning toward her, his eyes intensely searching her face.

"That's what I'm told. I was thinking I might 'accidentally' run into him and see if I could get him to sit down for an interview."

"That could be dangerous," Jaxon replied.

"Don't I know it," Ariadne said. "I certainly won't go anywhere out of the public view with him, but it'd be worth a try." As she spoke, the reporter glanced across the plaza and then froze. She nodded toward a tall, thin black man walking through the plaza toward the office. "That's him!"

Jaxon glanced over Ned's shoulder. "You sure? I can't see his face clearly."

"I'm sure," Ariadne replied. "When the Soviets caught him, they broke his legs and he walked with a funny hitch after that . . . sort of like John Wayne. That's him, all right. You going to take him down?"

Jaxon shook his head. "Look, I'm going to trust you with this, but just so you know, we believe a lot of lives could be at stake. We know he's involved, but he's not the only one or even the most important. We're hoping he'll lead us to the others, as well as to whatever is being planned. I'd appreciate it if you'd hold off on your plans to talk to him. It might drive him underground."

Ariadne sipped her drink before replying. "I know journalists have a reputation for getting the story at any cost. But most of us are responsible human beings, too. Just remember who scratched your back on this one when it's time to play little birdie."

Jaxon slapped a hundred-dollar bill on the bar. "I will. Now, do you mind if Ned keeps you company for a bit? I need to go see a man about a horse."

"Mind? If I didn't know Lucy—and if I wasn't trying to be a good girl for one Gilbert Murrow—I'd be on this boy like white on rice," Stupenagel said, smiling at a suddenly nervous-looking Ned Blanchett. "As it is I'm going to have to slow down on the *babash* or I might accidentally forget my newly discovered scruples." She licked her full red lips, which made Ned blush even brighter.

Jaxon laughed. "Well, try to keep your hands off the boy. He's got a job to do." He turned to Blanchett. "I'm going to go have a talk out of sight with Tran and Jojola. Keep your eye on the store and let me know on the cell when Omar reappears."

"Good luck getting service on your phone," Stupenagel added. "Mine's been spotty at best."

"Ned knows where to find me if the cell won't work," Jaxon replied. "And thanks again, Ariadne, I won't forget it."

"Say hi to Tran and John," Ariadne replied. She turned back to Ned. "Now, where were we . . . tall, dark, handsome, and oh so temptingly young?"

18

A TEAR ROLLED DOWN MARLENE'S FACE AS THE DRIVER OF the Lincoln, Detective Neary, turned right off of First Avenue onto Thirty-fourth and headed for the entrance of the Midtown Tunnel. "Remember when the kids were little and they would see who could hold their breath the longest whenever we'd drive through a tunnel?" she said, quietly changing the subject.

"Yeah, Zak cheated every time." Karp laughed. "He'd only pretend to hold his breath and then after Giancarlo and Lucy exhaled, he'd make a big show of continuing to hold on—turn red, struggle, moan, and finally gasp as he let it all out. It was quite a show."

Marlene smiled and nodded. "Yeah, and remember the argument the boys—they must have been about ten—had over whether it was the same hole you went into and came out of . . . just in a different place?"

"I don't remember that one," Karp admitted. "But it would make a good science fiction story."

"Zak argued that tunnels were really just one hole—the same at both ends—and that you go in one end, drive around for a little while, and then pop out of the same hole but near your destination." Marlene laughed, but then grew somber again as she looked out the window. "Life's kind of like that . . . you enter one end of it, drive around for a bit, and then pop out at your destination. If you look back, you can see the hole you came out of, but everything you saw and did along the way gets sort of hazy or is a series of snapshots. You really have no idea how you got there. They can tell you all they want that you drove through a tube under the East River, but all you see is the road, the walls, and other cars and people."

"Wow, getting a little existential, but I follow you," Karp said. "I do suppose that in many ways life looks the same on both ends. For one thing, you start with nothing and you leave with nothing. But if you're lucky, you find love, a family, and important work to do in between. If you can't remember every detail later in life, maybe it's because there were so many good ones, it's impossible to recall each and every one."

Marlene smiled and leaned over to rest her head on his shoulder. "That's my guy. Mr. Sunshine on a Cloudy Day."

Rain dripped like tears from the bare branches of the trees at Flushing Cemetery in Queens. Feeling a drop strike his bare head, Karp looked up at the lead-colored sky and then back at the sea of black umbrellas, hovering above the heads of those gathered around the gravesite that had been prepared to receive the body of Assistant District Attorney Stewart Reed.

Karp stole a glance at his wife, who was standing at his side. The expression on her face was tough to gauge as she stared straight ahead at the grave. But he knew that her mood didn't have everything to do with Reed's death and funeral. She was worried about Lucy.

It had been more than a week since their daughter had returned to New Mexico, and the only contact they'd had with her had been two text messages: one when she landed and another two days later saying she was fine and planned to enjoy some "meditative time" with friends in the mountains, without her cell phone. Marlene's attempts to reach Lucy by text and by calling had failed and it appeared that her cell phone was turned off.

Karp tried to reassure his wife that neither of Lucy's text messages had included the word "faith." She and Marlene had settled on the word sometime back as a way of telling each other that she needed help in case the messages were being monitored. Now Marlene lamented that it would have been better to use "faith" in all their correspondence, with the absence of the word indicating trouble.

When Karp tried to hint that she was being a little paranoid, it had not gone over well. And making matters worse, John Jojola was off, presumably with Jaxon and Ned, and so wasn't in Taos to check up on her. Jojola was the former chief of police at the Taos Pueblo, but he'd left the job a couple of years earlier and now Marlene didn't know who to call there *"without sounding like a hysterical mom."*

However, Marlene had continued to fret, so Karp promised her on the way to the funeral services that he'd call the sheriff of Taos County and ask him to do a welfare check on Lucy. His wife had nodded gratefully as tears sprang to her eyes. *"I'm sorry,"* she said, wiping at one on her cheek. *"I'm so tired of worrying about my kids, especially knowing that I have only myself to blame for some of what they've been through."*

Karp looked around at the other mourners, nodding to those he knew. The turnout from the DAO reflected Reed's popularity and their respect for him as a man and a prosecutor. All of the bureau chiefs were present, as were all of the ADAs from the Homicide Bureau who didn't have a trial. Many other ADAs and other office personnel were present, too.

Karp noted that a number of NYPD plainclothes detectives and uniformed officers stood in a cluster off to themselves. He knew that many of them had worked with Stewbie on cases and were stating with their presence that he was one of them—a rare tribute for anyone outside the thin blue line.

He spotted Kenny Katz standing with Sondra Bond, who had her hand on his arm. Kenny's face was drawn and his already deep-set eyes had even darker circles beneath them.

After the service, Karp glanced ahead at Reed's mother, a small, round-faced woman in a wheelchair, and Reed's sister, a tall, stern-looking woman dressed in the uniform of an army captain.

When he'd leaned over to shake the hand of Mrs. Gladys Reed in the receiving line, he noted the red hair and pale blue eyes that suggested she'd once been a pretty Irish-American girl. But her eyes were red-rimmed and weepy, yet when he introduced himself the grip on his hand tightened.

"My son did not kill himself, Mr. Karp," she stated, looking intensely into his eyes. "Suicide is a mortal sin and my Stewie was a good Roman Catholic. He was also a good son, and he knew how important it was to me that he be buried next to me and his father, God rest his soul. He would never have done anything to jeopardize that."

Karp didn't know quite what to say. "I understand, Mrs. Reed. I am so sorry for your loss and for our loss; we are all going to miss him."

"Do you really understand, Mr. Karp? They won't let him be buried at St. Joseph's," Mrs. Reed insisted, her voice cracking and desperate. "His father is there already, waiting, and I won't be long. But our little Stewie will not be with us. . . . Oh, sweet Jesus." A moan escaped the old woman, who then buried her face in her hands.

Reed's sister, Meghan, leaned over and put her arm around her mother. "It's okay, Mom. We know there's been a mistake. Stew will be with us in heaven."

"No, no, he won't," Mrs. Reed cried. "If he killed himself, he'll suffer the eternal hellfires."

"I don't believe that, Mom," Meghan said softly. "Even if Stew did this to himself, the God I love wouldn't be that cruel . . . no matter what you've been told by a priest." She stood up and looked Karp in the eye. "But I don't think Stew killed himself."

Karp nodded. "I have a hard time believing it myself."

Still looking him in the eye, Meghan asked, "Mr. Karp, would it be possible to have a moment with you after the services? Alone?"

"Of course," he replied. "And if there is anything I can do, or the DAO can do, just ask."

"We appreciate that, Mr. Karp," Meghan said. "And we may take you up on it."

After the receiving line, Karp viewed Stewart lying in his coffin. He looked as together as he had in life, dressed in one of his expensive tailored suits. He noticed that the mortician had done a good job of disguising whatever mark had been left by the noose.

A few minutes later, he met with Meghan Reed. Much of what she had to say he'd already been through a hundred times in his mind. She'd brought up again his Catholic faith—and its prohibitions against suicide—as well as his role as the doting son "who would have never hurt our mom like this."

Meghan said she'd talked to several of Stewart's friends outside of the DAO "and none of them ever felt the slightest inkling that my brother was suicidal. Yeah, he was disappointed in the hung jury, but he was happy that he was getting a second crack at that asshole Maplethorpe. In fact, he was getting downright antsy for the new trial and told Mom that he thought he'd found something important that might help."

Karp's radar went on alert. *Had Stewbie stumbled upon something?* "Did he tell her what that might be?"

Meghan shook her head. "No. He hadn't checked it out yet and told her it might or might not mean anything. But he was confident about the trial either way." The woman passed a hand across her eyes. "Mr. Karp, my brother and I were close. Even with me in Iraq, we spoke at least once a week. I would have known if he was contemplating this."

"When's the last time you talked to him?" Karp asked.

"Two days before he died. You want to know what we talked about? We talked about meeting in Italy next summer when I get my leave. He always wanted to see the Sistine Chapel and Rome. Now I ask you, does that sound like a man who is suicidal?"

All Karp could do was shake his head and agree with her. "But I have nothing else to go on," he added. "The police did a thorough investigation. I've known the detective who was in charge for more than thirty years and there's no one better. He insisted on a full write-up from the Medical Examiner's Office with an eye to foul play. But everything checked out . . . nothing in the toxicology report. None of the neighbors heard anything unusual."

"I know all that," Meghan agreed. "And all I can say to that, Mr. Karp, is that something is wrong with this picture."

The young woman reached into her handbag, pulled out a business card, and handed it to him. "My brother thought the world of you, Mr. Karp. He said you were the one man who would never stop pursuing justice. Will you at least think about this for my brother? My cell phone number is on the back."

Karp dropped Marlene off at the loft and returned to the office, where he sat back in his chair and propped his feet up on his desk. He glanced down at the yellow legal pad where he had written "Casa Blanca," "art of war," and "*It Happened in Brooklyn*," along with the warning "It's the worst that could happen."

My life seems full of riddles these days, he thought. On the one hand, there was Andy and his father. On the other, there was the riddle of Stewart Reed. *Something is wrong with this picture.* Meghan Reed's use of the same imagery that he'd been thinking in Judge Rosenmayer's court days earlier reverberated in his mind.

Karp closed his eyes and imagined the scene in Reed's apartment the night he died. He tried not to concentrate on any one detail but just let his mind's eye roam. He sat bolt upright in his chair and punched in the number for Fulton's phone.

A deep voice answered. "Fulton."

"Hi, Clay," Karp said. "You up for a drive to Queens?"

"Sure. What's up?"

"Probably nothing," Karp said. "Just following up on a request from Stewart Reed's sister."

"I'll get the car and meet you out front."

Karp hung up with Fulton and pulled Meghan Reed's business card from his wallet and called. "Miss Reed? It's District Attorney Karp. . . . Fine, thank you. . . . I was calling to ask if your mother has received Stewbie's personal effects. . . . You have? Would you mind if I dropped by in thirty minutes? There's something I'd like to check out. . . . I'd rather not say at the moment. . . . I'll fill you in when I get there."

Meghan Reed was waiting for them in the entry to the redbrick row house in Maspeth, an old blue-collar neighborhood in western Queens. He noted the Blue Star Flag in the window, indicating a member of the family was serving in a war zone. It reminded him of childhood walks he used to take with his mother around their old neighborhood in Brooklyn post–World War II. She pointed out that the blue stars in the windows represented local boys—the high school guys he'd looked up to and their older brothers—who were away fighting in places like North Africa, Guadalcanal, Italy, Saipan, Normandy, and Iwo Jima. Some of the houses they passed—*"too many,"* she once said, and started to cry—had gold stars in the windows, occasionally more than one. Those were the boys, she said, as she tried to pull herself together, *"who won't be coming home."*

It was his first realization that the life he enjoyed, the safety he always felt in his home, and his freedom that he experienced daily, had come at the expense of real people—young men like the baker's son, Sam Caputo, and Bobby McPherson, whose father was a New York firefighter, and the rabbi's kid, Irwin Brownstein. And it was a lesson he never forgot.

"By the way, I appreciate your service to this country," he said as Meghan stepped into the house and held the door open.

At first she looked surprised, then her expression softened. "Thank you," she said. "We don't hear that very often. I believe in what I do."

"Your brother also made sacrifices for this country," Karp said, without knowing why he said it. "He could have gone into private practice—made more money, worked fewer hours. But he believed that he was protecting the citizens of this county."

The young woman smiled and patted him on the shoulder. "I know he did, but thanks for saying it."

She turned and led him and Fulton into the tiny living room where Gladys Reed sat waiting in a large, overstuffed chair. It was as if Karp had stepped back into his parents' Brooklyn home in the 1950s; floral prints were in abundance—the furniture, drapes, and wallpaper—and a collection of Hummel porcelain figurines adorned the mantelpiece along with eight-by-ten photographs of her son and daughter.

"Mr. Karp, how lovely of you to drop by," Gladys Reed said. "I know you're so busy. I'm afraid the . . . the services . . . have left me exhausted. Would you or your friend care for a soda?"

"Thank you, but I'm good," Karp replied. "This is Detective Clay Fulton. He headed up the investigation into your son's death. Detective, would you care for a soda?"

"No, thank you," Fulton replied. "Upsets my stomach, and I'm not thirsty."

Karp's eyes drifted to another photograph on the wall—a black-and-white of a smiling young man in an army uniform.

"That's my Dan," Gladys said. "Stewart was only five and Meghan an infant when he shipped over to Vietnam." Her voice caught. "He never came home."

"You certainly did well raising your children," Karp replied.

"Thank you." The old woman smiled. "But to be honest, it was easy. They were both such good kids. Never any trouble really."

Meghan cleared her throat and said, "Mr. Karp, I'm sure you didn't come all this way to talk about our family. You said you had something you wanted to check out? Something to do with Stewie's personal effects?"

Karp nodded. "I don't want to get your hopes up. But something you said about this picture not being right jolted a memory. It might not mean anything, but I wanted to see if my memory was correct."

"Of course," Meghan said, and pointed to the staircase. "Stewie's room is upstairs. Some of his things are in storage. But his clothes and some other things, like his wallet and watch, are still in boxes in his room."

"That will be great," Karp said, and followed her up the stairs with Fulton behind him.

Walking into Stewart Reed's room was like entering the living space of a teenage boy. Apparently, his mother had kept it as it was when he left for law school. There were posters of rock musicians on the walls. A New York Mets baseball cap and another for the New York Jets hung on pegs. A large model of the Starship *Enterprise* was suspended with fishing line above a twin bed. Over in the corner, a bookshelf was lined with offerings that included *The Lord of the Rings, On the Road, The Naked and the Dead*, and *In Cold Blood*, all alphabetized by author's name. There were several photographs of Stewart on the walls and on the neatly ordered desk: him in the marching band uniform of Maspeth High School, and with different pretty young women, apparently just before going out on a date or to a dance.

Karp noticed that Reed was well dressed even as a boy and a teenager. "He certainly had a flair for style," he noted.

Meghan Reed laughed. "Yeah, he was always more of a clothes horse than I was," she said. "Some guys get jobs in high school so they can buy cars or stereos. But whatever Stewart wasn't putting away for college, he spent on his clothes. And pity the poor younger sister who accidentally spilled something on one of his shirts or stepped on the toe of his shoe." She pointed to several boxes in a corner opposite the bookshelf. "Those are the things brought from his apartment."

"Do you know if they contained the clothes he was wearing the night he died?"

Meghan's eyes widened for a moment, but then she shook her head. "No, I picked those up from the funeral home. The suit is hanging in the closet."

"What about his shoes?"

Meghan walked over to the closet, opened the door, and leaned over to retrieve a pair of dress shoes. "These?"

Karp stepped forward and carefully examined the Allen-Edmonds. Then he handed them to Fulton. "Clay, do you notice anything?"

The detective looked the shoes over and nodded. "Yeah, the toes and tops of the shoes are scuffed."

"That strike you in any way?"

"Only that I've known Stewart for close to ten years, and in all of that time, not once did I ever see him wear a pair of scuffed-up dress shoes. Hell, the man even kept his running shoes spotless. In fact, I never saw a hair out of place, a stain on his shirt or suitcoat. He was one fastidious cat, man."

Karp smiled. "Exactly."

Meghan leaned over to get a better look at the shoes and then looked back to the two men. "What's it mean?"

"Maybe nothing," Karp replied. "But that's what I was thinking about when I, too, thought that something wasn't right with the picture. When I saw Stewbie that night, I only glanced at what he was wearing. It didn't seem important, so I didn't make any note of it. But looking back, it suddenly struck me . . . Stewbie's shoes were scuffed. And I knew that was what was bothering me. Put it together with all the rest—the Catholic background, his character as a man—and it doesn't add up."

"So what's your next step?" Meghan asked.

"Well, I think I may want a second opinion on Stewbie's autopsy," Karp answered. "I need to get back to the office and make a call to Denver."

"Swanburg?" Fulton asked.

"Yeah, I want to bring Jack in on this," Karp replied. He turned to Meghan. "I really don't know if this will lead anywhere. But we'll follow it until the road leads somewhere or dead-ends."

"That's all we can ask," Meghan replied, and led them back down the stairs to where her mother was waiting.

When Karp leaned over to shake the older woman's hand, she reached up for him and hugged him. "Thank you, Mr. Karp. I'm not looking forward to spending eternity without my son."

"I can't guarantee anything, Mrs. Reed," Karp said. "But I promise you, I'll give it my all."

"I know you will, Mr. Karp. And I know you'll prove that my Stewie did not kill himself. There is a reason you came to my home today, Mr. Karp, it was the Lord who asked you to come."

As he and Fulton left the row house, Karp hoped that he hadn't given a false hope to the women inside. He had almost reached the Lincoln sedan when Meghan walked out of the door and called to him. She was carrying a briefcase, which she held out to him as she came down the steps of the landing.

"Mom wanted me to give you this. Apparently he left this over here that night when he picked up Mom for dinner and forgot it. He called her just before . . . before he died and said he'd pick it up the next day. She forgot about it until now. We don't know what's in it, but we hope that didn't cause a problem."

"I'm sure it's fine," Karp replied, taking the briefcase. "I'll take a look and see if there's anything that belongs at the DAO. Then I'll return it and any personal effects."

"Go ahead and give it to one of your guys who needs it,"

Meghan replied. "It's a pretty expensive one . . . Stewie always liked nice things. We gave it to him at Christmas a few years ago, but the engraved 'SR' tag comes off. Oh and here's the key to it from his key ring."

"Thank you," Karp replied. "I have someone in mind who I think would appreciate the thought that it was his."

Inside the Lincoln and headed back to Manhattan, Karp used the key to open the briefcase. There wasn't much inside of it. Just a photograph of a pretty brunette woman standing next to a young boy dressed in a cowboy hat, a vest with a sheriff's star pinned to the chest, and fringed chaps. The boy held a toy six-shooter, which he was pointing at the camera.

There was a yellow sticky note on the back of the photograph with the words "*pantaloni di cuoio dispari*" written in Reed's neat penmanship. He was reminded of the conversation in his office with Guma, Murrow, Katz, and Reed. *"I still have a copy of the photograph in the file, he's all dressed up like a little cowboy . . . in fact, I'm working on something one of our witnesses—that Italian guy, Hilario Gianneschi—said that may actually be related."*

Karp turned the photo back around and looked at the little boy with the gun. *What did Stewbie see in this photograph?* he wondered, and then took out his cell phone and punched in a number. A few rings later, a man answered. "Jack? Butch Karp. Have you got a minute?"

19

"You're a bad man," the voice said. "You're going to kill a lot of people."

"Quit sniveling," Erik said with disgust. "You've always been such a goody two-shoes."

The voice sounded young, like that of a boy. "One of us has to try to be nice," it replied. "Or we'll all go to hell because of you."

Erik laughed but it was not a pleasant sound, just cruel and mocking. "Well, what are you going to do about it, *little* brother? You've never had the balls to stand up to me. Oh, I forgot, as a perpetual ten-year-old, you don't have any balls."

"Oh yeah? I did that time at St. Patrick's Cathedral when you were going to do a bad thing to my friend Lucy. It ruined your big plans, too."

"And almost got us killed. I swear, Andy, you are such an idiot."

"I wanted to die," Andy retorted. "I wanted *us* to die. All of us. At least I would have done one good thing."

"I would have done one good thing," Erik sneered as he mimicked the boy's high-pitched voice. "I'd let you die if I could. You make me sick with your holier-than-thou bullshit, you snot-nosed little brat."

"At least I don't look like you," Andy taunted. "You're the boogeyman!"

The comment had the desired effect. Erik glared and then turned away to stare out the window of the Brooklyn Heights mansion at the Manhattan skyline, which was bathed in the copper light of the late afternoon autumn sun. He caught his reflection in the glass and shuddered, his ravaged lips pulling back from his perfect teeth in a snarl. He'd once been one of the most eligible and sought-after bachelors in New York City, the wealthy scion of the founder of a prestigious white-shoe law firm. Now he reminded himself of a snake shedding its scales, only instead of a fresh new skin, what lay beneath was a rotting, bloody, pus-marked horror mask. In another century, such a visage would have been attributed to leprosy, but that wasn't the case.

And it's Karp's fault, him and his fucking family, he thought. The hatred that roiled beneath his ruined countenance competed with the chill of fear that the thought of Karp dredged up. *Nemesis*. Ever since he'd met the man, the word had popped into his mind whenever he pictured his enemy's face or remembered how the district attorney foiled his plans. Nemesis—the Greek goddess of retributive justice, only in this case nemesis was six feet five, still taut and muscular, and the district attorney of New York.

Erik calmed himself by thinking of the girl he held prisoner. He'd intended on raping Lucy Karp in St. Patrick's and only his "little brother's" interference had prevented it. Still, he'd fled with her as his hostage, fantasizing how he would wait and then someday send Butch Karp photographs of his impregnated daughter. *Sweet revenge for dear old Dad.* But then that lunatic Grale showed up in the nick of time and the end result was Lucy's rescue and this . . . this . . . *this monstrosity of a face*.

There was a knock at the door. "Stay out of sight, Andy," he told the voice. "I don't need you fucking this up again." When Andy didn't respond, he shouted, "Come in!"

The door opened and Crawford entered. The congressman smiled and extended his hand as he walked across the floor. "So tonight's the big night."

Erik ignored the hand and comment, but noticed that Crawford kept his eyes averted from his ruined face. He reached for the silver mask and fastened it in place. "Is everything ready in Trinidad?"

"Yes," Crawford replied. "As soon as word is received that the Sheik is safely in our hands, everything else will be set in motion."

"The Sheik," Erik scoffed. "Everybody's so dramatic. What is this, a comic book? Is Karp Batman? Does that make me the Joker . . . or the Riddler? Perhaps we should refer to Nadya as Catwoman—she'd look great in a tight leather suit."

Crawford started to laugh but stopped when he saw the blue eyes behind the mask blazing with anger. "Do you think we can count on Grale showing up tonight with al-Sistani?" the congressman asked to cover his blunder.

Who knows when you're dealing with a madman? Erik thought, suppressing the little voice in his head that added, *Two madmen.* But he was quite sure that Grale would arrive as scheduled.

It was good to know an enemy's weakness. Ever since the St. Patrick's debacle, he'd been aware that Grale had a weakness for Lucy Karp. However, because he himself could not love a woman, and used them only for his pleasure, he had not at first thought of her as his opponent's Achilles' heel. Only when the traitor Treacher appeared at a certain import-export business and gave the password "Flashfire" as a sign that he was helping al-Sistani, and suggested that Lucy be taken hostage, had Erik seen the possibility.

The question had been whether to trust the filthy Judas who suggested it. Greed was something Erik understood. The promise of riches—indeed Treacher had already been paid an initial amount as promised by al-Sistani—had to be a terrible temptation for a bum on the streets. He himself would have jumped at the chance under similar circumstances, so he was inclined to believe it anyway.

Still, he didn't just buy the man's story without corroborating evidence. He'd been convinced by a spy he had among the ragged human offal who called themselves the Mole People. The spy told him that Grale was showing signs of increasing mental illness and a growing obsession with Lucy Karp. He seemed to consider himself the self-appointed guardian angel of the entire Karp family, except for the young woman he desired.

Perhaps he grows tired of spending cold nights alone beneath the streets of New York, Erik mused. *Who better to warm your bed than an unwilling wench?*

The depth of his obsession seemed confirmed when Lucy Karp's abduction was reported to Grale. The spy described Erik's enemy as having turned into a frothing-mad lunatic. And when he learned that one of his own, Treacher, had been behind it, he'd sworn to kill the man in the most horrible way he could devise.

Erik thought it funny to use Treacher as the go-between to carry his message: al-Sistani for Lucy Karp. *"If I return, he'll know the deal is on,"* Treacher had said, trembling before the dilapidated throne of David Grale. The madman had glared down at him, his hand around the handle of his long knife, the tip of which he'd buried in the arm of the chair when the preacher was brought before him. *"If I don't, there's no deal and Lucy dies."*

Treacher was allowed to return with a time and place for the exchange, as well as a counteroffer: al-Sistani for Lucy Karp *and* Edward Treacher.

"Don't worry," Erik had told the frightened man. *"I won't let anything happen to you. You're going to be a wealthy man, and I'll even help you disappear."*

Erik's spy had reported the meeting between Treacher and Grale, and how Grale had later sworn to cut his former friend's head off. It hardly mattered; if all went according to plan, neither Grale nor Treacher were going to survive the night. As he'd told Dean Newbury, Lucy Karp was more than just a commodity to be traded for al-Sistani; she was the sacrificial lamb he would use to lure Grale into a trap.

Erik shuddered with the anticipated pleasure of killing the man. If Karp was his *nemesis*, then Grale was the sword of retribution. When he was dead, Lucy Karp would be at Erik's mercy again. And there would still be enough time to torment Karp with knowing his daughter was suffering at his enemy's hands before the district attorney also met his fate.

"Grale will show," Erik assured Crawford.

"What about Karp?"

"What about him?"

"Well, I'm not superstitious," Crawford replied. "But that guy or some member of his family always seems to have your number."

Quick as a snake, Erik slapped the congressman across the face, hard enough to knock him to the floor. "I'll take care of Karp," he said. "Just make sure you've done your part, or I swear you'll wish you were dead."

Crawford got up on an elbow and rubbed his bleeding lip. He swallowed hard and nodded. "I understand," he said. "I'm ready."

"Good," Erik replied. "Now get out of here. I need a nap before I'm off to renew my acquaintance with Miss Karp and David Grale."

When the congressman had picked himself up and left, Erik turned back to the view of Manhattan. The sun had set and a gray mist was rising from the rivers and the harbor. The lights of the city's skyscrapers and the Brooklyn Bridge were winking on.

Erik rubbed his brow. He needed a nap; the headaches were getting worse—sometimes he seemed to even black out and couldn't account for time. He looked again at the skyline; it made him feel better to imagine how it was about to change.

Soon, he thought, *they'll bow before me like before a king, and then they'll all regret what was done to me. Karp most of all.*

Lucy felt another presence in the room where she sat hooded, naked, and bound to a chair, shivering in the dark, her hair still wet from the last visit by her torturer. But she had not heard the door open or anyone in the room, until the slight rustling of cloth, as if someone in a robe or dress was moving around her.

"Prepare yourself, my child, *he's* coming," a woman said softly in Spanish.

"St. Teresa?" Lucy's voice was tinged with fear. While to some, having a patron saint might sound reassuring, St. Teresa of Avila's presence meant that imminent, potentially fatal danger was near.

"Yes, it is I," the apparition replied. "You know who I'm talking about, don't you?"

Lucy tried to gather her thoughts to answer the saint. She had no idea where she was . . . *except I know we crossed a bridge,* she'd told herself. *I could hear it when the sound of the tires on the road changed. But New Jersey? Brooklyn? Queens?* The only man she'd seen since she'd been dragged into the building, stripped of her clothes, and searched was her torturer, Abu, a hulking Yemeni who rarely spoke except to interrogate her. When he was gone, the room was dark and silent; no outside noises or light penetrated the space. The only other human contact was the voice of a man who called himself Erik, who issued orders to Abu over a cellular speakerphone with a lisping yet somehow familiar voice.

Lucy shook her head. "I can't think," she told the saint.

After her abduction, she'd assumed that she would be questioned about what agency she worked for and who else was involved. So she was prepared and refused to answer. So they tortured her by waterboarding.

Abu would come into the room, lay the chair on its back with Lucy strapped in, and then pour water over the hood. It mimicked the process of drowning through forced suffocation and the inhalation of water; if she tried to breathe, all she got was water, down her nose, down her throat. Intellectually she understood that she was not really drowning, but there was no way as she gagged and convulsed to convince her body or her subconscious mind that she wasn't dying.

Her torturer seemed indifferent to what he was doing. Except for a brief comment before the first time—"for my brothers at Guantanamo"—he seemed to neither enjoy nor dislike tormenting her. He asked his questions dispassionately, and even when challenging or accusing her, his voice rarely displayed much emotion.

Lucy tried to resist. When she realized that she would not be able to hold out, she even hoped that Abu would make a mistake and kill her. But she soon realized that Abu was very skilled, and she would not be allowed to die—at least not until they had what they wanted. So she'd decided to begin reluctantly answering questions while she was still somewhat coherent and could control what she talked about.

Lucy first stalled by answering some of Abu's questions in a variety of the languages she was adept at speaking, as though she'd partially lost her mind but was trying to cooperate. At first this confused Abu, who stopped the torture apparently to confer with his superior and possibly interpret what she'd said, which were essentially nonsense rhymes. When he returned, he punished her with a session in which he didn't even bother to ask any questions. But he said that when he returned the next time, she would answer "truthfully in English" or the waterboarding would begin immediately.

When he returned, she answered his questions in English. But she did so as she'd been taught by one of Jaxon's men, a survival specialist, with partial truths and information that was either already known to her captors or harmless to her people. She said she worked as an interpreter for a VIP security firm run by former FBI agent Espey Jaxon. They did work for private companies and individuals, as well as the government.

"Then what were you doing in Dagestan?" Abu asked.

Lucy wasn't surprised. She thought her abduction would be tied to Nadya Malovo and that by answering at least somewhat truthfully, she would be perceived as cooperating without revealing any new information. *"I was there as an interpreter for a team attempting to catch a terrorist named Ajmaani."*

"You were there to assassinate this person," Abu accused.

"I was part of a team sent to kill her," she agreed. *"But my job was to interpret and help the team by speaking for them when necessary."*

"Why was the team sent to kill Ajmaani?"

Lucy shrugged against her bonds. *"She's a terrorist,"* she responded. *"If there was more to it than that, no one told me. We received information that she was in Dagestan, and our clients asked us to eliminate her."*

"The terrorist U.S. government, you mean," Abu said.

"I'm not given that information," she replied. *"I'm just an interpreter."*

Suddenly, Abu slapped her—hard but not as hard as she would have expected. Still, it was a rare demonstration of emotion. *"Liar!"* he said.

Lucy pretended to cry. *"That's what I was told,"* she insisted. *"If there was another reason, they didn't share it with me."*

"What do you know about the Sons of Man?"

Lucy shrugged as if the question had little meaning to her. *Though I'm learning something new*, she thought. *"Not much. Some right-wing end-of-the-worlders, I think. Mostly stuff for conspiracy buffs. Just some nutcases waiting for 'the revolution' to take over the world. To be honest, we've heard rumors, but they're below the radar compared to guys like Osama and freelance terrorists like Malovo."*

Once she started talking, Lucy was a font of useless information, playing her role to the hilt as just a low-level flunky for a private security company—one of hundreds that sprang up after 9-11, run by former federal agents looking to improve their retirement prospects. Then the questioning stopped. She wondered if she'd simply bored her captors, but she also had to admit that interrogating her had not seemed to be the priority.

In fact, it had been many hours since she had seen Abu or heard any sounds except the traffic. She wondered if she would now be killed and sometimes quietly cried for real. She wanted to see her parents and brothers and say all the things she'd been meaning to say. And most of all, she wanted to feel Ned's arms around her one more time and tell him that she was sorry that she would not be able to share a life with him, or give him the children they'd talked happily about teaching to ride.

Lucy felt the saint's hand on her shoulder. "Poor child, I remember the horror of the *toca*—the despicable *tortura del agua*—during trial portions of the Inquisition. Some misguided *inquisidores* believed that the use of water for torture had a profound religious significance." The saint sighed. "All these centuries and man still delights in the pain of others."

"Who's coming?" Lucy asked.

"You don't know? I think you do. You recognize his voice. His face . . . his old face has haunted you for a long time. He is the deceiver . . ."

"Satan?"

The saint paused. "No . . . the Great Deceiver doesn't like to do his own dirty work. He manifests himself through others, such as this one, whose face you once knew but won't now. Still, he has the same evil spirit he has always had."

"Why did you come to me now? Am I going to die?"

"That hasn't been determined yet," Teresa replied. "I'm here to tell you that you will again soon be faced with two choices. One is safer and may still accomplish what you set out to do, but it is uncertain. The second is fraught with danger, and you may die even if you succeed."

"Then why would I choose the second option?"

"Because he's the only one who can stop himself." Lucy felt the saint's hand suddenly tense and then her grip fade as her voice and presence receded. "No matter what, child, I will be with you. . . . *He* comes."

"Wait, I—" Lucy's reply was interrupted by the sound of the door opening. Over the past several days, that sound had come to be associated with the terror of drowning, and she shivered involuntarily with fear.

Someone walked across the room toward her. He moved with a stiff gait, as if one leg lagged, and his breathing seemed wet and labored.

"Ah, the lovely Miss Karp," he lisped. "I trust you have been enjoying Abu's hospitality."

Lucy recognized Erik's voice and didn't speak. A moment later, she felt the man grab the hood and yank it from her head. Although the light in the room was dim, after so long in the dark it still hurt her eyes and she blinked, trying to focus on the shape of the man in front of her.

Even as her sight cleared, she wondered if her mind was playing tricks on her. The man seemed to be wearing a silver mask. The mask was void of emotion one way or the other, just a blank slate, but the icy blue eyes beneath it glittered with malice.

"Why the disguise?" Lucy asked. "Do I know you?"

Erik tapped a shiny cheek with a finger. "Ah . . . 'that fate which condemns me to wallow in blood has also denied me the joys of the flesh. This face—the infection which poisons our love.'"

"Okay, I get it," Lucy replied as if bored. "The name Erik . . . the quote . . . you think you're the Phantom of the Opera. And who does that make me? Christine Daae? 'Who was that shape in the shadows? Whose is that face in the mask?' Either way you're a freak, and I know who you are . . . Kane." The name came out of her mouth as a curse.

Sociopath, former candidate for mayor of New York City, terrorist, and murderer, Andrew Kane seemed surprised. But then he threw back his head and laughed so hard that he began to cough. When at last he was able to stop, he lifted his mask and laughed again at the expression of repugnance on her face. "I see you like my new look. 'Pity comes too late, turn around and face your fate, an eternity of this before your eyes!'"

"I don't pity you," Lucy said. "The inside of the man finally emerged on the outside, that's all. But I do pity Andy having to live with you. Is he in there still, or have you managed to kill him and that last shred of decency from your twisted mind?"

Kane's ravaged face contorted for a moment as though he struggled for control. Then his scarred lips twisted into a half smile. "No, Andy's still with us, unfortunately, though if I could kill him without harming myself I would," he said. "But that's the sad thing about my particular version of schizophrenia—we're all in this together." He giggled. "What's the old saying? 'You can choose your friends, but you don't get to choose your relatives.' Well, with multiple personality disorder, I guess you could say you don't get to choose your body-mates, either."

Kane walked around behind Lucy, reaching out with his hand as he passed to caress her cheek and neck. "We'll have a lot of time to catch up. But aren't you the least bit curious what happened after we last saw each other . . . and why," he said, leaning over so that his glistening cheek was next to hers, "I look like this?"

"Not really," Lucy replied. "But I guess you're going to tell me anyway."

Kane smirked as he stood back up. "Well, you are a captive audience. You see after your friend Grale interrupted our 'elopement,' and he and I fell into the Harlem River, he managed to stick me quite deeply with that nasty long knife of his. Truly I was dead, sinking ever deeper into the depths. . . . I have no clear memory, except that at some point I was being carried upward as though by some unseen hand. I washed ashore, where I was discovered by a fisherman who I persuaded, with promises of riches, to take me to his house and to call a certain physician I knew. Apparently, it was touch and go for me for several weeks before they knew I would live, and by that time there was a problem with my new face."

Kane replaced the silver mask. "You see, in order to change my appearance after escaping from your father's man, Fulton, I arranged to have a face transplant. I'd seen a PBS show on a woman in France who'd been horribly disfigured in a car accident, but was then made whole with the transplant of a face from a cadaver. And I thought, *Why not me?* All very science fiction, and for a time it worked marvelously. The only problem is that facial transplants are still in their infancy and there are a lot of issues with the body rejecting the new muscle and skin. I was on heavy doses of antirejection drugs, but after my little run-in with Grale and subsequent dousing in that filthy river, it took a while to get the drugs, and by then they seemed to stop working. The transplant has been sloughing off ever since. So I've decided that the best thing to do is get my old face back. In fact, I'm spending millions for the latest technology. Those Pakistani doctors are geniuses, I tell you; they're going to regrow my facial tissues from my own stem cells, which would solve the rejection issue. I'll look like my old handsome self!"

"Handsome is as handsome does."

The high-pitched boy's voice surprised Kane and Lucy, who quickly tried to seize on his appearance. "Hi, Andy, are you there?"

Kane shook his head violently and staggered for a moment. Then looked up and smiled. "Sorry, Andy's been sent to time-out." He continued his patrol around the chair, a finger tracing the line of her cheek and stopping below her chin, which he lifted so as to stare into her eyes. "However, it could be some time for them to clone another me. So perhaps in the interim, I should choose a young masculine visage, perhaps that of a cowboy . . . you wouldn't know any cowboys, would you, Lucy?"

When she didn't answer, he held up a cell phone. "This is yours, I believe? I've been having some fun with it, texting your folks, who by the way think you're on a spiritual retreat with some Indians. Kind of fun having a direct line to your dad. I'm sure I'll find a way to work that into my plans."

"Go to hell," Lucy said, and tried to spit on him.

"I certainly hope so," Kane replied as he dodged her attempt. "All my friends will be there. But until then I have so much to accomplish."

Kane tried to make everything sound lighthearted. But Lucy thought his voice sounded strained, wound up like an old watch spring. She heard the saint's voice in her mind. *"Because he's the only one who can stop himself."*

"You're a monster," Lucy spat.

Interrupted, Kane looked at her hard for a moment before cocking his head to one side. "You're not the first person to say that today. I wish everyone would quit spending so much time pointing out the obvious. I mean, of course I'm a monster, just look at me." He stood back up and patted her on the cheek. "But you've yet to meet the real monster, my dear, soon . . ."

In the next instant, Kane howled with pain and rage as Lucy's teeth clamped down on one of his fingers. She bit as hard as she could, ignoring the sickening crunch of bone and ligament and the taste of warm blood as she shook her head.

It took Kane a moment to recover from the shock and strike her with his other hand as hard as he could. The force of the blow knocked her and the chair to the floor, which for the most part saved her from the worst of his kicks as he went berserk. "You fucking bitch!" he screamed, clutching his mangled finger with his good hand. "I'll kill you!"

"Andy, Andy, help me!" Lucy yelled. "You have to stop him!"

Kane kicked again, this time landing a blow to her knee that caused her to cry out in pain. "Andy, please! I need you! People need you!"

Lucy's attacker prepared to stomp on her, but paused with his foot raised. Trembling, Kane lowered his foot and then spoke with a different voice, taking on the personality of a ten-year-old, Andy. "Lucy," he said, "you have to get out of here!"

"I can't, Andy, I'm tied up," she replied. The boy sounded panicky and she was trying to talk as calmly as possible to settle him down. "Everything's okay, just untie me."

Andy began to do as he was told just as Abu came rushing through the door. The big man looked confused. "I heard a man yell," he said. "What are you doing? Is it time to go?"

"I'm untying her," Andy replied, his boyish voice high and squeaky. Suddenly he shuddered as if he'd touched a live wire.

Realizing her time with Andy was running out, Lucy pleaded. “Andy, tell me what he’s going to do . . .”

“I’ve been trying to tell your dad,” the boy whined, “but he’s not very good at riddles . . .”

“Andy! No more riddles, just tell me . . .”

“Stop me, you fool,” Kane shouted in his grown-up voice.

Not knowing what else to do, Abu drew a handgun and pointed it at Kane. “Stop or I’ll shoot,” he demanded.

“Go ahead,” said Andy. “Shoot! I double-dog-dare ya!”

“Not at me, you idiot!” Kane screamed. “Point the gun at the girl and shoot her if the boy says anything!”

Even more confused, Abu did as he was told. “Get away or she will die,” he said to Kane/Andy. He cocked the hammer back on the gun and took aim at Lucy’s head.

With a sigh, Andy’s head fell forward and he retreated into the mind as Kane regained control of the body they shared. Sweating visibly and flushed, he was nevertheless now calm as he looked at Lucy, but he spoke to his gunman.

“This woman is a witch,” he told the superstitious Yemeni. “If she ever speaks to me and I talk back to her like a little boy, it will mean she is casting a spell on me and you are to shoot her immediately. Do you understand?”

“Yes,” the big man replied, and glanced at Lucy with fear. “But if she’s a witch, shouldn’t we just shoot her now?”

Kane smiled and patted the big man on the shoulder. “Not quite yet, Abu, but soon, though I think you and I can be a little more imaginative than something as fast as a bullet. Now, I’m going to go disinfect this little bitch’s bite and then we can be on our way. Untie her and get her to the car. Let our people know that it’s time to take their places. Chop chop, places to go, mad monks to see.”

20

Across the river from where Andrew Kane stood looking at Manhattan, bathed in the copper coloring of an autumn afternoon, Clay Fulton pulled the Lincoln over to the curb on Waverly Place, and Karp stepped out. A few last leaves, yellow and red, hung from the trees in Washington Square Park, but most of the branches were empty, silently waiting for winter, which reminded Karp that Thanksgiving was approaching.

Just one week after the start of the Maplethorpe trial, he thought. *The jurors won't be in the mood to listen to any more than they have to, which should work in our favor.*

Jury selection was set to begin in a few days, and then they'd dig in up to the holiday break. *Wish it was you, not me, Stewbie*, he thought as he looked up at the old brick building where his friend had once lived. *And died*, he thought. *The question is how. And if it was murder, why?*

He hoped to have an answer to the first question in a few minutes from Jack Swanburg. A retired forensic pathologist, Swanburg was one of the founders of an eclectic little group of crime solvers called the Baker Street Irregulars. Mostly comprised of scientists from a variety of disciplines, as well as retired law enforcement officers, the Baker Street Irregulars used their expertise to assist agencies in solving difficult cases. It might be an entomologist—a scientist who studies insects—to determine the time of death by the maturity of fly larvae on a cadaver; or a geophysicist using a ground-penetrating radar machine to locate a body beneath ten inches of cement. Their strength was the variety and depth of their knowledge in so many different fields, so that when they put their heads together, they were—as Swanburg liked to say—"a many-headed Sherlock Holmes."

Marlene had actually first met the group several years before when a member of the group, Charlotte Gates, was helping John Jojola solve a series of child murders in New Mexico. Although they were initially reluctant to work with "amateur sleuths," the group's professionalism and successes had convinced first Marlene, and then Karp, that they weren't the usual volunteer detectives. And since that time, various members of the group, usually with Swanburg leading the team, had provided invaluable assistance to Karp with several cases that might not have been won without them.

After meeting with Stewart Reed's mother and sister at their home, Karp had called Swanburg, who caught the next plane out of Denver, Colorado, where the group was based. They'd talked about Reed over dinner at the loft that night with Kenny Katz and Marlene.

Swanburg, who at nearly seventy years old looked a bit like Santa Claus out of uniform with his full white beard, round belly, and bright red bulb of a nose, mostly listened. Then, wiping a last bit of Marlene's famous marinara sauce from around his mouth, he sat back, his eyes on the ceiling and chubby fingers tapping a rhythm on his ample stomach.

"I think you're right in that a suicide doesn't make sense from a psychological perspective," he'd said at last. *"A practicing Catholic, strong family ties, no history or suspicion of clinical depression or bipolarity. By all accounts, he was thinking rationally and productively at work, and as his cocounsel Kenny here noted, he was looking forward to the opportunity to win this one, not dreading it."*

Swanburg scratched his head and thought for a moment before

adding, *"I'd like to see those shoes. In fact, you might want to keep them as potential evidence."*

"Already done," Karp replied. *"I'll have them delivered."*

"Good, I figured as much, but you are getting a bit long in the tooth and you never know when your horse will quit running." The old man laughed. *"While we're at it, I don't suppose you've thought to obtain a court order to have Mr. Reed's body exhumed?"*

Karp nodded grimly. *"I asked his mother's permission this morning. Stewbie is currently at the Beth-Israel Hospital morgue."*

Swanburg raised his eyebrows. *"Not the Medical Examiner's Office?"*

Karp paused, then shook his head. *"I just thought it might be a good idea to keep this quiet. The ME's office isn't exactly Fort Knox when it comes to leaks to the press, and I don't want this splashed across the front page of the* Post*."*

"I understand," Swanburg said, and then looked sideways at his host. *"But there's more to it than that."*

"Yes," Karp acknowledged. *"If there's something that was missed by the assistant medical examiner who did the autopsy, I want to know what it was and how it could have been overlooked without raising suspicions."*

"Enough said," Swanburg replied. *"Now, if you don't mind, I'll head to my hotel and get some rest. I'm not getting any younger and need my beauty sleep before I head over to Beth-Israel in the morning."*

The next afternoon, Karp received a call from Swanburg. *"I've finished my examination of Mr. Reed,"* the old man said.

"Anything interesting?" Karp asked.

"Interesting? Yes. Definitive? We shall see," Swanburg replied. *"But before I say much more, I want to check out a couple of hunches at Mr. Reed's apartment. Think we could meet there in a couple of hours after you get off work?"*

Fulton had just joined Karp on the sidewalk when a yellow cab pulled up behind the sedan. Swanburg emerged from the cab with a briefcase and a pair of dress shoes in an evidence bag. "Evening, gents," the merry old man greeted them. "Butch, did I ever tell you one of my favorite Sherlock Holmes quotes, 'When you have eliminated the impossible, whatever remains, however improbable, must be the truth'?"

"Don't recall it, but it's a good one," Karp replied. "Why?"

Swanburg pointed to the door of the building. "Let's go find out," he said.

The three men walked into the building and up the stairs, where they were met at Reed's apartment by the building superintendent, who expressed his condolences. "He was a great tenant and real gentleman." Then he asked when they thought it would be all right to advertise the vacant apartment. "The cops told me I had to leave it as it was that night. But the building owners are all over me to get it rented."

Karp frowned. "We'll let you know." It came out as a growl, and the superintendent made a fast excuse and left.

The interior of the apartment was indeed as Karp remembered it. Reed had kept his home as immaculate as he'd kept his clothes. About the only thing out of place was the overturned stool beneath where Reed's body had hung.

Swanburg carefully walked around the perimeter of the room to reach the windows on the far side, where he opened the blinds to let the late afternoon sun pour in. He then retraced his steps to the living room entrance and knelt, looking back across the hardwood floors. Nodding, he looked up and said, "Butch, step over here, I'd like you to see something. . . . Now kneel down and look back. Notice anything?"

Karp did as asked and immediately saw that the wood of the floors was buffed to spotless perfection—except that in the reflection of the sun on the shiny surface he could see two nearly parallel tracks that led from the doorway to the overturned chair. "Scuff marks," he said.

"Bravo!" Swanburg replied. He handed the bag containing the shoes to Karp, who removed them gently and looked at the marks on the toes and tops.

"I believe that if I can scrape up enough of what's on the floor, it will be an exact match for the polish on the shoes," Swanburg said.

"Of course, you can scuff shoes by kicking something or by someone stepping on your toes. But imagine what it takes to get those marks on the top of the shoes. And by the way, under a microscope, it's clear that the scuff marks all run in the exact same direction, and approximately for the same length, from the ankle to the toes."

"Which means the scuff marks were caused by one incident," Karp said, leaping forward in the logic. "They're all on the top and toes of the shoes . . . which means he was lying on his stomach and was dragged across the floor."

"Precisely, my dear Watson." Swanburg beamed as he stood up and walked over to the stool. He pulled out a tape measure and noted the distance from the top of the seat to the bottom of a leg. "Clay, do you remember in your report how far Stewart's body hung above the floor?"

"I don't recall the exact number, but I do know my guy wrote it down."

"The report said nineteen inches from toes to floor," Swanburg replied, and then to their confused looks added, "From the seat of the chair to the floor is eighteen inches right on the nose. But the deceased was left swinging an inch higher than that. So either Stewart stood on the stool and then was able to jump up and stick his head through the noose before coming down . . . and then somehow kicked over a stool that was an inch lower than his toes . . ."

"Someone tried to make it look like he hung himself," Fulton growled.

"Looks that way," Swanburg agreed, "which coincides with the evidence that Stewart was dead before he was hung."

"How do you know that?" Karp asked.

"From my examination of the body this morning," Swanburg answered, as he opened his briefcase and brought out several photographs that he placed on the kitchen counter. "Whoever did this had a pretty good idea of how to hide a murder by making it look like a suicidal hanging. For instance, there was the mark left by the rope that was used—a length of common clothesline."

He pointed to one of the photographs. "Usually, the marks differ for a hanging, such as in the case of a suicide or execution, and a murder by manual strangulation, which would be the case if someone was garroted from behind. With a strangulation, the mark left by the rope would be horizontal across the throat and neck, as enormous pressure is generated from behind, such as in this photograph of a murder victim." He pointed to a different photograph. "However, in hanging, we see the mark starts at the front of the neck, but goes up at an oblique angle and behind the ear, as you can see in this photograph of a suicide. The different shape and placement of the mark is caused by the weight of the body pulling the rope up at an angle."

"What about with Stewbie?" Karp asked.

Swanburg pointed to a third photograph. "This is Mr. Reed."

Karp and Fulton peered down where the old man pointed. The photograph of the dead man's profile showed a slight reddish purple mark that began at the front of his throat and went up at an angle under his jawbone and behind his ear.

"So he did hang," Fulton noted.

"Slight correction, he was hung," Swanburg replied. "But that's not what killed him, though it took me a little bit of thinking to figure out what about this was bothering me. Then it came to me. The mark you see is in the correct position consistent with hanging, but it's not the right kind or size of mark."

"What do you mean?" Karp asked.

"Well, on examination, one sees that the mark is more of an abrasion than a bruise," Swanburg said. "The sort of wear and tear that you might expect on dead flesh. But there is almost no ecchymosis—that is, there was very little bleeding into and beneath the skin around where the rope made this mark."

"Etchy-moses?" Fulton shook his head as he stumbled over the word.

"Yes, ecchymosis. Let me back up a minute. Usually when a person commits suicide in the manner someone wanted us to think Mr. Reed did—that is, climbing on top of that stool, fastening a noose around his neck, and then kicking the stool over and dropping—death occurs almost instantaneously due to luxation, or fracture of the cervical vertebrae, most often at the C1–C2 juncture. It's virtual decapitation, without the body and head separating.

"As you know, when a person dies, their heart stops beating,"

Swanburg said, assuming his detached-scientist manner of speaking that made him an effective witness in court. "And if their heart stops beating, no more blood is being pumped, and if no more blood is being pumped, there can be no bruising, or more specifically, no ecchymosis, which occurs when blood vessels rupture and blood flows into subcutaneous tissue. So in the case of luxation, you might well only see the sort of abrasion that we have with Mr. Reed."

"I'm sensing a 'however' here," Karp said.

"Yes, indeed, and sorry if I'm taking the long road to home here," Swanburg replied, "but I'll get there in the end."

"By all means, continue," Karp replied, "I'm fascinated."

"Well, thank you, and there is a 'however.' Mr. Reed did not die from luxation. He died from asphyxiation, which in and of itself is not suspicious. In some cases of hanging suicides where there is no luxation, the victim either asphyxiates, strangles to death, or there's congestive apoplexy, which is when the pressure of the ligature around the neck prevents the return of blood from the brain and death occurs. But either way, the body reacts violently; there is a struggle for air and life—even if the victim wants to die, the body wants to live. There is thrashing around, kicking, perhaps even reaching with one's hands to remove the cord. In any event, the blood vessels rupture and we see the extensive vivid purple bruising around the rope caused by ecchymosis."

Swanburg tapped the second photograph of the suicide hanging victim, and then the photograph of Reed. "See the difference? The suicide died of asphyxiation, not luxation—note the large area of purple bruising, really nasty looking. Now look at the photograph of Stewart."

"Not even close," Fulton said. "Damn, how did we miss that?"

Swanburg shrugged. "I suspect that at the time the mark on Stewart's neck was easier to see and it was in the correct position. No reason to suspect a setup."

Karp looked up from the photograph into Swanburg's sky blue eyes. "So if hanging didn't cause the asphyxiation, what did?"

"Good question," Swanburg said. "And one I asked myself after I realized he was dead before he was hung. I still don't know the exact agent of cause, but I believe he was poisoned."

Swanburg pulled another photograph out of his briefcase. "This is Stewart's right buttock. Do you see a small purple bruise and tiny red smear?"

"Looks like a needle track," Fulton said. "I've seen 'em on enough junkies to last me a lifetime."

"You know what you're talking about," Swanburg said. "It's a needle track."

"Someone poisoned him with a hypodermic? What was in it?" Karp asked as Fulton swore.

"I don't know yet. Whatever it was, it was fast-acting. I assume it happened at the entrance to the apartment, perhaps as Stewart was returning home from—I believe he was having dinner with his mother, or upon answering a knock. I doubt the killer struck elsewhere and then lugged his body up the stairs, set him down, opened the door, and then dragged him into the apartment. It just doesn't fit the psychological profile. Anyway, I digress . . . the poison must have at least immobilized Stewart, if it didn't kill him instantly, so that he couldn't cry out or fight his attacker. People were in the building, but no one heard a thing."

"Jesus, what sort of shit are we looking at here?" Fulton exclaimed.

"Well, there are a number of possibilities, curare for one, an extremely toxic substance gathered from the skin of a certain frog in the Amazon," Swanburg suggested. "Or it could be some spook stuff from the good old days of the Cold War. The Russians were particularly fond of exotic poisons and means of delivering them—they had an umbrella that delivered a poison ricin pellet with just the tiniest pinprick when jabbed into the victim, as well as poison pens, and a very Bond-esque poisonous lipstick. Whatever the case, I've sent blood, hair, skin, and muscle samples off to one of the Baker Street Irregulars who owns a private forensics laboratory in Denver that usually tests for law enforcement and government agencies. It's not always possible to trace these things, but if anybody can find it, Griff can."

Karp walked over to the doorway and began reconstructing the crime. "So Stewbie goes to dinner with his mother, and then arrives home, maybe is letting himself in the door when the killer comes up from behind and sticks him with a hypodermic filled with some kind of fast-acting poison. Stewbie goes down on his stomach and dies as the killer drags him into the apartment, scuffing his shoes and leaving marks on the floor. The killer then fastens a noose around Stewbie's neck, throws the other end of the rope around the pipe, and then hauls him up, kicks over the stool, and . . . we have a suicide."

"Strong dude," Fulton interjected. "Stewart wasn't a big guy, but still, that's a lot to pull up if the killer was working alone. So we're looking for a big, strong guy or maybe more than one killer."

Karp frowned and walked over to the photographs. "Why didn't the assistant medical examiner see what you saw?"

Swanburg shrugged again. "I've been asking the same question. Without ecchymosis, he would have assumed luxation. But a cursory examination of the neck would have shown that wasn't the case, and that Stewart died from asphyxiation. Yet there is no bruising from the death throes."

"But what about the toxicology report? There was nothing in there out of the ordinary," Fulton pointed out.

"Some poisons are quickly metabolized by the body, even after death," Swanburg replied. "And some kinds wouldn't be detected unless you were specifically looking for them, or at least screening for rare poisons. The toxicology report I saw was a basic check for drugs and alcohol, and reasonably easy-to-spot poisons—like carbon monoxide. So it could have been missed. However, the needle track is fairly obvious, there was even a tiny smear of blood, but while you can see it on the photograph, which was taken by the AME, it wasn't noted in his report."

"So what does that say about the assistant medical examiner?" Karp asked.

Swanburg's eyes lost their twinkle and instead blazed with anger. "He's either lazy, incompetent . . . or someone paid him off to say it was a suicide."

"Which means someone hired a killer to kill Stewart and the AME is in on it," Fulton said as he clenched his jaw.

"But why?" Karp asked.

"Ah," Swanburg replied, "it's a riddle we need to solve."

21

Blindfolded and shivering from exhaustion, Lucy had been led out of a building to a waiting car. She could tell it was dark outside by looking toward the slight opening at the bottom of the blindfold, and it was cold. If she'd had to bet, she would have guessed it to be sometime in the early morning.

She was placed in the backseat with Abu on one side. They were soon joined by Kane, who rapped on a window and said, "Okay, let's go."

"Where are you taking me?" Lucy demanded.

"A little excursion to Central Park," Kane answered.

"Why?"

"To pick up a piece of the puzzle. And to set a trap with you as the bait."

"So what is it this time, Kane? Going to slaughter more innocent people? That's imaginative," she taunted. She knew that on top of being a murderous schizophrenic sociopath, he also had narcissistic personality disorder and loved to talk about himself, which she hoped might get him to reveal more than he should.

Kane giggled. "Now, now . . . we wouldn't want to be giving away any state secrets, would we? You'll just have to wait and see what I have planned. But rest assured, I've reserved a front-row seat for us to watch together. I wouldn't want to give away the surprise, but let's just say it will make 9-11 look like child's play and have much, much greater consequences."

Lucy had been surprised to learn that the Sons of Man council members weren't aware that the plan was Kane's. "In fact, except for that idiot Crawford, and a few loyal followers, they don't know I'm alive," he said with a laugh. They, too, thought he'd died at the Spuyten Duyvil, where the Harlem and Hudson rivers met. And he was content to let them think it until the moment came to reveal himself.

Apparently, he was concerned that he'd been betrayed by older members of the council, who balked at his plans to kill the Pope while blowing up St. Patrick's Cathedral, and that his enemies on the council would try to stop him again. So he worked behind the scenes using the congressman as his front man.

"Let's just say that New York will never be the same," he continued. "But that will hardly matter when this horrible attack is traced back to the Iranian government. You know we've just been dying to bomb those bearded freaks back to the Stone Age, and this will give my generals a reason to do it. Congress and the American public will cheer them on!"

Kane patted her knee. "You'll love this. The Muslim world will perceive the attack as yet another power move by the United States to establish a pro-Israeli hegemony in the region, and the Russians and Chinese will call it an oil grab, which will give them the go-ahead to roll up the little oil-rich countries on their borders. The big three super states—with most of Europe siding with us—will then pound the shit out of the towelheads and niggers, as well as the spics in Latin America. Granted, things may get a little tense between the big three when it's all over with the Third World and A-rab rabble, but our friends in the Kremlin will side with us against the Chinese, and then we'll be one big happy world order. So what do you think, brilliant, eh?"

"You'll never pull it off," Lucy scoffed. "You've overdosed on the Kool-Aid. You're either going to be killed or live the rest of your life sentenced to a rubber room."

"Oh, really?" Kane cackled. "In the face of fear, terrorists, and tumultuous economic times, my adoring public will be thrilled, thrilled, I tell you, when a few strong, determined Americans, led by yours truly, step forward to guide our country through these crises. And it will only cost them a few of their precious freedoms, most of which the sheep don't exercise anyway."

He shook his head as if he regretted what he had to say next. "As the pundits always warn and nobody listens, it is a slippery slope, and much harder to climb than it was to slide down. I've given quite a bit of study and thought to this and noticed that once a society gives up its core beliefs, it will rot from the inside and be susceptible to a strong man with a vision. Republican Rome grew fat and lazy and accepted Caesar and the despots who followed. Democratic Germany, smarting from World War I and desperate to regain its world power status—sound familiar?—handed the reins of government to a dictator, Adolf Hitler. A confused America of the early twenty-first century—beset by floods of illiterate immigrants, attacked by terrorists, and losing its grip as the world's number one economic and military power—gives in to imperial presidencies and tyrants in Congress, who promise a return to the good old days, or to empty promises of hope and 'change.' And each election year the sheep slip a bit further down the slope as power concentrates in the hands of the few. But it's only natural. People want to feel safe in their homes—with plenty of food on their tables and good, mindless entertainment on the television to help them forget what they used to believe. What's more, they will turn on anyone who threatens that peaceful existence and protect the government that gives it to them."

"The Thought Police and Big Brother," Lucy said with a scowl. "'Thoughtcrime does not entail death. Thoughtcrime IS death.' Not very original."

Kane shrugged. "Actually, I'm man enough to concede to a certain admiration of Mr. Orwell's fine novel, *1984*. When I first read it as a teenager, I thought it provided an excellent blueprint for the way our society, and that of the world, was heading and how it could be controlled. Indeed, even after the Sons of Man, with me at the helm, become Big Brother, we'll make sure 'the Russian threat,' and a smattering of terrorists, are kept around to cow the population.

There will be a car bombing here and there, a border skirmish over some obscure oil field, or a necessary ousting of a tinpot dictator with WMDs. Just enough to stir the pot, even if we have to make it all up, and fully televised with lots of heartfelt stories about the victims and their families. I've already seen a couple of prototypes for the newscasts, lots of bells and whistles, but quite touching really."

As they traveled, Lucy tried to keep track of the number and direction of their turns. She'd also noted when the sound of the tires on the road changed. *We're going back over a bridge into Manhattan, but which one? Let's see, when I was brought over from the city, the house where they kept me wasn't far from the bridge we crossed. We went straight over the bridge for a little bit and then made a left and went uphill and then made a couple more turns, probably a residential neighborhood. This time after a couple of turns, we went back downhill but traveled quite a ways . . . and since we're going to Central Park, I'm guessing we're now crossing on the Queensboro. . . . And that means the first bridge was the Brooklyn or Manhattan. . . . And that means I was being held in Brooklyn. But that's a big place. What am I missing? Come on, Lucy, think.*

It wasn't long after they passed over the bridge that the car slowed down and seemed to turn into a side street. There were a few police and fire department sirens in the distance and she could hear cabs honking, but at a leisurely pace that indicated there was little traffic on the road and no real reason to lean on the horn except boredom.

After the car stopped, Abu removed the blindfold. Then Lucy realized it was not a side street they'd turned onto but one of the small roads into the park. Apparently, they weren't concerned with being pulled over by the police, but Lucy recalled that Kane had men who'd infiltrated the NYPD and suspected there was a reason for the confidence.

Out of the car, Kane, Lucy, Abu, and the driver were met by a dozen other men who escorted them deep inside Central Park, which was cold and empty, with only the stars of a moonless night and a few lampposts to illuminate the grassy open spaces and the black, leafless trees that surrounded them.

Soon Lucy was standing with her captors in the shadow of the sixty-foot-tall obelisk known as Cleopatra's Needle, a 180-ton granite monument that was already more than three thousand years old in 1881 when it was brought to New York, a gift to the United States from Tewfik Pasha, the khedive of Egypt. She could just make out some of the hieroglyphics on the lower portion of the stone and noted Anubis, the jackal-headed god of the dead.

Lucy shivered and turned her eyes to where her captors were looking at the trees on the far side of a grassy area on the west side of the obelisk. She was standing next to Kane, who held on to a rope that had been tied around her neck. He in turn was flanked by Abu, while the other men stood in a circle around the needle, armed with silencer-fitted guns. She knew there were more of Kane's men in the woods, waiting to pounce on Grale.

Suddenly out of the dark, a tall, dark figure emerged, so near without having been seen that he was almost shot by Kane's nervous men. "*Don't shoot, friends*!" the man bellowed. "'*Blessed are the peacemakers, for they shall be called the sons of God!*' That's Matthew 5:9 for any of you who might be interested."

"Hold your fire," Kane ordered. "It's just the crazy preacher, spewing more bullshit. Come on, Treacher, time's a-wastin'."

Treacher walked out of the gloom, peering from face to face until he spotted who he was looking for. "Hello, Lucy," he said. "I'm sorry about all of this, but it will all be over soon."

"Don't speak to me, you bastard," she hissed. "I hope David cuts your heart out and feeds it to the rats!"

The preacher blanched in the light of Kane's flashlight and then bowed his head. "No doubt he will if he gets the chance. I do hope that someday you'll find it in your heart to forgive an old man who grew tired of sleeping in the cold and eating garbage."

"There are worse things," Lucy sneered. "But you'll pay a price for this. 'The righteous shall rejoice when he seeth the vengeance: he shall wash his feet in the blood of the wicked.' By the way, that's Psalm 58:10, *friend*."

"Glad to see you two are renewing your Bible studies." Kane's lisping voice interrupted the discussion. He was about to say something else when his cell phone buzzed. "Yes."

"They're approaching," a man said.

"You're sure? I don't want to spring a trap on just any old group of beggars."

"Tall guy in a hooded robe. Looks like he stepped out of the Middle Ages—beard, pale skin—a half dozen creepy-looking street people are following a few feet back."

"What about our prize?"

"al-Sistani is with him," the caller replied. "Grale has a rope around our guy's neck."

Kane laughed and gave a little tug on the rope tied to Lucy. "Turnabout's fair play, I guess. Wait until the exchange and then kill them all, but make sure al-Sistani is safe; after that, you know your orders."

"Yes, sir!"

Shadows appeared on the far side of the grassy area—a tall one, leading another shorter man, while others scurried from side to side, darting forward and then falling back. At one point, the shadows passed beneath one of the lampposts and for a moment were illuminated.

"It's him," Kane said, drawing a deep breath in through his ruined nose. "Tonight I'll taste his blood on my knife." There was a sound of a blade being drawn from a sheath and a glint of metal in the dark. He turned to Treacher and handed him the rope around Lucy's neck. "It's time, my fine filthy friend. Take her and bring al-Sistani back. Then I'll make you a wealthy man. Try anything and Abu here will shoot you dead on the spot."

Abu held up a rifle with a scope. Seeing it, Treacher bowed and then pointed the way for Lucy. "Come, my dear," he said. "Let's get this unpleasant business over with."

Lucy said nothing but followed the preacher toward where Grale stood with his men. At the same time, a short shadow separated itself from Grale and the others and started toward them, also leading another man.

Meeting halfway between the two groups, Treacher and the dwarf who led al-Sistani began to exchange ropes. Treacher had both ropes in one hand and then suddenly stepped back away from the dwarf's outstretched hand.

"What are you doing?" the dwarf snarled. "I'm supposed to take her to Grale. That's the deal."

"Not tonight, Paulito," Treacher growled, and raised his hand at the dwarf's head.

Too late, Paulito saw the small zip gun in the preacher's hand. "'Vengeance is mine, I will repay, says the Lord,'" Treacher said quietly, and released the pin that fired the bullet that punched a dime-size hole in the dwarf's forehead, the sound of the gunshot echoing as the little man's body crumpled to the ground. "That's Romans 12:19, friend."

Suddenly, the woods around the grassy area erupted with flashes and silenced gun reports, as well as the screams of men. Treacher dropped the rope attached to al-Sistani and pointed toward where Kane and his men were waiting. "Run, asshole!" he yelled.

Standing in the midst of the protective circle of his men, Kane watched as al-Sistani ran toward him. Then he was surprised and delighted when the preacher suddenly began pulling Lucy back toward him with the rope. He noticed that Grale and his men were running after the preacher, gaining on him quickly, but his men had not moved out of the woods to intercept the lunatic. *Something must have gone wrong,* he thought. "Cover the preacher and the girl," he ordered.

Abu barked out several commands and four members of the party split off to the sides, where they could fire at an angle at the pursuers without hitting Treacher or Lucy. Under fire, Grale and his men were forced to stop and retreat back into the deeper shadows, dragging a body with them.

"Well, Preacher, you are full of surprises," Kane said as Treacher came up huffing and puffing, yanking Lucy by her neck rope.

The preacher grinned. "I thought that there might be an extra reward for returning with both hostages."

"I'm sure I can arrange something suitable . . ." Kane smiled.

At that moment, an angry, desperate howl rolled toward them out of the dark. "*Lucy!!*" cried the voice.

Kane laughed. "Indeed, it's worth your weight in gold just to hear

Grale so upset. I'm guessing that he sniffed out my trap and may have won the battle in the woods."

Stepping forward in the direction his enemy had gone, Kane shouted, "Grale! Do you know who this is? It's your old friend, Kane! . . . Come, show yourself and let's finish this!"

There was no answer. Kane looked at Lucy and shrugged. "I guess love and lust have their limits. Apparently, you're not worth fighting to the death over."

Lucy kept her eyes on the ground and didn't reply, so Kane turned to Treacher and pointed his knife at him. "Time for you to join your friends."

"'*The Lord is my shepherd, I shall not want,*'" Treacher shouted, a meaty finger pointed skyward. "'*He makes me lie down in green pastures, He leads me beside still waters . . .*'"

"Oh, shut up," Kane said. "I'm not going to kill you myself, unless you continue to irritate me. . . . No, I think I'm going to leave your fate to your pal Grale. I hear he's sworn a particularly nasty one for you. Now start walking, and give my regards to David. Tell him I hope we get the chance to meet again soon."

Fear leaped into Treacher's eyes. He dropped to his knees. "No, please," he begged. "I did what I said I would do and more. I gave you Lucy back! You can keep the rest of the money, I have enough. Please don't make me face him!"

"I imagine that's pretty scary," Kane snickered. "But I can't have traitors, even if they were my traitors, hanging around. Simply can't be trusted, you know. Now go, or I will gut you and leave you for the Central Park rat packs to eat."

Treacher looked at the knife and then out toward the dark. He sighed. "I should have known better. Good-bye, Lucy."

Lucy looked up, hatred in her eyes. "Before he kills you, tell David that no matter what happens to me, I said to keep the faith and his time will come."

Treacher nodded. "It's the least I can do." He then straightened his shoulders and began walking down the path, his arms out in the form of a cross. "'*Even though I walk through the valley of the shadow of death, I fear no evil . . .*'"

"Christ but he's annoying . . ." Kane muttered.

"'. . . *for you are with me; your rod and your staff they comfort me,'*" Treacher shouted as he approached the circle of light beneath a lamp. "'*Surely goodness and mercy shall follow me . . .* '" He passed through the light and into the dark beyond. "'*All the days of my life . . .*'"

Suddenly, the preacher's voice stopped. Lucy, Kane, and his men continued to stare in the direction he had gone, wide-eyed and holding their breath as if waiting for a bubble to burst. Then a round object rolled from the dark into the light. A shaggy-haired head, blood shimmering on the full and grizzled beard.

Kane laughed and clapped his hands. "Well, I've done my civic duty and helped get a disgusting bum off the streets." He gave the rope tied to Lucy a tug. "Come, my dear Lucy, or shall I refer to you as Christine; time to take you to our lair. We've lots to do over the next week or so and need to get our beauty rest."

Lucy followed meekly, glancing up only once at the robed figure of a woman weeping in the shadows as they passed. *He's the only one . . .*

22

V. T. Newbury jogged through Central Park, pretend-ing not to have noticed the male and female joggers who'd been following him since leaving his Fifth Avenue office. He'd actually become quite good at picking out the tails assigned to his noon running routine. He assumed they were in the employ of his uncle, Dean, who apparently still didn't quite trust him.

First, there had been the young partner at the firm who just happened to bump into him wearing a tracksuit, as V.T. was about to head out one day, and the man suggested they run together. This was right after the attack on the New York Stock Exchange and his uncle was obviously keeping tabs on him. They jogged together that day but later V.T. told the man that he enjoyed the "alone time" and preferred to run by himself.

His uncle switched strategies and began keeping an eye on him from afar. Whoever he used for such things was smart enough to change it up; sometimes his pursuer was a man, a woman, a pair, and once even an extremely fit "young mother" pushing a state-of-the-art jogging stroller. But V.T. had suspected he'd be followed and made a game out of spotting them.

He never went on the same run two days in a row, so his uncle couldn't post spies along the route. That meant sending runners who could keep up with him, which made them easier to spot. V.T. had been an Ivy League rowing champ in his college days and prided himself on staying fit and trim. He ran at a good clip, and once he realized he was being followed, he amused himself by choosing odd routes and difficult paths, and then watching his pursuers try to keep up without exposing themselves.

Once, he'd sprinted around a corner and then doubled back, almost running into the woman with the jogging stroller. He got a good peek at the bundled doll being used as a prop, but pretended not to notice and apologized profusely to the flustered woman. "So very sorry. I took a wrong turn."

Still, he'd tried not to let on that he was aware of being followed. He wanted his uncle Dean to learn to trust him through benign reports from the spies. It was easy enough to shake pursuers when he needed to without making it obvious, such as the time he'd gone with Jaxon to see Karp. But most of what he did wasn't worth hiding or reporting as he went about the role of enjoying life as a wealthy, middle-aged partner in a prestigious law firm, and someone who was growing interested in his uncle's politics.

He and Dean had been spending many evenings together, talking over Cohiba cigars and snifters awash in Rémy Martin cognac about the family history, and its part in an intrepid band of "entrepreneurs, . . . perhaps a smuggler or two among them, ha-ha," from the Isle of Man who came to the young United States to make their fortune. The history lessons inevitably led to a discussion about the deteriorating state of the country and the world, and the need for "men of vision" to step up to the plate.

V.T. found it surprisingly easy to sound as if he was philosophically not that far removed from his uncle. He believed that it was true that the U.S. policy on immigration was a mess, and the lack of any cohesive policy to deal with it was frustrating. U.S. foreign policy was ambiguous and timid; no wonder the Russians, Muslims, and Chinese did what they liked—such as in Ossetia—and thumbed their noses at the U.S. nonresponse. No one could deny that the economy was in shambles, and yet the politicians seemed incapable of anything more than partisan bickering over who was at fault. And terrorists were most certainly at the doorstep, and yet U.S. leadership lacked the resolve to hunt them down and kill them in their lairs.

It was a shock for V.T. to realize that there were only a few degrees of separation between his uncle's philosophy and what he thought of as his liberal New England sensibilities. But at least he knew the counterarguments, though he kept them to himself. He suspected that these "shades of gray" were the general public perception that the Sons of Man would be counting on when they made their move for power. All they'd have to do would be to nudge the population a few steps toward "temporary emergency suspension" of constitutional protections and it would not be that far of a reach to totalitarianism.

Or to scapegoat one ethnicity, V.T. thought as he pounded down a path. *Or look the other way when thugs start breaking windows and murdering dissidents in their beds, and shipping people off to "relocation camps" in the country.*

Despite the spies who followed him, V.T. had felt a growing trust from his uncle as they continued their discussions. He'd been introduced to a number of very powerful men—politicians, military officers, and business executives—at the law firm and at dinner parties hosted by his uncle. He suspected that some, if not all, were connected to the Sons of Man, and watched what he said and did around them, aware that he was being judged.

Once, deep in his cups from the cognac, Dean had blearily clapped him on the shoulder as they were leaving the office and confessed, "I hope you won't take offense, but there are times when you are more like a son to me than my own Quillian."

The comment made V.T.'s skin crawl. His cousin, Quillian, had spurned his family and eventual place on the SOM council. Instead, he'd enlisted in the U.S. Marines and had been killed in Vietnam. *A better man than his father.* But what really galled V.T. was having to hide his hatred for the man he knew had killed his father. But he couldn't prove it—*yet*—so he'd plastered a smile on his face and clapped the old man back. "*Honored,*" he'd replied, all the time reminding himself that his goal was to help bring down the Sons of Man before they could accomplish their aims . . . *and charge this son of a bitch with my father's murder.*

The role-playing appeared to be working, as the old man seemed to relax his guard somewhat, such as leaving the notepad with "Malovo" and "Makhachkala" written on it on his desk, which had nearly meant a just end for a vicious terrorist. Some small items and comments, however, he ignored in case the old man was trying to trap him. During his meeting a month earlier with Jaxon and Karp, they'd all agreed that the fewer contacts he had with either of them, the better, and that rather than reporting every detail, he should use his judgment and risk exposure only for things that seemed to warrant it.

Such an instance occurred after-hours one evening when he was about to enter his uncle's office. He'd already told the old man that he was leaving but then remembered a case file he wanted to take home. As he was about to walk past Dean's office to his own, he overheard the old man place a telephone call.

"Chief Warrant Officer Adkins, please," his uncle said. *"Yes, my name is Vi Quisling."*

Why the false name? And that one in particular? V.T. wondered as he pulled a pen—actually a combination pen and recording device—from his pocket and clicked it.

There was a pause and then his uncle spoke again. *"Myr shegin dy ve, bee eh."* It was the Sons of Man motto spoken in Manx. What must be, will be. Apparently, the reply was satisfactory because the old man went on. *"The package is on the way. . . . No, there's been a change . . . five days later. Make it happen or forget the money."*

The old man hung up. After a slight pause, V.T. walked into the office, causing his uncle to start and scowl. *"Jesus Christ, Vinson, I thought everyone was gone! You nearly gave me a heart attack!"*

"Sorry about that, old chap," V.T. answered, and then shook his head and chuckled. *"Still at it when all the other partners and junior partners, as well as the rank and file, have gone home. Your energy and work ethic never cease to amaze me."*

The old man's scowl turned to a pleased smile at the compliment. *"You don't necessarily have to be smarter than the rest if you outwork them, I always say. Of course, it helps to be smarter and outwork the rubes. But yes . . . I had something I needed to tidy up*

. . . a large pension settlement for one of these investment banks that went under after that terrorist attack in September."

V.T. had used his judgment. His uncle had obviously lied about the "pension settlement" and had been talking in code to someone with a military rank. Chief warrant officer named Adkins. A mysterious package was arriving five days later. And then there was the name his uncle mentioned right before he hung up. Ivan or Iben—it was hard to tell on the tape—Jew-bare.

Using a false name had been the real kicker. At first "Vi Quisling" had seemed an odd choice. Vidkun Quisling was a Norwegian army officer and politician who had founded the Nasjonal Samling, a fascist party, and on the eve of the German invasion in 1940 he had declared himself prime minister and aligned with Adolf Hitler.

For most Norwegians, he was a traitor who not only seized power in a coup but participated in the capitulation of their country to the Nazis, the deportation of Norwegian Jews to concentration camps, and the execution of Norwegian patriots. He was arrested near the end of the war and executed for high treason. But to a member of the Sons of Man, V.T. assumed, he would be a hero—"a man of vision," as his uncle liked to say, who was willing to seize the reins when the moment was right, and knew how to deal with *problems,* like the Jews.

Although V.T. wondered at the wisdom of using an alias with such obvious connections, he knew it fit with the old man's twisted sense of humor and feeling of invincibility. However, the riddles were beyond him, so he decided that it was important enough to contact Karp and Jaxon and let them piece it together.

The last time they met, they worked out a plan on how to let Karp know he wanted to relay information. If he wanted to talk in person, V.T. would request that a clerk in the records division for the criminal courts pull a file on one of the cases he'd been working on when he left the DAO. If he just wanted to pass information, such as a recording, then a different case file would be pulled. This particular clerk had been told to contact Karp's office immediately if a request came through for them.

Which was why V.T. was now passing Cleopatra's Needle on his run through Central Park. He glanced over at a grassy space on the far side of the obelisk and saw that NYPD detectives were still on the scene. The news that morning had carried a story about a shooting in the park the night before. Apparently there had been one fatality—*which explains the body lying under a tarp surrounded by yellow crime scene tape*—and possibly more. *"There was a lot of blood,"* a spokesman for the NYPD had told the television stations. *"We believe it may be gang related."*

A few minutes later, V.T. pulled up at a bench near the *Alice in Wonderland* statue. The bench was occupied only by an old black derelict who sat snoring in the sun, apparently sleeping off the contents of the Old Grand-dad whiskey bottle in the brown bag at his feet. The man was dressed in several layers of old coats and pairs of pants and smelled like he preferred not to bathe. The young mothers with children and tourists visiting the famous statue avoided the bench.

V.T. put his foot up on the bench and leaned over to tie a shoe that was not untied. As he did, the MP3 music player in his jogging shirt pocket slipped out and bounced off the bench into a pile of leaves and other debris behind it.

"Damn," he said, and fished in the refuse until he found the device. He stood up and plugged it back into his earphone jack and replaced it in his shirt pocket. Glancing around and smiling as he watched children climb the toadstools, he noted his pursuers trying to catch their breath while keeping an eye on him.

Let's see how much more you have in the tank, he thought with a smile, and started off in the direction of Central Park West at a run. He patted the MP3. *Nice touch, Clay! A little John Coltrane for the finish line.*

After V.T. left, the old bum yawned and then lay down on his stomach to continue his nap. He stayed in the same position without moving for thirty minutes until he decided enough time had passed, then reached into the debris and closed his hand around V.T.'s MP3 player.

I know you appreciate good jazz, V.T., Detective Clay Fulton thought as he sat up, slipping the device into one of the filthy coats.

He stood and shuffled off to the men's restroom at the Conservatory Water pond, where he entered a stall and removed the filthy outer garments and placed the MP3 in his suit-coat pocket.

Stuffing the rags into a trash can, Fulton emerged from the men's room and looked around. As he walked east, he pulled a small radio from his pants pocket. "Neary."

"Yeah, boss?"

"Pick me up, and by the way if I see a hot-dog vendor, you interested?"

"Yeah, the guy at Seventy-fifth and Third has the best brats in the city, bar none. Make mine with the works. And just in case I never said this before, you're a swell guy, Clay, a real swell guy."

"Neary?"

"Yeah, boss?"

"Shut up."

23

Twenty minutes later, Fulton walked into Karp's of- fice. He held up the MP3. "Deep Throat sends his regards."

Karp looked up from where he was locked in conversation with Jack Swanburg and Kenny Katz. "Thanks, Clay," he said, holding out his hand for the MP3 and then placing it in his desk drawer. "I'll listen to it later."

"What's that, the missing eighteen minutes from the Nixon White House tapes?" Swanburg joked.

"I wish." Karp laughed. "Then I could quit this lousy job and write a book." Then his face turned serious. "Kenny just returned with a search warrant for the office and home of Dr. Kip Bergendorf, the assistant medical examiner who conducted the autopsy on Stewart Reed. "We're going to go serve it now. Want to join us?"

"You bet! Going to arrest him?" the big detective asked.

"Depends," Karp said. "Right now, we're going to sit him down and ask him a few questions. If he'll talk . . ."

Dr. Kip Bergendorf looked up from his desk in the small glassed-in office he shared with two other AMEs and nearly swallowed his gum when he saw the New York district attorney, accompanied by a young man with bushy hair and an old man in a full white beard, enter the New York Medical Examiner's Office. Karp spoke to one of the other AMEs who was milling around the entrance, and then looked up in his direction.

Bergendorf pretended not to notice as he stood up and left his cubicle to head for the exit behind him. He stopped at the door when a large black man suddenly appeared on the other side.

"Excuse me! Dr. Bergendorf? Could we have a word, please," Karp said in a loud voice as he came up behind the doctor.

"I, um, need to use the restroom," Bergendorf, a dumpy middle-aged man with a receding hairline, replied.

"It can wait," the big black man growled, flashing a gold NYPD detective's badge and handing him a document. "I'm Detective Clay Fulton and this is a search warrant for your office, including computer records; another is being served at your home in Newark."

"My wife's at home . . ." Bergendorf wailed. "This will really upset her."

"Well, if she's home, at least we won't have to bust the door down," Fulton replied.

Bergendorf turned to Karp. "Can I ask what this is about?"

"Sure," Karp responded. "It's about a homicide investigation."

"What homicide?" Bergendorf said, licking his lips nervously.

"That of Stewart Reed."

The AME turned white as the blood drained from his face. "But I did that autopsy, it was a suicide."

"It wasn't a suicide," said the older man with the beard. "He was murdered. Jack Swanburg's the name, pathology's the game, and as the man said, we'd like to ask you a few questions."

"Is there someplace we can sit quietly?" Karp asked. "Or would you rather we asked out here."

The AME looked around. Other AMEs were standing around their desks and talking in small groups as they stole glances in his direction. "We can go back in my cubicle, it's small but private."

"Lead the way," Fulton said, gesturing.

Ten minutes later, Swanburg had laid out his case, complete with graphs and charts. No luxation, death by asphyxiation, yet no ecchymosis. "Practically screams homicide," Swanburg noted. "Then there's the needle track on the buttocks. Remember that? You should, you took a photograph that included a blood smear."

Bergendorf just swallowed hard, so Swanburg continued. "Took a bit of looking, but my friend and colleague Griff—he's a forensic chemist, one of the best in the country—found it. A fast-acting neurotoxin injected into the muscle—immobilized him within seconds, killed through asphyxiation within six to eight minutes . . . before the killer hung him, thus no ecchymosis. The poison itself, which appears to have been one of those developed by the Soviets during the height of Cold War spy versus spy, had metabolized. Griff found what was left over from the metabolizing process and worked backward."

When Swanburg stopped, Bergendorf shrugged and smiled. "I don't know what to say. Good work. I obviously missed something. I've just been exhausted lately, we get so many cases and there isn't the time or resource to do a decent—"

"Can it, Bergendorf," Karp growled. "All Dr. Swanburg and I want to know is why and who?"

"I don't know what you're talking about," Bergendorf protested, and appeared ready to continue until Karp held up his hand.

"Before you say another thing, think about it," Karp warned. "You hit the radar, and we're going through your files here, and at your home—if there's something you kept that implicates you more, we're going to find it. Face it, Kip, you aided and abetted a murder of one of my men, you're going to swing in the big house big-time. Now I'll give you a choice: you can be a cooperating witness or an adverse defendant. Your call."

Bergendorf's hands trembled as he wiped the beads of sweat from his brow. "If I say anything, I'll be killed."

"It depends on what you say, but you might just qualify for witness protection in a prison in another state or at least administrative segregation at Attica," Fulton said. "Someplace where you might survive just getting to the lunchroom."

Bergendorf hesitated. "I want to call my wife," he said.

"Go ahead," Karp agreed. "You won't mind if we listen?"

The AME appeared about to say something, but then shook his head. "I just want to make sure she's all right." He pressed the numbers on his cell phone and everyone in the cubicle knew when she answered because she started screaming at him. All Bergendorf could get in was a weak apology. "I'll explain later. Just pack up the kids and go stay with your mother. It's going to be okay."

The woman screamed something else that caused Bergendorf to wince and close his cell phone. "Maybe I should call a lawyer?"

"You're free to do so and you're free to go," Karp replied. "You're not under arrest . . . yet. However, let me explain what will happen. If you ask for a lawyer, and that's your right, we won't be able to ask you any more questions. And that means we'll have to assume that you're unwilling to cooperate with us. Do you want to stop cooperating?"

Bergendorf started to cry. "No, I want to . . . help. I got a call from a guy to meet him at a bar. He's Russian or something, big guy, and I mean big . . . six-five, maybe three hundred pounds . . . got a face like a Neanderthal. Anyway, he tells me that on such-and-such a date, a body is going to be brought into the morgue, and all I have to do is look the other way and rule it a suicide."

"What was in it for you?" Karp asked.

"Twenty grand."

"So you noticed the lack of ecchymosis and yet no luxation?" Swanburg said.

"Yeah, sure," Bergendorf replied. "It was clearly a homicide."

Karp nodded. "Well, Mr. Kip Bergendorf, now it's official, you're under arrest. Detective Fulton will read you your rights and you will be escorted to the Tombs for booking."

As Fulton began to repeat the Miranda warnings to Bergendorf, the man sat back heavily in his chair. "Can't we work something out?" he cried. "What if I was to tell you that this Russian guy said to expect another body tonight? A woman this time."

That got everybody's attention. Karp leaned toward the man as if he might jump across the desk onto him. "I'm not making any deals with you, Bergendorf. But if you want to avoid a second charge of murder, then I suggest you talk."

"The Russian called again a couple of hours ago. He asked if I was working the afternoon shift and told me to be watching for a 'heroin overdose.'"

"He give you the name of the victim?" Fulton demanded.

"Carmina," Bergendorf replied. "Carmina Salinas, age twenty-four."

"She's an actress in Maplethorpe's play," Karp said. "Marlene thinks that she knows something, or Maplethorpe did something, but she's afraid to talk. Apparently, someone wants to make sure she doesn't have a change of heart. When is this supposed to happen?"

Bergendorf sniffled and then said, "Sometime after three."

Karp looked at his watch. "It's two forty-five." He pulled out his cell phone. "Clay, call Father Dugan, see if he has an address for Carmina Salinas."

"Who are you calling?" Katz asked.

"Marlene," Karp answered. "She was supposed to see Alejandro this afternoon. He's a friend of Carmina. He might be the fastest way to find her."

As Karp called his wife, and Fulton tried to reach the priest, Katz turned to Bergendorf. "Did this Russian say who he was working for?"

The AME shook his head. "No. Just that he had a job for me."

"Why would he know he could come to you for this?" Swanburg asked. "There must be a lot of AMEs who work here. Why you?"

Bergendorf licked his lips. "Let's just say I got involved with the wrong people and sold my soul."

The AME glanced over at Karp, who was just getting off the phone. "In fact, if you're willing to make a deal, Mr. Karp, I might be able to help with another case you should be interested in."

Karp glared at the AME. He was in no mood to negotiate with the weasel. "Yeah, what's that, Bergendorf? You talk, I'll decide later what it was worth."

"Does the name Newbury ring any bells?"

Marlene flipped her cell phone closed and rushed back into La Fonda Boricua, a Puerto Rican restaurant in East Harlem, where Alejandro Garcia flirted with the waitress, who was asking him to autograph her short skirt.

Up until thirty seconds ago, Marlene had been eating a delicious lunch of pork *chicharrones* in an effort to distract herself from worrying about Lucy. Her daughter had sent another text message saying she was still on a retreat and was only taking a break to send a quick message. "Be back in touch soon," the message ended.

Marlene was aware that if Lucy was with some of the Taos Indians on this retreat, cell phones weren't allowed. In fact, it was unusual for someone who wasn't a member of the tribe to be invited, which spoke to Lucy's standing with the tribe due to her work at the mission, as well as Jojola's putting in a good word for her.

In truth, Marlene wondered if Lucy was really on a secret mission for Jaxon and the whole "retreat" explanation was a ruse because she wasn't allowed to say. *Or she didn't want to worry us,* she'd thought when she had first walked into the restaurant for a late lunch with Garcia.

Then her cell phone went off to the ringtone of "When a Man Loves a Woman" by Percy Sledge. "It's Butch," she said, and laughed when Garcia wiggled his eyebrows suggestively.

"I certainly hope so, señora," Garcia replied. "I'd hate to think you were stepping out on the Man."

La Fonda Boricua was a busy, noisy restaurant and Marlene had to step outside to hear what Karp was telling her. But once she did, she didn't waste time asking questions. She rushed into the restaurant and pointed at Garcia. "We need to leave, now!"

"What's the rush? You forget your credit card and now we have to dine and dash?" He laughed, tossing a large bill on the table to cover the tab.

"Carmina's in danger," Marlene replied. "Do you know where she's at?"

Alejandro was on his feet in an instant and led the way out the door. "Probably at home in her apartment on Pleasant Avenue, getting ready for her show tonight. What's this shit about her being in danger?"

Before Marlene could answer, Garcia stepped out in front of a taxi. As the cabbie laid on the horn, he ran around to the passenger door and yanked it open. "Get out!" he shouted at the surprised Japanese tourist.

"What the fuck," the cabbie yelled. "Get away from my passenger!"

Garcia reached into his pocket and pulled out a bill. "Here's a hundred bucks," he said, handing it to the cabdriver. "There's another one if you can get me to One Sixteenth and Pleasant in two minutes or less!"

"You got it," the cabbie agreed. He turned to the tourist and gestured at the door. "You heard the man, get the fuck out of my cab!"

"Who's after her?" Garcia asked as he dialed Carmina's number on his cell phone.

"We're supposed to be looking for a very large Russian. Thick features," Marlene said, then clapped a hand to her forehead. "I ran into a guy that fits the description that time I met you and Carmina at St. Malachy's. He wanted directions to Radio City Music Hall."

"Sounds like a guy named Gregor, who works for Maplethorpe as a bodyguard," Alejandro said.

"Tell Carmina to leave the apartment and go somewhere with other people around," Marlene said. "I'm going to call Butch and he'll send the cops."

Alejandro nodded, and after a few moments he slammed the cell phone shut. "Dammit, she's not picking up," he cursed. He banged on the partition between him and the driver. "Pedal to the metal, hombre, or that hundred goes back in my pocket."

The driver punched the gas pedal and leaned on the horn as he slipped in and out of lanes. "Okay, but you also pay the ticket if I get pulled over."

"No problem, just don't stop until you get there!"

Carmina looked through the peephole at the large man in the Elkins Plumbing and Heating uniform outside her apartment door. He had a cap on and she couldn't see his face very well. "What do you want?"

"Superintendent sent me," he said in a bored, heavily accented voice. "There have been complaints about no heat."

"I'm not having any problems," Carmina replied. "You can check me off the list."

"Sorry, but super says I have to check all apartments. Please, lady, I lose my job if I don't check all."

Carmina rolled her eyes. All she wanted was a bath and a nap before the evening performance of *Putin.* But this guy wasn't going to go away, so she unlatched the dead bolt and removed the security chain to let him in. "Make it fast, please."

She turned around and led the way into her living room before turning around and getting a good look at the man. "Gregor? What the hell are you doing?" Suddenly, she realized she was in danger and made a dash for the front door.

However, the big man was agile as a tiger and grabbed her by the arm with one hand while his other snapped a plastic bag over her head. "Where you going, little Carmina?" he said as he brought his hand up and helped secure the bottom of the bag around her throat as she gasped for air.

Gregor was enjoying his work. There were many beautiful women who worked in the theater, but none of them would have anything to do with him. *They're all bitches, including this one,* he thought as the girl tried to stomp on his feet and scratched at his gloved hands. As he'd worked out how he would arrange this "suicide," he'd considered raping her as well. But first he had to render her unconscious, then arrange to make it look like she'd overdosed on heroin.

Not the first whore in Spanish Harlem to mix up her dose, he thought.

The girl fought like a wildcat, and it was all he could do to keep the bag over her face, and her hands from ripping it away. But expending that energy also had the effect of her running out of air that much faster, and soon she sagged to the floor.

Gregor dragged the girl into her bedroom and placed her on the bed. He then took the rubber tube out of his pocket and fastened it around her arm. Working quickly, he brought out a small plastic bag filled with white powder, which he poured onto a spoon and melted with his lighter. *Enough to kill a horse,* he thought as he sucked the liquid into a hypodermic, *but not so fast I can't have a little fun before the body goes cold.*

Carmina moaned and started to stir as he tapped on the vein in her arm that was enlarged due to the tube. "Sweet dreams," he said as he leaned over to insert the needle.

There was a crash of a door giving way to force. Snarling, Gregor threw down the hypodermic and started to rush out of the room with his gun drawn. But he ran straight into a short, muscular young man coming the other way.

Gregor recognized Carmina's boyfriend even as Garcia's charge knocked him off his feet, the gun clattering away. The young man landed on top of him and rained down several blows. But Gregor had been trained by the best in the Soviet KGB special forces unit. He threw a devastating elbow to the young man's head that knocked him off, and, quick for a three-hundred-pound man, he jumped to his feet and landed a heavy kick to Garcia's midsection.

As Garcia went down in a heap, Gregor leaned over and picked up his gun. He sighted along the barrel at the young man's head and started to pull the trigger. But the gunshot that followed was not from his weapon. He felt a powerful blow in his ribs despite the armored vest he always wore.

With a primordial scream, he turned and saw a petite woman aiming a small handgun at him. She pulled the trigger again but nothing happened. Gregor smiled. "Is jammed, no?" he said.

Marlene worked the slide back on her semiautomatic as Gregor leveled his gun. For a second time, however, he was unable to pull the trigger. This time it wasn't a powerful blow that stopped him, but the tiny prick of a needle piercing his massive right leg. He looked back to see the young man squeeze the hypodermic plunger and snarled. But before he could do or say anything else, the nearly pure heroin that had been injected into his saphenous vein arrived at his heart like a runaway freight train, and for all intents and purposes, he was dead before he hit the floor.

A loud moan escaped Carmina, and Alejandro rushed to her side. He tore the tube off her arm and smiled as her eyes fluttered open. "Alejandro?" she said weakly.

"*Querida,* I'm here," Alejandro replied as tears rushed into his eyes.

She smiled and brushed at one of the tears on his cheek. "Late as usual," she said, and pulled his head toward her, kissing him tenderly. There was a sound in the doorway, and they both turned to see Marlene.

"Your husband still need a witness?" Carmina asked.

"I'm sure he'd appreciate it," Marlene replied. "He's the one who got us over here in time."

Marlene looked over at the hulking body of Gregor lying on the floor. "I guess he won't being watching the Rockettes at Radio City anymore."

24

At a nod from his security man outside, Omar Abdullah emerged from the office of Trinidad & Tobago Dairy Products, Inc., and looked quickly around. The sun was setting, painting the tropical night orange and red, and the lights were just coming on in the plaza and surrounding businesses.

When he'd arrived that evening, hoping to hear good news, he'd immediately taken a mental picture of the people in the plaza outside the office, looking for anyone who seemed *too* interested. He couldn't be too careful. The national security antiterrorism personnel for Trinidad were well trained, and he was a wanted man.

However, he'd also been gone from the island for many years; he'd aged and a hard life had changed the young man he'd been when he left. Plus, there were plenty of true believers willing to help him, many of them having infiltrated the government and its agencies. The people of his village weren't all supportive of the idea of an Islamic revolution, but they were intimidated by those who were and just in case, he'd moved almost every night to avoid being pinpointed for a raid.

Now the hiding and running was over. *Allah be praised*, he'd finally received the news that his good friend and leader, Amir al-Sistani, had been rescued and the "spectacular" event was going to proceed. *Allahu akbar! God is great! His will be done!* The day of his martyrdom was drawing close.

Tired of constantly being hunted by the Americans and their allies, as well as living in training camps and the ghettos of the Middle East and Africa, he'd decided that it was time to join the Prophet in the presence of Allah. He looked forward to the pleasures promised to those who died in the cause of Islam, and he was pleased that the beginning of the end of his life should start where he had been born, in Trinidad, the son of a simple Muslim farmer and his equally simple wife.

His parents were moderately religious—his father prayed five times a day, observed the holy days, and his mother knew her place as his chattel. They were too simple to understand the politics of Islamic fundamentalism, or appreciate that the battle between Islam and the West was at hand; but they'd listened to the village imam and sent their young son to religious school, where the radical teachers taught him to hate.

He'd been a young man in the ranks of Jamaat al Muslimeen since the great coup that had almost succeeded in creating an Islamic state in Trinidad. Then he fled to Afghanistan to avoid arrest and join the jihad against the godless Soviets. After the victory, he'd remained at the invitation of the Taliban, helping train the growing ranks of al-Qaeda until the U.S. invasion forced him into the Pakistan tribal areas.

Now he was back in Trinidad and ready to begin his final journey, having said his good-byes to his ancient parents, friends, and the young jihadis who worshiped his name and wanted to be like him. The only cause for alarm had been the day when Ariadne Stupenagel arrived in the village where he was hiding. He was certain that he'd been found out and his former lover was there to expose him.

Abdullah was prepared to abduct and kill her. He felt no pity for the woman he'd once professed his love to, only disgust for the man he had been in those days when he'd allowed himself to be seduced by an infidel whore. But his spies told him that while she asked questions about the resurgent Islamic fundamentalist movement in Trinidad, she didn't ask about him. He decided that her appearance was probably a coincidence, and that it was even somehow fitting that his last lover had, in American lingo, "come to see him off."

Still, just in case Ariadne was working for the U.S. government and not a newspaper as she claimed, he'd kept men following her every move. But so far she'd done nothing to cause further suspicion. Yes, she'd been asking questions about "radical" Islam and the religious schools, but sympathizers in the prime minister's office said her questions, while probing, had not indicated she had any specific knowledge about Abdullah or his plans.

It was no surprise that a journalist was asking these questions. The West's concerns about the spread of Islamic fundamentalism in the Caribbean and the transport of liquid natural gas was no secret in the world of terrorism and counterterrorism. In fact, the surprising thing was that it had been all but ignored by the Western media. The press and the U.S. government still spent more time worrying about those old washed-up communist revolutionaries in Cuba than the real threat looming below the soft underbelly of the United States.

So the fact that Ariadne, who he grudgingly acknowledged had been a tough, fearless journalist when he knew her, was on the story came as no surprise. *But her warning will come too late,* he thought with satisfaction.

Then she'd surprised him several nights before when he'd first checked in at the dairy products office. The man he had watching her called to say that the whore was apparently trying to pick up two men she met at a bar across the main plaza from the office. *"The joke is on her. I think they're homosexuals, may Allah burn their souls in hell."*

"Did she follow me here?" he'd asked.

"No, she was already sitting next to the men when you arrived," the spy said. *"She didn't react when you arrived in the plaza. She was too busy showing her large, unclean breasts and uncovered legs to the faggots."*

A little later, the spy had reported that the older of the men left soon after, but his young companion remained with the woman. *"Apparently, the young one has at least some interest in women, though she seems to be the aggressor. The other whores are angry."*

Abdullah shook his head with disgust and tried not to think of the sudden images of Ariadne's naked body that had flooded into his mind. She'd had a large sexual appetite and thought she could seduce any man . . . *even a homosexual, if he had even a smidgen of manhood in him.*

Now, as he walked down the sidewalk away from the office, Abdullah glanced across the plaza at the bar. Ariadne was nowhere in sight. His man would remain behind in case she made some sudden move. Soon they would be out of contact, but the young jihadi would know what to do. Port of Spain could be a rough place; Ariadne wouldn't be the first tourist murdered for her purse by some unknown assailant.

Abdullah dismissed any thought of Ariadne or anyone else stopping him as he marched toward the loading docks. He believed with all his heart that the release of al-Sistani was a sign from Allah that his path was blessed. No Trinidad security force, no American agents or Russian spies—and no filthy female journalist—would keep him from his destiny.

Abdullah was so confident, which rubbed off on his men, who relaxed their vigilance, that he still did not see the three dark shapes who shadowed him.

John Jojola and Tran Vinh Do followed the terrorist with the help of an officer of the Trinidad national security force who was a native of Port of Spain and knew the streets well. Yasin Salim, the officer, was young and dedicated; he, too, was Muslim but angrily denounced the radicals "who give good Muslims a bad name."

After picking up Abdullah's trail the night Stupenagel spotted him, they'd been able to watch his movements from afar, constantly switching the surveillance teams, all of which reported to Jaxon. Cell phone chatter among Muslims sympathetic to Jamaat had picked up considerably and Abdullah seemed to be at the center of it. Then they got word that whatever was going on, was happening that night.

Jaxon decided to split up his team. He and Blanchett would watch the oil and natural gas shipping facilities located south of Port of Spain. It was a large series of facilities, but they knew where to focus. The spies had named a large LNG tanker, *The Nile,* as possibly being involved. In the meantime, Jojola, who still had his T-shirt stand, and Tran would keep an eye on the Trinidad & Tobago Dairy Products office and Abdullah.

Yasin Salim quickly guessed that Abdullah was heading for the Port of Spain loading docks. While the petrochemical and oil and gas shipping facilities were kept far away to prevent a catastrophic accident, most regular shipping was conducted at the main docks in the city.

This made it easier to shadow Abdullah. Instead of just following, the three men were able to split up and take up posts along the way, so that Jojola was actually watching the docks when the target arrived and was joined by his comrades. Security was light and they were soon crouched in the shadow of a small warehouse looking toward the activity on the docks.

Jojola pointed to a small cargo ship that was being prepared to set sail. Several large cargo containers were still being loaded and men were filtering aboard. But otherwise, lines were being cast off and a tugboat waited a few yards out in the dark harbor, its lights trained on its next job.

"He went aboard that ship," Jojola said. "The . . . how's that pronounced? The *I-ben Jew-bare*?"

"A reefer," Tran whispered.

"A what? Reefer? They're shipping marijuana?" Jojola asked. His wide bronze face looked puzzled.

Tran rolled his eyes. "You've been out in the desert sun too long. Not reefer as in 'marijuana reefer' . . . and by the way, kids these days don't say reefer, its ganja or weed. Man, you're behind the times . . ."

"Leave it to a Vietnamese gangster to be intimately familiar with all the latest drug terminology," Jojola retorted, "but you were saying about a reefer?"

"A reefer—a refrigerated ship—especially fitted for shipping goods that need to be kept cold or frozen," Tran explained. He pointed at the logo of one of the containers being loaded. "Trinidad & Tobago Dairy Products."

"So what's Omar doing on a reefer? Going to poison a ship full of milk?" Jojola asked.

"Wouldn't put it past him, but I don't know," Tran replied. "I'm going to call Jaxon and let him know where we are and see what he wants us to do."

Tran pulled out his cell phone and punched in the number. He watched the cell phone screen for a moment and then cursed. "I can't get a damn signal," he swore.

At the same time, a car pulled up to the ship and a blond woman stepped out. She kept her head down and hurried aboard.

"Holy shit!" Jojola exclaimed. "It's Nadya!"

"You sure?" Tran asked.

"Damn straight," the Indian replied. "I've had a few good looks at her, including in Dagestan. But I knew it was her just the way she moved . . . like a predator."

The three men watched the ship for a few more minutes. Only two more containers were left on the dock.

"What do you think they're up to?" Tran asked.

"I don't know, but I'm tired of letting this bitch get away," Jojola replied as he started to rise from his hiding place.

"What the hell are you doing?" Tran hissed.

"I'm going to get on that ship," his friend replied. "Whatever she and Omar are up to, it can't be good."

"You crazy Indian! Let's call in the Coast Guard," Tran insisted.

Jojola thought about it. "Go call Jaxon and let him make the decision. Maybe he wants to follow these guys and see where they're going. I don't think there's much danger from this ship. Maybe they're meeting up with other terrorists and we can nab the whole bunch."

"I can't call Jaxon from here," Tran replied as he got up, too. "I don't have cell service, and besides, who says I'm going to let you go alone and get all the glory? I'm tired of listening to you about how you kicked our Viet Cong butts all over the Mekong when everybody knows we were the ones who kicked your asses. I'm not about to let you lord this over me."

Jojola smiled. He and Tran had once been blood enemies, but

now they were more like blood brothers. "Fine, it's all about you," he said. "But someone needs to let Jaxon know what we're up to so that he can send the cavalry."

Tran turned to Salim, who'd been listening to their debate with his mouth hanging open. Apparently, the Trinidad national security forces didn't carry on like the two odd Americans. "Do you have a cell phone?" Tran asked him.

Salim shook his head. "They don't work well and are easy to intercept," he replied.

"Well, Jaxon's private number is programmed into my phone," Tran said as he handed the device to the young man. "When you get a signal—you'll see little bars up there in the left-hand corner—hit the Send button. Jaxon should answer quickly; tell him we went aboard the *I-ben Jew-bare* and that Nadya Malovo and Omar Abdullah are aboard. We'll stay out of sight until he makes his move." Tran looked at Jojola. "Right?"

Jojola smiled. "Whatever you say, Kemosabe. Ready?"

"As I'll ever be," Tran replied with a groan. "I'm getting too old for this." He looked again at Salim. "You got it down?"

The young man nodded. "Nadya Malovo. Omar Abdullah. The *I-ben Jew-bare*."

Tran gave him a thumbs-up and then followed Jojola as they wove their way from hiding place to hiding place until they reached the spot of the dock that was nearly even with the stern's covered subdeck and separated from it by only by a few feet. Jojola quickly shimmied across the large hawser and dropped onto the subdeck, where he waited for his companion.

Tran looked with misgiving at the hawser but was preparing to cross when there was a shout from somewhere toward the bow. The Vietnamese gangster turned and saw a man looking at him.

"What are you doing?" the man shouted.

"Getting ready," Tran shouted back, and pointed at the rope.

"Where are the others? The ship is ready to go!"

Tran shrugged. His best guess was that a dock crew would be appearing soon to cast off the hawser.

As the man continued to walk to Tran, there was another shout from above. This time it was a woman's accented voice. "What's going on? Why the delay?" she yelled down at the man on the dock, who looked up.

"It's Malovo," Jojola hissed from the shadows of the subdeck.

"The lazy dock crew only sent one man," the guard shouted up.

Tran looked quickly down as first Malovo's face and then Abdullah's appeared over the railing halfway down the ship. "You, come here, where is the rest of the workers?" she shouted.

Tran shrugged without looking up. He was trying to decide whether he should run and risk raising the alarm with the two terrorists or try to bluff his way through this, when yet another female voice rang out in the dark.

"Excuse me, but I'm looking for an old friend, Omar Abdullah. I heard he might be aboard?"

Tran glanced quickly in the direction of the voice and saw Ariadne Stupenagel marching down the dock as though late for an appointment. The guard on the dock moved quickly to intercept her, forgetting about Tran for the moment.

"What's she doing?" Tran whispered.

"Buying us time, you old idiot," Jojola whispered back. "Now get your butt over here before they remember you."

Thirty minutes earlier, Ariadne Stupenagel had gone for a stroll outside of her hotel. As she expected, the man who'd been tailing her followed.

She'd first noticed him the night she'd met Jaxon and Blanchett at the bar. She and Ned had closed the place down and then tottered out toward the street at three a.m. Or at least she tottered, Blanchett was moving with his usual grace.

The cowboy had appeared to down several drinks during the course of the evening, but actually had been quietly exchanging his barely tasted cocktails with hers as she drained them. She estimated she'd had four or five times as much to drink as he had, which explained the tottering.

Blanchett had escorted her to a cab and made sure she got in the backseat. As the cab pulled away, she'd looked back to wave good night and that's when she spotted the young black man who'd stepped out to the curb and hailed a cab of his own. She'd noticed him earlier in the bar but thought perhaps he was watching her out of lust. So it was with a prick to her pride that she saw him turn to see where Blanchett was going before he got in his cab, and she realized that her "admirer" was actually tailing her.

Wondering if she was about to become one of the kidnapping statistics, Stupenagel told her cabbie to speed up. "Turn left at the corner and stop halfway down the block."

When they stopped, she turned in her seat to see the other cab speed around the corner. It was obvious when her pursuer saw her as the other cab suddenly slowed, but then continued down the road until it pulled over two blocks away on the opposite side of the street.

Stupenagel didn't want the tail to know he'd been had—better to know her enemy's face than to have to spot his replacement—so she hopped out of the cab for a moment and pretended to be trying to place a call on her cell phone. She made a big show of not getting through—stamping back and forth on the sidewalk and signaling to her cabdriver that she would just be another moment. Finally, she'd thrown her hands up in frustration and climbed back in the cab, which she directed to her hotel, certain that her tail was following.

In the days that followed, the journalist had kept her word to Jaxon and avoided confronting Abdullah. Instead, she'd gone about her business as a reporter doing a general assignment story on Islamic fundamentalism in Trinidad. Sure that her questions and statements would get back to Abdullah—she'd been around enough spies in her life to recognize when someone was listening while pretending not to—she'd kept her inquiries unspecific and avoided using Abdullah's name.

A liberal application of booze and flirtation had developed good sources within the national security agency and so she learned that something big was afoot. The best source—a captain who'd suggested that perhaps sometime he could visit her in New York—had called that night to say that she might want to keep her eye on the office of the Trinidad & Tobago Dairy Products company. But first she had to get rid of the tail.

No problemo, Stupenagel thought, as her walk took her into a commercial area that was nearly devoid of other pedestrians as night overtook the city. She'd been taking care of herself in some of the roughest places in the world for years, and now chose an alley to slip down, hesitating just enough to make sure the tail saw.

Earlier that day, she'd gone to the Bank of Trinidad and purchased several rolls of Trinidad fifty-cent coins, which she'd stuffed into a sock. Finding a dark doorway in the alley, she took the sock out of her purse and waited. It wasn't long before she heard the quick footsteps of the young man.

As he passed her hiding place, she stepped out and swung the sock expertly into the side of his head. There was a satisfying crack and stunned grunt, followed by the man's collapse. She dragged his body out of sight behind a row of trash cans and returned to the street, leaving the sock full of coins on a windowsill, hopefully for one of Port of Spain's many street urchins to find.

Stupenagel had arrived at the plaza in time to see Abdullah step out of his office and begin walking toward the docks. Hanging back, she'd also seen Jojola, Tran, and a young man she didn't know following the terrorist.

Arriving at the docks, Stupenagel found a place to hide and watch the pursued and the pursuers. She'd been surprised and excited when Nadya Malovo arrived. *I'm going to get the frickin' Pulitzer for this,* she thought. But she had to be careful and stay out of sight; she'd had run-ins with Malovo in the past and the other woman was bound to recognize her.

She was still watching when Jojola and Tran made their way to the stern of the ship, with the Indian slipping quickly aboard while Tran hesitated. Then he'd been seen by the guard whose shouts had alerted the always suspicious Malovo. When Abdullah appeared at the rail and it looked like Tran was about to get caught, Stupenagel decided to act.

Well, Stupe, she thought as she stepped away from her hiding place and began walking toward the ship, *you're either going to get the Pulitzer and a Medal of Honor for this, or you're going to get dead.*

"Excuse me," she shouted, "but I'm looking for an old friend, Omar Abdullah. I heard he might be aboard?"

Abdullah's eyes looked like they might bug out of his head, which would have been funny in a safer situation, but at the moment it made her sick to her stomach. She saw him turn and say something to Malovo, who gave some orders before moving out of sight.

The guard had pulled his gun and had it trained on her head as she walked toward him. "Stop there," he demanded, "and put your purse on the ground. You are my prisoner."

"Prisoner? I beg your pardon, my name is Ariadne Stupenagel, and I'm a reporter for the *New York Guardian*," she said. "I'm working on a story about the Islamic revolution in Trinidad and was wondering if—"

The man grabbed her by the arm and yanked her toward the ship. "Shut up! You are to go aboard now!"

"Watch it, bub," she retorted as the guard hustled her toward the gangplank. "These are Guccis I'm wearing. They're worth more than you make in a year, I bet, and if I break a heel, you're getting the bill."

After the woman was taken aboard the ship, which had then quickly left port, Yasin Salim stepped out of the shadows.

It was true that he hated the radical Islamists, but he was no friend of the West, either. He was a dedicated socialist, who worked secretly for the Russian secret service.

Salim had received no direct orders to interfere with the Americans tracking Abdullah. Just watch and report back to the Russian ambassador in Port of Spain. However, as the general strategy of Moscow was to encourage strife between the West and Islam in the Caribbean, he felt good about what he did next. He took three running steps in the direction of the harbor and then threw Tran's cell phone as far out into the water as he could.

25

"THE PEOPLE CALL FRANK CARDAMONE."

As Karp stood in front of the prosecution desk and waited for his witness to appear, he turned toward the jury and smiled slightly to let them know he appreciated their patience. His expression didn't change, but he was pleased to see them smile back, or nod, waiting expectantly for him to begin.

Just into the afternoon session of the first day of the Maplethorpe trial, Karp was pleased with the composition—and attentiveness—of the jury. There were seven women, five men—four black, six white, an Asian, and a Puerto Rican—sitting in the jury box with the four alternates seated alongside. But gender and race were not what had mattered to him the week before when he was selecting the jurors.

When Katz asked him what he was looking for in this particular jury, he'd replied, *"The retail shop–owner, small-business types."* He didn't want philosophers or advocates or "big picture" sorts of people; he needed people who got by in life by being careful with the details. They counted nickels and dimes, believed in hard work, and didn't fall for get-rich-quick schemes. *"And they see through bullshitters the minute they walk in the door."*

Anytime somebody enters a small business in New York City,

he told Katz, "*that shopkeeper has two thoughts going through her head. 'Is this person here to buy something, or is he going to rape, rob, and kill me?' They're constantly reading other people, and they know when someone is sincere, or someone is lying to them. If the defense has a righteous case, they see it, but if someone is feeding them the Big Lie, they'll see that as well. But it's a two-way street—we have to read them, too, and see how they're reacting, and understand where they're coming from. Most important, are they comfortable with me as the representative of the People?*"

Karp said that the essential point was that the jurors would evaluate the demeanor of all the witnesses giving testimony. "And that's something you cannot learn from reading the record. Appellate courts won't see it, either. But demeanor evidence—does the witness appear to be telling the truth?—would be very important."

The doors at the back of the courtroom opened and Detective Frank Cardamone entered. The detective reminded Karp of a terrier with his square head, craggy features, and the set of his jaw, and now he looked over the crowd in the courtroom as though he'd like to take a bite out of several of them. Especially the press.

During their strategy sessions, Karp and Katz had discussed the merits of whether to start with the concierge, Hilario "Harry" Gianneschi, or Cardamone, the detective in charge of the case. There was something to be said for either strategy, but in the end, Karp had decided on the detective.

There were facts that he wanted to establish with Cardamone that would then resonate when Gianneschi took the stand. And he thought the concierge's testimony would have more impact when it came immediately after Carmina Salinas's appearance. *Especially the puzzle piece that Stewbie found before he was murdered*, Karp thought.

Cardamone fit right into his plan to keep the prosecution case on a strict diet. He planned to call the detective as his sole law enforcement witness for the crime scene and subsequent investigation.

During the first trial, Stewart Reed had carefully reconstructed the crime scene and detailed the forensic evidence found there by calling to the stand a dozen witnesses—from the first officers on the scene, to the paramedics, to each of the crime scene investigation specialists, to the detectives assigned to the case, including Cardamone. Some of them had spent less time on the stand than it had taken to call them, swear them in, and hear them recite their credentials.

It was a classic way to handle such a case. Leave no stone unturned. Assemble an army to counter the defense's army with victory going to the last man standing. *"But it played to Leonard's strengths and strategy,"* Karp said to Katz, *"by adding to the confusion. This is a simple, straightforward case, which we can make abundantly clear by emphasizing that this was a simple, straightforward crime scene in the eyes of a simple, straightforward detective like Frank."*

Cardamone was a twenty-three-year veteran, a no-nonsense cop whether he was on the streets or sitting on the witness stand. While some police officers and detectives made it a point of trying to "win over" a jury, sometimes with disastrous results, Cardamone played it straight. He could have been the role model for the television detective played by Jack Webb on *Dragnet*, with his just-the-facts-ma'am demeanor. And Karp thought he was perfect for this trial—clear, concise, and unflappable during cross-examination.

Karp fed Cardamone the questions and then stepped back to let the detective state the facts in his concise, unemotional style. Cardamone testified that when he arrived at the scene at the Poliziano Fiera Hotel it had already been secured by the first officers, who'd made sure that nothing was touched or changed. A crime scene photographer was already working, taking photographs "that later comported with my evaluation of the scene when I arrived."

Karp handed Cardamone six crime scene photographs placed inside a three-ring binder. "Are People's Exhibits One through Six, previously marked for identification, some of those photos?"

The detective leafed through the binder carefully and then nodded his head. "Yes, sir."

"Do these photos fairly and accurately represent the scene inside the defendant's apartment as you observed it when you first arrived there?"

"Yes, sir."

"Your Honor, I ask that People's Exhibits One through Six now be admitted into evidence," Karp said. He held up a folder of the same photographs.

"Objection," Leonard said. "There is no reason to submit . . . what? Six, eight, ten photographs? Many of which depict the same thing, just at different angles, particularly of the deceased's body. The number and graphic nature of these photographs is intended only to inflame the jury's emotions."

"Overruled," Rosenmayer replied without waiting for Karp. "We've already been over this pretrial, Counselor, and pared the number down to this. Let's not waste the jury's time by arguing points that have previously been decided; your objection has already been preserved in the record, so let's continue with no further delay."

Couldn't have said it better, Karp thought as he looked back up at Cardamone. "Detective, please describe for the jury what appears in People's Exhibit One."

"This is a photograph of the deceased, looking at her pretty much head-on. As you can see, she is sitting in a large, floral-print chair," the detective said.

The photograph wasn't for the squeamish. Gail Perez sat with her legs akimbo, her arms dangling lifelessly, her head turned slightly to the left, which actually hid the large exit wound on the back left side of her skull.

"Detective, would you please describe what the deceased is wearing," Karp said.

"Well, for starters, she has the strap of a purse around her left shoulder with the purse sitting on her lap."

"As if she intended to leave?"

"Objection!" Leonard came out of his seat with a scowl. "Calls for speculation. Neither the district attorney nor the witness has any idea of whether Miss Perez is coming, going, or just liked to keep a grip on her purse."

"Sustained."

Karp nodded. "Okay, she is sitting in a chair with a purse on her lap, the strap around her shoulder."

"Yes, that's correct."

"Does she appear to be in any state of undress?"

"Objection! What does that matter and how would the witness know?"

Karp shrugged. "It matters because in his opening statement Mr. Leonard speculated that there was quote 'a romantic reason' for Miss Perez's presence in the apartment. I was inquiring if the detective noted what might potentially be evidence to indicate that was true. And as to how the detective would know . . . I'd guess some sort of physical appearance of her clothing—buttons undone, an unclosed zipper—might lend itself to that theory."

"Overruled."

"Thank you, Your Honor," Karp replied. "Detective, would you please answer the question. Does it appear that Miss Perez is in any state of undress that you can see?"

"No."

"No buttons undone? No unclosed zipper? Bra remained fastened?"

"No. No. And yes."

"Is she wearing shoes?"

"Yes."

"What sort of shoes?"

"They appear to be . . . I don't know, I guess you'd call them high heels?"

"So she isn't sitting there, a button or two undone, her shoes kicked off . . ."

"Objection."

"Overruled."

"No, she appears to be completely dressed and is wearing her shoes."

Karp held up Exhibit 2.

"This is a photograph of the deceased from her left side," the detective responded. "The exit wound—that large, bloody area toward the back left of her skull—can be seen."

"And what about Exhibit Three, this photo?"

"A close-up of the side of the deceased's face, the wound clearly visible."

"Detective, have you seen the ballistics report for this case?"

"Yes. I've studied it thoroughly."

"What can you tell us about the trajectory of the bullet?"

"The gun was discharged with the barrel inside the mouth of the deceased. The bullet traveled slightly downward from a roughly central position toward the back left side of the deceased's head."

"And what caliber was this gun?"

"A .45."

"Did investigators recover the weapon?"

"Yes. According to a witness, the defendant was holding—"

"Objection! Is this witness going to be testifying for all the other witnesses, including putting words in their mouths?"

"Sustained."

Karp shrugged. "I'll ask that in a different way. Detective, where was the gun found when police officers took possession of it?"

"It had been placed on the kitchen counter inside the defendant's apartment."

"Was this any particular sort of .45?"

"Yes. A .45 caliber Peacemaker . . . what the general public might think of as a cowboy's gun from the Old West."

"The sort of gun the cowboys and sheriffs and bad guys have in their holsters in Western movies?"

"That's correct."

Karp held up another photograph, People's Exhibit 4. "Would you describe what we're seeing here?"

"Yes," the detective responded. "This photograph was taken from behind the deceased. As you can see, there is a lot of blood that has sprayed somewhat forward and to the young woman's left."

"And this photograph, Exhibit Five?"

"A wall some five feet behind the deceased. The stain on the wall is from blood and brain tissue."

"Was the bullet located?"

"Yes, it was in the wall."

Karp allowed himself to look puzzled. "Detective, can you explain to the jury how it is that there's blood behind, as well as slightly to the front and left of the deceased?"

"Well, yes," Cardamone replied. "The force of the bullet blew a hole in the back of her skull, carrying blood and other tissue with it. However, in passing from front to back it also struck major blood vessels in the back of her throat, causing the deceased to hemorrhage blood forward out of her mouth in the direction her head was turned."

"So her head would have been turning toward the left as the gun discharged?"

"That's correct."

"So the gun goes into her mouth, it discharges, the bullet travels from the center toward the back left side of her skull, which it exits and enters the wall, her head jerks or turns toward the left, and blood hemorrhages out."

"That's pretty much it, yes."

Karp had one more, seemingly innocuous question about a wide-angle photograph, Exhibit 6, that showed most of the death scene—Gail Perez slumped like a life-size doll in the chair, a large stain of blood to her left, an end table on her right.

"Detective, if I can ask you to turn your attention to the table next to Miss Perez," Karp began, "it appears that there is a framed photograph on the table. Do you recall seeing it?"

As he asked his question, Karp turned so that he could see Maplethorpe's reaction, which was to blanch and ball his hands, which had been resting on the table, into fists.

"I remember seeing it," the detective said. "I believe that it was a photograph of the defendant when he was a boy standing with his mother."

"Do you remember anything else about it?" Karp asked.

"Objection," Leonard said. "I don't see the point of this. Are we going to discuss the artwork on the walls as well?"

"Mr. Karp?" the judge asked, clearly puzzled himself.

"Just trying to be thorough, Your Honor, but I'll move on."

Karp turned to Cardamone and asked, "When officers responded to the scene, what was the defendant wearing?"

"He was wearing a button-down shirt and blue jeans."

"And during a search of the apartment, did you and your fellow officers discover a smoking jacket?"

"Yes."

"What, if anything, did you observe on the smoking jacket?"

"There were bloodstains on the right sleeve."

"And where was this bloodstained smoking jacket found?"

"Objection! Your Honor, may we approach the bench?" Leonard asked.

"Certainly," Rosenmayer replied without much enthusiasm, though he gestured to the area in front of him.

When Karp joined him, Leonard whispered angrily, "Mr. Karp is asking this question in order to elicit a response, the sole purpose of which is to insinuate that my client intended to hide something, when the truth of the matter is that in a state of shock, he saw the blood, was appalled, took it off, and tossed it. He wasn't trying to hide anything, but if Mr. Karp is allowed to ask this question, that's what it will look like."

"If I remember correctly from the first trial, the smoking jacket landed under the bed," the judge replied. He then turned to Karp. "So what's your response to Mr. Leonard's assertions?"

Karp shrugged. "It's a simple question as to where evidence was located during a criminal investigation. If Mr. Leonard is so convinced as to what it does or does not 'insinuate,' he's welcome to put his client on the stand and let him say how it got there."

Leonard glared at Karp. "You're trying to force my client to take the stand."

"Oh, I'm sure you can get one of your shrinks to explain Mr. Maplethorpe's thinking when he balled up the jacket and hid it—or accidentally tossed it—under the bed," Karp replied. "It might cost a bit more, but I'd bet any one of them would be willing to render an opinion."

"Gentlemen! Knock it off," Rosenmayer said quietly but forcefully. He then closed his eyes for a moment and sighed. "I'm going to overrule the objection. The location of evidence obtained by the police in a criminal investigation is both relevant and allowable."

Leonard stomped back to his seat, his cowboy boots clomping heavily in disgust. He glanced at the jury as though he expected them to share his disgust, and he shook his head sadly.

Karp looked back up at Detective Cardamone, who had a bemused smile on his rugged features. "Okay, Detective, where was the smoking jacket located?"

"It was under the bed in the master bedroom."

Karp held up a plastic bag containing the smoking jacket and handed it to Detective Cardamone, who examined the contents.

"Is that the smoking jacket you just described?"

"Yes, sir, it is."

"Your Honor, I ask that the smoking jacket, People's Exhibit Seven, be admitted into evidence."

Rosenmayer looked at Leonard. But the defense attorney shook his head and stifled a partial yawn. "No objection. Excuse me, Your Honor, I didn't mean any disrespect, we've been working late hours."

The judge smiled sardonically. "I understand, Counselor. I hope you won't object if Mr. Karp also finds it necessary to yawn at some point in the trial. I'm betting both sides have been burning the midnight oil."

"Now, Detective, would you please describe for the jury the type of bloodstain you see on the jacket, People's Exhibit Seven," Karp asked.

Cardamone held up the right sleeve of the jacket. "I would describe this as flecks of blood."

"Not a large amount?"

"No, not really."

"Not a smear?"

"No, just a few flecks."

"Detective, when you arrived at the apartment, did you notice anything unusual about the pants the defendant was wearing?"

Cardamone arched his eyebrows, as if this was something new, and shook his head. "Not to my knowledge. Just regular old blue jeans."

"Not leather?"

"No, sir. Denim."

"Detective Cardamone, who is Hilario Gianneschi?"

"Hilario Gianneschi, also known as Harry Gianneschi, was working as the concierge at the hotel that night when the defendant called and asked him to come up to his suite. He was the first to see the deceased and Mr. Maplethorpe, who told him—"

"Objection," Leonard said. "Once again, this witness is apparently going to speak for everyone. I might as well let him have my job, too." The courtroom spectators tittered, and Leonard smiled. "But seriously, if this witness, Mr. Gianneschi, is going to testify, why don't we just let him speak for himself?"

"Your Honor," Karp jumped right in, "Detective Cardamone is intimately familiar with all of the witnesses and police reports in this case. His answer does go directly to a follow-up question I have regarding what Mr. Maplethorpe was wearing when police officers arrived, and what he did with clothing he was wearing when Miss Perez died. So I respectfully request that you permit this line of inquiry subject to connection."

"Very well, Mr. Karp, proceed, but make sure you connect later on. You know, I'll be watching," the judge said.

"Thank you, Your Honor," Karp said. "Detective Cardamone, do you recall statements made by Mr. Gianneschi several days after Miss Perez died?"

"Yes. We asked him to come to the precinct to answer a few follow-up questions."

"And during this interview, did Mr. Gianneschi make a statement about the pants that Mr. Maplethorpe was wearing when he arrived at the apartment?"

"Yes."

"And did the defendant describe these pants in his native tongue, which is Italian?"

"Yes."

"And he described this article of clothing as '*pantaloni di cuoio dispari,*' if I'm pronouncing that correctly."

"Not bad," the detective replied. "He said that the defendant was dressed in '*pantaloni di cuoio dispari,*' which means—"

"Objection!" This time Leonard shouted as he rose from his seat. "I don't believe that Detective Cardamone has been qualified in this courtroom as an expert witness in the field of linguistics or as a speaker of Italian. I insist that he be prohibited from acting as either."

The judge looked at Karp and raised his eyebrows. "What say you?"

Instead of answering, Karp turned to Cardamone. "Detective, could you tell the court how you were able to translate this expression?"

"Yeah, my folks are first-generation immigrants from Florence," Cardamone replied. "I was speaking and reading Italian before I put together my first sentence in English."

Leonard snorted loud enough to be heard by everyone in the courtroom. "That's all fine and good," he said. "But we have no idea if he's telling us the truth, or perhaps his Italian has gone downhill, or if his interpretation would be matched by a 'real' expert."

"Your Honor, I submit respectfully that Mr. Cardamone would be considered by any court as an expert in Italian," Karp growled. "He's been speaking it all of his life with his family. If the court would like to conduct a voir dire on that, I certainly would have no objection."

Eyes blazing, Karp continued, "And if Mr. Leonard thinks that I would pull a fast one on this court and this jury, all he has to do is add to his assembly line of highly paid experts to attest to the alleged inaccuracy of Mr. Cardamone's interpretation."

Karp stopped and stared at Rosenmayer. The judge sat back in his chair, staring back at Karp, then addressed Leonard. "Mr. Leonard, I believe we heard a challenge. I will allow this evidence and permit you to call an expert, well-paid or otherwise, to refute Detective Cardamone's translation, if you deem it necessary. So, Mr. Leonard, your objection is overruled."

"Thank you, Your Honor," Karp replied. *And thank you, Mr. Leonard, for helping me make the jury curious about the interpretation of* 'pantaloni di cuoio dispari.'

Karp then asked Cardamone what the phrase meant.

"It means 'strange or crazy leather pants,'" the detective said.

Karp then ended his questioning of Cardamone by asking about the medical examiner's autopsy report.

"Detective, was there any evidence of drugs or excessive alcohol in the victim's system?"

"Her blood alcohol content was within the legal limit for

operating a car in the state of New York," Cardamone answered. "Otherwise, there was ibuprofen—a mild, over-the-counter pain medication—but no other detected drugs."

"No prescription medication for depression or anxiety?"

"None."

"How about cocaine, heroin, or methamphetamine?"

"Nope."

"Marijuana?"

The detective shook his head. "Not a trace. And marijuana leaves a detectable residue for thirty days."

Karp's entire direct examination of Detective Cardamone took less than an hour. But Leonard spent twice that long nitpicking at every little detail of the investigation and Cardamone's testimony.

The defense attorney ended his cross-examination by asking the detective, "Can you tell us beyond any doubt that Gail Perez *did not* place a gun in her mouth and pull the trigger?"

"Yes, sir," the detective replied. "It's not my job to speculate about the facts of a case when the evidence demonstrates beyond any doubt that the defendant blew Miss Perez away."

Karp had to hide his smile at the detective's clever shot at Leonard's trial strategy. *Touché, Frank.*

Leonard virtually leaped out of his boots and shouted at Judge Rosenmayer. "I move to strike the witness's statements as totally not responsive and self-serving, and I make a formal motion right here and now to dismiss this case!"

Rosenmayer leaned over the bench. "Oh no, Mr. Leonard, the record will reflect that Detective Cardamone couldn't have been more spot-on in answering your question. Be careful, Mr. Leonard, when you open a door, sometimes it shuts rather abruptly. Now, would you like to explore just how Detective Cardamone came to his conclusion?"

Leonard offered a faltering smile and dismissively muttered, "I have no further questions of this man."

26

The pretty young Hispanic woman on the witness stand wiped her tears and blew her nose. She was obviously having a difficult time getting her emotions under control as Karp stood patiently next to the lectern between the stand and jury box.

After Cardamone stepped down from the witness stand, Rosenmayer had called for the afternoon break. When they returned, Karp had called Gail Perez's sister, Tina, to take the stand, but he'd only made it through the first series of questions before she started to cry.

Come on, Tina, I need you to pull it together, he thought. Whereas Frank Cardamone was the prosecution's sole representative of the police investigation, Tina Perez was there as his only voice for her sister's character.

Prior to the trial, Karp had explained to Katz that normally, having to retry a case worked against the prosecution more than it did the defense. During a first trial, the defense got to see the entire prosecution case, learning its weak points, which it could attempt to exploit the second time around.

"That's when the defense has a legitimate case, including real evidence to suggest reasonable doubt," he'd said. *"However, when the defense doesn't have a legitimate case—as in this instance—and*

is relying solely on something like the Big Lie, we get to see their strategy."

After reading the transcripts of the witness testimony, Karp had decided to pare all the character witnesses down to just Tina Perez. The question now as she sipped from a cup of water that Karp had poured for her was whether she could hold it together, or if he'd be forced to call other character witnesses.

"Are you ready to proceed, Miss Perez?" he asked gently.

"Yes, sir. Thank you . . . it's still hard," she said apologetically. "I miss her."

"I understand completely, Miss Perez," Karp replied. "And I'm sorry to put you through this. We were discussing your sister's childhood, and you told the jurors that she was a happy kid, full of energy, and that as she grew up, she looked out for you—her kid sister—especially after your parents passed away. I'd like to turn now to her career. How important was it to your sister, Gail, to—and I quote—'be a star' on Broadway?"

A pretty brunette with her sister's green eyes, Tina tilted her head to the side and thought about the question for a moment. "Even in high school, she'd work two or three jobs so that she could afford acting classes and voice lessons. And starting somewhere around her senior year, she went to every casting call she could sneak into. Even if she knew that she wouldn't get a part, she went anyway for the experience. . . . I remember the first time she got a role that paid a little bit of money, she was so thrilled."

"How old was she?" Karp asked.

"Maybe twenty-one or twenty-two."

"Were there other paying parts after that?"

Tina nodded her head emphatically. "Nothing big, but quite a few, plus she started to get some modeling work."

"Your sister was a beautiful woman," Karp stated.

"Yes, she was very beautiful, inside and out."

Karp picked up a "glamour shot" of Gail Perez and handed it to Tina. "Miss Perez, does People's Exhibit Eight, marked for identification, fairly and accurately represent a so-called modeling photograph of your sister, the deceased, Gail Perez?"

Holding the photograph with both hands, Tina nodded her head and stifled a sob. "Yes, it is."

"Your Honor, I ask that this photograph, People's Exhibit Eight, be received in evidence," Karp said.

Rosenmayer looked over at Leonard, who waved his hand without looking up from a document he was reading. "No objection."

Karp handed the photograph to the jury foreman and then turned back to the witness stand. "Miss Perez, did your sister ever become a 'big star' on Broadway?"

Tina shook her head. "No. Mostly smaller parts, but with that and her modeling, she paid the bills, and she loved what she was doing."

"Did she ever seem down about only getting the small parts . . . not being a star?"

"Well, there was a time, especially when she was starting out, when she'd complain that someone got a role she felt that she should have had," Tina replied. "She said some girls would do anything . . . you know, sexual . . . to get a part."

"Was your sister one of those girls?" Karp asked.

The reaction was exactly as he'd hoped and why he'd sprung it on her without warning. Tina's eyes flashed with anger and her voice tightened as she looked hard at the defense table. "No. Never. She told me there wasn't a part that was worth her self-respect."

"Did losing parts to those other women bring her down?"

"Like I said, at first she complained. But later on, she figured that at least she was working onstage when most girls who have the same dream never make it past auditions. She was okay with it, and was even talking about getting her certificate so she could teach drama in high school or maybe a community college."

"Miss Perez, how often did you and your sister talk?"

"Pretty much every day," Tina replied. "After Mom died of breast cancer in 1988, Dad only lasted a few more years before he just went to sleep one night and never woke up. We figured it was a broken heart . . . and maybe the cigarettes. After that, it was just me . . ." The young woman's voice cracked and she had to stop. "I'm sorry . . ."

"That's okay," Karp said. As he turned away to allow her a few moments to compose herself, he noted that several of the jurors were dabbing at their eyes, too. "Take your time."

"Thank you," Tina replied at last. "Anyway, it was just me and Gail. We were sisters and best friends. We talked all the time, even when I went away to school at Smith College in Northampton, Massachusetts."

"Wow, that's an expensive private college, isn't it?" Karp asked as if surprised, though he'd intended to bring it up.

"It is," Tina replied. "But I got scholarships for part of it—Gail was real tough on me about getting good grades in high school—and she paid the rest."

"So your sister was earning enough to pay her bills, and some of yours," Karp said.

"Yes. She always took care of me."

Karp nodded and checked something off on the legal pad he kept at the lectern. "You said you talked nearly every day. What would you talk about?"

"Everything." Tina smiled. "Work, boys—or I should say men—homework, dreams . . . everything."

"Did she keep secrets from you? Maybe things she didn't want to worry you about?"

Tina shook her head. "No. Well, maybe when I was younger, and we'd just lost Mom and then Dad. She had a lot of responsibility on her shoulders back then, and she just wanted me to do well in school and be happy. But especially after a little time had passed, we talked about everything. And if she was down about something, she'd tell me and we'd deal with it."

"Was she down often?"

Again, Tina shook her head. "No. You really had to know her, but she was always an upbeat sort of person, very outgoing. If you met her, you'd never forget her. But if she didn't get a part she really wanted, or some jerk dumped her, she'd call me and we'd have a good sister cry, but even that usually ended with us laughing about 'idiot men and *bastardos*.'"

"Do you think you would have known if she was suffering from a mental issue, such as clinical depression?" Karp asked.

"Absolutely," Tina replied. "To be honest, I take a small dose of Xanax for anxiety. We talked a lot about it after a doctor prescribed it for me, Gail did a lot of research on the Internet, and we decided it might help."

"Do you know if your sister took any prescription medication for anxiety or depression or any other mental illness?"

"I know she didn't because we discussed it when she took me to the doctor to see why I was having such a hard time. He asked her if she was taking anything, and she said no, that she didn't need it."

"Miss Perez, turning to the day your sister died . . ."

"Yes."

"Did you talk to her?"

"I called her that morning before I went to school."

"Did she say anything about her plans?"

"She said she was having dinner that night with some big producer who was going to talk to her about a possible role in his new show."

"Did she name this producer?"

"No. Or if she did, it went in one ear and out the other."

"Was she excited?"

"Very."

"So excited that if later that night, after dinner, she went back to this producer's apartment and learned that he only wanted to have sex with her—"

"Objection! That is a mischaracterization of my client intended to paint him in an unfavorable light."

Karp turned to the judge and said, "I'd refer Mr. Leonard to his opening statement, where he all but accused Gail Perez of offering sex for a role in the defendant's musical and that the defendant's only interest, according to Mr. Leonard, was 'romantic,' which I'm taking to mean didn't include sending flowers."

The judge nodded. "You opened that door also, Mr. Leonard; I'll allow it."

Karp looked back at Tina Perez. "If your sister was so excited about the possibility of getting this part, only to learn that Mr. Maplethorpe just wanted to have sex and that she was not being considered, would she have made the effort to locate Mr. Maplethorpe's gun, stick it in her mouth, and then shoot herself?"

"*Never!*" Tina Perez shouted, before calming herself. "That's ridiculous. She'd lost out on big parts before; it's part of that business. And Maplethorpe wouldn't have been the first loathsome little man to use the opportunity for a big role to try to get in her pants."

Leonard jumped to his feet, sputtering with indignation. "I'll ask that the witness's last remarks be stricken from the record. The sole purpose of this line of questioning is the character assassination of my client."

Up to this point, Karp had kept his cool and let the defense attorney run his mouth. But now he roared back. "If there is any character assassination going on in this courtroom, Mr. Leonard, I would suggest that you and your client look in the mirror!"

Rosenmayer had heard enough and banged his gavel down three times in quick succession. "That's enough!" he thundered. "Gentlemen, approach the bench!"

With Karp and Leonard standing in front of him, the judge glared from one man to the other. "You are both experienced, extremely capable professionals, and you know better than to engage in this sort of extraneous hyperbole," he said in a low, stern voice meant only for their ears. "I want you to knock it off and avoid repeating this sort of crap, or I'll toss the offender in jail so fast that two hours later his skull will still be waiting for his brain to show up. Am I clear?"

"Yes, sir," both attorneys answered as one.

"Good, then, Mr. Leonard, I'm denying your request that Miss Perez's comments be stricken, so let's resume and carry on like the gentlemen I know you both to be," the judge warned.

Karp walked to the prosecution table, where he stood facing Katz. "That was fun," he said in a voice barely audible to his co-counsel.

"Twenty lashes with a cat-o'-nine?" Katz joked. Conscious of the judge's continuing glare, he managed to avoid smiling as he spoke, though his eyes twinkled with merriment.

"Worth every stripe," Karp replied with a wink, and turned back to the witness stand.

"Miss Perez, I believe I asked you if not getting a part would have been enough for your sister to want to kill herself, and you responded in the negative. So if someone was to describe your sister as some pathetic, washed-up actress-wannabe who would whore herself for a chance to be a star . . . and was so unstable and desperate—as well as apparently vindictive—that she would end her life in the apartment of a man she hardly knew, what would be your response?"

Tina looked beyond Karp to where Maplethorpe was sitting, perched forward at the defense table as if preparing to jump up and object like a lawyer. But her gaze froze him and he had to look down and away. "I would say he was a liar," she replied icily.

Karp walked back to the prosecution table. "Your Honor, I have one more photograph, People's Exhibit Nine, that I would like to have admitted into evidence."

"I don't remember this photograph." Leonard frowned as Karp handed it to him.

"We received it only today when Miss Perez brought it to us," Karp replied. "She said it's how she wants people to remember her sister. It depicts Gail Perez onstage in a production of *Annie Get Your Gun*."

Guy Leonard looked shocked. "A photograph of a woman who killed herself with a gun, holding a gun? I hardly think that's appropriate for a jury to consider as evidence, and I object to its inclusion."

Judge Rosenmayer looked puzzled as he twisted his lips into a pucker, before adding, "It does seem a bit odd, Mr. Karp."

"I understand, Your Honor," Karp replied. "Notwithstanding that it's a beautiful photograph of a lovely young woman singing as her eyes look upward, I actually have a more pedestrian purpose for asking that it be included."

"And what is that, Mr. Karp?"

"Actually, my purpose has more to do with a particular fact about this photograph having to do with a question I am about to ask Miss Perez about her sister," Karp continued.

For perhaps the first time in the trial, the judge laughed. "Everyone loves a good mystery, Mr. Karp, but you're going to have to be a bit more forthcoming than that." He motioned for the photograph, which Karp retrieved from Leonard and handed to Rosenmayer. "Why don't you ask your question, and then I'll rule on whether to admit the photograph," he said with a sly smile.

Karp returned the smile with a small bow. "Fair enough. Miss Perez, was your sister left-handed?"

"She was," Tina replied slowly, as if wondering where he was going with this. "My mom used to tell her that it made her special, so I used to try to do things left-handed, though I'm naturally right-handed."

Karp turned to the judge and said, "Your Honor, in the photograph Gail Perez is pointing a gun in the air as she sings. I'd like the jury to see the photograph that corroborates Tina Perez's testimony that her sister was left-handed."

"Does that matter, Mr. Karp?" Rosenmayer asked.

"Oh, I believe so, Your Honor." Karp nodded. "And I intend to demonstrate that to the jury."

"I'll allow it. The record will reflect that this photograph is received in evidence as . . . Mr. Karp, what number are we up to?"

"People's Exhibit Nine, Your Honor."

"Very well, you may show the witness the photograph and then distribute it to the jury."

"Thank you, Your Honor," Karp said, and did just that. As he walked from the jury box back toward the witness stand, he asked, "Miss Perez, what hand is your sister holding the gun in?"

"Her left," Tina replied.

"Was it common for her to use her left hand more than her right?"

"She did everything left-handed . . . wrote, drew . . ." Tina suddenly laughed. "And pulled my hair when she was mad at me."

Karp laughed with the rest of the courtroom. "I have a couple of boys like that," he said as he turned to the defense table. "No further questions, Your Honor."

Leonard seemed subdued when he began his cross-examination of Tina Perez, which disappointed Karp, who'd hoped that he would start off by harassing a young woman with whom the jurors were obviously empathetic.

"Miss Perez, you told the jury that you are living in Northampton, which is what, five hours' drive from Manhattan?"

"Yes, about five hours by car," Tina replied.

"And I take it that going to school, you spend most of your time there."

"That's correct. I try to come home pretty often, but it's expensive and we are . . . we were . . . both pretty busy."

"So at such a distance, and leading busy, active lives that kept you physically apart, isn't it possible that things were going on in your sister's life that she didn't want to bother you with?"

"Like what?" Tina scowled.

"Like losing roles to other actresses," he said. "Or getting older in what we all know is a young person's game . . . especially for women."

"Actually, she was working more now than in her twenties," Tina said defensively.

"Still, isn't it fair," Leonard retorted, "to say that if a woman doesn't 'make it' by a certain age, it's tougher to get a job than it is for a man of the same age?"

"I've heard that's true," Tina agreed. "But Gail was okay with getting older and maybe fewer roles in the future. I think she was hoping to find somebody to settle down with and maybe move on . . . teach drama."

"But still . . ." Leonard said, holding up a finger as if trying to make a point in a debate. "Still, there's that hope: 'If I can just get a break, I'll show them I can be a star. It's not too late.' And if you hold on to that dream . . . after all those acting classes, and voice lessons, and working menial jobs just to pay the rent . . . and put up with all those auditions and the unfairness of people with less talent getting the roles you—"

Karp objected. "Mr. Leonard is making speeches, not asking questions. Maybe he could get to the point."

"Sustained. Mr. Leonard, a question please."

"Certainly, Your Honor," Leonard replied. "I like to think of what I was saying as adding context, but I'll move on to my question. Miss Perez, did you talk to your sister the night she died?"

"No, I spoke to her that morning."

"So you had no firm idea of what was going through her mind at approximately eleven that night?"

"I know she wouldn't have been thinking about killing herself."

"Really?" Leonard said as if surprised. "Miss Perez, have you ever attempted to kill yourself?"

"Objection," Karp said, rising to his feet. The alarm bells were starting to go off in his head. "It's one thing for Mr. Leonard to put Gail Perez on trial, and another to dig into the personal life of Tina Perez."

"I'll allow it," Rosenmayer said. "But get to the point quickly, Mr. Leonard."

"I will if Miss Perez will answer the question, Miss Perez," Leonard replied, moving toward the witness stand until he was only a foot or so away.

Tina Perez looked down at her lap. "No."

"No?" Leonard said as he held up a paper. "I have here a medical record from the medical clinic at Smith College that says you were admitted two months before your sister took her own life due to an overdose of Xanax and alcohol."

"Objection!" Karp yelled, leaping to his feet. "Medical records are confidential and can only be obtained with consent or a warrant from the court. I'd like Mr. Leonard to produce either before he starts waving confidential records around and discussing personal medical history. The witness is not on trial here . . . or isn't supposed to be."

"Mr. Leonard, do you have a court order, or Miss Perez's permission, to possess her confidential medical file?" Rosenmayer scowled.

"It was slipped under the door of our law office when we arrived at work this morning," Leonard claimed.

"How convenient," Karp retorted. "Your Honor, I'm going to object to this document and ask that the jury be instructed to ignore everything that has been said about it or Miss Perez."

"Sustained," Rosenmayer said angrily. "Mr. Leonard, please surrender that document to my clerk as well as any copies or other documents that fall under anyone's right to privacy."

"Your Honor, it is not our fault that this document—"

"You heard me, Mr. Leonard!" the judge demanded.

Leonard bowed. "Of course, Your Honor." He then made a show of handing the medical report to the clerk. Then he turned to the judge and asked as though nothing had happened, "May I resume my cross-examination?"

Rosenmayer glared at Leonard and looked like he might say something, but then thought better of it and nodded. "Yes, Mr. Leonard, but beware, you are on thin ice."

"I'll remember that, Your Honor," Leonard said before whirling to face Tina Perez again. "So Miss Perez, I'll ask you one more time, have you ever tried to commit suicide?"

Tina Perez looked from Karp to Leonard and shrugged. "You just read that to everyone. But it's not what it seems. I was homesick, and my boyfriend had just dumped me for another girl back home, I started drinking and wasn't thinking clearly . . ."

"Objection," Karp said, this time coming to his feet. "He's using the medical record to question the witness. It might as well have been admitted into evidence!"

Leonard shrugged. "I didn't say anything about the record. In fact, I returned to a question I asked before there was any mention of a record. It is the witness who just referred to this record *after* I was required to hand it over to the court. How can I be blamed for what your witness said?"

Karp didn't answer except by turning to the judge. "Your Honor, Mr. Leonard's protestations of innocence to the contrary, he knows what he was doing, and I ask that you prohibit this line of questioning."

Rosenmayer looked from lawyer to lawyer and then shook his head. "We're watching a couple of pro tennis players here, folks," he said. "This time, Mr. Karp, I have to overrule you. I know what he did, too, but he did it cleverly. Mr. Leonard, you may ask your question again."

"Thank you, Your Honor, I appreciate the analogy," Leonard said with a smile. Then his face hardened as he turned back to the witness stand. "Miss Perez, please!" he scolded. "Did you try to kill yourself?"

"No . . . not really . . . maybe that's what I was thinking, but not what I wanted," she tried to explain. "It was an accident."

"People who unsuccessfully attempt suicide often say things like that," Leonard said. "My question to you now is: did your sister know you were thinking about killing yourself at that time?"

Tina shook her head. "Of course not. She only found out later when the hospital called her."

Leonard backed up as if he scored a major point in the debate and then drew himself up to his full height as he turned to the jury. "So even though you talked to your sister pretty much every day—about everything—the evening you overdosed on pills and booze, you did not tell her you were contemplating suicide."

Tina Perez bit her trembling lip. "That's correct."

"Then isn't it possible that you wouldn't have known if your sister was contemplating suicide on the night she died?"

"I don't believe that."

"I'm not asking you what you believe, Miss Perez. I'm asking you, given what you just told us about your own experience with this, isn't it possible your sister may not have given you any warning either?"

Tina Perez sighed and then began to cry quietly. "I suppose it's possible."

Leonard glanced over at Karp, his mouth twisted into a triumphant half smile. "Thank you. No further questions."

"My bad," Kenny apologized as he bit into one of the meat knishes Darla Milquetost had sent a law clerk to buy from a vendor in the park across Centre Street. "Tina Perez was my responsibility to re-interview, and I missed it."

"Missed what?" Karp asked.

"The suicide thing," Katz said. "But I asked her if she'd ever attempted it and she said no."

"Just like the first time she was asked by Leonard," Karp noted. "You heard her, it was an accident; she doesn't see it as a suicide attempt because she didn't really want to die. But Leonard had the benefit of some sleazeball getting him that medical record—and I hope she sues his ass later. Anyway, lesson learned."

"Thanks, boss. I'll do better next time. What was that about being left-handed?" Katz asked.

Karp grinned. His young ADA protégé was not part of the preparations involving the Medical Examiner's Office and the cause-of-death issues because they'd seemed so self-evident. "I'm going to let you think about it in light of what else we know. Get back to me."

"Oh yes, Zen Master Karp." Katz laughed as he wiped a stray bit of yellow mustard from his mouth. He pulled an apple out of his briefcase, which had belonged to Stewart Reed, and bit into it. "Are you going to try to get the cowboy picture in now?"

Karp wiggled his eyebrows. "You betcha," he said.

The "cowboy picture" was the framed photograph that Karp had noted in the crime scene photographs he'd asked Detective Frank Cardamone about. It was the same photograph that had been in Stewart Reed's briefcase with the sticky note that said "*pantaloni di cuoio dispari*."

"*Well,* 'dispari' *means 'odd' or 'strange' and* 'pantaloni di cuoio' *are leather pants,*'" Marlene had told him when he came home that night from the Reeds' house in Queens. "*Kind of a strange way of saying it. What was he trying to get at? Maplethorpe was wearing tight leather pants? Or maybe he was wearing buttless pants with his ass hanging out.*"

Karp had laughed about his wife's description and didn't think about it until he looked again later at the photograph of young Maplethorpe standing with his mother. "*I still have a copy of the photograph in the file; he's all dressed up like a little cowboy,*" Stewbie had noted at that meeting before he died. And that's when Karp noticed the chaps. The boy in the photograph was wearing play versions of chaps worn by real cowboys.

Everyone had missed it. Whoever the police used to interpret the expression for the transcript of the interview had simply noted "leather pants" and left it at that. At the first trial, Gianneschi had been asked if Maplethorpe was wearing leather pants when the concierge arrived at the apartment. He'd replied yes, but no one asked him about the type of leather pants.

"But what if he meant that Maplethorpe was wearing leather chaps when he pulled out his cowboy six-shooter . . . and next thing you know, Gail Perez is dead," Karp said to Katz when they were discussing the photograph later.

"Maybe I'm dense here," Katz replied, *"but where are you going with this?"*

"Not sure yet," Karp said with a shrug. *"Maybe Maplethorpe was into some kinky costumed sex act involving leather and guns?"*

"Okay, so he's into the S&M cowboy crowd, probably not so unusual with the theater set. But it helps our case how . . . ?"

Karp made a few notes on a yellow legal pad and then said, *"Well, if our argument is that Maplethorpe may not have intended to kill Gail Perez that evening, but his reckless behavior created the circumstances that led to him shooting her, maybe role-playing figures in."*

"I'm pretty familiar with the evidence seized at the house, but I don't remember any leather chaps," Katz said.

"They didn't know to look for them," Karp said. *"I'm sure they searched for any clothing with bloodstains, and they found the smoking jacket under the bed. But what if Maplethorpe put the chaps away? Obviously, he's a clotheshorse and the cops executing the search warrant wouldn't have confiscated something unless they had a reason to."*

"Nobody put it together until Stewbie saw that photograph, which Leonard submitted as part of a strategy in case they went for an insanity defense. Apparently, there is something about that photograph that set Maplethorpe off."

Katz looked sideways at Karp. *"The Water Pitcher Incident?"*

"The same," Karp agreed.

"You old fox! Are you going to bait Maplethorpe by getting the photograph admitted now?"

Karp grinned. *"The thought's crossed my mind. But there's more to it than just trying to get under Maplethorpe's skin."*

"The role-playing."

"You got it. And I think Stewbie did, too. His last official act in this case was to ask Judge Rosenmayer for a search warrant on Maplethorpe's apartment. His request was very narrow; he said he would be looking for 'leather pants, leather chaps.' And that was it."

"So what's the next step?"

"I want to talk to Hilario Gianneschi. And I'm taking the photograph."

27

"I THINK I'M GOING TO BE SICK."

Tran peered over at Jojola in the dim lighting beneath the tarpaulin covering the lifeboat where they'd holed up three days earlier. They were hungry—having eaten only a partial loaf of stale bread and a can of sardines Tran had managed to swipe from the ship's kitchen late the second night. There'd been plenty to drink with the rainwater that seeped in under the cover during frequent squalls, but the rain also made them cold.

The worst part, however, had been the cramped quarters of the lifeboat. At least that was the worst part for Tran.

The seasickness was what was getting to Jojola. Even in the partial illumination of a deck light several yards away, the Indian's usual bronze-hued face had a greenish cast to it. "Don't even think about it," Tran warned. "It already stinks in here from the last time. . . . I thought you Native Americans were supposed to be tough. You get seasick like some child."

"You might recall," Jojola groaned, "if your senior dementia hasn't robbed you of all your faculties, that my people live in an arid climate. The biggest body of water we had until whitey showed up and started putting up reservoirs in the desert were rivers you could throw rocks across. And the land didn't go up and down under your feet like a fat man's belly. We're not doing much good here, either, so Jaxon can show up any moment as far as I'm concerned. I wonder when the cavalry's going to arrive."

"Me, too," Tran agreed. Ever since they'd come aboard, they'd done little more than hide. The reefer wasn't a large craft, nor did she seem to have a very large crew from what little Tran and Jojola had been able to gather by sneaking around after dark. There weren't that many unsecured places they could hide, and the crew was certain to notice any strangers among them.

Perhaps, as a Trojan horse, they'd be of use when Jaxon and the U.S. Navy caught up to the ship. But right now the only thing they could do was stay out of sight.

Tran guessed that somewhere beyond the horizon or in the skies overhead, they were being tracked by U.S. Navy vessels and aircraft. "They're probably waiting for Malovo and Abdullah to tip their hand as to what they intend, or possibly setting a trap for other conspirators," he said.

"Well, then I wish they'd all—bad guys and good guys—hurry up," Jojola replied. "I don't have anything left in my stomach, or I'd already have lost it. But one more set of swells like that last one, and I'm going to puke my guts up through my nose."

"Nice imagery," Tran said, disgusted. "And I think medically impossible."

As if to further Jojola's torment, the ship's engines, which had been turning over at a dull roar since leaving Trinidad, suddenly shuddered and labored at a much slower pace. The ship began to wallow.

"That does it," Jojola complained, "I'm giving myself up so they can put me out of my misery."

"They'll put us both out of our misery, now hush," Tran said, and held still as he listened. After a moment, he nodded. "We've definitely slowed, which is why the ship is rocking more."

"I'd rather have my fingernails pulled out."

"That can be arranged when we get back home. Right now, something's up."

"How do you know?"

"We're in the middle of the ocean, not even close to land judging by the direction and size of the swells, but we're slowing down on purpose," Tran replied.

Jojola didn't question how he figured this out. Tran knew his way around ships. First as a "boat person" fleeing Vietnam after the triumphant North Vietnamese began purging former Viet Cong guerrillas from the country. And later as a "successful businessman in the import-export trade" with his own fleet of ships.

"Maybe this is what their plan is all about," Tran said. "I'm going to go check it out."

"I'm coming, too," Jojola said. "I can use the fresh air."

The two men slipped out from under the tarp. But Jojola wobbled and then sat down heavily on the steel deck.

Tran knelt next to him. "You're not going anywhere," he said. "Do you still have your knife?"

Jojola nodded. They'd been prevented from carrying guns in Trinidad, as they were only supposed to be there as observers assisting the national security agency's antiterrorism teams. But the Indian had keep his long, razor-sharp fighting knife tucked in a sheath behind his broad back.

"Good. Then wait here. Get some air, but stay out of sight."

With that, the Vietnamese gangster stood and disappeared. He worked his way forward from the stern, where the lifeboat was stowed, and over to the port side, where he saw crew members hurrying about in the dark.

Whatever they were preparing for, they were hampered by heavy seas and a light rain. He noticed that they kept staring out over the waves. But if they could see something, he couldn't make it out from farther back in the shadows of the superstructure.

Suddenly, Tran found himself bathed in a dazzling bright light that blazed out of the night. At the same time, lights from the reefer illuminated the massive shape that rode on the waves thirty yards away.

Tran actually jumped back as the sudden materializing of the supertanker made it appear that the small cargo ship was about to be squashed like a bug. But he quickly realized that the tanker was running parallel to the smaller reefer and maintaining a constant distance. Instead of a collision course, it was more like a mother elephant running alongside her calf. It was not until he saw the mother's "trunk" reaching out of the dark that he started to catch on to what was happening.

We're refueling? he wondered. *But we just left Trinidad.*

For a moment a swell lifted the reefer up to where he got a better view of the behemoth across the water. He saw the four domelike structures jutting out of the main deck of the bigger ship and his mind made the next leap. *It's an LNG tanker. We're taking on liquefied natural gas. I've got to find a way to let Jaxon—*

Tran's thoughts were interrupted by the feel of steel pressed to the back of his head and a woman's voice.

"We meet again, Azahari Mujahid, or whatever your real name is," Malovo sneered. "Now put your hands on the wall while my man frisks you."

Standing outside on the flying bridge, Ariadne Stupenagel gazed in amazement at the LNG supertanker as it plunged up and down through the heavy seas in tandem with the smaller ship. She stumbled a little and her guard, a young Sudanese man named Ebenezer, reached out to steady her. She was still wearing her Gucci heels, having complained to her captors that "if I have to die, a girl wants to go well dressed."

"Thank you, Eb," she said with a shy smile. He started to smile in return but then remembered his duty as a jihadi, and frowned as he stepped back and lifted the nose of the MAC-10 submachine gun.

"So what's a good-looking holy warrior like you doing in a place like this?" she asked.

Ebenezer backed farther away. "Do not speak to me, woman," he demanded, though his teenage voice lacked authority.

They both turned to look when the hatch opened from the main bridge below. The scarred, bearded face of Omar Abdullah appeared, followed by the rest of his body, as soon as he saw the coast was clear.

"Couldn't resist another look, big boy?" Stupenagel said in her best Mae West impersonation.

Abdullah scowled and spoke to Ebenezer. "Leave us."

"Uh, don't I have any say in this?" Stupenagel continued. "I was sort of getting attached to Eb. You know how I like younger men."

Abdullah's eyes blazed. "You're a witch and a whore. But soon you will answer to Allah for your sins."

"What about yours? The last I remember, you were comparing my fine white ass to the moon over the Caribbean on a warm summer night." She winked at Ebenezer, who'd stopped to listen to the exchange with his mouth hanging open. "Bet you didn't know the Big O here was such a poet, did ya, Eb? Yep, he tended to wax rather enthusiastically when he was boinkin' this fine little piece of infidel booty."

"I said go below!" Abdullah yelled at the young man, who jumped and ran for the hatch. He then turned to the journalist. "You bewitched me once before, but never again."

"Bewitched, my ass," Stupenagel scoffed. "You were just as horny as I was. And you know what, Omar? What we had there, for a little while, was pretty good. Of course, that was back when you laughed and enjoyed life, even with the Soviets breathing down your neck. Back then you believed in something other than the deaths of innocent women and children."

"I believed in Allah then as I do now."

"Bullshit! You believed in Allah and the rightness of a cause to keep a small country from falling into the hands of a totalitarian regime. I remember how you used to talk about returning to Trinidad someday and running for parliament. You said you'd had enough of war and wanted to create a Muslim state through peaceful means."

"The world changed."

"Really? Or was it you who changed? Don't you remember watching the moon rise over the Panjshir Valley, wrapped in our little sheepskin blankets?"

Abdullah's eyes softened for a moment, but then they hardened, even angrier than before. "Silence! Yes, I've changed. That man you knew was filled with evil desires and had lost the way of Allah. The Soviets taught me in their torture chamber that I needed to purify myself and understand that women only weaken the resolve of a mujahedeen. And so I see you as you really are now . . . a demon in the body of a woman sent to distract me from my true calling. But Allah has sent you to me again so that you can join me on my final voyage, and we will both be cleansed in the holy fire of Allah."

"What?" Stupenagel exclaimed. "I thought this was one of those Caribbean booze cruises. It's a Muslim crew? No wonder I can't get a drink."

"Enough with the stupid jokes!" Abdullah snarled and motioned to the hatch. "Go below. We've caught your associate and it's time the two of you were reunited."

Tran fell painfully to his knees, unable to catch himself because his wrists were bound behind him, when his guards shoved him through the door and onto the bridge. He got back up on his own and was then shoved against a bulkhead, where he watched the crew and officers who were occupied with the delicate operation of fueling at sea. He noted that while most of the crew and even officers of the ship appeared to be Middle Eastern or black, the man at the helm was a Caucasian.

Stepping onto the bridge, Malovo saw his glance and explained. "Allow me to introduce Sasha Sukarov, an officer in the navy of the once glorious Soviet Union. He was executive officer of a fuel tanker and an expert at this sort of procedure. His counterpart on board the tanker is also former Soviet navy. They make more money now, eh, Sasha?"

Sukarov grinned at Malovo. "*Da*, lot more money," he said before returning his attention to business.

Malovo stepped in front of Tran and slapped him hard across the face. "That's for ruining my plans and nearly getting me killed last September," she said. During the attack on the New York Stock Exchange, she had been in charge of destroying the NYSE backup computer in a high-security building in Brooklyn. However, she'd been thwarted at the last minute by Tran—who'd been posing as the terrorist named Azahari Mujahid—Jojola, and her former lover-turned-archenemy Ivgeny Karchovski.

"Pleasure to have been of service," Tran replied, spitting out the blood he tasted in his mouth.

Malovo stepped closer until her face was just a few inches from Tran's. "So what are you, Chinese?"

"Don't be insulting," Tran replied. "I'm Vietnamese."

Malovo laughed. "Excuse me, Vietnamese. But then you subhuman Asians all look alike to me. Speaking of subhuman, where's your friend, Abu Samar?" she asked, referring to Jojola's alias during the NYSE incident.

Tran shrugged. "He's not so good with ships; he gets seasick. I left him in Trinidad."

"I take it he's not Vietnamese," Malovo said. "What was he? Pakistani? Indonesian?"

"American Indian."

Malovo looked surprised. "You mean like in cowboy movies? I love cowboy movies, especially Indians on the warpath." She patted her mouth and mimicked a war dance. "Woo-woo-woo-woo!"

"Yeah, that kind of Indian," Tran said. "And the next time you two meet, he told me he's going to take your scalp with that wicked long knife of his. Just like in the movies. . . . Hey, do you think it might hurt?"

Malovo's smile twitched and her eyes wavered, but just for a moment and then she scoffed. "The Americans must be getting desperate recruiting old Chinamen and fat Indians to fight terrorism."

"No, they just didn't figure you were worth wasting the time of their best agents." Tran shrugged apologetically. "So they sent me. Sorry, that has to be bad for the ego."

"Ha, that is a good one." Malovo laughed. "And the woman . . . Stupid-neegel . . . who pretends to be a journalist!"

"She is a journalist."

Malovo sneered. "She's an American spy just like you. We know all about the two of you sneaking on board. In fact, here she is now."

Tran turned in the direction Malovo pointed and saw Ariadne coming down the ladder from the flying bridge. He thought quickly. *The two of us? They must not know about Jojola.*

Tran shrugged. "Hello, partner," he said pointedly to Stupenagel. "I guess they've got us." He turned back to Malovo. "You do realize that our people know where we are, and you might as well give up.

Make this easy and we'll put in a good word for you with the executioner to make it quick."

Malovo smirked. "Did I forget to tell you?" she said. "Your message to your boss never got sent. The man you asked to relay the information actually works for a man in the Russian embassy, who happens to be employed by the people I work with. We didn't realize you were on board because we've been maintaining radio silence. However, the message was passed to us from our friends on the tanker, telling us to watch for two spies. That's how I knew to look for you. We already captured the first spy when this stupid woman pretended to be a journalist to get on board."

Tran quickly put out of his mind the image of what he would do to the traitor Salim. *If I live that long.* He hoped that Jojola would manage to stay away from the searchers, buoyed by the fact that Malovo and her men believed that they already had the "two spies" mentioned in the message.

"So now that you have us, how about letting us in on what you're up to," Stupenagel said. "I'd like to quote you in my story before some fed puts a bullet in your brain."

Malovo chuckled and shook her head. "I'm glad we found you," she said. "It will make the next few days more enjoyable to listen to your jokes. But sure, you're not going anywhere, so I'll tell you what to expect."

The original plan, she said, had been to arrive in New York harbor the day after Thanksgiving. "It's called Black Friday, no?" she said as she took out a pack of cigarettes and shook one out. "Biggest shopping day of the year. Lots of traffic on bridges and roads."

Malovo placed the cigarette in her mouth and dug a lighter out of a pants pocket. "You may have noticed that we are taking on liquefied natural gas, very dangerous, this stuff. Now imagine a bomb the size of this ship, floating up the East River. Suddenly, there is a rupture in the hull and liquid escapes and turns into a gas cloud surrounding the ship. . . . It's very important that the rupture does not ignite the gas until a cloud forms, otherwise it's just a big blowtorch as gas escapes. But when the cloud is ignited at the exact right moment"—Malovo lit her cigarette and took a deep drag—

"whoosh, it's a giant fireball—hot as the sun—burns everything for a mile. Now it would be Blackened Friday . . . good joke, no?"

The main obstacle for the plan, Malovo said, had been getting the right ship. The use of LNG supertankers as weapons of mass destruction had been on intelligence agencies' radar long before the attack on the World Trade Center. But 9-11 had caused security precautions to increase even more until getting a tanker close enough to a population center was "nearly impossible . . . though someday I expect it will be accomplished."

"But for now, we needed a ship that would not draw such attention," Malovo continued. "No one suspects a small reefer designed to transport milk, no? At most, a cursory check by the Coast Guard, especially if the right hands are greased to look the other way."

"A milk ship can't haul LNG," Stupenagel said. "The refrigeration system can't get cold enough."

"You are correct," Malovo answered. "The gas must be transported at minus 163 degrees centigrade, or minus 260 degrees Fahrenheit, to keep it in liquid form, which also reduces its volume by six hundred times."

Malovo patted the bulkhead. "But this is no ordinary milk ship. She is very special and has been converted into a mini-LNG tanker at a shipyard in Saudi Arabia owned by our friend Amir al-Sistani."

"al-Sistani, the guy who masterminded the stock exchange attack?" Stupenagel asked.

"Yes," Malovo said. "So sad that that did not work, or this would not be so necessary. But unfortunately, it failed, and even worse, that madman David Grale captured al-Sistani and almost ruined this plan."

"How's that?" Tran asked.

"al-Sistani is a clever man," Malovo replied. "When he heard of the alternate plan should his fail, he offered to refit one of his milk ships so that it could carry LNG and be fueled at sea by a larger tanker. But he plans it so that it could not happen—ship would not be available—unless he was safe. He, of course, was thinking that he might be captured by U.S. authorities, and my employers would have to pull strings to allow him to escape or be sent to a friendly country. So Grale threw his plans off until we could arrange for him to escape, and unfortunately, this has delayed us so that we cannot arrive on Black Friday."

Malovo shrugged. "But it's okay. Even though a small ship won't be as big a fire as a tanker . . . it will still be a terrible fire and there will be many deaths. And after all, image is more important than actual casualties, is it not?"

"So you plan to kill a bunch of people and damage some buildings and maybe a bridge or two," Stupenagel said. "What exactly do you hope to accomplish by that except piss off the American public so that they hunt down every Islamic fanatic and roast his ass?"

"Exactly." Malovo smiled. "They will be very angry. Especially when it is learned that this ship is owned by men with business connections to Commander-General Muhammad Ali Jafari of the Iranian Revolutionary Guard. They will be so angry when a certain U.S. congressman provides these proofs, they will approve an attack on Iran, which of course will throw the entire Middle East into chaos. Maybe even a nuclear attack on Israel."

"So what do your employers get out of it?" Stupenagel said.

Malovo looked surprised. "Out of chaos, order," she said. "The keys to the White House, the Kremlin, Ten Downing and Westminster, the Palais Bourbon, the Bundestag, and Congress."

"And you? I don't suppose the world is lucky enough to count on you going out in a blaze of glory," Tran said.

Malovo smirked and looked around. Omar Abdullah was occupied with the helmsman, and the other guards had remained back with their guns trained on the prisoners. She moved closer so that only Stupenagel and Tran could hear.

"Me? I'm in it for the money. But I'll make sure you have front-row seats before I leave."

28

"Mr. Karp, we're ready for your next witness," Judge Rosenmayer said when the jury was seated on the morning of the second day of the trial.

"Thank you, Your Honor, the People call Carmina Salinas," Karp announced.

Having expected the move, Leonard was already on his feet. "Your Honor, with all due respect, I must once again object to the appearance of this witness."

After Carmina was attacked by Gregor Capuchin and decided to testify in the Maplethorpe trial, Karp had immediately interviewed her and then notified the court and defense counsel that he would be calling her as a witness. Leonard responded by filing a motion in limine, which essentially was a motion to prohibit her from testifying regarding any "similar prior bad acts" allegedly committed by his client, Maplethorpe.

Judge Rosenmayer had immediately held a hearing on Leonard's motion, and the defense attorney had started by complaining that the addition of Carmina Salinas was "late in the game" for the defense to properly prepare. And, he said, the sole purpose of her testimony would be an "outrageous attempt" by the prosecution to link his client to another man's crime.

"What do you mean by that?" the judge had asked.

"Apparently, Miss Salinas claims to have been recently attacked by one Gregor Capuchin, who as it happens is, or was, an independent contractor hired for Mr. Maplethorpe's protection by the people financing his current hit Broadway musical," Leonard said. *"I fear that the real intent of calling her as a witness is to try to link my client to this alleged attack—guilt by association, you might say."*

Rosenmayer raised his eyebrows and looked at Karp. *"And how do you respond?"*

"First, there's no 'alleged' to this attack," Karp said. *"Gregor Capuchin, a man employed by Mr. Maplethorpe as a bodyguard, assaulted Miss Salinas in her apartment—placing a plastic bag over her head to render her unconscious—and was preparing to inject her with a lethal dose of heroin when he was stopped."*

"And where is Mr. Capuchin now?" the judge asked.

"He was killed during the struggle to save Miss Salinas," Karp replied.

Rosenmayer's eyebrows shot up and knitted. He looked over at Maplethorpe with a scowl on his face, but the producer shook his head sadly without looking up. *"So, Mr. Karp, are you saying that you want Miss Salinas to testify about this attack? I can see why the defense might be alarmed by the implications."*

Karp shook his head. *"Not at all, Your Honor. Mr. Maplethorpe has not been charged in connection with this crime. If my office later brings charges against him in relation to what happened to Miss Salinas, the charges will be separate from this case. In fact, if it makes the defense rest easier, we will stipulate that there will be no mention of Gregor Capuchin or this assault during Miss Salinas's testimony."*

"Then what will she be testifying to?" Rosenmayer asked.

"Miss Salinas will be testifying to a different assault—this one perpetrated by Mr. Maplethorpe on her—approximately a month ago," Karp said.

The judge turned back to Leonard. *"And your argument against this?"*

Leonard acted as if he was surprised that the judge even needed to ask. *"It's a form of double jeopardy. He's charged with one crime, yet if this woman testifies he'll, in a very real sense, be on trial for two separate and distinct crimes. The courts have held that in order for the State to use 'similar bad acts' statutes, the crimes must be so alike in nature as to be indistinguishable—as far as motive, behavior, and especially in this instance, result. I've read through the transcript of Miss Salinas's interview with the district attorney and she makes these outrageous allegations regarding Mr. Maplethorpe's behavior, for which there is no evidence of anything similar in the Perez case. Furthermore, there's an obvious difference between what my client is actually charged with—homicide—and what Miss Salinas is claiming, which is at worst a misdemeanor sexual assault . . . essentially that he exposed himself to her."*

"Mr. Karp?"

"First of all, Your Honor, what Miss Salinas 'alleges' is quite a bit more serious than a 'misdemeanor sexual assault,'" Karp said. *"My argument in support of Miss Salinas's testimony regarding 'prior bad acts' is not based on the assertion that the crimes were identical in nature, particularly the end result. In fact, the entire People's case rests on the contention that through his reckless and irresponsible behavior, Mr. Maplethorpe created the circumstances that led to the murder of Miss Perez. He then repeated this reckless and irresponsible behavior with Miss Salinas and it is only through the grace of God that she was not killed, too. The defendant created a violent and reckless environment, motivated by lust, that resulted in the murder of the deceased."*

"What about Mr. Leonard's assertions that there is no evidence that what Miss Salinas would describe was part of this 'reckless and irresponsible' behavior you say was also responsible for the death of Miss Perez?"

"Taken subject to connection with subsequent evidence, Your Honor, the People will prove it was. I am asking to be permitted to create my mosaic one tile at a time," Karp replied.

At the hearing Rosenmayer had denied Leonard's motion in limine and ruled that Carmina Salinas could testify *"as long as neither she, nor the district attorney, talk about the alleged assault by Mr. Capuchin."*

* * *

Carmina looked around the spectator section until she saw Alejandro Garcia sitting two rows behind the prosecution table. They smiled at each other, and then she strode purposefully up to the witness stand to be sworn in.

After the attack on her, it was all Carmina could do to keep Alejandro from going after Maplethorpe himself. *"Those Inca Boyz, gangbanging days are over, Alejandro. You can't go shoot someone. I'm not visiting you in Attica,"* she'd told him. He finally agreed to see how the trial went first. *"But bets are off if Maplethorpe walks,"* said the former gang leader known by the nickname Boom.

After Carmina was seated, Karp began by setting the scene on the night she and Garcia met Maplethorpe at the Poliziano Fiera Hotel for the *Putin: The Musical* preproduction cast party. "Did you have anything to drink that night—anything alcoholic?"

"Yes, I had two or three drinks," Carmina replied.

"Is that a lot for you?"

Carmina shrugged. "These days, yes, though when I was a kid I used to get wasted, and three drinks would have been nothin'."

The spectators and jury laughed lightly. "But these days, two or three drinks are about your limit?" Karp asked with a smile.

"Yeah," she replied. "Actually, I don't drink much anymore at all. But it was a cast party, and I was feeling pretty good about getting a part."

"And Mr. Maplethorpe gave you that part," Karp said.

"Yes. The director would have had some input, but him mostly."

"At some point during the evening, did Mr. Maplethorpe invite you up to his penthouse apartment in the hotel?"

"Yes. He said there was going to be a private after-party with some of the other cast members."

"How were you feeling at the time?"

"To be honest, a little woozy and light-headed," Carmina responded.

"From the alcohol?"

"Well, yeah, the alcohol, but it seemed more than that—"

"Objection!" Leonard said quickly. "The witness is about to delve into the realm of speculation for which there is no evidence."

Karp waited for the judge to respond. Although Carmina believed that she'd been slipped a drug in her drink, and Karp thought it entirely possible, she had not been tested for its presence, and he expected the judge to keep her from alluding to the possibility.

"Sustained. Mr. Karp, please proceed."

"Yes, Your Honor," Karp replied. "Miss Salinas, do I understand that you accompanied Mr. Maplethorpe to his suite?"

"Yes."

"Was anyone else in the apartment?"

"No."

"But I thought this was supposed to be a party for other members of the cast as well?"

"So did I. He said they would be there later."

"What happened next?"

Carmina tilted her head to the side as she thought about the question. "I wasn't feeling so good so I sat down on the couch. He sat down next to me and told me what a good actress I was and that if I worked with him, he could make me a star."

"And how did you feel about that?"

"Good. I mean, what actress wouldn't want to hear that from a famous producer?"

"Did he make you feel uncomfortable?"

"Not until he tried to kiss me."

"He tried to kiss you. How did you respond to that?"

"I wouldn't let him," she said.

"Did you attempt to leave?"

Carmina shook her head. "No. I told him I wasn't interested . . . that I have someone I'm in love with," she said, glancing quickly at Garcia. "It wasn't the first time a man tried to kiss me when I wasn't interested. But I can handle myself without having to overreact."

"Did he persist?"

"No, at first he looked mad, but then he apologized and fixed me another drink."

"Did you drink it?"

"I sipped. It was a rum and Coke, I think."

"What did he do next?"

"He told me to relax and that he was going to change into his party clothes before the other guests arrived."

"Go on . . ."

"Well, I may have passed out for a minute or something because the next thing I knew, he was coming down the stairs to the living room wearing a cowboy costume."

"A cowboy costume? What do you mean?"

"Well, it was strange," she said. "He was sort of giggling—I thought maybe he'd had a few too many himself—but anyway, he was wearing a cowboy hat, and cowboy boots, and he had a gun in a holster."

"What sort of pants was he wearing?"

"Well, at first I couldn't tell because he had on a . . . what do you call a silky man's robe, like what Hugh Hefner wears all the time?"

"A smoking jacket?"

"Yes, a smoking jacket . . . and the holster went around it like a belt."

"So when did you see his pants?"

"I was sort of waking up and trying to figure out what he was doing and he came up and stood in front of me. Then he opened the smoking jacket and said, 'If you don't want to kiss me on the lips, then how about kissing . . .'"

Carmina hesitated and looked over at the jurors.

"It's okay, Carmina," Karp assured her. "I know this is embarrassing, but we need to know exactly what was said."

The young woman nodded. "He said, 'Then how about kissing my dick.'"

"What was he wearing under the smoking jacket?"

"Chaps," Carmina replied. "Leather chaps and nothing else . . . nothing covering his . . . privates."

"Oh, my word," Maplethorpe suddenly blurted out. "Do we really have to listen to this nonsense?"

At first surprised by the outburst, Rosenmayer quickly recovered and slammed his gavel down. "Mr. Leonard, the defendant will refrain from making any statements. Mr. Maplethorpe, I expect you to control any such outbursts."

"Yes, Your Honor," both men responded. The producer turned in his seat toward his fans in the rows behind him and rolled his eyes as he shook his head.

"That includes playing to the crowd, Mr. Maplethorpe!" the judge demanded.

Flushing at the admonishment, Maplethorpe turned back around with a sullen look on his face. With a final hard look at the defendant, Rosenmayer turned back to the prosecutor. "You may continue, Mr. Karp."

"Thank you, Your Honor," Karp replied. "Miss Salinas, do I understand that Mr. Maplethorpe was wearing only chaps beneath the smoking jacket?"

"That's right. Just leather chaps . . . like a cowboy, except I think they probably wear pants under them."

Karp laughed. "I imagine riding a horse with just chaps might be a little uncomfortable," he said to additional laughter from everyone else in the courtroom, except those sitting at the defense table and Maplethorpe's retinue.

"Your Honor," Leonard complained, "this is hardly a matter for levity. A man's life is at stake here."

The smile disappeared from the judge's face. "You're quite right, Mr. Leonard. Although I find that at times during a trial it's beneficial for us to laugh and release some of the stress we're all under, we are aware of the gravity of these proceedings and will move on. Mr. Karp, your next question, please?"

"Miss Salinas, did I understand you correctly that Mr. Maplethorpe exposed himself to you and then asked you to engage in oral sex?"

"Yes, that's right."

"And did you?"

Carmina scowled. "Hell, no!"

"What did you do?"

"I started to get up, but he pushed me back in the chair."

"Did he say anything?"

"He said I couldn't leave. He said, 'Nobody leaves me unless I say they can.'"

"Did you feel threatened?"

Carmina nodded. "Yes, he had his hand on his gun and he had sort of a wild look on his face."

"Was the gun still in the holster?"

"Yes, but his hand was around the handle."

"Which hand?"

"What?"

"Which hand was on the gun?"

"Ummm . . . his right hand."

"The gun and holster were on the right side, too?"

"Yes. Same side."

"What did you do when he said you couldn't leave?"

"I tried to get up anyway. He started to yell at me, but then his cell phone rang."

"Did he answer?"

"Not at first, but then he did."

"Do you know who called?"

"No. Somebody who wanted to come up to the apartment."

"What did he say?"

"He said 'Not now.' But I got up and slipped past him. I figured he wouldn't try nothin' while he was on the phone."

"Did he let you go?"

Carmina nodded. "He said, 'Wait. I was just kidding.' But I kept moving and didn't stop until I got home."

Karp walked over to the lectern to check his notes. After leafing through several pages, he turned back to the witness stand. "Miss Salinas, after this incident you continued to work for Mr. Maplethorpe in his play, is that correct?"

"Yes."

Karp looked puzzled. "Considering what happened, why would you do that?"

Carmina shrugged. "I figured it was over. In the theater business you deal with some real freaks . . ."

There was an angry murmur as she looked over at the spectator section behind Maplethorpe. "Objection," Leonard said. "The witness is labeling my client, who happens to enjoy an esteemed reputation as a citizen of this great city, a 'freak' in order to cast him in a bad light with the jury."

"She was asked a question and is voicing her opinion," Karp replied. "Free speech, especially in a court of law, is still allowed in this country. Why don't we leave it to the jury to decide whether her opinion is valid?"

"Overruled, but let's keep to the point, please."

"As you were saying, Miss Salinas . . ." Karp encouraged.

"I was saying that as far as I was concerned, it was over. He'd played his weird little game of cowboy—maybe it's a fantasy or something—but I wasn't hurt or even that scared."

"But Miss Salinas, weren't you aware of the charges facing Mr. Maplethorpe regarding the death of Miss Gail Perez?"

Carmina nodded and looked at Alejandro. "But I was confused about what really happened. I figured that maybe he tried to have sex with her, but why would she kill herself over that and why would he kill her because she didn't want to fuck him? Nothing made any sense."

"Why didn't you report this to the police?"

Carmina's face blushed pink as she shrugged. "I wanted the job. It's a good part, and *any* parts are tough to come by in this town. There's a lot of beautiful, talented girls out there, and some of them will do whatever it takes to get those parts."

"Including oral sex?" Karp asked.

"Yeah, and more," Carmina agreed.

"Did Mr. Maplethorpe ever bring up the assault?"

"Once," Carmina replied. "A few days later, he called me into his office at the theater and said that he hoped that I understood that he'd had a few too many drinks and was not himself. He'd meant the whole thing to come off as 'funny' but it didn't work. He apologized. But then he said that if I wanted to give up my part in the musical, he'd understand, or he said we could just forget the whole thing."

"And how did you take that last part?"

"He was telling me that if I said anything, I'd be fired."

"And what was your response?"

"I said okay. You have to understand, being onstage was more important to me than some fruitcake making a pass at me. I just wanted to forget about that."

"Did he mention it again?"

"Not in so many words," Carmina replied. "But he kept saying that I should remember our 'deal.' And whenever he saw me standing around anyone, he'd talk about how he was going to make me a star someday."

"Wasn't there another reason you didn't want to testify?"

Suddenly tears sprang into Carmina's eyes and she grabbed a tissue to wipe at them. "Yeah. I told my boyfriend and my priest that I didn't want to testify because I knew that if I did, I'd never work on Broadway again."

"Why is that?"

"Because I'd be the actress who testified against a big-time producer," she said quietly. "They'd say I had sex with him and was getting even because I didn't get the part I wanted. Every other producer and director in this city will be thinking, 'I wonder if she'll say I raped her because she didn't get a part.' Theater people are a tight-knit community in some ways, and really vicious in others. I'd be the girl who turned on one of them, and a slut who put out and then accused someone when I didn't get my way. There are a lot of dirty little secrets in the theater; the term 'casting couch' didn't just appear out of thin air."

"So the other reason you didn't want to testify was because you believed your dream of being a Broadway actress would be over?" Karp said.

"Yes," Carmina replied, her voice just barely audible. "It probably is now."

"Why do you say that?"

"Yesterday I was replaced by another girl," she replied. "The director said it was because I was missing my marks and I was off-key, but I know the real reason."

"So why did you decide to testify?"

Karp gave Carmina a telling look. This was a dangerous moment. He'd been over it several times just that morning with Carmina. *"You cannot under any circumstances, unless the defense lawyer brings it up first, mention or even hint at the assault by Gregor Capuchin. I will ask you why you decided to testify. I'm not going to put words in your mouth, but whatever you decide to say in response, do not talk about Capuchin or being attacked."*

Over at the defense table, Leonard tensed, hoping she would make a mistake, and readied to pounce when she did. He would leap to his feet and demand a mistrial and that Carmina's testimony be stricken from the record. He would certainly have more grounds for an appeal if he lost the case.

Carmina bit her lip as she looked first at the jurors, then at Alejandro, and finally at Maplethorpe. "Because I needed to tell the truth."

Karp, without showing his relief, faced Rosenmayer, stood firmly, and said, "I have no further questions."

Leonard stood behind Maplethorpe, his hands on his client's shoulders, as he gazed for a long moment at Carmina. Then he shook his head.

"Miss Salinas, if I remember correctly, you told Mr. Karp that you'd had three or four drinks that night before going to Mr. Maplethorpe's apartment."

"I believe I said two or three," Carmina responded.

"I see, and what if I was to tell you that other witnesses will testify that it was more like five or six?"

"They would be mistaken."

"I see," Leonard repeated. "And however many drinks you had, it was more than you are used to . . . at least now that you've matured?"

"That's correct."

"Then wouldn't it be possible that, perhaps, you might have forgotten how many drinks you had?"

Carmina shook her head. "No. I've thought about it a lot . . . I distinctly remember two—one when my boyfriend was there and another just after he left—and I think one more after that."

"You think?"

"That's what I think."

"But you can't remember the third drink distinctly?"

"I remember having another drink. I don't remember exactly what time it was."

"So your memory is vague?"

"In that regard, yes," Carmina replied. "But I know it wasn't more than three."

"I see," Leonard said again, in such a way as to clearly demonstrate that he didn't believe her.

"So at some point, you agreed to accompany Mr. Maplethorpe to his apartment?"

"Yes, he said he was going to have a private party with some people after the cast party."

"And you happened to be one of the people he invited?"

"Yes. He said the others were coming in a little bit."

"I see." Leonard moved out from behind the defense table and strolled in front of the jury with his hand stroking his chin, as though he was in deep thought. He stopped and faced Carmina. "Miss Salinas . . . how old are you?"

"Twenty-three."

"Twenty-three . . . so you've been around."

Carmina's eyebrows knit in a frown. "What do you mean by that?"

Leonard shrugged. "Just what I said . . . you've been around. I take it you're not a virgin?"

Karp objected. "Miss Salinas's sex life is not on trial here."

"Your Honor," Leonard countered. "There's a question as to whether Mr. Maplethorpe attempted to sexually assault this woman by exposing himself and asking her to perform a sex act, or whether Miss Salinas's actions could have been construed by my client as those of a willing participant."

"I'll allow the witness to answer the question," Rosenmayer said. "But don't linger here too long, Mr. Leonard."

"I don't intend to, Your Honor," Leonard replied. "So answer the question, Miss Salinas. Are you a virgin?"

"No."

"How many sexual partners have you had?"

Karp interrupted. "Wait a minute, what's going on here? This is the same character assassination the defense has engaged in with respect to the deceased."

"Overruled, I'll allow it, Mr. Karp. But Mr. Leonard, are we about through here?"

"Just about. How many, Miss Salinas?"

Carmina looked at Karp but there was nothing he could do. "Three."

"Three," Leonard repeated, as if he'd just been told the moon was made of cheese. "As in two or three drinks, or three or four or five or six drinks?"

"Three."

"And Miss Salinas, have you ever had sex with someone who you worked for in the theater?"

Carmina looked at Karp again, but he said nothing. She glanced at Alejandro, who sat looking down at the floor. She bit her lip and nodded. "I used to go out with the director of an off-Broadway play I was in."

"I see. Did you start to have sex with him before or after you got the part?"

"It wasn't like that," she said. "I went to the audition and he called me up a couple of days later and asked me out."

"Did you have the part yet?"

"The producer was still making his decision."

"In other words, you started 'dating' the director before you got the part?"

"Yes. But that wasn't the reason. Mike, the director, wasn't in charge of casting."

"I see. However, you then got the part?"

Carmina nodded. "Yes."

Leonard turned away from Carmina and faced the jury. "Miss Salinas, you've been around," he said, emphasizing the phrase again. "You've had sexual relations with a man who was essentially your boss and had great influence on your role in a play. What did you think was going to happen when Mr. Maplethorpe invited you to his apartment alone?"

"I didn't know we were going to be alone."

Leonard gave the jury a look like he was dealing with a recalcitrant child. "But no one went with you, correct?"

"Correct."

"And there was no one else there when you arrived, correct?"

"Correct."

"Then why didn't you leave?"

Carmina shrugged. "I thought other people were coming."

"Even after Mr. Maplethorpe allegedly tried to kiss you?"

"Yes."

"So no one's there, Mr. Maplethorpe makes a pass at you, and still no one arrives . . . but you stayed?"

"Yes."

"And had another drink while Mr. Maplethorpe went to change his clothes?"

"Yes."

"I see. And it didn't strike you that he wanted to have sex with you?"

"I think he did. But I told him no and that was when he stopped."

"Are you sure you asked him to stop?"

Carmina nodded. "Yes, I told him to stop."

"You didn't consider having sex with him in order to get a better role in the play?"

"No! That's not true!"

"Then why didn't you leave?"

"I told you! I thought it was settled—he apologized and I was going to let it go. He'd been drinking . . . it was no big deal."

"No big deal," Leonard repeated. "So you stayed and accepted another drink . . . was this number four or five?"

"It was number four," Carmina replied. "I had three before we went to his apartment."

"I see. And you were feeling a little tipsy . . . and you told Mr. Karp that you may have even passed out for a few minutes."

"Yes."

"And then you wake just as Mr. Maplethorpe comes down the stairs in a—and I quote—'cowboy costume'?"

"Yes."

"Even though he expected other guests to arrive at any moment?"

"That's what he'd told me."

"And what you believed."

"I didn't have any reason not to."

"Not even after he made a pass at you . . . you still believed that other people were about to arrive?"

"Yes."

"And he's wearing this outlandish cowboy costume, including a pair of leather chaps with nothing on underneath?"

"Yes."

"I see. And even though you'd already rejected one advance, which was simply to kiss you, he now allegedly stands in front of you and demands fellatio, or as you so eloquently put it, to 'kiss my dick.' Is that right?"

"That's what he said."

"I see. And of course, you refused to do this?"

"Yes. I tried to leave."

"Ah, right, and he pushed you back down on the couch."

"Yes."

"And placed his hand on his gun?"

"Yes."

"I see," Leonard said. "Miss Salinas, did Mr. Maplethorpe actually threaten you with this gun?"

"He had his hand on it when he told me I couldn't leave."

"And you took that as a threat?"

"Wouldn't you?"

Leonard shrugged. "I wasn't there, Miss Salinas. I couldn't say. The question is did you take this as a threat?"

"Yes."

"So a man threatens you with a gun and demands that you perform oral sex . . . but you didn't think this was something that should be reported to the police?"

"I . . . I didn't think it was necessary," Carmina replied. "And I wanted to keep my job."

"I see. In your mind, a small role in a Broadway musical outweighs armed sexual assault?"

"That's not what I said."

"But it is, Miss Salinas. And yet this alleged crime doesn't rate calling the police because having sex with an employer in order to get a role you want isn't new to you, is it, Miss Salinas?"

"Objection, argumentative," Karp said.

"Sustained," Rosenmayer agreed. "Rephrase or move on, Counselor."

"Miss Salinas, after this alleged incident, did you keep your role in the play?"

"Yes."

"So Mr. Maplethorpe made no attempt to punish you for refusing to have sex with him."

"No, he did not."

"On the other hand, you didn't get a better role than the one you already had, correct?"

"I kept the same role. It's a good role."

Leonard checked several items off his legal pad with great flourish. "Miss Salinas, in this story of yours, did Mr. Maplethorpe pull the gun out of the holster?"

"No."

"Did he attempt to place the barrel of this gun in your mouth?"

"No."

"Did he place it in your mouth and then pull the trigger?"

"Obviously not."

"That's right . . . obviously, he did none of these things. Thank you, Miss Salinas, you have given us nothing, and I have nothing else."

Karp rose for redirect with his blood boiling. *Stay cool*, he told himself, *don't rise to the bait or you're going to give him credibility*.

"Miss Salinas, how long did your relationship with this other director last?"

"Almost two years."

"How long did the play run?"

Carmina laughed unexpectedly. "About a month. It wasn't a very good play."

Karp smiled. "Apparently, the relationship was better than the play?"

"Yes, but we eventually went our separate ways."

"Did you have sex with this other man because you wanted a role in his play?"

Carmina shook her head. "No. I had sex with him because I liked him. That's why I continued to see him after the play was closed."

"Miss Salinas, do you remember what happened in Mr. Maplethorpe's apartment that night?"

"Clearly."

"Did Mr. Maplethorpe attempt to kiss you?"

"Yes."

"Did he change into a 'cowboy costume' that included chaps with no pants on underneath?"

"Yes."

"Did he then ask you to perform fellatio?"

"Yes."

"Did you refuse?"

"Yes."

"Did you try to leave?"

"Yes."

"Did he tell you, 'Nobody leaves me unless I say they can'?"

"Yes."

"Did he look angry when he said this?"

"Yes."

"Did he have his hand on the butt of a gun when he said this?"

"Yes."

"Did you feel threatened?"

"Yes."

"What did you do?"

"I left."

"Why didn't you tell the police?"

"I didn't think it was necessary; he apologized."

"Did anyone from my office or the New York Police Department ever discuss whether Mr. Maplethorpe was wearing chaps the night Miss Perez died?"

Carmina looked puzzled, then shook her head. "No, I didn't know that he did."

"You didn't read about it in the newspaper or see it on television?"

"No. I never saw anything about chaps."

Karp tossed his legal notepad onto the prosecution table and paused to let the jury catch up. He turned to look at them to ask his final questions. "Miss Salinas, were you worried that telling the authorities about Mr. Maplethorpe's actions would prevent you from working on the stage again?"

"Yes."

"Were you worried that you would be perceived as a slut who tried to use sex to get a better role in Mr. Maplethorpe's play?"

"Yes," Carmina replied quietly, on the edge of tears.

"Isn't that exactly what Mr. Leonard just did?"

The defense attorney leaped to his feet. "Objection!"

Before the judge could respond, Karp held up his hand. "That's okay, Your Honor, I'll withdraw the question. I'll let the jury come to its own considered conclusion."

29

"Mr. Gianneschi, what was Mr. Maplethorpe's reaction when you asked if he needed you to call an ambulance?"

They were a half hour into the direct testimony of Hilario Gianneschi, which so far had covered everything up to getting the call from Maplethorpe that he needed help. That included identifying Gail Perez as the woman he had seen get on the elevator with the defendant. "She was laughing, but she seemed like she did not want to be there."

"What do you mean by that?" Karp asked.

"Like she did not want to be with that man. I know when a woman wants to be with a man, this was not like that."

When they'd talked about Gianneschi's testimony before the trial, Katz wondered if they should bring Perez's demeanor up. *"They could read that like she had something weighing her down . . . she's resigned. Or even bipolar or something . . . laughing one moment, down in the dumps the next."*

Karp acknowledged that there was a danger of the jury reaching that conclusion. *"But it would be more dangerous if the defense brings it up and it looks like we tried to hide it,"* he'd told Katz. *"We'll stick to our game plan. Clear, simple, here are the facts, noth-*

ing to hide. Make the defense look deceptive with all their bells and whistles and opinions."

Karp had also spent several minutes establishing that while accented, Gianneschi's English was more than just adequate. He accomplished this by getting him to talk a little bit about himself and his job at the upscale, swank hotel in Tribeca. And then asked him about his dreams for the future. "I want to fall in love, take her to Italy to meet my mother, and then return to America, maybe someday go to college and"—he laughed, his white teeth flashing—"make lots of babies and grow old with my wife in the country."

There wasn't a woman in the courtroom—or jury box, Karp thought—who hadn't melted at least a little bit with that. Then, when Gianneschi talked about his desire to become a citizen, he was positively eloquent. "I like it here a lot. I love the people. Here you are limited only by your dreams and you have only yourself to blame if you fail. I want that opportunity. I want to be an American."

That brought them up to Maplethorpe's call for help. "Mr. Gianneschi, what was Mr. Maplethorpe's reaction when you asked if he needed you to call an ambulance?"

"He shouted, '*No!* Don't call anyone. Just come here.'"

"What did you see when you arrived at Mr. Maplethorpe's apartment?"

"Mr. Maplethorpe."

"Was he holding a gun?"

"Yes."

"Which hand?"

Gianneschi thought for a moment, then said, "His right."

"Did he say anything to you?"

"Yes, he say, 'I've been bad.' And then he say, 'Tell her I didn't mean to do it.'"

"He said that he'd been bad?"

"Yes."

"Not that there was an accident? Or that Miss Perez had done something bad?"

"No. Neither of those."

"And he said, 'Tell her that I'—meaning Mr. Maplethorpe—'didn't mean to do it'?"

"Yes, that's right. Then I asked him what he means by this."

"And he responded how?"

"He says, 'I think I killed her.' That's what he says."

"Mr. Gianneschi, this is very important," Karp said. "It's important to Miss Perez and it's important to the defendant over there"—he pointed at Maplethorpe—"that we get this exactly right, word for word . . ."

"Yes, of course."

"He told you, in these exact words, 'I think I killed her.'"

"Yes, exactly."

"Did the defendant say that he'd accidentally shot someone?"

"No."

"Did he say he'd accidentally killed someone?"

"No."

"And Mr. Gianneschi, think very carefully . . ."

"Okay."

"Did the defendant say that she had shot herself?"

"No."

"Did he say that she found a gun in his apartment, put it in her mouth, and then pulled the trigger?"

"No," Gianneschi replied. He was starting to sound exasperated, which was what Karp wanted. "He said, 'I . . . think . . . I . . . killed her.' That's all. That's what he said. Okay?"

"Mr. Gianneschi, what was Mr. Maplethorpe wearing when you arrived at the apartment?"

"A smoking jacket with dots on it," Gianneschi replied, as Karp walked over to the evidence table and picked up the bag containing the polka-dotted garment.

"Does this look like it?" Karp asked.

"Yes, that is it."

"Was he wearing pants?"

Gianneschi made an equivocating gesture with his hand. "Um, they are kind of pants."

Karp walked over to the prosecution table, where Katz handed him several pieces of paper. "Mr. Gianneschi, I have here pages nineteen and twenty from your interview with a police detective three days after Miss Perez was shot and killed. Do you recall that interview?"

"Yes. He asked me many questions."

"Please take a look at these pages," Karp said, handing them to Gianneschi. "And then I'm going to ask you a few questions." At the defense table, Leonard snapped his fingers and one of his subordinates scrambled to find the pages Karp had identified.

The young Italian spent a minute reading the transcript and then looked up. "Okay, I am ready."

"Good. Okay, if you would go to line seventeen on page nineteen, the police detective asks you about the pants . . . how did you describe them?"

"I could not think of the words in English, so I say they are *pantaloni di cuoio dispari.*"

"And what does that mean in English?"

"It means . . . um . . . strange, uh, weird . . . leather pants."

"Strange or weird leather pants."

"Yes."

"Hold on here just a cotton-picking minute," Leonard said, standing with pages from the transcript in his hand. "It only says here 'leather pants.' I don't see anything about *pantaloni di* . . . whatever he said."

"Mr. Karp, do you wish to explain the apparent discrepancy?" Rosenmayer asked.

"Yes, Your Honor," Karp replied. "Mr. Leonard must be referring to the original transcription of the taped interview with Mr. Gianneschi, which was inaccurate. He was supplied with a copy of the revised transcription . . . when exactly, Mr. Katz?"

Although they'd planned for this moment, Kenny Katz made a big show of leafing through several pieces of paper before finding what he was looking for. "It was signed for by Mr. Leonard a week ago. It was prefaced with a letter explaining the discrepancy."

Karp held up the transcript. "This is the revised copy of the transcript, including a translation of the phrase '*pantaloni di cuoio dispari*' certified by three outside linguists who speak Italian. It does indeed translate to 'strange or weird leather pants.' The People are asking that this transcription be accepted into evidence, as well as a tape recording of the original interview with Mr. Gianneschi, which, by the way, defense counsel has had in his possession for more than six months."

"How was this discovered?" the judge asked.

"Well, Mr. Reed found the mistake sometime before his death," Karp said. "In fact, you may recall a warrant he requested to search Mr. Maplethorpe's apartment for leather pants."

"I do recall that," Rosenmayer agreed.

"I found a note that Mr. Reed left behind with some of his work with the phrase *'pantaloni di cuoio dispari.'* I then listened to the tape of the interview with Mr. Gianneschi. So I decided to ask Mr. Gianneschi about it. He recalled at that time making the statement, as well as described to me what he meant by it. Which is what I was getting to before Mr. Leonard objected."

Rosenmayer looked over at where Leonard was fuming. "Counselor, did you receive this transcript and tape?"

"I may have," Leonard conceded. "But I don't have time to listen to Karp's tapes and read every piece of paper the district attorney shoots my way."

"I've read every piece of paper you've sent to my office," Karp replied. "Which at last count outnumbered the paperwork we've sent you by about twenty to one, including notice received this morning of a new defense witness, a Mr. Mike Cowsill, the former boyfriend of Carmina Salinas who Mr. Leonard made much ado about earlier this afternoon."

"Your Honor, there is a huge difference between adding a witness and slipping some paperwork under the door and expecting me to read it," Leonard complained.

"I'm going to overrule your objection, Mr. Leonard," Rosenmayer said. "Keeping up with the paperwork, which is all part of the pretrial discovery that you demanded by way of formal motion, is a very important part of the job. And you really should have vetted the prosecution copy of the transcript against the tape you have had in your possession. What if the DA really had been trying to pull a fast one?"

Leonard sat down heavily and tossed his pen on his pad as

though giving up. Karp allowed himself only a little smile at that as he turned back to Gianneschi.

"Mr. Gianneschi, you said that the defendant was wearing strange leather pants. What did you mean by 'strange'?"

"I mean"—Gianneschi waved a hand over his groin area—"there is nothing here to cover him." He shrugged apologetically at the jury. "*Scusami,* I could see his *pene e testicoli* . . . his, um, cock and balls." He blushed as several spectators giggled before a look from Rosenmayer silenced them.

"You could see his sex organs?" Karp asked.

"Yes."

"Was this because his pants were unbuttoned, or his zipper was down?" Karp asked.

Gianneschi shook his head and waved his hand over his own lap. "No. There was . . . ummm . . . no cloth."

"And have you since recalled or been told what such leather garments are called?"

Gianneschi nodded. "Yes, they are '*pantaloni del cowboy.*'"

"In English, please."

"Like cowboy pants you see in the movies. I think they are called chaps."

"He was wearing leather chaps when you arrived at his apartment?"

"Yes."

"Was he wearing these chaps when the police arrived?"

"No," Gianneschi said, shaking his head. "He changed. He was wearing blue jeans."

"Thank you, Mr. Gianneschi," Karp said. "I have no more questions."

"Can I go?" Gianneschi asked.

"No, sorry, that man over there—his name is Mr. Leonard—is going to ask you a few questions, too," Karp replied.

"Oh, great!" Gianneschi said with such feeling that everyone laughed, including the people sitting in the pews behind Maplethorpe.

Even Leonard smiled. "I'll try to be gentle, Mr. Gianneschi."

"I appreciate that," Gianneschi replied to more chuckles.

But suddenly, Leonard's demeanor changed. "Mr. Gianneschi, you're an illegal alien, are you not?"

Gianneschi's smile disappeared and he looked frightened. "Yes. I am here illegally."

"Illegally. That makes you a criminal, doesn't it?"

The young Italian looked confused and shook his head. "No, I am not a criminal. I do not rob. I do not steal."

"Are you breaking the law by residing in the United States without permission?" Leonard asked.

"Yes, I guess so," Gianneschi conceded.

"That makes you a criminal, Mr. Gianneschi," Leonard said. "And doesn't it also make you a liar?"

Gianneschi looked outraged. "I am not a liar," he insisted. "I am a good Catholic. I do not lie."

"When you got your student visa, Mr. Gianneschi, did you agree to obey the laws of this country?" Leonard said.

"Yes."

"Did those laws include that if you were not attending college, then your visa was no longer valid?"

"I guess, but I work instead . . ."

"Did you have a work visa?"

Gianneschi shook his head. "No."

"Then you lied when you said you would obey the laws of this country?"

"I guess this is true," Gianneschi said sullenly.

"And isn't it true that you used another name, and a false Social Security number, when filling out the tax forms for your employer's tax records?"

"Yes, or I can't get paid. The government keeps the tax money."

"Well, isn't it lying to pretend you are someone you are not?"

"Yes."

"And isn't it lying to use a Social Security number that's not yours?"

"Yes."

"Then by your own admission, you're a liar?"

"Yes."

"So then why should this jury believe anything you just said when questioned by Mr. Karp?"

"Because it's the truth?"

"I see. But didn't we just agree that the truth is you are a criminal and a liar?"

Gianneschi looked at the jurors. "Then I would tell the jury that even a criminal and a liar can tell the truth."

For a moment, Leonard seemed put off by Gianneschi's answer. He took a moment to scribble something in his notebook as he gathered himself. "A criminal and a liar, Mr. Gianneschi," the defense lawyer muttered. He tossed his pen back on the lectern. "Mr. Gianneschi, your first language is Italian, correct?"

"Yes. I speak Italian before I speak English."

"Do you find yourself sometimes translating things people say to you in English into Italian so that you can understand what they meant better?"

Gianneschi thought about it for a moment and then nodded. "*Sì*, I sometimes think to myself what an English word would be in Italian and then I know better how to answer in English."

"If that's true," Leonard continued, "isn't it possible that Mr. Maplethorpe said those things to you in English and that you translated them into Italian, and then translated them again back into English when the police asked you what he said?"

Gianneschi looked confused. "I did not understand you. Could you repeat, please?"

Leonard gave a knowing glance at the jurors. "Sure. I said, 'Isn't it possible that Mr. Maplethorpe said those things to you in English and that you translated them into Italian' . . . You with me so far?"

"Yes."

"And then you translated the Italian words back into English when the police questioned you?"

Gianneschi realized what Leonard was getting at. "Ah, I see what you are saying," he said. "But no. He said these things exactly as I told Mr. Karp. He said he'd done something bad. That he wanted me to tell her that he didn't mean to do it. And he say, 'I think I killed her.' Are you with *me* so far?"

The young man's unexpected rejoinder seemed to suck the air out of the courtroom. Mouths hung open, every eye traveling from Gianneschi to Leonard to see how the defense attorney would react. Then someone in the spectator section whistled and said, "Oooh, *pysch,*" which caused the courtroom to erupt in laughter.

It took Rosenmayer several minutes to restore order, including tossing the offending spectator out of the courtroom.

At last Gianneschi was allowed to get down from the stand. Karp watched him go and then turned to the judge. "Your Honor, Mr. Gianneschi was our last witness. That concludes the People's case."

Leonard and the rest of the defense team, as well as Maplethorpe, looked up in shock. Even the jurors appeared to be pleasantly surprised; they'd been told to expect the trial to last weeks, as the first trial had. Gathering his composure, the defense attorney addressed the judge. "Your Honor, perhaps we should discuss this outside the hearing of the jury."

"I think that's wise," Rosenmayer agreed. He turned to the jury and excused them for the night.

When the jurors had happily trooped out of the courtroom, Leonard whirled to face Karp. "That's it?" he said. "Aren't you going to call any of the experts on your witness list?"

Karp shrugged his broad shoulders. "Not on direct. Maybe as rebuttal to your experts." He looked at Rosenmayer. "There is one last piece of housekeeping before we break. A last piece of evidence I would like to have admitted when the jury returns."

"And what's that, Mr. Karp?" Rosenmayer asked.

Karp walked over to the prosecution table, where Kenny Katz handed him several copies of a black-and-white photograph. He handed one to the judge and one to Leonard.

As expected, Leonard got to his feet. "I object, Your Honor, what's the relevance of this?"

Rosenmayer looked at Karp. "Want to explain?"

"Actually, Your Honor, this photograph is already part of the evidence," Karp said. "You'll recall the testimony of Detective Frank Cardamone regarding a framed photograph that can be seen on the end table at the crime scene. He said it was a photograph of the defendant as a child standing with his mother."

Karp walked over toward the judge. "As you can see, in this photograph, the defendant is dressed up as a cowboy—hat, gun in holster, boots . . . and chaps. It is our contention that the reckless environment created by the defendant, coupled with his penchant for violent, lustful conduct, which led to the death of Miss Perez, is a type of role-playing related to this photograph. In a pretrial hearing, before the first trial, you may also recall Mr. Maplethorpe suddenly grew violent and had to be subdued when the defense introduced this photograph and noted that Mr. Maplethorpe's mother had left him as a boy—"

"Leave my mother out of this, Karp!"

Even though Karp expected to get a rise out of Maplethorpe with the photograph, he, like everyone else in the courtroom, was shocked as the defendant jumped up from his seat and screamed as he pointed at him. *"Not one more word!"*

Leonard rose from his seat and grabbed Maplethorpe by the elbow. "It's okay," he assured his client. "Don't let him—"

Suddenly, the defense attorney started to shriek. Without a word, Maplethorpe had turned and stabbed Leonard in the thigh with his pen.

"You should have stopped, Karp," Maplethorpe complained a moment before two large court officers jumped on him and knocked him to the ground.

Several of Maplethorpe's followers screamed and tried to rush to his assistance only to be wrestled to the ground by more security officers, handcuffed, and dragged from the courtroom. General bedlam ensued for several minutes, as the defendant was hauled shrieking and kicking out of the courtroom, before it was over.

As a paramedic attended to the puncture wound in Leonard's leg, the judge shook his head, stood up, and gathered his notebook and papers. As he started to leave the dais, he said, "Now that we're off the record, Mr. Karp, has anyone ever told you that on occasion you can be annoying?" Rosenmayer smiled and added, "You don't have to answer."

But Karp cleared his throat. "Yes, as a matter of fact," he admitted. "Your Honor, if I may, before we leave, you haven't yet ruled on Mr. Leonard's objection to the photograph."

Leonard looked up as though dazed. "You've got to be kidding. That photograph has nearly got me killed twice."

"Third time's a charm." Karp smiled. "But actually, no, I'm not kidding."

The judge thought about it for a moment. "In light of two witnesses' testimony regarding chaps, and what would appear to be a connection between the defendant's past, that particular article of clothing, and his current propensity for violence, I'm going to overrule the objection. I believe relevance has been established. I would suggest that you stay some distance from your client on Monday, Mr. Leonard."

Five minutes later, the courtroom was clear except for Karp and Katz, who shook his head. "That went well," he said.

Karp patted him on the back. "Yeah? What makes you think that?" Laughing, the two men left the courtroom.

30

Karp sat on a stool at the island in his kitchen rubbing his stomach, which he'd filled with turkey, prime rib, stuffing, mashed potatoes and gravy, and cranberry Jell-O mold, his favorite, made from his mother-in-law's recipe. Thanksgiving was Karp's favorite holiday, and while he'd warned himself of the consequences of his actions, he'd gone ahead and indulged in two generous pieces of chocolate and banana cream pie brought by the Sobelmans. Now he was paying the piper.

The others who'd gathered at the Karp-Ciampi loft to celebrate the holiday were busy in the living room, engaged in noisy, overly energetic word games. They included the twins; Marlene; Kenny Katz and his girlfriend, Sondra; Moishe and his wife, Goldie; as well as Guma, who had shown up, unexpectantly and a little red-faced, with Darla Milquetost.

"Why, Guma," Karp had teased when he got him aside before dinner, *"I do believe you've developed a soft spot for my receptionist. I hope your intentions are honorable."*

Guma tried to blow it off as a humanitarian gesture. *"She's been having a hard time since her boyfriend took off for parts unknown. I thought she might be lonely, and you said I could bring someone."*

"By all means." Karp laughed. *"And a good choice. I would have*

invited her myself if I'd thought about it. But on Thanksgivings past 'bringing someone' usually meant whichever stripper or barfly you went to bed with the night before."

"Maybe I've matured," Guma replied defensively.

"Or, more likely, you've identified Darla as easy pickings, hence my question about your intentions," Karp shot back.

That was two hours ago and Karp was no longer in the mood for teasing Guma, or word games. His poor stomach gurgled and rumbled as he attempted to take his mind off his gastronomic distress by retreating to the kitchen to make a few notes to himself about the previous day in court and the start of the defense case.

Karp knew that when the trial resumed on Monday the true test of his "minimalist" strategy would come. He was reminded of the DVD retrospective the defense presented the other day in court that began with the narrator, who Karp thought sounded like the guy who records voice-overs for NFL Films, setting the scene: "In a small town in Ohio, where a young boy once saw a traveling Broadway production of *The Music Man*, and dreamed of life in the theater . . ." The DVD featured scenes from some of Maplethorpe's more famous productions, and interspersed were testimonials of famous Broadway and civic personalities.

The defense would be trying to overwhelm the jury with all sorts of bombastic expert witnesses with important-sounding credentials and lots of letters after their names, from shrinks to blood-splatter-pattern analysts. It would be up to him to cut through their bullshit without adding to their credibility.

As he looked over his notes, he felt prepared and looked forward to the resumption of the trial. But then he glanced at the margins of one page on his notepad and suddenly felt at a loss again. He'd written the words "Casa Blanca," "art of war," and "*It Happened in Brooklyn*" on the page, as if writing them would create some sort of magic and he'd understand. But he was no closer now than the day he first heard from Andy.

They meant something, of that he was sure. *"In Casa Blanca plans are made that have to do with the art of war."* But what did they mean? There were plenty of white houses in Brooklyn but none that stood out in the context of a potential terrorist attack. Or seemed to have any relationship to an ancient book of military strategy.

"Oh, and he said to tell you to think about the view." Dirty Warren was sure that was what the man said, and Karp had gone over it a thousand times in his head. Did he mean the view of Manhattan from Brooklyn? In that case, the view was principally of the downtown skyline and the Brooklyn and Manhattan bridges. Or was it supposed to be the view of Brooklyn from the Manhattan side of the East River, in which case the scenery ran the gamut from industrial waterfront, as far as the ship repair facilities, to the same two bridges down to Brooklyn Heights. Whichever way he looked—and he'd stood on both sides of the river plenty lately doing just that—nothing stood out.

The riddles were just too vague, but more than that, he felt like he was missing something. That the clue he needed was right in front of him, but he couldn't see it.

And what did any of it have to do with the tape he'd received from V.T.? Just thinking about that made him feel guilty. After all of V.T.'s troubles and Fulton's efforts, he'd tossed the recording in his desk drawer and forgot about it in the wake of the attack on Carmina Salinas and the subsequent arrest of AME Kip Bergendorf. Then the trial started and it wasn't until Wednesday evening as he was leaving for home that he'd opened his drawer and there it was. He hadn't even had a chance yet to tell V.T. about Bergendorf.

Karp had listened to the recording several times since, with no more understanding of what it meant than he had of Andy's riddles. "The package is on the way." *What package . . . a person, a bomb, an illicit case of Cuban cigars?* "No, there's been a change . . . five days later." *Later than what? Sounds like a target date got pushed back. But from what to what? And then there was the name . . . Ivan or Iben Jew-bare.* The first name was unclear and the second he had only a poor quality phonetic pronunciation. He'd had Fulton run a dozen different variations on both names through the national crime computer database, but nothing had come of it.

Karp would have liked to talk to Jaxon about all of it, but he hadn't heard from the agent—or, for that matter, from Ned Blanchett or Lucy. The fact that Lucy still had not called convinced Marlene that she was off on this secret mission with the men but hadn't wanted to worry her parents. "Next time I see that little brat," his wife steamed, "I'm going to let her know in no uncertain terms that this is worse than knowing she's off chasing terrorists."

All day Karp had worried that whatever all of it meant, the target date was Thanksgiving. As part of the Five Borough Anti-Terrorism Task Force, he was well aware that NYPD and federal law enforcement had been worried for years that the annual Macy's parade, with tens of thousands of people packed into a small area, was a prime target for a terrorist chemical or gas attack or a car bomb. But without any specific threat, there was nothing much he could do other than to ask Fulton to pass on to the NYPD higher-ups that there was an unspecified threat to add to their concerns. But the morning, when the crowd was at its zenith, had passed without incident.

What about tomorrow? The day after Thanksgiving was the busiest shopping day of the year. Known as Black Friday because it was the day merchants "went into the black" in profits for the year, there were actually more people in the city, on the sidewalks and in the stores, than on Thanksgiving. Of course, both scenarios ignored the fact that neither the parade nor Black Friday's crowds were in Brooklyn.

And if the attack was moved back five days—that could mean Tuesday or *Wednesday or*—Karp stopped; the whole thing was giving him a headache to match the pain in his stomach. He became aware of an argument between Zak and Giancarlo in the other room.

The boys' relationship had remained strained ever since Elisa Robyn asked Giancarlo to the dance. Or more accurately, ever since he'd accepted.

Zak was used to being the center of attention when it came to the two boys. The boisterous, competitive athlete, he wasn't used to coming in second to his brother. He hadn't said anything more about it—at least nothing that Karp had heard—but he'd started doing more things on his own or with other friends. The two boys had been nearly inseparable from the womb to now, and Zak's sudden independence said a lot about his level of resentment.

Giancarlo, on the other hand, wasn't helping matters any. Despite all his musical and academic talents, when it came to "guy stuff," he'd always been in the shadow of his bigger, stronger brother. However, "winning the girl" had changed that and he wasn't shy about rubbing it in Zak's face, especially when his brother said anything about Elisa and Giancarlo being "two-faced phonies."

Marlene had tried to talk to Giancarlo about why Zak was reacting that way. But while he'd always been the twin who was the most likely to see both sides in an argument, he wasn't having it this time. *"He's being a big baby,"* he'd said to Marlene. *"She likes me and she doesn't like him. And no wonder, all he can do is act like a macho jerk, running around flexing his muscles and saying stupid stuff. I shouldn't have to walk on eggshells; he's the one who should knock it off."*

Karp figured they'd eventually get over it. Elisa Robyn would move on. Zak would get a girlfriend of his own. However, it was driving Marlene crazy. She'd come from a big, loud but loving Italian family.

Now she was trying to moderate an argument between the twins while their guests pretended not to notice.

"What's going on?" Karp asked, though he wasn't sure he wanted to get in the middle of it. *A nap sounds good right about now.*

"We're playing a riddle game and Zak's pissed because his team lost," Giancarlo complained.

"And Giancarlo guessed the winning answer," Marlene pointed out. "But nobody else got it either, Zak. Come on, be a good sport."

"It was a stupid riddle," Zak sulked.

"What was the riddle?" Karp asked in spite of his headache,

"Think of words ending in 'gry.' Angry and hungry are two of them," Marlene read from a game card. "There are only three words in the English language. What is the third word? The word is something that everybody uses every day. If you have listened carefully, I've already told you what it is."

Karp thought about it. "Can I use my legal pad?"

"Sure," Marlene said. "Shall I repeat it for you?"

As Marlene read it again, Karp wrote the riddle down. He stared at it for a minute as the others began to heckle him. He glanced up at the top of the page where he'd written "cut through the bullshit" and underlined it twice. Then it became clear to him.

"Well, the key to this is to realize that the answer here is surrounded by distractions," he said, then looked at Katz. "Sort of like in the Maplethorpe trial. So start by disregarding the first two sentences, which are: 'Think of words ending in 'gry.' Angry and hungry are two of them.' They have nothing to do with this case . . . I mean, riddle."

"You can take the lawyer out of the courtroom, but . . ." Katz said to general laughter from everyone except Zak.

"Yeah, yeah . . . now listen carefully to what you have left: 'There are only three words in the English language. What is the third word?' The rest of the riddle is all true but irrelevant. So the answer is: language. Language is the third word of 'the English language.' It's also something we use every day."

The others clapped. "Showoff," Zak muttered. "Just like Giancarlo."

Marlene scowled. "Zak, knock it off."

The company shifted uncomfortably in their seats and tried to find something else to look at. The Sobelmans held hands and smiled, while Kenny and Sondra got "maybe kids aren't such a good idea" expressions on their faces. Only Darla Milquetost, who appeared to have been enjoying the Zinfandel port that Katz had brought over, and Guma seemed oblivious as they whispered in each other's ears and giggled on the couch.

"Okay, smart guy, try another one," Marlene said to break the ice. She pulled another card from a box. "Who said 'A riddle wrapped up in an enigma' and what does it mean?"

"It means 'a puzzle that is difficult to solve,'" Karp said. "And I believe it was Winston Churchill, but I don't think that's an accurate quotation."

"Well, that's what it says is the right answer," Marlene replied, reading the back of the card.

"But I think they got it wrong."

Katz laughed. "Now he's challenging the trivia experts at Hasbro!"

"Quit while you're ahead, *boychick*," Moishe said.

"How can he be a boy and a chick?" Zak scowled.

"*Boychick* is a Yiddish term of endearment for a boy," Moishe explained.

"He's not a boy," Zak countered. "He's *old.*"

"Not as old as I am, *boychick* number two." Moishe laughed. "Now *that* is old."

"Dad's right!" Giancarlo said suddenly, looking up from his laptop computer.

"About what this time?" Zak replied.

"I searched the Internet for the quote 'a riddle wrapped up in an enigma' and this is what it says: 'A form of a Winston Churchill quote in a 1939 radio broadcast: 'I cannot forecast to you the action of Russia. It is a riddle, wrapped in a mystery, inside an enigma; but perhaps there is a key. That key is Russian national interest.'"

"Ah, that's right," Moishe said. "I remember it on the radio right before the war. It was the start of the bad years. That was very good, Butch. You know your history."

All the eyes in the room turned to Karp, who stood with his chin cupped in his hand, staring at the floor. "Okay, I got one for all of you," he said.

"Bring it on, *boychick*," Marlene said.

"'In Casa Blanca plans are made that have to do with the art of war. One can be a house, the other is usually not an art. But when you look at both what do you see? And so does the deadly connection between the two sides.'"

Karp looked over at Marlene. She was the only one in the room who knew the significance of the riddle. She gave him an apprising look, but the rest of the people in the room furrowed their brows in thought and mouthed the words like incantations. It did not surprise him that Katz was the first to speak.

"Well, let's go back to the old legal pad theory of riddle solving," Kenny said. "What if the first two sentences are just distractions? Well, in this case they're more than that because they give us 'Casa

Blanca' and 'art of war.' But otherwise, they're just there to disguise the real question."

"Why not *The Art of War*?" Sondra asked. "Isn't that the full name of the book? Not 'Art of War.'"

"Yes, but is he talking about the book? Or just 'art of war'? Anyway, just bear with me, I think I have the answer, so I might be fudging some of this. I am but a lowly apprentice and not yet a Zen master."

"Continue, grasshopper," Karp said with a smile, thinking, *The boy learns fast*.

"So okay, if we get rid of the clutter and concentrate on the question—slightly altered: *But when you look at Casa Blanca and art of war what do you see?*"

The room was silent. Then Giancarlo shouted, "They're the same at both ends!"

"Don't be an idiot," Zak said, and sulked, receiving a glare from his mother.

Karp nodded. "Go on, G-man, what do you mean by that?"

"They're the same at both ends," the boy repeated himself. "Casa Blanca begins and ends with *ca*; Art of War begins and ends with *ar*."

"So they're the same at both ends, what does that mean?" Marlene asked.

Karp shook his head and smiled. "That's the real riddle. All this time, I've been telling Kenny that we'll win our case by simplifying, but then I turned around and worked this thing to death and came up with all sorts of hidden meanings, when it's really quite simple. In fact, it took me until a moment ago and the other riddle to look at this, really just look, without trying to make it more complex than it is. That's when I got the 'they look the same at both ends' clue. So then I'm thinking, 'Okay, the deadly connection will see that whatever we're both looking at is the same at both ends. So what?' And then it struck me that I was still overthinking it. The 'connection' between the 'two sides' isn't some person standing between Islam and the West, or anything like that. In fact, the connection isn't a person or group at all. It's just a connection . . . something that brings two sides into contact . . . such as a road between one place and another. So then I'm thinking, 'What road or path looks the same on both ends?' And Zak, you came up with the answer to this one."

"I did?" Zak replied, looking both pleased and confused.

"Yep," Karp said. "Marlene, do you remember our conversation on the way to Stewbie's funeral and what Zak once said about tunnels?"

A light dawned on Marlene's expression and she smiled. "He said that they were really just the same on both ends. That you went in one end and you came out of the same end near your destination."

"I said that?" Zak asked. He smiled and gave Giancarlo a smug look.

"You did, which is why I think the 'connection' between the two sides is a tunnel, or maybe a bridge; they both look the same on both ends," Karp went on. "And since my other clue in solving the bigger riddle is '*It Happened in Brooklyn,*' my guess is that the answer is either the Brooklyn-Battery Tunnel, or the Brooklyn, Manhattan, or Williamsburg bridge."

"So what's deadly about a tunnel or a bridge?" Darla Milquetost said, slurring just a bit.

Everyone looked at her, and then looked back at Karp. He shrugged. "That's the part that worries me."

Two hours later, the company had left and the boys were in bed, leaving Karp and Marlene in the kitchen talking about the riddle and what it might mean.

"At least I think I know where the danger lies," Karp said.

"But when?"

Karp thought about it and shook his head. "I thought it might be today, or maybe tomorrow. I'm going to talk to the mayor and the chief of police and see if they want to bump up security at the tunnel and bridges. But it could be next week . . . or next year for all I know."

"Do you think the threat is real? Or just some nut who likes to make riddles that sound bad?"

"I don't know that, either," Karp replied. "But Jaxon seemed to take it seriously before he left. That bit about Dagestan had him worried. And this Andy said 'it's the worst thing that could happen,' which I'd hate to imagine."

The conversation was interrupted by a buzzing that meant someone was downstairs at the loft entrance. Karp walked over to where he could see the security monitor.

"Thank God," he said. "It's Jaxon and Ned."

"Lucy's not with them?" Marlene asked, disappointed.

"No, babe, but maybe they can tell us where she is," he said, pressing the lock release. "Come on up, guys, looks chilly out there."

A minute later, Jaxon and Blanchett were standing in the kitchen as Marlene poured two cups of coffee.

"Sorry you missed Thanksgiving dinner," Karp said, "but what brings you here at this hour?"

"Sorry to barge in," Jaxon said. "We just got back, but I need to ask you a question and didn't want to do it over the phone. Have you heard from Jojola or Tran?"

"No," Karp said, looking at Marlene, who shook her head. "What's up?"

Jaxon's face tightened. "They're missing. We were on a mission in the Caribbean. They were supposed to be following a terrorist named Omar Abdullah. But we haven't heard from them in nearly a week. One of the locals who was working with them says they were tracking Abdullah into the bush and sent this other guy, his name is Salim, back to let us know . . . cell phones don't work there. But they've vanished and an all-out manhunt hasn't turned up any clues."

"What about if they had to follow this guy off what I presume is an island?" Karp asked.

"I've thought about it," Jaxon replied. "Maybe they followed him or were taken hostage. I've been trying to get a handle on what aircraft or ships left the island around the time they disappeared. There's nothing with any of the airlines; they couldn't have left without being noticed. But that doesn't rule out private aircraft or the ships, and unfortunately, it's a busy port. I got a list of the ships that left but I don't have much hope of finding them that way. I guess we're going to have to keep looking and hope they turn up."

"Is this the same mission that Lucy's on?" Marlene interrupted.

Jaxon gave Marlene a funny look. "Lucy wasn't on this mission."

"Lucy's home in New Mexico," Blanchett added.

"You've talked to her?" Marlene asked, surprised and a little irritated that her daughter had spoken to her fiancé but hadn't answered her mom's messages.

"Well, no, but that's where she was headed after I left."

Marlene frowned. "That's what we thought, too. But we haven't spoken to her since. Just two text messages saying she was going on a spiritual retreat with some Taos Indians."

"In November?" Blanchett said. Now it was his turn to frown. "The Taos people generally move into the old pueblo on the reservation during the winter and avoid contact with the outside world. Members of the tribe only—not even someone they like as much as Lucy."

"You're not lying to me about her being on this mission, are you, Espey?" Marlene demanded. "Because if you are, and I find out about it, I'm going to tear you a new one."

"Scout's honor," Jaxon promised.

"Can I use your phone?" Blanchett asked.

"Of course," Marlene replied. "Who are you calling?"

"The airlines. I need to catch the first plane out of here for New Mexico."

31

Karp and Marlene looked up as Jaxon and Blanchett entered the DA's office from the door leading to the private elevator. They could tell that both men were on edge.

Blanchett had called Saturday to say that he had information about Lucy but was flying back to New York on Monday to talk about it rather than say anything over the phone. *"It's not good news,"* he'd said, obviously worried but doing his best to remain cool. *"However, it's not entirely bad, either. Fact is, I don't know what to make of it."*

"So what's the good news/bad news?" Marlene demanded.

Jaxon looked at Blanchett and nodded. "When I got back to the ranch on Friday, I didn't see any sign that Lucy had been there since we left," Blanchett said. "I checked with the sheriff and even got one of the Taos reservation police officers to ask if anybody had seen her. No one had, even though the airline said that someone used her ticket. I was getting pretty frantic, then I checked our mailbox on Saturday morning and found a note from the mailman saying I had a certified letter waiting for me at the post office. I barely got there before they closed at noon."

The young man pulled an envelope out of the pocket of his sheepskin coat and handed it to Marlene.

"'My darling Ned,'" she began reading, "'if you get this it means that I'm still not back from my trip to see an old friend as I expected. The boss knows who I mean and why I went. Tell my parents that I'll be okay and that I'm sorry I lied. But I thought I had to do this. Tell Mom to keep the faith and give Booger a treat soon. And tell Dad to keep doing his word games. I love you, Ned, I want to be your wife, so come home safe to me. Luce.'"

Marlene teared up at the last sentence and looked at Jaxon. "She's talking in code, so I guess that means that she was worried someone might intercept this, but assuming you're 'the boss,' what's the rest of it mean to you?"

Jaxon was quiet for a moment, then sighed. "Before we left for the Caribbean, Lucy told me she wanted to find Grale and talk to him about releasing al-Sistani to us," he said. "But I told her that under no condition was she to make contact with him without a team along to ensure her protection. I guess she decided to ignore my orders and is going forward with her plan."

"She's always been headstrong," Karp noted. "I can only hope that this time it's not going to backfire on her. I noticed she started by saying that if Ned got the letter, it meant that she wasn't able to get back in time to retrieve it, which means something had come up to change her original plan."

"She also gives another hint by saying 'as I expected,'" Jaxon added. "So she knew the situation was fluid."

"Or that something's gone wrong," Marlene said.

Karp looked at her, saw the strain, and nodded. "It could be. But it also sounds like she does have a plan, even if confronted by the unexpected, and went out of her way in this note to tell us that she would be okay. I haven't given her enough credit sometimes in the past—but that's one tough young woman and if she tells me that she had to do this, I'm going to trust that she weighed the consequences carefully and has a good reason."

Marlene smiled through her tears. "You're really sweet and special. Always looking out for everybody else. . . . The other night he finds a way to pump up Zak when the kid needed it most and wasn't getting it from his mom. Today, he finds a way to keep me from having a nervous breakdown."

"Hope he can do the same for me. What did Lucy mean by telling you to 'keep the faith and give Booger a treat soon'?" Jaxon asked.

"She was using our code word for danger and telling me to get into contact with the Walking Booger—one of the street people who seems to have a direct connection to Grale—and 'soon' means as soon as I get the message. But she couldn't have known when that would be, so we may already be out of time."

"What's the treat?"

"Booger likes the brownies at the Housing Works Bookstore Café down the block from our loft. He calls them 'treats,'" Marlene said. "Guess I'll hang out there until he shows."

"Can I go with you or at least send a team to keep an eye on things? You won't even know they're there," Jaxon said.

Marlene shook her head. "No. Stay away. If your people show up in that neighborhood, Grale's people will know. If he wanted to make contact with you, he would have reached out to you. But she directed that comment specifically to me, and it's obvious she's worked out a plan with Grale."

Jaxon looked at Karp. "So that leaves the last comment telling you to keep at your word games. Want to hazard a guess at what that means?"

"I know what it means," Karp replied. "It means that 'the worst thing that could happen' is connected to whatever Lucy's doing with Grale."

Karp's intercom buzzed. "Mr. Karp, there's a Mr. Ray Guma here to see you."

Darla Milquetost left her finger on the button a moment longer than she should have, so those in Karp's office heard her giggle and say "Stop!"

"Just a moment, Darla, and pour some water on him . . . that usually cools him off for a minute or two," Karp said.

The other three left by the private door and Karp pressed the intercom button. "Darla, you may show Mr. Guma in."

"Sure, Mr. Karp," the receptionist cooed. "Mr. Guma, Mr. Karp says you may go in now." She giggled—"stop that . . . go!"

A moment later, Guma sauntered into the office, a wicked grin on his face. "Ready? I was going to walk you to court today."

"Goom, you really have to stop . . . you're ruining a perfectly good receptionist," Karp pleaded. "First she's going to be all atwitter, and useless, and then you're going to break her heart, and she'll really be useless. I need a cold, efficient secretary, not a woman in love."

"I can't help that I have that sort of effect on my paramours," Guma boasted. "And who knows, perhaps Madam Milquetost is the One."

"Uh-huh, if I want to hear lies this early in the morning, I'll go listen to Mr. Guy Leonard," Karp replied.

Guma made a grand gesture toward the door. "Let us be off," he said, then stopped and sniffed. "Isn't that Marlene's perfume I smell? Have we been, perhaps, misbehaving in the DA's inner sanctum this morning?"

Karp thought about Lucy, the madman David Grale, and al-Sistani. "No, Goom, I should only be so lucky. But let's go, I can only deal with one evil man at a time."

Katz was waiting for Karp when he arrived in the courtroom a few minutes later. "Welcome to Character Assassination Day," he said in a low voice.

"We'll see who assassinates whom," Karp said grimly.

"You okay?" Katz asked.

"Never better, Kenny. I'm just getting my game face on."

"What game? Rugby?"

Karp laughed, which relaxed him a little bit. "It might end up looking like that; now watch and learn, my boy, watch and learn."

Character Assassination Day began with Leonard's assault on the deceased, Gail Perez, when he called psychiatrist Latisha Gordon-Winker to the stand. He spent the next forty-five minutes on Dr. Gordon-Winker's bona fides as "one of the foremost authorities in the world on depression and bipolar disease," and author of the bestseller *Of Two Minds: My Own Battle With Bipolarity,* as well as "hundreds of important academic papers on this subject."

When Leonard moved to have Gordon-Winker, a thin, haughty-looking black woman whose face seemed set in a permanent sneer, accepted as an expert witness on the subject of depression and bipolar disease, Karp hardly bothered to look up from his notepad as he said "No objection." It was a pattern he planned to follow throughout the day. "The less obstructionist, the better," he explained to Katz. "The more the merrier, that way they can dig a deeper hole."

Karp watched calmly as Leonard spent over an hour with his "expert" witness, trying to paint the picture of Gail Perez as deeply depressed and, in fact, borderline bipolar. When, at last, it was time for cross-examination, he hardly questioned Gordon-Winker, except to say, "Your opinion that Gail Perez was depressed or bipolar can be shown to be true . . . a proven fact?"

"Well, no. It's an educated opinion from a medical expert."

"But it's not a fact, is it?"

"I can't prove it to you, no."

"So, it's fair to say that other so-called experts might very well have different opinions about Miss Perez's mental state? Meaning these experts could very well testify that Miss Perez did not suffer from any mental disease or defect?"

"They might . . . but they'd be wrong."

"In your opinion, of course."

"Yes. Of course."

"I have no further questions."

Leonard had used the remainder of the morning session trying to rehabilitate Dr. Gordon-Winker through redirect. Most of which consisted of repeating what she'd already said.

After lunch, Leonard had called a well-known psychologist, "Dr. Bill" Pecker, who had his own television show in the New York area and had recently written a book, *The Casting Couch: Sex, Stars, and the Great White Way.*

"Dr. Bill," Leonard said with a smile, "what do you mean by the term 'casting couch'?"

Dr. Bill, a small, balding, pear-shaped man, was brought in to question whether or not Gail Perez used Maplethorpe sexually to procure her role in his play. After listening to Leonard's detailed questioning, Karp first embarrassed Dr. Bill by refuting his qualifications and then hit him and the defense where it hurt.

"Doctor, can you give us one single fact—something irrefutable, something that can be proven to be true—about anything you just said? Not an opinion, not an educated guess, just a fact?"

"If you're talking about something I can prove with empirical evidence, then no," Pecker said. "Psychology is not a hard science; much of what we do is based on the study of anecdotal evidence, from which we draw conclusions."

"I see," Karp said. "In other words, you make things up based on what you've read, or heard, or been told, without having any idea whether they are factual or not."

"That's not true," Pecker argued.

"Dr. Pecker, were you in Mr. Maplethorpe's apartment the night Carmina Salinas was there?"

"No, of course not."

"I was just checking," Karp replied. "You seem so sure about what happened, I thought maybe you were a fly on the wall." He let the image hang in the air for a moment before adding, "I have no further questions for the . . . *doctor*."

32

DEAN NEWBURY DRUMMED HIS FINGERS ON THE LONG wooden table in the private conference room down the long hall and past the reception area from his office. As he waited for his appointment to arrive, he studied the symbol inlaid in gold in the center of the table. It depicted a shield from which three running legs, placed equidistantly, protruded around the circumference. The triskele was an ancient symbol whose origin was lost in the mists of time, but it was part of the Isle of Man flag, as well as the symbol for its long-lost sons.

Whichever way you throw it, he recalled of the triskele legend, *it lands on its feet.* Just like the Sons of Man, whose council members wore rings with the triskele emblem as a sign of their united purpose. Despite many setbacks, including the fiasco at the New York Stock Exchange, he would know in just a few days whether that purpose would reach its culmination in his lifetime. *And whether you'll be part of the council when we reap the benefits.*

At the moment, however, he was an old man who wished he was home in bed instead of waiting on that idiot congressman, Denton Crawford, at ten o'clock at night. Still, it was probably better to meet after-hours, if they had to meet at all.

The conference room was only accessible via a solid steel security door from the reception areas or a VIP-only elevator to a private, guarded garage beneath the Fifth Avenue building's main garage. "I don't see why we need to meet at all," he'd groused to Crawford when the man called that afternoon. "Everything's in place. The proper people have been paid to look the other way. The package will be delivered according to the new schedule."

However, Crawford had insisted they needed to talk and so here he was. Newbury glanced up when the monitor for the security camera in the parking garage winked on at the arrival of a dark Mercedes. As only a very few people had access to the garage, he knew that Crawford had arrived. He watched as the chauffeur got out and opened the door for his passenger, who stepped from the vehicle wearing a fedora and a heavy trench coat. *Look at that fool, he thinks he's playing spy games,* he thought. *Surely even if he's successful the other council members and SOM families won't approve his ascension into leadership. If he can be controlled, perhaps he'd be a more manageable replacement for V.T.*

Dean Newbury didn't even bother to look up when the monitor for the private elevator whirred into action, but instead got up and made himself a stiff whiskey and soda at the bar. The first sip was scorching its way down his throat when he heard the sound of the elevator arriving and then the titanium lock on the security door clicking open.

Newbury looked up expecting to see Crawford and scowled when a man wearing a silver mask stepped into the room. "Who the hell are you?" he demanded.

"What?" the man lisped as he stepped up to the far end of the table. "Don't you recognize me, my old mentor, Dean?"

The tumbler of whiskey slipped from Newbury's hand and crashed to the floor. "You," he whispered. Suddenly, it all made sense. The bold, merciless plan. Even Crawford as the front man; he'd always been one of Kane's toadies. "We thought you were dead."

"Ah, but I am risen." Kane laughed and removed his mask, taking pleasure in the shudder it elicited from Newbury. "A little worse for wear, as you can see, but I'll soon rectify that. Right now, this face serves my purpose."

"Where's Crawford?" Newbury asked.

"Probably asleep in bed with his favorite call girl in D.C.," Kane replied, "a busty little brunette named DeeDee, I believe, and waiting on his instructions from me."

Newbury let it sink in. As if there could have been any doubt, Kane had just told him who was the mastermind behind Operation Flashfire and, if it succeeded, in the driver's seat for leadership of the Sons of Man. Dealing with Crawford would have been one thing, but as an adversary, Kane was on another level entirely. *One I will not be able to control,* he thought.

"I can see you're disappointed in my resurrection," Kane continued. "Now that hurts. After all, I was once your protégé when that disloyal son of yours got himself killed in that war *we* started. How ironic, the Sons of Man go through all that trouble to foment revolution in the sixties and one of its favorite sons dies as a result. But that's all ancient history. A more immediate concern is that you seem to have replaced me so quickly as to be unseemly with your nephew, V.T. Of course, I have no idea why in the hell you think he can be trusted."

"I had hoped that blood would be thick enough," Newbury replied. "And if not, I have my own uses for him."

Kane frowned. "I had best not find that your uses ran counter to my plans," he warned. "Even your old cronies on the council won't save you if you interfered with an approved plan. And even if you didn't, but your nephew turns out to have been a spy, you'll be held personally responsible."

"I'll take care of my nephew in whatever way is appropriate," Newbury replied. "I killed my own brother, didn't I?"

The decision on V.T. came with a small pang of regret. He'd come to recognize that an old man's desire to have the Newbury name continue on in a leadership role with the Sons of Man had clouded his judgment. V.T. was a liability and would have to be removed. Still, he'd enjoyed their dinners and conversations.

Just that afternoon, he'd walked in on V.T. as his nephew was playing with a remote-controlled truck in his office. "*What's this? Goofing off on company time?*" he'd pretended to scold.

V.T. looked up, embarrassed. "*Oh hi, Uncle Dean. Yeah, sorry, I should be slaving away over torts, but I just bought this little beauty off a street vendor in front of the building. I always loved these when I was a kid and couldn't resist."*

"Quillian did, too," Newbury said, surprised that the memory caused a pain in his chest. *"Anyway, don't worry about it. You've been working a lot of late hours. As a partner, you really don't have to do that all the time, you know."*

"Now how would it look if I let my dear old uncle put in more time than I did," V.T. said with a smile. *"An ingrate, that's what, after all you've done for me. When I think that I could still be working at the DAO even worse hours for a mere pittance of the pay and little or no thanks, I thank my lucky stars you stepped up to the plate."*

"I'm glad I could talk some sense into you, my boy," Dean had replied with a chuckle. *"I look forward to many more years together."* He'd known that was a lie—he'd already decided that V.T. would never be completely trustworthy—but it sounded good at the time.

"I'd be happy to take care of him for you," Kane said. "I have some old scores to settle with your nephew. You do know he led Karp's white-collar crimes bureau that started all my troubles."

"I said I'd take care of him myself." Dean scowled. "It's a family matter, and the family will deal with it."

Kane grinned, a ghastly look on his ruined face. "Got to love that old-fashioned concept of family justice; I know a little bit about that myself. But just make sure you do deal with it. One of the first orders of business when I assume my rightful place at the head of the council will be a general housecleaning. I'm afraid we've gotten soft, even a little dotty, and we'll need to be a lean, mean fighting machine over the next few years. The problem with hereditary seats on the council is eventually you get a lot of deadwood, like Crawford; it's time for some fresh, young blood."

"Careful, Kane, you're not sitting in my chair just yet," Newbury said. "And in the meantime, what are you going to do about Karp? The cowboy was spotted in New Mexico this past weekend, and then took a plane back to New York. So we have to assume that they know Lucy Karp never arrived. That's going to turn up the heat."

"I'm not worried about District Attorney Butch Karp," Kane said.

He held up a cell phone. "We're in constant communication. It's as if I can reach out and touch him."

"What about David Grale?" Newbury asked, and for a moment thought he saw fear in Kane's eyes. But the man quickly recovered.

"Grale is a madman," Kane replied. "He's in no position to do anything about my plan. And if he tried, well, I still have Lucy Karp in my possession. He won't do anything to endanger her life. Unfortunately, the spy I had embedded with these so-called Mole People is dead. I had hoped to use him to hunt them all down in their filthy sewers after things had settled down again. But it doesn't matter, I'll find another way to settle my debt with Grale."

Ten minutes later, after a quick review of the plans, Kane said he was leaving.

"And al-Sistani?" Newbury said. "Are you going to let him go?"

"What, and have someone out there who can tell the world what we're really up to? Hell no," Kane said. "As soon as our package is delivered, he's toast . . . so to speak. The idiot almost got us followed by that madman Grale; he actually had a GPS tracking device in his shoe. It was from a dog collar, if you can believe that shit. My man Abu found it with a hand sensor before we got home, but that could have been bad. I'm going to enjoy watching the little towelhead fry for that alone."

Newbury squinted at Kane as the younger man walked toward the door. "I don't understand why you wanted to meet in the first place," he said. "This was an unnecessary risk."

"You don't understand?" Kane replied, as though surprised. Then he laughed. "Why, to gloat, old man, and tell you to your face that your time is almost over. Soon you'll be put out to pasture . . . and that's if you're lucky. *Myr shegin dy ve, bee eh,* right? What must be, will be."

Marlene looked up from the old couch in the back of the Housing Works Bookstore. It was ten o'clock, she'd been there for an hour, and there was still no sign of the Walking Booger.

She was trying to decide whether to get another cup of coffee—*guaranteeing that she wouldn't get any sleep tonight, if worrying about Lucy wasn't already going to do it*—when she heard the little bell above the front door ring. An enormous shaggy head poked in to survey the place, which was followed by the body of the Walking Booger.

There was no mistaking him. He was a giant of a man, even taller than Karp and Treacher, and probably as heavy as both men combined, though there was some question as to how much of that bulk was man and how much was the layers of filthy clothing he piled on. He appeared to be covered in thick, dirty hair from head to foot—if the tufts that jutted from his sleeves and covered his hands, neck, and face were any indication—and resembled a bear. A dirty, smelly bear.

Apparently homeless and preferring it that way, the Walking Booger got his nickname due to the fact that he usually had a grimy finger shoved up his nose. Such was the case when he spotted her. "'arlene! 'ood to 'ee you," he shouted in his usual muffled Boogerspeak, and smiled. He shuffled forward but instead of stopping where she sat, he moved right on past to the counter, where he told the barista, "A 'reat and a 'ot chocolate, pleas'. The 'ady will pay."

The barista looked over at Marlene, who nodded. "Whatever he wants. Nice to see you, too, Booger."

When he had his brownie and hot chocolate, Booger shambled over to where Marlene was sitting and plopped down across from her on a chair that groaned under his weight. His unmistakable odor washed over her and for a moment she wondered if she might pass out.

She forgot about how he smelled, however, as she watched him break off a piece of brownie between two crusty fingers, one of which had been involved in the recent nasal excavation, and pop it into the hole that appeared in his beard below his nose. As he chewed, he looked at her and smiled, or at least she thought he was smiling—it was difficult to tell through all the hair.

"So I had a message from Lucy that you wanted a treat?" Marlene said.

Booger nodded enthusiastically as he pinched off another piece of brownie and devoured it. "Yes, 'reats are 'ood. . . . 'ucy a great 'irl."

"Yes, she is," Marlene agreed. "But I can't find her. Are you going to help me?"

Nodding, the giant stuffed the rest of the brownie into his mouth, licked his fingers, and then slurped noisily at his hot chocolate until it was gone. He then stood up, wiped his hands on his filthy coat, and said, "Come 'ith me, 'arlene."

Halfway to the door, he stopped and leaned over to look her in the eye. "'oh-one 'ollow us, 'kay?"

"No one will follow, I promise," Marlene said, and followed him out into the night air.

Thirty minutes later, after dodging through a maze of alleys and dark streets, they arrived at the Bowery Mission in the East Village. Booger pointed to a side door in an alley and said, "'ock on the door. 'avid wants to 'ee 'ou."

"Uh, thanks, Booger," Marlene said, and did as she was told. The door opened and she found herself looking at the magnified blue eyes and pointed nose of Dirty Warren.

"Fu-fu-fucking ass tits . . . there you are," the little news vendor said. "Booger sure took his sweet time getting you here. Oh boy, oh boy . . . !"

"Thanks, but am I supposed to be meeting David?" she replied.

"Yeah, down the end of the hall . . . scumbag douche . . . first door on the right."

Marlene walked to the end of the hall and knocked on the door. She didn't bother to wait for the reply before entering.

David Grale sat in a large chair across the room next to an ancient floor lamp that cast dim light and did little to reach the dark circles beneath his haunted eyes. He looked worse than ever, she thought, gaunt and emaciated. "Hello, Marlene," he said. "Sorry about the walk, but I can't be too careful. Everybody wants a piece of this poor boy."

"Hello, David. Where's my daughter?"

Grale looked at her for a moment with his glittering dark eyes. "I don't know just yet, but I have reason to hope that all is not lost. However, I have to tell you some bad news . . . Kane's alive and he has Lucy."

Marlene groped for a chair and sat down, feeling suddenly nauseous and dizzy. "Kane has Lucy? How did it happen?"

Grale sighed and tried to explain. He said that he'd known in his heart that Kane wasn't dead. "I could feel him, like a malignant tumor you can't see but know is growing inside of you. But I wanted to believe that it was just my imagination, all those years of trying to catch and kill the demon that inhabits that body. But I was distracted by these other evil plots and evil men."

One such plot involved the Sons of Man, and Amir al-Sistani was the key to finding out what they had planned and stopping them. "I decided to use him to draw them out, but I couldn't just let him go and follow him. They'd know that something was up. I was trying to think of a way to accomplish this when Lucy asked to talk to me. We met the night her boyfriend left with Jaxon. I was waiting in the alley near the loft when she came around the corner with Gilgamesh."

Lucy's original goal was to ask him to release al-Sistani to Jaxon. *"We think he may have information about a large-scale terrorist attack on U.S. soil,"* she'd pleaded.

"Where is Jaxon?" he replied. He didn't trust law enforcement agencies; they'd all been infiltrated by agents for the Sons of Man, and it had nearly cost him his life several times. *"How do I know they won't just let al-Sistani go? Maybe that's part of their plan . . . make sure he lives to fight another day."*

"Jaxon's different," Lucy replied.

"Maybe," he said. *"I'd like to think so after working with him to stop the attack on the stock exchange. But what about his men? And just because he has al-Sistani doesn't mean he'll be allowed to interrogate or prosecute him. But why not ask me himself? Why send you . . . doesn't he know I'm a dangerous lunatic . . . a 'murderous vigilante,' I believe the* Times *called me?"*

"He doesn't know I'm here," she replied. *"In fact, he ordered me not to try to contact you. You're right, he does think you're mentally unstable and, perhaps without even meaning to, hurt me."*

Grale's face saddened as he finished relaying that last sentence, and Marlene saw how the comment had cut him. She also heard it in his voice when he said, "I told her that I could never hurt her.

Nor, if I could help it, would anybody else ever harm her." He sighed, part of which came out as a deep, rumbling cough from his thin chest. "But I'm afraid I may have failed at that."

"What happened?" Marlene said.

"I told her about my idea of following al-Sistani to the source of the danger. She thought about it for a minute and then came up with her plan. She said she wanted me to feign increasing madness"—Grale laughed—"not a very far stretch, and that I was growing obsessed with her. I knew that I had a spy among my people who was reporting to his unknown master about al-Sistani. We'd followed him one night to a meeting with his contact, who we later abducted and . . . made him want to talk to us . . . he didn't have the name of who he worked for, just some powerful person, who I now know is Kane but didn't then."

Grale had been hoping to use the spy to reach this mystery terrorist when Lucy came to him with her idea. She wanted to be "kidnapped" by the enemy and held hostage until exchanged for al-Sistani. *"They'll believe they have the upper hand,"* she'd said. *"And not suspect that al-Sistani is a Trojan horse."*

Grale leaned forward and looked earnestly into Marlene's eyes. "I hope you'll believe me when I say I told her no. I said it was too risky. But that feisty girl I once knew has turned into a tough-minded young woman, who told me that she was willing to risk her life if it meant saving hundreds or thousands of other lives. She gave me a choice. I could hand over al-Sistani to Jaxon, and she'd go happily home to New Mexico, or she was going to find a way to get herself kidnapped and then I'd have to make the exchange. At least this way, she said, I could protect her. . . . But she was wrong."

With the spy's help word got back to Kane that Grale was mad and infatuated with Lucy. Then it was arranged to have her kidnapped by Kane's men with the help of "an old friend . . . Edward Treacher. If there is one bright spot in any of this, Edward received a rather handsome advance for his treason, which has been largely donated to this mission, though Edward did need a new coat and boots."

"That doesn't tell me what happened to my daughter," Marlene replied.

Grale looked down at the floor. "The plan was that an exchange of prisoners would be arranged. That I'd get Lucy for my connubial bed . . . which would make you my mother-in-law."

"David, please, get to the point?"

"Ah yes, sorry, my mind wanders sometimes these days," he replied. "Anyway, I'd get Lucy, and Kane would get al-Sistani . . . with one of those microchip GPS locators that can be found in pet collars inserted into a shoe."

"So what went wrong? Why isn't my daughter home in New Mexico?"

Grale shook his head. "I don't know. The exchange was going along as I thought it would. I knew they would try to ambush me and keep Lucy, so we had their people in our sights before we began the prisoner exchange. They were no problem, but then for some reason, Lucy insisted on going back to Kane."

"Why?"

"Apparently she has some plan," Grale replied. "She passed a message to my man and then demanded to go back to Kane."

"What was this message?"

"Hold on, I'll let you hear it from the man who heard it," he said, and then shouted, "*Edward! Would you come in now, please*?"

The door opened and Edward Treacher stepped in, ducking slightly as he passed under the transom. "'Father, forgive them, for they know not what they do. . . . ' That's Luke 23:34 and I think a little more than appropriate at this moment. Hello, Marlene."

Treacher recounted how he'd led Lucy by a rope and collar to the clearing where he met up with Paulito, the dwarf, and al-Sistani. "Paulito was the spy," Grale said. "But his purpose had been served, and we could not allow him to shout a warning to Kane."

"'The truth shall set you free . . . ' the truth and a slug from a .45 derringer," Treacher said. "That's John 8:32 by the way. Lucy told me there wasn't much time, but she had to go back and needed me to remember her messages."

Treacher's eyes looked around wildly, as if he was back at Cleopatra's Needle. "I told her there was no way. I begged her to go with me to David. But she wouldn't listen. She said she was going to run back if I didn't take her and that would look suspicious. She said she had a plan—that 'he is the only one who can stop himself' and that she was the only one who knew how to make him."

"I still don't understand," Marlene said.

"I don't think anyone does yet," Grale said. "But there's more . . . Edward, tell her the messages."

"Of course, one was that she believed that she was being held in Brooklyn, possibly Brooklyn Heights. She said, 'Somewhere with a view. He said I'd have ringside seats.' And she said that her dad should expect a call from Kane on her cell phone and to tell Jaxon because he'd know what to do. Then she made me take her back. I'm sorry, I tried to tell her."

"I understand, Edward," Marlene said. "It sounds like she had you between a rock and a hard place. In fact, that was a big risk for you to take her back to Kane. How did you know he wouldn't just kill you?"

"Lots of good people are taking risks for good causes these days," Treacher said. "If Lucy was willing to risk going back to that monster, then I could make it look like I was trying to make a buck by cheating David. Plus, I used the ol' Br'er Rabbit reverse psychology gambit."

"Br'er Rabbit?"

"Yes, you know, from the Uncle Remus folktales," Treacher said. "It's not very PC these days, but remember the story about the time when Br'er Fox and Br'er Bear caught Br'er Rabbit and were trying to decide what to do with him? They talked about roasting him, and hanging him, and drowning him, which he said was fine with him—'hang me as high as you want'—as long as they didn't throw him in the briar patch. 'Anything but the briar patch.' So of course the two dummies threw him in the briar patch only to find out that Br'er Rabbit had been born and bred there. And that's how he escaped. So I pleaded with Kane not to send me back to David Grale. I cried that I was only trying to make a buck and that Grale would have my head. 'Please don't make me go down there.' Which, of course, got me flung into the briar patch."

"But since it wouldn't do to have Edward survive," Grale interjected, "which might make Kane suspicious, we cut off Edward's head and rolled it under one of the streetlamps."

"Actually, I borrowed the head from an old friend who's a night watchman at Madame Tussauds wax museum on Forty-second Street," Treacher continued. "He let me have the head of Hagrid, that big, hairy fellow from the Harry Potter movies. I have to say I don't think I look quite that bad, but it was good enough when covered with some ketchup to fool Kane at a distance. I am going to be in some trouble, as David saw fit to roll the head across the hard ground and it suffered some damage, with rocks and debris stuck in the wax."

"That's very imaginative," Marlene said. "But if I can get back to the subject, did my daughter say anything else?"

"She told me to tell David that no matter what happens to her, she said to keep the faith and his time will come."

"I know faith is code for her being in danger," Marlene said, "but what does she mean by your time will come?"

"I'm not absolutely sure," Grale said. "I think she thought of it last minute and had to be a bit more oblique in front of Kane when she said it. But I believe she was telling me to find her, but when I do to wait until the right moment to strike. Where that will be and when, I'm still trying to ascertain."

Marlene stood up and Grale rose, too. "What about al-Sistani," she asked, "and the tracking device in his shoe?"

"We were able to trace it to Fulton Ferry Park beneath the Brooklyn Bridge. We located the shoe, but it was on a bum who found it in a Dumpster in the park."

Marlene was silent for a moment, looking at the robed man who stood in front of her. She never knew quite what to make of him. Vigilante. Avenging Angel. Killer. "Why didn't you come in and talk to Jaxon before my daughter thought this was the only way?"

Grale shrugged. "I thought about it, but decided against it. One, it would put him in an awkward position as a law officer in the company of an accused serial killer—me—doesn't matter if they were all evil demons disguised as men, that's not how the law sees it. But more important, what if Kane or any of the others involved are arrested and it comes out in the trial that Jaxon relied on information given to him by that same serial killer and religious wacko, some of it obtained through torture? I'm not a lawyer, but couldn't that get the charges dismissed?"

Marlene nodded. "It's possible." Then without warning she reached out and slapped Grale hard across his face. "But that's for playing God and leaving my daughter in the hands of a sociopath."

Grale slowly wiped the blood from his mouth. "I deserved that and worse," he said. "And I'm sure I'll have to answer to a higher authority if something happens to Lucy."

"That may be, David," Marlene said icily, "but first you'll have to answer to me."

33

"KANE'S ALIVE AND HE'S GOT LUCY."

No matter how many times Karp repeated the words Marlene had said to him when she got home the night before, they still made his heart pound. Each time, he had to remind himself of the little speech he'd given just the day before about trusting Lucy's instincts and decision making. *But that was before Kane slithered back into the picture.*

Just the thought of the man set his blood boiling. Kane was a man who slaughtered a schoolbus full of children and tried to murder thousands of other people in St. Patrick's Cathedral, without batting an eyelid. And Karp knew his mortal battle with Kane wouldn't be over until either he or Kane, or both, was dead.

Karp just prayed as he looked around the courtroom, trying to get his thoughts focused on the trial, that his daughter would not be a casualty along the way. For a moment it seemed surreal. Kenny Katz was toying with an apple at the prosecution table. On his dais, Judge Rosenmayer was looking over a note Karp had passed to the judge's law clerk. He looked up and nodded to Karp.

"If we have no other business, I'll ask that the jury be brought in," Rosenmayer said.

Focus, Karp, it's showtime. But Kane's alive and he has my little girl!

Just a half hour earlier in his office, after Marlene had gone over her meeting with Grale the night before, Jaxon had suggested that he might want to ask the judge to postpone the trial. *"I don't see how you're going to be able to concentrate on Maplethorpe with Kane and Lucy on your mind,"* he'd said. *"And if you do get a call from Kane on Lucy's phone, we're going to want to be right on it."*

However, Marlene had a different opinion. *"I think you need to just push on with the trial,"* she'd said. *"Nothing's probably going to happen right this minute, and you're just going to sit around fretting. Plus, I wonder how carefully Kane is watching what we do. If you go ahead like nothing is different—instead of postponing a major trial and locking down with law enforcement authorities—maybe he'll relax his guard."*

In the meantime, she said, he could keep his cell phone on vibrate, *"and let Kenny monitor it. Maybe talk to Rosenmayer before he summons the jury and tell him that you may need to ask for an emergency recess at some point. Tell him it's a national security issue, and he won't ask a bunch of questions."*

After hearing Marlene out, Jaxon changed his mind. *"On second thought, she's right. I'll have my surveillance guys hook you up so that we can hear whatever you say and, if you don't mind having a small transmitter in your ear—can't even see the thing—we can talk to you. We'll make it something you activate if Kane calls or you need us."*

Jaxon explained that he needed to know the moment he picked up a call from Lucy's cell phone. *"A lot of people don't know this, but some of the newer, higher-end cell phones come with global positioning system technology,"* he'd said. *"A lot of this started after the 9-11 attacks to help law enforcement and firefighters locate people who make emergency calls on their cells. But it can be used to locate someone making other calls, too. Lucy's got one of those phones."*

"So if she calls, you'll be able to pinpoint the location?" Karp asked.

Jaxon nodded. *"If there's a good signal with transmission towers nearby, which is basically how we locate where the signal is coming from, we can narrow it down to two hundred, maybe even a hundred feet. Hopefully that will be enough. But it does take some time to get an exact fix, so you'll want to keep whoever's calling on the line as long as possible. This would be especially true if they're traveling, because then, obviously, we'll be tracking a moving target. It's not an exact thing, but I think from that message that's what Lucy's counting on."*

Karp looked at Marlene, who gave him a tearful smile. At least this sounded hopeful. *"Speaking of calls, any word from Jojola or Tran?"* he'd asked.

Jaxon's face grew grim and he shook his head. *"Nothing,"* he'd said. *"We're still hoping that they're simply out of communication range and following some hot lead they don't want to abandon. That's one of the problems with amateurs; they tend to freelance and break all the rules. On the other hand, I know those two might be getting up there a bit, but there aren't a lot of young guys who can handle those two old jungle fighters, either."*

The agent had done his best to try to make the last part of his statement sound confident, but Karp caught the tightness in his voice. He knew that Jaxon was thinking that the worst-case scenario was also the most likely. But he still had a job to do.

"Where are you off to while I'm in court?" Karp asked.

"We're going to set up shop quietly over in Brooklyn Heights," Jaxon replied. *"It's an educated guess, but I want to be as close as possible to where she and Kane might be when that call comes."*

As Jaxon got up, Blanchett, who'd been sitting quietly, his face taut, rose to go with him. But the older man turned and said, *"Ned, I'm going to leave you here with the district attorney."*

Blanchett's face turned angry. *"What? No way, sir! If you're in Brooklyn looking for Lucy, I want to be there, too."*

"Sorry, son, you're emotionally involved—we all are to a degree, but you more than even me, and I can't have two of us thinking with our hearts and not our heads," Jaxon said. *"But more than that,*

I need you on the scene here. If that call comes in, I want you by Karp's side and making sure that nothing happens to him. And keep your rifle handy, maybe Kane will want to meet with Butch, and you may get a shot."

Ned looked hard at Jaxon for a moment but then dropped his head. "*Yes, sir,*" he said.

The last part may have convinced Blanchett, but Karp knew that Jaxon was also looking out for the young man in case they found Lucy and she was hurt . . . or worse.

"The defense calls . . ."

Kane's alive and he has my little girl! Focus, Karp, now is not the time!

Portly and bald with a long, gray beard, Dr. Anthony Belli waddled up to the witness stand ready to challenge Hilario Gianneschi's "interpretation" of what Maplethorpe said to him the night of Gail Perez's death.

As he told the jury, he was a professor of languages, "specializing in English-as-a-second-language adaptation, and North Mediterranean languages," at Columbia University. "I am fluent in Italian, Greek, French, and Spanish with a basic understanding of Arabic and Croatian."

Belli testified that it was common for people speaking English as a second language to interpret what they heard in English in their native tongue, and that sometimes it doesn't always translate exactly.

When it came time for Karp to question Belli, Karp easily dismissed this as a mere opinion and, during cross-examination, managed to get Belli to admit—albeit reluctantly—that Hilario Gianneschi's English was more than adequate.

Next, the defense called another shrink, this one specializing in post-traumatic stress disorder. Psychologist Willow Spring, a large woman with a mop of blond hair, wore a tie-dye dress and described herself as a "Buddhist Freudian." She equated the interaction between Maplethorpe and Gianneschi as a "perfect storm of PTSD . . . one a witness to a gruesome suicide, the other a witness to its immediate aftermath, on a psychological collision course."

Spring said she'd interviewed Maplethorpe in a clinical setting using hypnosis. "When he was under, he had a quite different account of what he said to Gianneschi."

"Is there a reason to believe that he would give a *factual* account?" Leonard said, emphasizing the word "factual" as he looked over at Karp.

"Yes, the cool thing about hypnosis is that people don't lie," she said.

"Then would you please tell the jury what you learned," Leonard said.

"You betcha . . . well, for one thing he remembered calling Mr. Gianneschi and asking him to summon help," Spring said. "This beautiful young woman who he hoped would find him attractive as a male had located a gun and shot herself in the head. A horrible, horrible tragedy and yet another reason handguns should be banned."

Leonard ignored the handgun comment—not able to tell where the jury stood on that—and asked what happened next.

"Instead of summoning an ambulance, the concierge came himself," Spring said. "Beginning to feel the first effects of PTSD, which are a confused state and disassociation from what just happened, Mr. Maplethorpe waited at his door, hoping paramedics would arrive to save the day. But instead, Mr. Gianneschi came alone."

"At which point he says something about something 'bad,' depending on what version you believe," Leonard said.

"Well, of course he feels bad about what just happened, it was his gun and he left it lying carelessly around," Spring said.

"Does he think he's killed her?"

Spring shook her mop of curly blond hair. "No, it's obvious he doesn't, because he says something to the effect of 'Please tell her.' Well, you can't tell a dead person anything. So no, he thinks she's still alive.'"

"What if Mr. Gianneschi heard correctly and Mr. Maplethorpe wanted him to say he was sorry?"

"Of course he's sorry. He's sorry that he didn't give her a role in his play. He's sorry that she misinterpreted his intentions. He's sorry he had a gun. He's sorry she shot herself. He's got a lot to be sorry about. It's also sort of like a child who thinks that by saying he is sorry the results can somehow be reversed. Unfortunately, large-caliber gunshot wounds don't work that way."

Compounding the issue, Spring said, was the fact that Hilario Gianneschi was also suffering post-traumatic stress disorder. "He saw a body. He saw blood. He saw a gun. So when he heard the word 'bad,' he assumed he was being told that Mr. Maplethorpe had done something bad. Then when Mr. Maplethorpe said he felt sorry for what had just happened through his negligence, Mr. Gianneschi heard an admission of guilt. And when Mr. Maplethorpe said something along the lines of thinking she might be dead, Mr. Gianneschi, his mind trying to disassociate from the horror, hears 'I think I killed her.'"

Leonard limped over to the lectern, where he arranged his note cards in some sort of mysterious order, like a gypsy reading fortunes. "Could there be another explanation for hearing 'I think I killed her'?"

"Yes." Spring nodded. "Mr. Maplethorpe, with his extreme feelings of guilt, may have actually said 'I think I killed her.'"

"Does he mean it?"

Spring shook her head. "Not in the literal way," she said. "But for those reasons I just described, in a figurative way, yes. He's going to have to live the rest of his life knowing that he did not have that gun secured; I believe there are even laws about such things."

Leonard shoved all his note cards into one pile, as if he'd seen all he needed to see. "You're telling the jury that Mr. Maplethorpe felt so guilty about leaving his gun available that he actually was confessing to that, not murder."

Spring nodded. "That's exactly what I'm saying, if he actually said 'I think I killed her.' However, I want to emphasize that if I was a betting woman—given Mr. Gianneschi's language difficulties, as well as both men suffering from PTSD—it's more likely that he is misquoting what was actually said, and that would be more along the lines of 'I think she's dead.'"

Leonard waved his note cards at Spring. "Ms. Spring, have you looked over Mr. Gianneschi's interview with the police, and did anything about it jump out at you?"

"Well, I think it's pretty clear that this was an interview with a man who is very aware that he's in this country illegally," Spring replied. "He understands that if he doesn't cooperate with the authorities—if he doesn't tell the police what they want to hear—things could go rough for him, and he might find himself in handcuffs and on the next plane to Italy."

"So if the police interrogators sit him down and show him a photograph of a child in a cowboy outfit found in Mr. Maplethorpe's apartment and ask him if anything looks familiar . . ."

"He's going to want to give them the answer he thinks they want, such as saying that Mr. Maplethorpe was wearing something similar."

"Thank you, Ms. Spring. No further questions."

Karp was on his feet before Leonard sat down. "Ms. Spring, taking into account everything you just said, how much of it was factual and how much of it was opinion?"

Spring looked surprised by the question. "I like to think I base my opinion on fact."

"Is that like a film based on fact?" Karp retorted. "Where they change things just a little . . . or a lot . . . we really don't know."

"No, I wasn't changing anything. I just looked at what I was given and rendered an opinion."

"And is that opinion subject to change?"

"I'm not sure what you mean."

"Well, you just told the jury that Mr. Maplethorpe might have said 'I think she's dead,' which in your opinion Mr. Gianneschi misquoted as 'I think I killed her.' But then you said that if Mr. Maplethorpe actually did say 'I think I killed her,' which is what Mr. Gianneschi testified to in this courtroom—no ifs, ands, or buts—then your opinion was that he said this because he was feeling guilty for leaving his gun lying around. So your opinion is subject to change depending on which version is true?"

Spring pursed her lips and blew out, then looked up at the ceiling.

"Ms. Spring, did you understand my question?"

"I'm thinking," Spring replied testily.

"And your answer is . . ."

"You're twisting it all around, but sure, anyone's opinion can change if the facts change."

"But aren't facts something you know to be true, or can prove to be true?"

Spring pouted. "That sounds like one definition of the truth."

"What other definition do you have? Perhaps you could share that with the jury."

Spring glared at Leonard, and when he didn't speak said, "No, what you said is good enough."

"So how much of what you said do we know to be true or can prove to be true?"

"Like I said, Mr. Karp," she replied, "I did my best to give my professional opinion. I will leave it up to the jury whether to accept that as fact."

Karp smiled widely. "Now *that's* a fact, Ms. Spring. No further questions."

During the lunch break, Karp went back to his office alone. "I need to make a couple of calls," he told Katz and Blanchett, who'd sat in the courtroom all morning. "Why don't you guys go grab a bite?"

Karp entered his office and sat down in his chair. His cell phone had not gone off during the morning session. He pressed a button twice on the small transmitter in his pocket—"*twice to chat, three times in an emergency,*" the tech had said.

Suddenly, Jaxon's voice was in his head. "Yeah, Butch, anything?"

"Nope," he replied. "Just testing. How about you?"

"Nothing yet. Hang in there. . . . And Butch?"

"Yeah?"

"Sorry I got Lucy into this," the agent said, his voice faltering. Uncle Espey had known Lucy since childhood.

Karp felt tears in his eyes. "She's a big girl," he said. "I hope after this, she'll decide that being a rancher's wife is plenty exciting. But it's her choice."

The rest of the lunch break, Karp sat back in his chair with his feet on the desk and his eyes closed. He tried to focus on the next witness, but instead, images of Lucy flooded into his head. The precocious child who talked to adults like they were the children and she the old soul. But not too old that she didn't love to crawl into bed with her parents and snuggle down. There was the egghead who by the age of seven spoke seven languages and was beginning Chinese, and was well ahead of her classmates in just about every other subject, too. And the young teen who'd cried on his shoulder until his suit coat was soaked because some boy at school told her she had "a face like a horse." He recalled the young woman working in soup kitchens, who'd taken the pantheon of sociopaths, terrorists, and killers who'd threatened her or her eccentric family in stride. *The woman who'd looked so happy the night she and Ned announced their engagement.*

Karp started at the sound of a knock on the door. He realized that he'd actually fallen asleep. "Yeah, come in," he said, glancing at the clock.

Katz opened the door. "You ready to go?"

Karp swung his feet off the desk and stood. "I'm always ready to go," he said.

34

NADYA MALOVO WATCHED AS THE U.S. COAST GUARD PATROL boat came alongside the wallowing ship just as the sun was creeping above the pink-tinted horizon. *Red sky at morning, sailors take warning,* she thought. *An appropriate bit of folklore for today.*

As she made her final preparations, Malovo automatically assessed the enemy's strength. *Eighty-seven-foot Marine Protector Class coastal patrol boat, burns 165 gallons of diesel an hour at top speed of twenty-six knots. Armament consists of two .50-caliber machine guns fore and aft, and small arms distributed to ten-member crew. Can launch an inflatable boarding party boat out a ramp at the back while under way.*

Malovo whirled to where Stupenagel and Tran stood handcuffed next to each other, guarded by two men with AK-47s. Tran's face was bloody and swollen from the beating he'd taken from Malovo. Stupenagel was none the worse for wear, except that her long blond hair had been cut short and her face washed clean of makeup. "Take these two below and keep them where we discussed until the ship is under way again."

"Then what?" said the younger of the two guards, a small man with unsteady, red-rimmed eyes who nervously fingered the trigger of his assault rifle.

"Shoot him," Malovo said, pointing at Tran, "but in the legs. I want him alive when you dump him overboard for the sharks to finish. Good-bye, whatever your name is, little Vietnamese man. Too bad Ivgeny is not here to try to rescue you this time. I would like to feed him to the sharks, too . . . piece by piece. . . . Ah, well, someday perhaps."

"What about her," said the older guard, a big man with an enormous belly.

"When the Coast Guard leaves, bring her back and tie her to the rail at the front of the bridge so that she is easy to see," Malovo said. "She is my understudy. Don't you think that from a distance, she looks like me? Her hair is short like mine. She's a little fatter, but they won't get too good a look before it's too late. Then when she is gone, in their eyes, Ajmaani will be, too." *And they will stop looking for Nadya Malovo*, she thought.

The big blond shook off the little man's hand. "Touch me again and I'm going to kick your ass over the railing," she snarled, and then looked at Malovo. "See you in hell, bitch."

Malovo grinned. "Save me a spot next to the fire when you get there first," she said, laughing.

As the guards hustled the two prisoners below, Malovo turned to the captain and Omar Abdullah. "I'm going to my cabin," she said. "You both know what to do."

"It will be done," Abdullah replied. "The great day is upon us! *Allahu akbar*!"

"*Allahu akbar*!" the other men on the bridge responded.

"Yes, God is great," Malovo said as she left the bridge. *But I'll take the money over religion any day.*

A few minutes later, Chief Warrant Officer Ron Adkins stood where Malovo had been, looking over the passports of the men on the bridge. He was accompanied by six armed seamen, four of whom checked the passports of the remainder of the cargo ship crew on the deck.

The U.S. Coast Guard chief handed the passports back to the

man who'd identified himself as the captain. "What seems to be the problem?" Adkins asked.

The milk transport had radioed that it was having difficulty with steering and requested permission to head for the closest ship repair facility, which happened to be the Brooklyn shipyards on the East River. Adkins's ship was patrolling in the area and responded to the distress signal for a quick security check before allowing the ship to proceed to Brooklyn.

Adkins was well aware that vessels entering American waters are supposed to provide advance notice to the Coast Guard of at least twenty-four hours—ninety-six for liquefied natural gas tankers. In addition, they are required to provide the ship's cargo list, the names and passport numbers of each crew member, details about the ship's ownership and agents, and a list of recent ports of call. But there wouldn't be time for this vessel.

"We're having difficulties with the electrohydraulic drive for the rudder," the captain said. "We do okay on smooth seas, but I worry if we run into foul weather, the helm may lose control."

Adkins looked at a clipboard. "It looks like you're headed to Nova Scotia? With milk and milk products?"

The captain nodded. "Yes. Fortunately, there is no problem with our refrigeration units."

"Why in the world would anyone ship milk from Trinidad to Nova Scotia?" one of the sailors with Adkins asked.

"Who knows, Jamieson," Adkins responded. "Ours is not to reason why . . ."

"Yes, sir."

"Okay, Captain, your papers appear to be in order," Adkins said. "But let's have a look around. Jamieson, check the cabins. Rodriguez, you come with me."

The captain escorted Adkins and his man on a quick but efficient check of the remainder of the ship, including a cursory glance at where some of the men were working belowdecks on the hydraulic drive. Neither Adkins nor Rodriguez was familiar enough with the terrorist watch list to recognize Omar Abdullah, nor interested in a small storage room in which Tran had been left bound and gagged.

When they came to the refrigeration units for the enormous stainless steel milk tanks, Rodriguez whistled in admiration. "Boy, this is state of the art, especially for an old tub like this."

"New owners want to provide only the freshest milk." The captain smiled.

Rodriguez looked closely at a temperature gauge. "Thirty-six degrees Fahrenheit," he said. "Man, a glass of cold milk sounds real good about now. Don't suppose these babies come with a spout?"

The captain laughed. "Oh no, no sipping allowed."

When the three men arrived back on the bridge, they found Jamieson standing with a beautiful blond woman. She looked frightened.

"I found her hiding in one of the cabins, sir," Jamieson said. "Her passport is a little shaky."

Adkins stepped closer to look at the woman. She was obviously in her forties, though proof positive that some women improve with age. Her skin was tan, her blue eyes clear and steady, and she had a body most twenty-year-old women would kill for, he thought.

No wonder the old geezer is willing to pay big bucks to sneak her into the country, he thought. *That and whatever they're hiding in those milk tanks . . . cocaine, probably, with the money they're paying me. But the old boy wants this fine little piece of ass off the ship before they deal with U.S. Customs.*

Adkins was a career man, but he was looking at retirement in five years on a pension that would barely keep a roof over his head. But a simple act of helping an old man sneak his Russian mail-order bride into the country and looking the other way during this security inspection was going to buy him a nice place on Nantucket, where he'd spend the rest of his days fishing from a new boat, swilling beer, and chasing women. What did he care if the niggers in Harlem smoked crack from Trinidad until they OD'd.

"Weren't you aware that you were supposed to present your passport?" he asked after he'd perfunctorily glanced at hers. "And I didn't see any Mary Blithe on the crew list."

"I didn't think passengers had to," she said with an accent that didn't fit the name Mary Blithe.

"A passenger? On a milk transport?" Jamieson said.

"Stand down, sailor," Adkins ordered.

"Yes, sir."

"So why are you hiding on a milk transport bound for Nova Scotia?" Adkins asked.

The woman began to cry. "I'm sorry," she wailed. "I just want to see my family in Canada but I cannot receive visa because of one-time mistake in Moscow . . . for prostitution."

Adkins acted as if he needed to think about it for a moment, and then reached a decision. "Mr. Jamieson and Rodriguez, please escort Miss . . . Blithe to our vessel. I'm sorry, young lady, but I'm going to have to ask you to come with us. If the INS doesn't care, you can reboard this vessel when she departs from the ship repair facility and let the Canadian authorities deal with you."

Turning to the captain, Adkins said, "You may proceed to the Brooklyn shipyards. When you approach New York Harbor, you will be met by tugboats to guide you in. You are to maintain the course my navigator sends you and not deviate from it. Do you understand?"

The captain saluted. "Yes, I understand. No deviations. Straight for the shipyards. Thank you very much, sir."

"What kind of speed are you making?"

"No more than ten knots," the captain replied. "More than that and she is difficult to control."

"And Captain," Adkins said with a wink no one else saw. "If it turns out that there are problems with Miss Blithe, you may have some explaining to do."

"I am sorry I ever agreed to give her passage," the man replied. "She offered a great deal of money and showed me a passport. How was I to know that she was a disgusting prostitute trying to sneak into Canada? I am just a poor ship's captain."

"Yeah, yeah, just hope you don't have to explain it to the FBI," Adkins said. "Now if you'll excuse me."

Jamieson spoke up. "Chief Adkins, do you want me to radio over to the ship and have one of our women standing by to search her?"

Adkins thought about it. The old man, Dean Newbury, had given him specific instructions; no one was to search the woman or her things. He'd hinted that she might be carrying contraband diamonds from South Africa. *So maybe she's a courier, not his mistress,* Adkins thought. *No matter, it's not my business; I'm being paid good money to follow instructions.*

"I don't think it will be necessary, Jamieson," the chief warrant officer replied. "She looks harmless enough, and it's probably not going to go well for her. We'll turn her over to Immigration when we get back to port; until then place her in one of the cabins and put a guard on the door."

"Yes, sir," Jamieson replied. *Boy, is the chief getting soft in his old age*, he thought, *but I have to admit, she is one good-looking MILF. Wonder if he's hoping to tap that before we get back to shore.*

Jojola awoke at the sound of a large engine starting up. It took him a moment to realize in the dim morning light that the engine belonged to another boat.

Good guys or bad guys? he wondered. Just then a large swell passed beneath the reefer, rocking it like a baby in a cradle, and his stomach flopped. He was lying among a dozen or so life jackets hanging in a heavy net above the fantail deck of the ship, which had the unfortunate habit of swaying even more than the deck or his previous hideout in the lifeboat. *I hope it's the good guys, because I can't take much more of this. Please, spirits of the earth, if you let me live long enough to return to the land, I will never leave it again.*

He wondered how Tran was faring with Malovo. When his friend didn't show up that night, he'd gone looking for him and saw his capture. There was nothing he could do at the time; while his hunting knife was a formidable weapon, it was no match for Malovo and a half dozen men with automatic weapons.

The fact that Malovo had not killed Tran outright and hauled him off with his wrists tied together gave Jojola reason to believe that she would at least keep him alive for questioning. The old Viet Cong guerrilla was a tough old bird; Jojola just had to hope he'd last until he could do something to rescue him. *Tonight when it's dark and I have a fighting chance*, he thought, *or the good guys show up! I wonder what's keeping Jaxon.*

As much as he wanted to believe that the sound of the engine he heard might be Jaxon and a boarding party, he knew that the lack of resistance from the reefer meant that help had not arrived. The other boat's engine suddenly roared louder and then began to recede. *Whoever it was,* he thought, *they're leaving. At least I won't have to fight two ships full of terrorists.*

A few minutes later, he heard an even larger engine crank up and head away. *Hope I didn't just blow my chance to call in the cavalry.* He'd cut partway through the ropes to one side of the net so that if he was discovered, a quick slash with his knife and he'd be able to drop to the deck and at least make a last stand.

He knew after Tran was captured that search parties would scour the rest of the ship; Tran wouldn't give him up, but they'd come looking just in case. But he also hoped that the search would be cursory and the crew preoccupied with whatever evil plan they were hatching with a milk transport ship filled with liquefied natural gas.

So he stayed away from the lifeboat and hid himself as best he could among the life jackets. The expected search parties had passed below, but as hoped, they only glanced around and none of them looked up. One of the searchers pulled out a pipe and lit up a bowl of what smelled like hashish that he passed around. *Smoke up, boys,* Jojola thought. *I can use all the help I can get.*

Jojola was contemplating getting down from his perch long enough to stretch and work some of the kinks out of his muscles when he heard voices coming from inside the ship. A few moments later, Tran appeared below him followed by two men with assault rifles. The big one pointed his gun at Tran.

"Go stand over near the railing," the man ordered.

"Go fuck yourself," Tran replied, turning around to face his assassins. "I'm not going to make this easy. You're going to hurt your back when you have to bend over and pick me up and throw me over the side."

The big man scowled and started to aim when the smaller terrorist put his hand on the man's arm. "Let's smoke some hash first. Then you shoot him in one leg, and I'll shoot him in the other. It will be more fun watching the sharks eat him when we're high. Besides, tonight we'll be in Paradise, and they may not have any hashish there."

The big man smiled and nodded. "They have everything in Paradise," he said. He kept his gun pointed at Tran. "I'll watch him. Go ahead and get it ready."

The smaller man put his gun down and pulled his pipe out of his pants, as well as a small foil wrapper, which he carefully unfolded. He removed a piece of hashish and placed it in the pipe, and then produced a lighter. A few quick puffs later, and the smaller man had it going, holding it up to his companion's lips.

"Hey, how about giving the condemned man a little of that?" Tran said.

The smaller man looked at the bigger man and shrugged. "Why not? Perhaps the sharks will like their meat better with hash in it." He stepped over to Tran, careful not to get in the way of his comrade's line of fire, and placed the pipe in the Vietnamese man's mouth.

Tran took a couple of puffs, then smiled. "You know, you guys are all right, and if you let me go right now, I'll ask my friend not to kill you both."

The big man laughed. "Ha! Next you will tell me that your friend is standing behind me," he said. "I saw that in an American movie once. Only there really was a man standing behind the bad guy, who was too stupid to turn around and shoot him."

"Well, close," Tran said. "Actually, he's right above you."

The man laughed again and took aim at Tran's right leg. But then there was a sound above his head of ropes parting and before he could react, something heavy had landed on his shoulders. Next was a burning pain in his neck, and when he tried to breathe in, he couldn't get any air. He dropped his rifle as his hands clasped his throat, which for some reason was slippery with warm liquid, and he pitched forward.

About the time that Jojola landed on the big man's back, the smile left the face of the smaller man. It took a moment for him to realize that his companion's throat had just been cut from ear to ear; then he screamed and tried to run for his rifle.

However, as the smaller man turned his back on him, Tran reached out with a foot and swept the man's feet out from under him. The small man went down hard, striking his head on the steel deck, and was knocked unconscious.

Jojola grinned as he wiped the blood off his knife on the big man's shirt. "Geez, you look like shit," he said.

"Yeah, I'd say the same, but you always look like shit," Tran replied with a smile.

"Hey, that's not a nice thing to say to the man who just saved your miserable hide," Jojola said.

"Save my— Are you crazy, I had it all worked out," Tran said, holding out his wrists so that Jojola could cut the rope that bound them. "I lured the one near me and was going to use him as a human shield to reach the big one with the gun. I would have then crushed his larynx with a perfect kick to the throat and then dispatched the smaller one by strangling him."

"Wow," Jojola said. "How much of that stuff did you smoke?"

Tran grinned. "Only a couple of puffs. But that's pretty good shit. Want to try some?"

"I'll take your word for it," Jojola said. "Drugs are bad for your health. Just ask these two guys."

Just then the small man moaned. Tran looked at him and then stripped out of his shirt and pants.

"Um, I hate to ask what you're doing now," Jojola said.

"Just help me get his clothes off, dummy," Tran replied.

"Why? You like his style?"

Tran rolled his eyes. "No, but the captain of this ship expects to hear me get executed and then see my body floating in the water for the sharks. So that's what he's going to get."

"Ah, I see the method behind your madness," Jojola said, and leaned over the semiconscious man and tugged his pants off.

A minute later, they had the other man dressed in Tran's clothes and standing up, albeit unsteadily, next to the railing. The man suddenly realized what was happening and his eyes filled with terror. "Please, do not kill me," he said to Tran. "I gave you hashish."

"You were also going to shoot me in the legs and feed me to the sharks," Tran said.

"That was Ibrahim's doing," the man said, pointing to the dead man on the deck. "I was going to let you jump. And at least have a chance."

"You're a liar," Tran said, and aimed the assault rifle at the man's chest. "Now tell me, when is the attack going to take place and what is the target?"

"Tonight," the man squealed. "I do not know the target, just a glorious blow for Allah against the Great Satan! We will all die together."

"So if you were so willing to die tonight, why are you afraid now?" Jojola asked.

The smaller man looked troubled. "I don't want to die alone."

"Too bad," Tran replied, and pulled the trigger, letting off a burst. The bullets struck the target in the chest and propelled him over the side of the stern railing of the ship.

"That was harsh," Jojola said, walking over to the rail and looking down to where the man's body bobbed to the surface in the ship's wake.

"Captain's expecting an execution and a body," Tran replied. "At least he's dead. That's more than he was going to do for me."

"So what next? Do we make like pirates and take the ship?"

Tran shook his head. "Too many men," he said. "We might get a bunch of them, but they'd get us, too. Plus Malovo's on board, and she's no hash-toking dummy."

"What do we do?" Jojola asked.

"They're planning on sailing this ship up the East River and blowing it up," Tran replied. "Malovo explained it all to me when she was kicking my ass around. Apparently, there's a small specialized bomb attached down in the room that has the supposed milk tanks. It's designed to rupture the hull and the tanks at the same time without igniting the gas when it pours out."

"Why?"

"They want a cloud of the gas to form around the ship. Then they'll ignite it. Otherwise it just burns as it escapes like a big Roman candle."

"Doesn't sound like a good thing."

"It won't be. If they get this next to buildings and bridges, hundreds or even thousands could die in an instant."

"How do we stop them?"

Tran thought about it. "I think we have to try to disarm the special bomb, or keep them from setting it off."

"How do you propose to do that if they have so many guys with guns?"

Tran pointed to the other assault rifle. "As we taught you Americans in my native land, two well-armed, dedicated men can hold off the biggest army in the world if they outsmart their big, oafish enemy."

"Don't look at me when you say that," Jojola said. "I counted plenty coup against you people."

"Plenty coup? Since when did you start talking like Jack Palance in *Arrowhead*? But can we fight about this later? We have a bomb to disarm."

"Okay, but don't think I'm going to let that slight to my heritage go when this is over," Jojola replied. "You know there are things I could say about your funny little black pajamas and those goofy-looking cone-head hats."

"You're still an idiot," Tran said, shaking his head as he led the way into the ship.

"And you're still high."

35

"DR. BRAUNSCHWEIGER, IS THERE A PARTICULAR FIELD OF psychological study that you specialize in?" Guy Leonard rocked back on his cowboy boots with his thumbs hooked into his pants pockets and gazed up at the gray-haired, severe-looking woman in black horn-rimmed glasses.

It was the fourth day of the defense case. *And unfortunately*, he thought, *it will be the last.* He'd planned to parade another six to eight witnesses in front of the jury, use two or three more days. But it had suddenly dawned on him that Karp was baiting him with his "minimalist" approach. What he had mistaken for going through the motions, as he'd seen in other DAs he'd faced across the country, was a strategic plan.

When he told Maplethorpe that morning that he planned to wrap it up today with two witnesses, the producer had pitched a fit. *"But our witnesses did a fantastic job last time,"* he'd whined. *"Even if it's another hung jury, Karp would never go after me again. The press would have a field day with wasting taxpayer dollars about some washed-up actress nobody really cares about."*

But Leonard had stuck to his guns. *"You're in the theater,"* he explained. *"Surely you've heard the quote from* Hamlet, *'The lady doth protest too much, methinks.' He's trying to make it look like we're putting all these people on the stand because we don't have any real evidence."*

"Well, that's what we're doing, isn't it?" Maplethorpe said.

"Yes, but we don't want it to look that way," Leonard replied. *"Or the jurors might start wondering what we're trying to hide. In the first trial, that ADA Reed put on almost as many witnesses as we did, so it wasn't so noticeable. But Karp is clearing some of the trees out of the forest, and we can't let it look like once he's done with ours, his are the only ones left standing."*

Maplethorpe had sniffed a little longer about "getting what I paid for," but he'd eventually gone along with it. However, Leonard reminded himself not to let his guard down around his client . . . *or who knows what the little freak will try to hit me with.*

Once he recognized Karp's plan and saw the DA's cross-examinations cut to the chase with his expert witnesses—*"Can you name a single fact?"*—Leonard would have closed the defense case immediately. But he felt he needed the last two witnesses, so he'd started by calling Marta Braunschweiger, PhD, to the witness stand.

"I specialize in suicidology, the study of suicide," Braunschweiger replied.

"Is there any one aspect of this field that you are particularly esteemed in academic circles for?" Leonard asked.

"Well, I am probably best known for my book, *A City to Die For: Suicide Tourism in New York,* which was actually a bestseller on the *New York Times* list for several weeks," Braunschweiger said tersely, a little perturbed that the lawyer had tried to slip right on past giving her book a plug as agreed. "It was a compilation of case studies involving people who travel to Manhattan for the express purpose of killing themselves here—usually by jumping from tall buildings, like the Empire State, or hanging themselves in famous hotels, often where famous people also died. It's really a fascinating—"

"Ah, yes, Doctor, I'm sorry to interrupt, but I think I was referring to your most recent work," Leonard said. "I understand that is fascinating as well, and more on point, I think, with our purpose here today."

Braunschweiger stopped and stared for a moment at Leonard like a frog eyeing a bug. "Yesssssss, of courssssse," she replied, stretching out the *s* sounds so that she sounded vaguely like a snake hissing.

"Could you tell the jury what that is, please?"

"My current work focuses on RSS."

"RSS?" Leonard replied, as if it was the first time he'd heard the acronym.

"Revenge suicide syndrome," Braunschweiger said.

"Revenge suicide syndrome," Leonard replied, furrowing his brow. "I don't think I've ever heard of it."

Except for when you had me testify at the last trial, you boob, Braunschweiger thought as she smiled and replied. "That's because although we've all heard the anecdotes, there was no terminology for it until I was able to identify and define this as a syndrome, that is to say: 'a group of symptoms that collectively indicate or characterize a disease, psychological disorder, or other abnormal condition.' In the case of RSS, we're talking about suicide as a means of exacting revenge on one or more persons, or even a community or something as anomalous as 'society as a whole.'"

"And are you considered a leading expert in this field?" Leonard asked.

Braunschweiger smiled again. "I would say that I am *the* leading expert in this field. I'm the one who identified the characteristics that make it a syndrome; I'm the one who coined the term revenge suicide syndrome, RSS; and I'm the one who spent years collecting the data, collating it, postulating a theory, and then publishing the findings."

"So are there some characteristics that piled all together make up this syndrome?" Leonard asked.

"Yes, quite a number, but we can discuss the main ones," the psychologist said. "One characteristic is revenge as a motive for killing oneself. This can range from committing suicide to make someone else feel guilty that you were driven to such extremes, to actually staging your suicide to make it look like a murder in order to frame the object of your revenge."

"But why would someone do this? Killing oneself seems a rather drastic way to carry out revenge."

Braunschweiger arched her eyebrows. "It is rather drastic," she acknowledged. "It's probably the most drastic statement a person can make. We've all read stories about someone killing themselves for love, but were they really doing it because they didn't want to live anymore . . . or because they wanted to injure the person who didn't return their love?"

"But why end your own life for revenge. If you're angry, why not just shoot the person?"

"There are several reasons. Usually people who commit revenge suicide are also suffering from depression, or bipolar disorder, both of which often involve suicidal ideation. So they're already inclined that way. But they may have cultural or moral obstacles to taking someone else's life. Or they may love this other person and couldn't cause them physical harm, just mental anguish. Or the idea of putting the alleged offending soul in prison for the rest of his life for a crime he *knows* he didn't commit is the best revenge they can imagine."

"What about murder-suicide?"

"We do see that, of course. 'If I can't have you, no one can . . . but I'm also not going to live without you . . . or I'm afraid of going to prison, so first you and then me.' But that's not the same as revenge suicide. A very important characteristic of RSS is that the 'victim' of the revenge suicider continues to live, whether it's live with the guilt or live in prison."

"And this is RSS?" Leonard asked.

Braunschweiger nodded and sniffed. "Well, it's a very simple explanation meant for laypeople."

"Doctor, when we first began this conversation, you noted that we've all heard about RSS, we just didn't know to call it that, or that it was a syndrome. What did you mean by that?"

"What I meant was that taken individually, it is sometimes very difficult to identify a suicide as RSS," Braunschweiger said. "I've documented hundreds of cases and have barely touched the tip of the iceberg, but no one stopped to think that they had a common motive—revenge. Yet, we've all read a story about a teenager who kills himself and leaves behind a note blaming his parents. They may have been the most loving parents in the world, and yet they will have to live with the hell of that note for the rest of their lives.

Or we've heard about the jilted lover who shoots himself at his former girlfriend's wedding to another man. That woman will never forget what he did to her wedding day. And of course there's the wife of the wealthy philanderer. She could just kill herself, but that makes it too easy on him. He gets the younger trophy wife without having to sneak around anymore, and gets to keep his money and freedom. But what if she makes it look like he killed her? She doesn't have to live with the shame anymore, and he rots in prison with plenty of time to think about how he did her wrong. It really is the perfect revenge in some ways."

Leonard slowly walked toward the jury with his head down. "Dr. Braunschweiger, have you had the opportunity to examine the relevant transcripts?"

Braunschweiger removed her glasses and appeared to clean the lenses. She replaced them and answered. "Yes, I have."

"And what, if any, conclusion have you reached?"

"That this was a textbook example of RSS," Braunschweiger said. "Let's examine the facts. We have a—how shall I say this—a 'second-tier' actress who is getting older, the roles—which were never great—that she does get are getting fewer and smaller. And she knows that it's just going to get worse. She sees younger women get roles she feels she deserves, and it festers inside of her, though she tries to hide it behind an overly sunny personality, which is also a symptom of her bipolar disorder. She's been used by men for her body, and she's allowed it in order to move forward in her career. But she can see the writing on the wall; even on the casting couch, these powerful men want younger bodies."

"How does this affect someone like Gail Perez?"

"Well, you get to the point where it's hard to get up in the morning," Braunschweiger said. "It's just not worth it. At the low lows, you wonder if suicide is the best answer. You're done with the stress. Friends and family can stop worrying about you. Perhaps she knows someone close to her who has attempted suicide, and it plants that seed."

Braunschweiger, who had obviously been coached by the defense, mimed a two-handed grip on a gun. "She puts it in her mouth. She hears Mr. Maplethorpe shout 'No' and thinks, 'Good, he's watching; he'll have to live with the memory when he's rotting in jail for my murder.' And she pulls the trigger."

The psychologist looked over at Maplethorpe and shook her head sadly, as if he was the victim. Maplethorpe, who'd been nodding as she spoke, wiped at his eyes with a large red handkerchief he'd pulled from his forest green suit, and then blew his nose loudly. Several of the spectators behind him were also weeping, and one of them muttered loud enough for everyone in the court to hear: "That vindictive bitch!"

Leonard looked back at where the statement had come from and sadly nodded his head, as though someone had finally had the courage to say the truth. "No further questions," he said softly, and sat down.

Karp sat for a moment at the prosecution table, tapping his pencil on the legal pad in front of him. He seemed to be collecting his thoughts, but he was actually channeling the disgust and anger that seethed in him after listening to Braunschweiger's testimony.

The continued bastardization of the legal system, as exemplified by Leonard's Big Lie defense, rankled him today more than ever. His daughter was in the hands of a killer. New York City was once again a big bull's-eye for terrorists. And now he and every person in that courtroom had to listen to a clever defense attorney not so much advocate on behalf of his client, but create an illusion of truth from a pack of lies that if successful trivialized all the sacrifices other people had made and were making in defense of that legal system. People like his daughter, and Jojola and Tran, and Captain Meghan Reed, were willing to lay down their lives to preserve travesties like F. Lloyd Maplethorpe getting away with murder.

Karp took in a deep breath and let it out slowly as he stood. He wasn't trying to rid himself of his anger—this jury needed to see his righteous indignation—but he needed to wield it like a rapier, not a cudgel. Carefully laying his pencil down, he rose from his chair but remained standing where he was as he addressed the witness.

"Do you have a single shred of real evidence that Gail Perez was suicidal?" he asked, his voice firm but under control.

"There are a number of factors that added together point—"

"I wasn't asking for you to take a bunch of 'factors' you stirred in a pot to come up with some theory of what might have happened," Karp said. "I asked if you have a single shred of real evidence that Gail Perez killed herself. A suicide note? Something she said to someone? In fact, did she say something to Mr. Maplethorpe that might indicate she was thinking about sticking a gun in her mouth and pulling the trigger?"

"I have no idea what she may have said to Mr. Maplethorpe," Braunschweiger answered.

"Well, don't you think that if she said 'I'm going to kill myself,' he might have reported that to the police?" Karp responded.

"That makes sense, I guess."

"You guess," Karp repeated. "So I return to my original question, which you have yet to answer. Do you have a single shred of evidence that Miss Perez killed herself?"

"No, one single item, no."

"A note?"

"No."

"Something she said?"

"No."

"A videotape she left behind? Or maybe one from Mr. Maplethorpe's apartment?"

"No. It's just that in my professional opinion—"

"I did not ask for your opinion!" Karp thundered suddenly, then dropped his voice again. "I asked for a single verifiable fact. And now what I want to know is: without a single verifiable fact, where do you get off calling Gail Perez a vindictive whore?"

"That's not what I said," Braunschweiger said, a shocked look on her face.

"Let's look at what you said," Karp shot back. "You said this was a 'textbook' example of this so-called revenge suicide syndrome. You said she went to a man's apartment to have sex with him, that man over there"—Karp pointed across the aisle at Maplethorpe so that every juror in the box looked at the pale-faced defendant as he nervously licked his thin lips—"a man thirty years her senior, hoping that he would give her a job. Tell me, Dr. Braunschweiger, when a woman has sex in exchange for money or something else, is that a definition of a whore?"

"Well, I wouldn't want to unnecessarily disparage—"

"Unnecessarily disparage?" Karp tossed it back at her. "But that's what you've been doing in this courtroom since you got up on that stand!"

"Objection! Your Honor, the district attorney is insultingly and unnecessarily argumentative."

"I'm questioning an unresponsive witness," Karp retorted, turning to Rosenmayer. "I ask her a simple question and she 'guesses,' or prevaricates, or simply refuses to answer."

"I'll overrule the objection," Rosenmayer said. "The record will show that the witness has been unresponsive."

"Thank you, Your Honor," Karp said, and turned immediately back to the witness. "So, Dr. Braunschweiger, do you have any evidence, not opinion or guess, that Gail Perez was such, to use your words, a 'vindictive whore' . . ."

"Yes," said the spectator who'd said it before.

Karp whirled and pointed at the man, whose eyes grew huge. "Your Honor, I'd ask that this man be removed from the courtroom!"

"Sir, you're out of here!" Rosenmayer agreed, rising from his seat and motioning to the security guards to apprehend the offender.

"I didn't mean it!" the man squealed. He tried to slide away from the approaching guard but was shoved back by his compatriots, who didn't want to share his fate.

With the pleading man dragged from the court, screeching his undying affection for Maplethorpe, Karp stood staring at Braunschweiger, who nervously cleaned her glasses, put them on, took them off, and cleaned them again before replacing them.

"You were saying, Mr. Karp," Rosenmayer said.

"I was asking the witness if she had any real evidence that Gail Perez was such a vindictive whore that after allowing herself to be used by *that* man," he said, pointing again at the defendant, "she killed herself to get back at him—knowing the devastation it would cause her sister, and the trauma she would inflict on a Hilario Gianneschi, the police and crime scene investigators called to the scene, and the maids who would have to clean blood and brain tissue from carpets and a wall?"

"She was not thinking clearly," Braunschweiger said.

"That's not what I asked you," Karp said. "I asked if you had any evidence of any of that."

Braunschweiger hesitated, then she shook her head. "I don't have the sort of evidence you are looking for, Mr. Karp."

"What I'm looking for here is the truth," Karp replied. "Do you have any of that?"

Leonard roared to his feet. "Your Honor, the district attorney's conduct is an outrage!"

"The only outrage is that without a shred, a scintilla, a single bit of evidence, this woman takes an oath to tell the truth and gets up on that stand and labels a young woman she's never met, who died because she was shot by that man, a vindictive whore!" Karp shouted back.

"Gentlemen, I want to see both of you before me now, please," Rosenmayer said, keeping his voice moderated. When he had both attorneys in front of him he held up his hand. "Whatever you're going to say, I don't want to hear it. I'm just going to warn both of you that I'm not going to let this get out of hand. There are already enough emotions running amok in this courtroom without you two adding to it. Am I understood?"

"Yes, Your Honor," both attorneys responded.

"Good, now let's move on," the judge said.

Karp returned to the side of the jury box. "Doctor," he said, not angrily but forcibly enough that Braunschweiger jumped and stared like she thought he might attack her. "Do you have any evidence that Gail Perez was angry with Mr. Maplethorpe?"

"Well, the revenge suicide syndrome assumes that—" She looked at Karp's face and stopped. "No, I do not have any evidence that Miss Perez was angry with Mr. Maplethorpe."

"So essentially everything you told us you made up out of whole cloth?" Karp said without emotion.

"That's not quite right."

"Any evidence that she killed herself?"

"No."

"Nothing to show that she was angry with the defendant?"

"No."

"And you coined the phrase revenge suicide syndrome?"

"Yes."

"RSS."

"Yes."

"Does anybody else in the field of psychology use this term?"

"Well, it's relatively new . . . I first wrote about it in my book . . ."

"I'm not interested in your book. I want to know if anybody else in the field of psychology uses this term?"

"Not yet," Braunschweiger said. "I plan to present my paper on RSS at the American Association of Psychology convention in January."

"In other words, you're the only psychologist who gives any credence to revenge suicide syndrome," Karp said.

"I wouldn't say that."

"Name one . . . and remember that you're under oath."

Braunschweiger closed her mouth, then sighed. "I can't off the top of my head."

"Then why should this jury give it any credence?"

The psychologist didn't answer, but gave Leonard a withering look.

"So, Doctor, if you didn't have facts or evidence as a reason to say these truly despicable things about Gail Perez, what did you have?"

Braunschweiger looked at Leonard and arched her eyebrows. Karp recognized the "I'm not going down alone" look and smiled slightly.

"I formed my opinion on what I was told by Mr. Leonard and from reading the record."

"I'd like for you to point out in the record where it says that Gail Perez killed herself."

"I can't."

"I'd like for you to point out in the record where it says that Gail Perez was angry at Mr. Maplethorpe."

"I can't."

"I'd like for you to point out in the record where it says that Gail Perez killed herself in order to exact revenge on Mr. Maplethorpe."

Braunschweiger removed her glasses and cleaned them.

"Doctor, do you want to answer the question?" Karp leaned forward with his knuckles on the table.

Braunschweiger replaced her glasses and tilted her head. A slight ironic smile played across her lips. "I can't."

"You can't answer the question or—"

The psychologist snapped. "Let's not be obtuse, Mr. Karp. I can't point out where in the record it shows that Miss Perez killed herself because she was angry with Mr. Maplethorpe."

"Just trying to be clear, Doctor," Karp replied dryly. "So that means you must have formed your opinion based on what Mr. Leonard told you."

"And my professional experience."

"What in your professional experience gives you the right to come into this courtroom and besmirch the character of the deceased, Gail Perez?" Silence fell across the courtroom. "No further questions."

Leonard had tried his best on redirect to right the ship that had been Marta Braunschweiger by pointing out that "many currently accepted psychological maxims initially began as one person's theory that later gained widespread acceptance."

"That's correct," Braunschweiger replied. But it was clear that all she wanted was to get down from the witness stand. She even started to rise when he finished, only to freeze like a deer in the headlights when Karp cleared his throat.

"I have a couple more questions," he said.

Braunschweiger sat back down with a sigh. "Yes, Mr. Karp."

"Just to clarify, again, how many other psychologists use revenge suicide syndrome as a widely accepted theory in their practices?"

"None, Mr. Karp."

"And how many facts do you have to back up your assertions?"

"None, Mr. Karp, just my professional opinion."

"Thank you," Karp responded. "No further questions."

The psychologist stepped down quickly from the witness stand and stalked across the well of the court, passing between the prosecution and defense tables and down the aisle between the spectators without looking to one side or the other. She pushed the courtroom door open with a bang that caused several of the spectators to snigger.

Rosenmayer watched her leave with a bemused look on his face. He finally shook his head and turned to Leonard. "Call your next witness."

Leonard rose and turned to the back of the courtroom. "We call Frank Okuza."

The door opened and a small, young-looking Japanese man peered in, glancing around as if to make sure it was safe to enter. He smiled broadly and stepped forward quickly to the witness stand.

Leonard introduced him as a "bloodstain pattern analysis" expert certified by the International Association for Identification. "Can you tell the jury what is meant by bloodstain pattern analysis?" the defense attorney asked.

"Yes," Okuza said. "Bloodstain pattern analysis, or as we say, BPA, draws on the scientific disciplines of biology, chemistry, math, and physics to study the evidence left by bloodstains, particularly from suspected crime scenes."

"Is this a well-established field of forensic science?"

"Quite. It's been around for a number of years, though recent advances in DNA and other testing have really revolutionized the field. There was a 1936 Charlie Chan movie where he taught the Honolulu police about BPA, so it's been around a while."

"Can . . . BPA . . . be trusted to yield scientifically factual information?"

"Absolutely," Okuza said with a big smile. "If an analyst follows the scientific process, this applied science can produce rock-solid evidence for investigators."

"What are some of the things a bloodstain pattern analyst can determine?"

Okuza chuckled. "Well, there are quite a number, so how about I name some of them?"

"That would be fine."

"Okay, well, first the location and description of individual bloodstains and patterns—from large pools to microscopic droplets that can't be seen with the unaided eye," the little man replied. "I can tell the direction a blood droplet was traveling by calculating angles of impact, and the area of origin. I will be able to describe the object used in an attack, such as a sharp edge, or a blunt instrument, or a firearm. And I can give a pretty good picture of the positioning of the deceased, the perpetrator if there is one, perhaps a witness, and other objects during the event. And often I can determine the sequence of events."

"Very well," Leonard said. "Have you gone over the photographs taken in Mr. Maplethorpe's apartment the night of Gail Perez's death?"

"Yes, I have."

"And have you reviewed the police reports, and the testimony given so far in this court?"

"Up to the witness prior to me," Okuza replied.

"And have you applied the scientific process to what you know and come up with a conclusion?" Leonard asked.

"I have," Okuza said, and then turned solemnly to the jury. "It is my belief that the deceased killed herself with a single shot from a .45 caliber handgun."

"And how did you reach that opinion?"

"By looking at this as a whole. One point was that the deceased had blood on both of her hands, which indicates a trajectory coming from her mouth and striking her hands. Also, the accused, Mr. Maplethorpe, had a few blood flecks on the right arm of his smoking jacket, indicating that his right hand may have been extended, as though to grab the gun. But he was standing far enough away that very little blood struck the arm, and nowhere else on the jacket."

"What else can you tell us?"

"The bullet struck the major blood vessels at the back of her throat, causing a massive hemmorhage out of her mouth onto the floor to her left. As she died her head then slumped toward her chest/left shoulder."

Leonard walked over to the defense table, where he picked up a wooden gun. "Mr. Okuza, would you please demonstrate the manner in which, according to the scientific process of bloodstain pattern analysis, Miss Perez killed herself?"

"No problem," he said, taking the gun with his right hand and sticking it in his mouth, and then grabbing the barrel with the other hand. "Like so. It explains the bloodstain pattern on both of her hands as blood exploded out of her mouth."

"And would you demonstrate how the blood from her mouth ends up to her left?"

"Sure. When I place the gun in my mouth, you say 'Bang,' and I'll show you what happened," Okuza replied, and stuck the gun in his mouth.

"Bang!" Leonard said.

Okuza snapped his head back and to the left, and then let his head fall forward into roughly the same position Gail Perez's head had been. The little man stayed that way for a moment, and then sat up again with a smile on his face.

"And that is in your best scientific judgment how Miss Perez died?"

Okuza nodded. "That's what the evidence shows."

"Thank you, no further questions," Leonard said, retrieving the gun from Okuza and sitting back down at the defense table.

Karp rose from his seat and walked up to the lectern, where he studied his legal pad for a moment and then looked up at the witness. "The name of the Charlie Chan movie was *Charlie Chan at the Race Track.*"

Okuza blinked. "Okay, if you say so."

"It's a hobby," Karp said with a shrug. "Mr. Okuza, do the results of every bloodstain pattern analysis qualify as incontrovertible evidence?"

Okuza sipped water from a cup and shook his head. "No. There are a number of things that can happen that make a positive analysis impossible, such as someone disturbing the crime scene before the evidence is gathered."

"But you followed, and I quote, 'the scientific process' to arrive at your conclusion?" Karp asked.

"Yes, sir," Okuza answered.

"And does this scientific process include going through various scenarios so that you can either rule them out or include them as possibilities?"

"Uh, yes, generally," Okuza said. "However, you can eliminate some scenarios simply by things you already know. For instance, if I know that the wound was caused by a bullet, I don't have to run through the scenarios that would involve a knife."

"A pretty broad example, Mr. Okuza."

"Yes, but it serves as a demonstration of what I mean," Okuza responded.

Karp walked over to the defense table and picked up the wooden gun. "May I?"

"By all means," Leonard replied.

Karp started to walk to the witness stand but apparently thought of something and returned to the prosecution table to check his notes, laying the gun on the table. He then turned toward the judge. "I'd like to ask that the witness step down from the stand for a demonstration."

Rosenmayer looked over at the defense table. "Any problem with that?"

"I don't understand what purpose is served, but no objection," Leonard responded.

"Thank you, Mr. Leonard," Karp said. "The purpose is that this demonstration will involve two of us."

Okuza smiled and hopped down from the witness stand like he'd been invited to participate in a game show. As he approached, Karp picked up one of the chairs from the prosecution table and moved it into the well facing the spectator section. He looked over his shoulder and said, "Mr. Okuza, would you mind getting the gun for me?"

"Sure, no problem." The witness walked over to the prosecution table and picked up the gun.

"Have a seat, please," Karp said, and gestured to the chair.

Okuza complied with a grin. He was facing the spectator section, with his right side to the jurors.

"Mr. Okuza, before we get started, I noticed that you picked up the gun from the table with your left hand," Karp said. "Are you left-handed?"

Okuza nodded. "As a matter of fact I am."

"But you've since transferred it to your right hand."

"I assumed we were going to reenact the scenario," Okuza said.

"We are," Karp agreed. "I was just noticing that you had to make a conscious effort to put the gun in your right hand, even though you're left-handed."

"I didn't really give it much thought," Okuza replied, his smile fading. "But the trajectory of the bullet—"

"Yes, we've heard, Mr. Okuza," Karp said. "The bullet tracks from center to left. So, Mr. Okuza, if you would, please show the jury again how you believe Miss Perez placed the gun in her mouth."

"Like this," Okuza replied, and put the gun in his mouth.

"Mr. Okuza, I notice that you turned your head slightly to the right when you did that, is that simply the most natural way to do that?"

"Yes, I guess so," Okuza agreed.

"And so according to the scenario you worked out, Miss Perez then pulled the trigger and the force of the bullet made her jerk her head to the left."

"Yes."

"And a few flecks of blood strike the sleeve of the jacket worn by the defendant, who is standing some distance back but reaching forward with his right hand."

"That's correct."

"What if Miss Perez was left-handed?"

Okuza furrowed his brow. "What?"

"I asked, 'What if Miss Perez was left-handed?'"

"I don't understand," Okuza replied.

"Well, let's do this, then," Karp said. "Put the gun in your left hand and let's try that scenario."

"But . . ."

"Just humor me," Karp said.

Okuza shrugged and transferred the gun into his left hand. He then put the gun in his mouth.

"I notice that you've turned your head slightly to the left," Karp said.

"Yes, as you said before, it's natural to do that rather than sit looking straight forward and trying to bend your wrist around to the front."

"According to the evidence, Mr. Okuza, what's wrong with the scenario you just demonstrated?"

"Well, in this scenario, I would expect the bullet to have a trajectory traveling from center to slightly over to the right," Okuza said, "the opposite of what happened."

"Okay . . . oh, when you picked up the gun from the prosecution table with your left hand, was that because you do most things left-handed?"

"Sure. Like most people I have a dominant hand."

Karp held out his right hand for the gun, which Okuza delivered with a smile. "Okay, Mr. Okuza, now I'm going to act out a somewhat different scenario. I'm going to put the gun in your mouth. But first, put your hands up in front of your face like you are pleading for your life or trying to defend yourself."

Okuza's eyes rolled, but he managed a half smile. "No problem," he said. "Just try not to chip the crowns." He raised his hands as requested.

"I'll do my best, Mr. Okuza," Karp replied. "Open your mouth."

The little man did as he was told, looking at Karp like he was a dentist with a drill. Karp then jammed the gun into Okuza's mouth—not hard, but enough to make him sit back in the chair.

"Okay Mr. Okuza, on the count of three, I'm going to pretend to shoot. One. Two. Three . . ." Suddenly, Karp shouted, "*Bang!*"

Startled, Okuza jerked his head toward his left, away from the gun.

Okuza looked back at Karp, his eyes wide with surprise and fear. He tried to force a smile but it was halfhearted.

"Mr. Okuza, do you know what you just did when I shouted 'bang'?" Karp asked.

"I moved my head like this," Okuza said, turning to the left.

"And if this had been a real gun, and I'd pulled the trigger when you did that—and remember I was holding the gun in my right hand—would blood hemorrhaging from your mouth strike your hands?"

Okuza thought about it and nodded. "Sure. It happens very quick, almost instantaneously."

"And by turning your head to the left, away from the pressure and threat of the gun, would most of the blood miss me standing in front of you?"

Again, Okuza stopped and thought about it. "If I turned my head far enough to the side, yes, just as it would if the force of the bullet had jerked her head to the left."

"So it's possible that a few flecks of blood would have landed on the outside of my right sleeve, and the rest on the floor to your left?"

"It's possible."

"Mr. Okuza, when you were coming up with your conclusion for Mr. Leonard, did you follow the scientific process and attempt to verify or dismiss a scenario in which Mr. Maplethorpe held the gun in his right hand and stuck it in Miss Perez's mouth as she held her hands up to resist?"

"No . . . I . . . I didn't consider the possibility that she turned her head as the gun was fired."

"Mr. Okuza, do you think that a left-handed person would probably use her left hand to hold the gun if she was going to put it in her mouth and pull the trigger?"

"Objection," Leonard said without getting to his feet. "Calls for speculation."

Karp laughed. "The entire defense case calls for speculation," he said. "Every defense witness on the stand has speculated. . . . They've speculated about whether Hilario Gianneschi heard what he heard and understood what he heard; they've speculated that because he's an illegal alien, he's also a liar. They've speculated about Miss Perez's moral character and her mental stability. They've speculated about everything, except whether Mr. Maplethorpe killed her."

Judge Rosenmayer thought about it for a moment. "Overruled. I believe that the witness testified to being able to make his determination regarding a number of variables, including the positioning of objects during the event. Surely, the position of the gun could conceivably be one of those variables."

"So, Mr. Okuza, would you think that a left-handed person would be more likely to shoot herself using her left hand?"

"I'd say it's probably more likely," he agreed. "But it's not an absolute certainty. She may have used her right hand, or both hands for that matter."

Karp pointed at the witness as if he'd made an excellent point. "That's right, Mr. Okuza, it's just one of at least two and maybe more possibilities, isn't it?"

"Yes," Okuza acknowledged.

"And the truth is that while you and I can look at the bloodstain pattern and come up with different possibilities about what actually happened, we don't know with absolute certainty, do we? As a matter of fact, you cannot state to a reasonable degree of medical certainty that she used her right hand, left hand, or both hands, isn't that true?"

Okuza bit his lower lip and looked over at the defense table. "I believe that one fits what I know about the scene more than the others, but no, I don't know with absolute certainty."

"Thank you, Mr. Okuza, for an honest answer," Karp said.

36

The cell phone on Karp's desk buzzed with what seemed an unusual degree of urgency. *Or is it just that I'm getting jumpier by the minute,* he wondered as he reached for it.

Following Okuza's testimony, Leonard had suddenly and unexpectedly rested the defense case with a half dozen of the witnesses he'd called in the first trial still waiting in the wings. *"I think he may be on to us,"* Karp had said with a wink to Katz.

Karp was glad that the trial phase was just about over. However, he was a little disappointed; he'd hoped that he'd provoked Maplethorpe into taking the stand. But after some angry muttering over at the defense table, the defendant had slumped back into his seat with his arms folded across his chest and allowed his attorney to rest the defense case.

Rosenmayer had looked at his watch and dismissed the jury for the rest of the day. *"We'll return tomorrow morning and the attorneys will present their summations, after which I will charge you on the law and then you'll be asked to begin your deliberations."* The judge and the attorneys in the absence of the jury had then spent another hour going over his instructions to the jury, which would follow the summations.

Karp returned to his office to go over his summation one last time. Murrow, who had listened, then stepped out to place another call to the U.S. embassy in Trinidad. The poor guy was going crazy. He hadn't heard from Stupenagel in more than a week, which was not entirely unusual for the investigative reporter when she traveled to Third World countries on assignment, but Trinidad was a modern country with lots of oil and gas money pumping up the economy. She hadn't said anything about going undercover or not calling him, and Karp's aide was getting a little frantic and was trying to get the U.S. embassy involved in looking for her.

Karp looked at the cell phone's caller ID and immediately hit the button to connect with Jaxon.

"Yeah, Butch," the agent answered immediately.

"I'm getting a call from Lucy's phone," Karp said.

"We're on it."

Karp answered the phone. "Lucy?"

"Dad! You need to listen to me!"

It was at once a relief to hear her voice and know she was alive, but he could also hear the fear and urgency in her words. "I'm here, honey, what do you need?"

"I'm sitting here with Andy," she replied. "You remember Andy? He's Kane's little brother?"

"Yes, of course."

"And you remember how he helped me when his brother was going to hurt me in St. Patrick's Cathedral?"

Karp picked up on the game she was playing. "Yes, that was good of him. Is he helping you now?"

"He's helping all of us," she replied. "But Dad, we don't have much time before his big brother comes back."

"Lucy, get out of there!" Karp said, trying to keep his voice calm.

"I will, Dad, but I can't right now," she said. "There's going to be an attack. Today, I think."

"Where?"

"I don't know that yet," she replied. "Or how."

"Ask Andy if it's the Brooklyn-Battery Tunnel . . . it's the same at both ends like 'Casa Blanca' and 'art of war.' Or is it one of the bridges?"

"He says that's for him to know and you to find out," Lucy replied. "He's acting very immature. But Andy likes riddles and you're going to have to solve his or he won't help. But he says we're going to have to hurry because his big brother is coming back."

Karp felt a fresh wave of fear for his daughter wash over him. "The next answer was the movie *It Happened in Brooklyn.* Same at both ends, Brooklyn—the Brooklyn-Battery Tunnel. Or one of the bridges. What am I not getting?"

"He says that to start with that wasn't the next riddle."

Karp frowned. There was the note in his pocket. The riddle about Casa Blanca and art of war. "He told me to ask you about Dagestan?"

"That's not it either. Hurry, Dad, Kane could show up at any moment."

Puzzled, Karp tried to recall every word he'd heard since the beggar stuck the note in his pocket. Then it dawned on him. Andy kept repeating his warning using the same curious phrasing. "He said, 'It's the worst that could happen.'"

"Right, that was the next riddle. And because you didn't get that one, Andy says you haven't figured out the correct answer for the movie riddle."

"Ask him for another clue. Lucy . . ."

"Dad . . . Kane's back."

Karp heard a bellow of rage and a blow being struck. "Give me that, you bitch!"

The next sound Karp heard was the lisping voice of Andrew Kane. "You want another clue, Karp?" the sociopath screamed. "I'll give you a call when I think you're ready for one." Then the cell phone went dead.

Karp leaned back in his chair. The father in him wanted to scream in rage and fear for his child. But now was not the time. "Did you find her, Espey?" he asked.

"Not quite," said the voice in his ear. "But definitely Brooklyn Heights. We're getting close. Sounds like he's going to call again. We'll be waiting. Any idea on the riddles?"

Karp looked down at the words on his legal pad. "Casa Blanca.

Art of war. *It Happened in Brooklyn.* Tunnel? Bridges? And now he added: It's the worst that could happen." "Not yet," he replied. "I'm going to think about it for a bit."

"We'll do everything we can to get her back, Butch," Jaxon said. "He's keeping her alive for a reason. We have time."

"I hope, Espey," Karp replied. "But it's more than about Lucy. If I know Kane, something big and bad is coming at us. A lot of people could get hurt or killed, and it's likely to be the start of a whole lot worse. Find Lucy, but let's make sure we stop Kane first."

The little voice in his ear was quiet for so long that Karp wondered if Jaxon had gone off air. "Espey?"

"Yeah, Butch, I'm here," the agent said. "Just, uh, having a moment. Where's Ned?"

"He's in the outer office reading a magazine," Karp said. "I'm going to let him know that I heard from Lucy. He seems to be doing pretty well, though . . . I'd say he's, oh, what's the word I'm looking for? . . . Grim. Grim and determined."

"Good. Knowing Lucy was able to make a call will keep him focused. I think he'll be okay, but keep him close."

"I will," Karp replied.

"Okay, then, let's keep the transmitters on full-time now," Jaxon said. "I don't want to take any chances with missing something. Tell Ned to turn his on, too. If Kane calls again, keep him on as long as possible."

"Sure," Karp said. *If he calls again . . .* Tears threatened to come to his eyes but he willed them away. "I'm going to give some thought to these riddles now."

Karp paused for a moment and then wrote something on a note card that he placed in an envelope, then he pressed the intercom button. "Darla, would you have Ned come in here, please?"

A few seconds passed before there was a knock on the door followed by the appearance of Ned Blanchett. It was obvious the young man wasn't getting much sleep; his startling blue eyes had dark circles beneath them and his cheeks were flushed. But those same eyes were clear and his jaw set.

The night before, after Ned had retired to Lucy's old room to try to get some sleep, Marlene had wondered aloud if the young man should still be on duty. Karp had not been convinced himself at first. But as he'd realized and said to Marlene, *"There are only two things we can do for Ned right now. Sedate him so that he doesn't know what's happening. Or keep him involved. I think he'd choose the latter. And you know, not to sound too much like our daughter, ever since Ned came into Lucy's life, it's been his fate to be her knight in shining armor. I'm not in a place at the moment to think that's just coincidence."*

"Yes, sir?" Blanchett asked.

"Whatever happened to 'Dad'?" Karp asked.

Blanchett smiled. "Maybe away from the office, sir."

"Fair enough. I wanted to let you know that I just got a call from Lucy."

Blanchett's eyes immediately lit up and a slight smile came to his face. "She escaped?"

Karp shook his head, sorry to see the effect it had on Ned. "No. But she called of her own volition. I think she's okay for now. And Jaxon says he's close; we're hoping that we get another call so he can pinpoint the location. Keep your head up, Ned." He decided not to tell Blanchett about the blow he'd heard delivered over the phone.

"You, too, sir," Blanchett replied. "Anything else?"

"Oh, yeah," Karp said, holding out the envelope, "would you take this down to that little news vendor in front of the building on Centre Street?"

"The one who cusses up a storm all the time," Blanchett said with a smile. "Warren?"

"Yeah, that's the one," Karp said. "See that he gets it right away. Tell him it's from me and it's for David."

Blanchett tilted his head to the side to look at Karp but didn't say anything more. He took the envelope and left the office.

Karp closed his eyes and put his shoes up on the desk. *"The worst that could happen." What is it with that particular phrasing? Jesus, this really is a riddle wrapped in an enigma . . . a difficult puzzle.*

Suddenly he sat upright. Using his office phone, he dialed the number to his house.

"Karp and Ciampi residence, Zak speaking," a bored teenage voice answered.

"Zak, is that you?"

"Who else would answer the phone 'Zak speaking'?"

Karp rolled his eyes. "This is Dad. Where are you?"

"My room," Zak replied. "By myself. Giancarlo's hanging out with what's-her-name somewhere. I hope she dumps him."

"That's the spirit. After we get off the phone you might want to make one of those voodoo dolls and stab it with pins," Karp said. "But I need your help right now, Zak. This is important."

Karp almost felt Zak's interest snapping to attention. "Yeah? Like what?"

"Remember on Thanksgiving when we were playing that riddle game?"

"You mean, when you and Giancarlo were showing off in front of everyone?"

"Yeah, that time," Karp replied. "Anyway, Giancarlo plugged some words into the Internet or something and came up with the correct quote."

"So what," Zak replied. He was beginning to get the idea that this was going to be an "isn't Giancarlo wonderful" session and the wall was going up.

"Well, I need you to search for a phrase for me," Karp said.

"Why don't you wait for Giancarlo to come home. He's the brainiac."

"Zak, I don't have any more time for this, lives are at stake, do you understand?" Karp said firmly.

"Lives? Yeah, sure, what do you need me to look up?" Zak said, suddenly all business.

"'It's the worst that could happen,'" Karp said. He could hear Zak typing in the background.

"Well, you're in luck, there's only a few million hits," Zak replied.

"Like what?"

"Let's see, there's an ad from a divorce lawyer that says 'Divorce is the worst thing that could happen to you in your life.'"

"No, the word 'thing' isn't part of the phrase," Karp said. "What else?"

"Well, there's a lot of websites that start off with 'What's the worst that can happen?' Such as this Dale Carnegie course that starts off,

'First ask yourself: What's the worst thing that can happen?' Does that sound right?"

"Not yet. And it's got to be all the words in that order: 'It's the worst that could happen,' see anything exactly like that?"

"Here's some old song called 'It's the Worst That Can Happen.' Geez, it was from 1968 . . . that's practically the Stone Age."

"Hey, watch it, kiddo," Karp growled. "What's it say about it?"

"Let's see, it was written by a guy named Jimmy Webb."

"Doesn't click with anything," Karp said, drumming his fingers on the desk. "What else? Any lyrics?"

"The first line . . . 'It might be the best thing for you but it's the worst that could happen to me.' OMG, you really listened to stuff like that?"

"OMG?"

"Oh my God," Zak said, verbally rolling his eyes at his dinosaur father.

"Forgive my ignorance," Karp replied. *Let's see, what's the next clue. Oh yeah,* It happened in Brooklyn.

"Anything in there about Brooklyn?"

"Only if you're interested in boring trivia, like Jimmy Webb wrote the song but the guys who made it famous were Johnny Maestro and the Brooklyn Bridge. What a dumb name—"

Zak was interrupted by his father's excited shout. "Zak, you got it! You're a genius!"

"I do okay?"

Karp recognized the insecurity in his son's voice and for a moment all the terrorist bombs in the world didn't matter. "Zak, I love you more than you'll ever know. I think you may have just saved the world. I gotta go—I'll tell you about it later."

"Thanks, Dad," Zak replied, and Karp could almost feel the glow over the phone.

Karp punched in Fulton's number. "Clay, it's me, and Jaxon's listening in," he said. "I think the target is the Brooklyn Bridge."

"I'll call it in as a bomb threat," Fulton replied, "and get the bridge cleared."

"I have a federal response team on the way, too," Jaxon added.

As Karp hung up, something was still nagging at him. With all the clutter, he wasn't quite seeing what he needed to see. He was sure he was right that the Brooklyn Bridge was the target. It made sense with the other pieces of evidence, including what Lucy told Treacher about believing that she was being held in Brooklyn, *"Somewhere with a view. He said I'd have ringside seats."* The Heights certainly had the best view of the Brooklyn Bridge on that side of the East River.

"View," he repeated aloud. There was a second part of the *"It Happened in Brooklyn"* riddle, according to Dirty Warren. *"Oh, and he said to tell you to think about the . . . motherfucking . . . view."*

Somewhere from the recesses of his memory, Karp recalled as a little boy watching *It Happened in Brooklyn* with his mother on a Saturday afternoon. It was not as good as a Western for a kid, but his mother had hummed the title song for the rest of the day and talked dreamily about Frank Sinatra, who'd sung it.

Many years had passed since, but Karp could hear the Chairman of the Board crooning the words: *"What a lovely view from . . . heaven looks at you from . . . the Brooklyn Bridge."*

Karp punched in the number for Fulton again. "Clay, get the car. . . . I need to check out the view from the Brooklyn Bridge." As he rose from his chair, he looked upward and said, "Thanks, Mom. I needed the help."

37

The young man sitting in the rented truck at the corner of Adams and Tillary streets in Brooklyn jumped when his cell phone started playing Public Enemy's "Don't Believe the Hype."

"Hello?" he answered, and listened for a moment before repeating after the man on the other end of the line. "*Allahu akbar.*"

Born and raised in the projects of Bedford-Stuyvesant, one of the worst slums in New York during his childhood, he'd been easy pickings for the agents of radical Islam. By junior high he was a member of the Rolling 777s, a Black Muslim gang that had originated in Harlem but was branching throughout the five boroughs. Not that Islam gave him anything more than the nothing that he already had, but it promised a better afterlife and he was ready to go.

He got out of the truck and went around to the back, where he opened the sliding panel high enough to see beneath, reach in with his arm, and flip the switch that armed the detonator that would ignite the fuel oil–and–fertilizer bomb. Walking back to the driver's door, he paused for a moment, looking up at the gathering clouds above, dark and threatening as evening fell. He sniffed the air. *Smells like snow is on the way*, he thought. *Folks are in for a storm tonight*.

He climbed back into the cab of the truck and pulled away from the curb on Tillary. As he turned left on Adams and headed north for the Brooklyn Bridge, he glanced down at the transmitter on the seat next to him. All he had to do was turn it on and press the button. There'd be a flash but no pain, the man in the silver mask had assured him. *"And then you'll wake up in Paradise."*

The young man was less than halfway across the bridge when he saw the other truck heading south. For a moment he caught a glimpse of his counterpart, who was looking back at him. He waved, wondering if he looked as lonely and scared as the other guy.

Damn, he's early, he thought, *going to get there before I do.* He stepped on the gas and got right up on the car in front, but it was no use; traffic was heavy heading into the city in the early evening with Christmas shopping in full swing. He couldn't go around either because he was hemmed in by a big yellow Brooklyn City School District bus filled with laughing, smiling teenagers. *Probably going into Manhattan for a basketball game or something.*

A few snowflakes landed on the windshield. He watched them melt. *I'm like a snowflake,* he thought, *here for a moment and then gone. No one will even remember what I looked like.* The young man looked again to his left and noticed that people on the pedestrian walk were starting to run. Police officers hurried among them, shouting instructions and directing people. *So the word's out,* he thought. *The man in the mask said it might happen but it wouldn't matter.*

Everybody was trying to get off the bridge—except for the police officers, and more of them were arriving, some with jackets that read BOMB SQUAD in big yellow letters on the back. He noticed a very tall white man who was running up the road on the other side of the bridge; some other men were with him, including one who appeared to be carrying a rifle. Then he was past them.

The young man was three-fourths of the way across the bridge, the heart of New York City lit up for the Christmas holidays and laid open to him, when he heard the muffled *crump* of the big explosion behind him. He was surprised to feel the tremor even on his side of the bridge. In his side mirror, he saw a ball of orange fire shoot up into the sky followed by a billowing black cloud. *So that's what it will look like,* he thought as he reached for the transmitter and turned it on.

He saw that over on the pedestrian bridge people had stopped their flight and turned around to face Brooklyn and the smoke. He glanced up at the school bus. Young faces were pressed to the glass, fear and confusion in their eyes. He wondered why their expressions didn't bring him any joy; after all, kids like them never had much to do with him when he was growing up in Bed-Stuy, the son of junkies. Instead, he felt sorry for them.

The young man slowed so that the school bus pulled ahead. Behind him an angry, frightened driver leaned on the horn. He then slammed on his brakes and cut the wheel hard to the right. The cars in the left and right lanes behind him couldn't stop in time and slammed into the truck.

As he felt the impact, the young man hoped that the school bus was far enough ahead. "*Allahu akbar!*" he shouted, and pressed the button.

Karp was standing in shock with Murrow, Fulton, and Blanchett, staring off toward the Brooklyn side of the bridge as the plume of smoke rose in front of them, when there was a flash and then the shock wave and roar of the second explosion behind them. A hot, heavy wind followed, almost knocking him down.

"Oh my God," Murrow, who had fallen to the ground, cried out. Ten minutes earlier, he'd seen Karp leaving his office in a rush and demanded to follow. "*I'm tired of sitting around waiting for her call. I've got to do something or go crazy,*" Murrow had said.

They'd abandoned the car at the traffic jam caused by arriving police officers who were trying to prevent traffic from going onto the bridge. Then they started running to reach the center of the bridge because Karp said he needed to see the view.

Now they all looked back in shock at the smoke and fire, twisted steel, and vehicles strewn about like autumn leaves. Snow mixed with ash and smoke partially obscured the scene, but they could see bodies, and people screaming and running or simply standing in disbelief and shock.

"Jesus, what was that?" Jaxon shouted in Karp's earpiece.

"Bombs on either end of the Brooklyn Bridge," Karp said. "I didn't figure it out in time."

There was a moment of silence before Jaxon said, "None of us did, Butch. But there will be time for recriminations later. Right now, this isn't over. We need to catch Kane to prevent this from happening again. Any word? I would think that he'd want to gloat."

"Not yet. I'll let you know."

Blanchett and Fulton started to head in the direction of the second explosion, responding to people in distress. But Karp called them back. "There will be other people to help," he said. "I need you with me."

Jaxon's comment *"this isn't over"* repeated itself in his mind. He saw people on the far side of the bridge running back toward the middle. And others on both sides getting out of their cars—either abandoning them and running away, or simply standing there. He knew it would take more than a couple of car bombs to knock down the Brooklyn Bridge. *And Kane would know that, too. That's why he hasn't called to gloat. He wants to drag it out and set me up for his big moment. Then he'll call.*

"It's a trap," he yelled to his companions. "They want people stuck on the bridge. Clay, get these cops to clear everybody out of here. Ned, Gilbert, stick with me. . . . Espey, he's going to call again, so stay tuned."

Karp ran for the center of the bridge, where he found a lieutenant with the NYPD bomb squad. "I think we haven't seen the worst of it yet," he said to the officer.

The lieutenant nodded. "Either way, we're not taking any chances. I've got my people all over and under the bridge now, including guys in boats. Harbor Patrol is going to keep all water traffic away; we've got to get the civilians out of here."

The officer moved off shouting orders, as Karp walked over and got up on the narrow walkway that ran along the rail. He looked downstream over the East River toward New York Harbor. Partly shrouded by the lightly falling snow, the Statue of Liberty lifted her lamp.

What a lovely view from . . . heaven looks at you from . . . the

Brooklyn Bridge. . . . But what am I supposed to see? A flotilla of holy warriors on yachts shouting Islamic slogans and firing AK-47s into the air as they launched a suicide attack? A hijacked jetliner screaming in low to crash into the bridge?

Nothing looked out of place, except for the police boats that were cruising back and forth, intercepting the barges, ships, and pleasure craft to keep them at a safe distance from the bridge. Farther out in the harbor, he could see a medium-size ship sitting with a tugboat on either side. *Probably bound for the shipyards*, he thought. But no supertankers or Iranian gunboats.

Karp pulled out his cell phone and flipped it open. He hesitated for a moment, and then pressed a speed dial number he'd never used before. The call was answered by a male voice.

"Ivgeny? . . . Hi, it's Butch. You've heard? Yes, car bombs on the Brooklyn Bridge. I need to ask a big favor."

Omar Abdullah stood next to Ariadne Stupenagel on the bridge of the ship, watching the twin pillars of smoke rise from either end of the Brooklyn Bridge. "*Allahu akbar*!" he shouted.

"You murderous pieces of shit," Stupenagel cried, tears streaming down her face. "You must feel real proud of yourself, sneaking up like a coward and killing innocent people, including women and children."

"Innocent? There are no innocent Americans," Abdullah sneered. "The United States has been making war on Muslim countries for fifty years. I don't see those same tears for Muslim children murdered in Palestine. Or in Afghanistan. Or Iraq."

"Don't try to wrap murder in the flag of self-defense or retributive justice," Stupenagel shot back. "No one else *targets* civilians. And if civilians are sometimes killed, you brave warriors who hide in their houses and surround yourselves with their children for shields and propaganda are to blame. You just embarrass yourself when you try to pretend that unarmed civilians are somehow a legitimate military target. You're no better than any other low-life killer who sneaks up behind someone in the dark. What happened? You used to be a warrior, Omar, but now all you are is a craven criminal."

Abdullah raised his hand to slap Stupenagel, but she didn't flinch or try to pull away from the blow. "Go ahead, attacking defenseless women is all you're good for anymore," she spat. "My hands are tied behind my back, just the way you like it. Let me go, and I'll kick your ass. But that's what you're afraid of, isn't it, you piece of crap? You're not about to take on anybody who can fight back."

The terrorist looked around. The other men were pretending to go about their business or were looking off in another direction, but he knew they were taking it all in. He lowered his hand and turned back toward the bridge, now outlined in lights that twinkled on as the evening darkened. "Prepare for the assault," he ordered. He reached for a portable radio and pressed the button to speak. "Everyone take your positions. Bomb team, get ready."

Stupenagel shook her head. "You know what else, Omar," she said. "You're just a tool. You and your men are just being used by evil people who could care less about your religion or your politics. Speaking of which, where's Nadya? I haven't seen her around, bet she jumped ship like the rat she is."

"Nadya? You mean Ajmaani," Abdullah said. "She is a great warrior for Islam."

"Her name is Nadya Malovo and she works for the Russians, you dolt," Stupenagel shot back. "Or at least she was. Now she's working for a multinational power group that's using you little radical Muslim lemmings to stir things up. Why do you think she keeps turning up for all the little escapades? But you don't see her hanging around for the big bang, do you?"

"The leaders must survive to continue jihad," Abdullah replied, noticing that the men had stopped pretending not to listen.

"What a joke." Stupenagel laughed. "Are you listening? Tell me you didn't use to be this stupid—that the guy I fell for was just a moron with nice muscles?"

"Shut up!" Abdullah yelled. "I've heard enough. You're a woman, everything you say is twisted."

"Boy, did you buy the whole spiel. Well, let me tell you something about what happens when you die today. The mullahs got it wrong, just like Christian ministers who tell murderers that they can be forgiven and go to heaven got it wrong." She smirked. "It doesn't really work that way. Where you're going is reserved for murderers . . . for people who destroy Allah's greatest gift . . . and it's cold and dark and alone and forever. That's it. Not even a bit of hellfire to give you warmth or light. Enjoy."

Abdullah struck Stupenagel in her stomach, knocking the wind out of her. "Shut up, I told you," he screamed.

The reporter remained bent over as she fought to catch her breath. Then slowly, she straightened up until she was looking Abdullah in the eye. "Is that all you got? Forget me kicking your ass, my boyfriend, who is a better, kinder, gentler man than you ever dreamed of being, could kick your ass blindfolded . . . and I can kick *his* ass," she said. "But he's not going to get the chance because I'm going to kill you myself. I just don't know how yet."

Abdullah shoved his face in hers and stood for a moment, clenching and unclenching his fists. He wanted to kill her but knew it would make him look weak in front of the men, attacking a woman whose wrists were bound behind her after she called him out.

With a supreme effort to control his anger, he turned toward the captain and yelled, "Attack! *Allahu akbar. Allahu akbar! Allahu akbar!*"

The captain and other men on the bridge joined Abdullah in shouting. "All ahead, full!" the captain ordered the helmsman, who rang up the engine room to crank up the slowly turning propellers.

At the stern of the ship, a young crewman who'd been waiting for the signal ran to the fantail only to slip and fall on the blood that covered the deck. Then he remembered that the Asian had been shot and dumped overboard. He took a large green flag with a golden crescent moon emblazoned on it from a bag he carried and ran it out the flagpole that jutted from the stern.

Up on the bridge, Abdullah smiled as the ship began to move forward. One of the tugs tooted its horn in alarm and the ship-to-ship radio crackled to life. "Please disengage your propellers, you are under way . . ." The terrorist reached out and flipped the switch that cut the radio.

Walking up to Stupenagel, he addressed her coldly, calmly. "We shall see who's a warrior and who's not." He spoke into his handheld radio. "Bomb team, is the device armed?"

A click was followed by the sound of gunfire and a man screaming in pain. "Armed men are in the room. They killed the guards and just shot two of my men."

"I'm sending more men," Abdullah yelled into the radio, nodding to several men, who ran off. "Do whatever it takes, make any sacrifice. Get to the bomb."

Abdullah glared at Stupenagel, who smiled and said, "Guess maybe God isn't on your side."

The terrorist's eyes narrowed, but instead of getting angry, he smiled. "You're wrong," he said. "God *is* on my side. There is more than one path to Paradise."

Kane stood looking through the telescope at the ship in the harbor, waiting for the signal. When he saw the green flag unfurled, he smiled and turned to face Lucy, who sat naked and bound in a chair facing the myriad lights of the Manhattan skyline. The hulking Abu stood near her, stealing glances at her breasts and legs, wondering if the boss would let him . . .

"Want a look?" Kane asked the young woman. "It's really quite beautiful."

Lucy kept her eyes on the Brooklyn Bridge. "I don't get off watching cowards murder people."

"No?" Kane said as if surprised. "Imagine that . . . I do." He pointed to the ship. "That's a floating bomb and it's going to sail right up under the Brooklyn Bridge and roast your old man. It's Christmas come early; hell, it's even snowing."

"I hope your bomb is big enough to come through this window and turn you into a smoking ember," Lucy replied.

Kane walked over to the big window and tapped on it. "Multilayered polycarbonate laminate. Bulletproof, fireproof, and it would take a direct hit from a pretty good-size bomb to get through. I had it installed so that we could watch the fireworks in perfect safety. Now, if I'd been able to get a big tanker full of liquefied natural gas on the East River, it might have been a bit too warm in here, even if we didn't burn to the ground like some of our neighbors probably will. This ship will turn the Brooklyn Bridge into molten steel, take out every window along the waterfront, and incinerate all forms of life, including our friend al-Sistani out there."

Lucy looked where he was pointing and saw al-Sistani was tied to a chair on the concrete deck outside the house. He struggled against the ropes and seemed to be yelling something, but the house was soundproof. Kane and Abu had placed bets on whether he would die immediately or suffer for a while when the ship blew up.

"But don't worry," Kane continued. "It won't be *too* big. You and me and Abu will all be snug as bugs in a rug. But thanks for the thought."

Hobbling back to the telescope, Kane turned it toward the Brooklyn Bridge. "Ah, there's your dad now. I was beginning to worry that he wouldn't figure out all of Andy's riddles."

Lucy frowned. "You knew?"

"Jesus Christ, who do you think is the dominant personality here?" Kane laughed. "Are you really that stupid? Of course I knew he wanted to warn your dad, the traitorous little do-gooder. I probably couldn't have stopped him entirely; he does keep trying to get out and it does take an effort to keep him submerged. So I let him make up his stupid riddles, and even went along with the hand-delivered messages, just so long as it kept him from spilling the beans entirely. In fact, I thought it would be fun to find a way to kill the invincible Karp-daddy at the same moment of my triumphant return to my favorite city in the whole wide world."

Kane pulled out Lucy's cell phone and leaned against the picture window in front of her. "Let's give him a call, shall we?" He hit the speed dial button for Karp. "Hi, Butch! It's your future son-in-law. How do you like the show so far?"

Winking at Lucy, Kane giggled. "Now, now, what good are empty threats? But hey, I've got another riddle for you. This is for the jackpot. . . . 'What do you get when a famous Muslim traveler crosses the Nile? I'll give you a hint: Longfellow said it best.' I'll call back in a few and see if you've figured it out. But a lot of lives could depend on it, including your daughter's. Want to say hi?"

Kane held the cell phone out toward Lucy. "Say hi to dear old Dad?"

"Do the right thing, Dad," Lucy shouted.

"My, my, how altruistic," Kane said, snapping the phone shut. "That ought to keep him there. Isn't this fun?"

Karp closed the cell phone but kept it in his hand. "You got him, Espey?"

"Not quite," Jaxon said. "I think we've narrowed it to a row of houses on Pierrepont Place. I hope he calls again. I want to narrow this down. We're going to have to go in fast and heavy, and we're only going to get one shot at this."

Jaxon didn't have to finish the thought. *If Lucy's going to survive.* But Karp knew. "I think he'll call. But it might be the last chance. Keep working on it, I've got to figure out this other riddle."

Karp punched the number for his home. "Zak?"

"Dad!" his son replied. "They bombed the Brooklyn Bridge. It's all over the news. I guess I didn't save the world?"

"You can, Zak," Karp said. "I'm okay and everything's going to be all right. But I need your help again. Are you still at your computer?"

"Yeah."

"Search for this phrase: 'famous Muslim traveler.'"

"There's a few names that come up," Zak replied. "I'm not sure how to pronounce these but . . . looks like I-ben Arabi. I-ben Battuta. I-ben Jew-bare . . ."

"Wait! That one," Karp said. "How do you spell it?"

"I-B-N . . . J-U-B-A-I-R."

"Thanks, Zak, you did it again, love ya," Karp yelled. "I'll get back to you."

Closing the cell phone, Karp spoke aloud. "Jaxon, did you get that?"

"Yeah, what are you thinking?"

"Kane's riddle," Karp said. "I think he was referring to Longfellow's famous quote about ships passing in the night. Do you have access to that list of ships that left Trinidad when Jojola and Tran disappeared? Maybe they were on to something."

"Hold on a sec," Jaxon said. That was followed by silence and then he came back on the line. "I'm patched in to one of my computer guys at the office. Give him the names of the ships."

"The *Ibn Jubair* . . . that's I-B-N and J-U-B-A-I-R, and *The Nile*."

"I can tell you right now that *The Nile* was one of them," Jaxon said. "That was the ship that Ned and I were watching the last night we saw Jojola and Tran. It's a big liquefied natural gas tanker. We had reports that something was up involving the ship. But nothing came of the tip. Got anything, Greg?"

"Yeah, just came up. The *Ibn Jubair* is a medium-size refrigerated cargo vessel. It was supposed to be heading for Nova Scotia. But was contacted by the U.S. Coast Guard early this morning off the coast, reported mechanical problems. . . . Let's see, was diverting to . . . the Brooklyn shipyards."

"Shit!" Karp exclaimed. "Is there any chance those two ships crossed paths and *The Nile* could have transferred gas into the *Jubair*?"

"They left within a few hours of each other," Greg replied. "And had similar routes. The *Jubair* to Nova Scotia. The *Nile* to the floating transfer facility in the Long Island Sound."

"Jaxon, I'd tell somebody about that tanker," Karp said.

"Already on it. What about the *Ibn Jubair*?"

Karp turned to Blanchett, who'd been standing by trying to decipher what was happening. "Ned, do you think you could get your scope on that ship out there?" he said, pointing to the cargo ship sandwiched between the tugboats. "And tell me the name?"

Blanchett opened the case containing his sniper rifle and pulled out the scope, which he trained on the ship. "It's tough to see with the snow and haze," he said. "Hold on a sec. . . . It's the *Ibn Jubair*!"

"Jaxon, did you hear that!"

"I'm on it," Jaxon replied. Karp heard him yelling to others. "Call the airbase, give them this code . . . and tell them to scramble fighters, we have a hostile ship in New York Harbor, possibly loaded with liquefied natural gas. And Greg, you get on the line to the Coast Guard and Harbor Patrol. Same message." The agent turned his attention back to Karp. "I don't know how they did it—it takes a special refrigeration unit to get cold enough to store LNG—but if that ship is filled with gas and they set it off under this bridge or next to the waterfront in lower Manhattan—"

Blanchett interrupted. "More bad news," he said. "The ship is moving toward us."

As Karp and the others watched, small figures of men appeared on the forward deck of the ship. One stood up next to the railing and a moment later a gray line of smoke marked the path of the rocket-fired grenade into the wheelhouse of the tugboat. A single heartbeat passed and then the wheelhouse exploded. The tugboat veered wildly away from the *Ibn Jubair*. Meanwhile, on the other side, the remaining tugboat was trying to get away as men on the deck of the ship raked it with automatic-weapon fire. Smoking and on fire, the tug finally broke free and headed away at full speed like a singed cat.

Slowly, a white wake grew around the bow of the *Ibn Jubair* as it began to pick up speed. Karp looked around; there were still hundreds of people trying to get off the bridge, and who knew how many thousands in all the glassed-in rooms and offices of the skyscrapers, and driving in cars, along the waterfront.

"Espey, whatever happens, catch Kane," Karp said. "Or this will just be the start of something much worse."

"I promise, Butch. Now leave; there's nothing more for you to do there. Let NYPD and the air force deal with this. If they can't, you did everything you could."

"Can't do it, Espey," Karp said. "This is personal to Kane. He's somewhere he can see me. I've got to keep his eye on me and get him to call again."

Karp turned to Blanchett. "I think you better go, Ned. You, too, Gilbert and Clay."

The three others ignored him and looked out at the ship in the harbor. "We're staying," Murrow said.

Karp smiled. He patted Blanchett on the back. "Ned, you might want to get your rifle ready," he said. "I don't know why, but as Lucy might say, maybe there's a reason you're here."

Blanchett nodded. "Been thinking the same thing. Don't know

how I'm going to stop a ship with a .50 caliber, but maybe I can pick up a few of those assholes. All I know is that if the bear is trying to eat you and all you have is a rock, you throw the rock."

"Look for the leaders," Karp replied. "Maybe you can put them in a panic if the main guy is gone."

Karp flipped open his cell phone again. "Ivgeny," he said when his cousin answered. "Here's the situation."

"Bomb team, have you killed the infidels?" Omar Abdullah yelled into the radio. But there was only silence. "Bomb team, report!"

More silence, and then a voice. "Why, hello, Omar. I'm afraid the bomb team is indisposed at the moment. In fact, you might want to send a few more. Tran and I are tied at three each, and we need a tie-breaker or three. No even numbers, please."

"Give me that," said another voice Abdullah recognized as the Asian. "What's the matter, Omar, cat got your tongue? Or maybe Stupenagel has your tongue? I heard she's been hanging around some loose company."

"Hey, watch it, Tran!" Stupenagel laughed. "You should see the look on Omar's face. Priceless!"

Abdullah's eyes blazed with fury. "Make more jokes. You're just going to die with the rest of us," he said, and slammed the radio against a bulkhead. He turned to Stupenagel and grabbed her chin. "You do know you're going to die, don't you?" he snarled. "You'll never see your wonderful boyfriend or anyone else you love ever again. No matter what else happens, I am going to make sure that you in particular never live to see another sunrise, even if I have to kill you with my hands."

"I know that, Omar," Stupenagel replied softly. There were tears in her eyes but her voice was firm. "I've already accepted that. But I'm happy. The boys have fucked up your plan."

Omar's cruel eyes glittered but he smiled. "They have only made it more difficult." He turned to the captain. "Aim for the docks between the last tall building and the bridge. We'll rupture the tanks by running into them."

The captain nodded. He and the rest of the crew had volunteered for this suicide mission. "Police boats approaching," he said.

Abdullah picked up the microphone for the ship's broadcast system. "Prepare to repel the infidels." He then watched with pride as his men assumed the positions they'd trained for while at sea—some manned searchlights, others set up .50 caliber machine guns, or checked their assault rifles, grenade launchers, or handheld rockets before finding cover from which to fight. Not only would his men have the advantage of shooting down on the police, he knew from the Internet that the Harbor Patrol was lightly armed. He also knew that the Coast Guard—at least those who hadn't been paid off—were busy monitoring "hazardous" shipping, not some broken-down old milk wagon.

An NYPD helicopter suddenly appeared off the starboard bow and shined a spotlight on the bridge. "*Ibn Jubair*, cut your engines, lay down your arms, and prepare to be boarded," said the pilot over the loudspeaker.

Abdullah nodded to a young man who'd been standing near the door with an over-the-shoulder missile launcher. The young man stepped out of the bridge and sighted and fired the missile, which buried itself in the copter and exploded.

As the helicopter whirled away from the ship and crashed in the water, the men on the *Ibn Jubair* cheered. Then they began firing at the Harbor Patrol boats that were approaching at high speed over the dark water, the twilight suddenly blazing with tracers and spotlights. A rocket grenade caught a police boat broadside and left it dead and smoking as its crew jumped overboard or lay where they'd fallen.

It was soon clear that the police were outgunned and unable to approach the slow but inexorable ship. There'd always been a plan just in case the small bomb attached to the hull and linked to the tanks of gas malfunctioned. Even a change in target if it looked like the Brooklyn Bridge was too far. The skyscrapers of lower Manhattan along FDR Drive crowded along the waterfront, thousands of windows and who knew how many lives exposed to the flash fire of an exploding LNG ship.

"There are your warriors of Islam," he shouted at Stupenagel, pointing to his men.

"Yeah, just like any other scumbags waiting in a dark alley," she sneered. "And I don't see you out there, risking your ass. Just a bunch of poor ignorant slobs who've been sold a bill of goods."

Enraged, Abdullah decided it was time to kill the woman. *Why should I have to go through this hell before I get to Paradise?* he thought, and started to reach for his gun. But just then the captain shouted.

"Tugboats!"

"Tugboats?" Abdullah forgot about Stupenagel for the moment and looked toward where the captain was pointing up the East River. Two big tugboats had passed under the Brooklyn Bridge and were bearing down on the *Ibn Jubair*. He grabbed a pair of binoculars and trained them on the new arrivals.

Immediately, he saw these weren't just any old tugboats. They were both carrying many armed men. One of them, a very tall man with a black eye patch, stood on the bow. The man turned and waved to someone on the bridge.

Abdullah followed the man's gaze to where a knot of four or five men stood at the center of the bridge. He did a double take. One of the men on the bridge and the man in the tugboat at first looked to be the same man, except for the eye patch.

Twins? he wondered, then shook his head. *It doesn't matter. They're both going to die.*

38

As he passed under the Brooklyn Bridge and out into the harbor, Ivgeny Karchovski turned and looked up at his cousin Butch Karp. He lifted a hand and saw Butch wave back. Then he turned and faced the ship to assess the situation.

He'd just been informed about the bombings by one of his men when Butch called and asked for a "favor." It surprised him because his cousin maintained an arm's-length relationship with the Karchovski family, understandable given their divergent career paths. There'd been a few quiet dinners with Butch and Marlene, or visits from the twin boys to their "uncle Vladimir," since circumstances had reunited the two sides of the family a few years back. But it was always understood—and Ivgeny's father and head of the Karchovski mob, Vladimir, had insisted—that they respect Butch's position as district attorney and not jeopardize that.

However, he understood within the first few words from Butch that this was a special occasion. The attack he knew about, but his cousin said he was worried that a bigger attack was on the way and it would come over the water from the harbor.

Karchovski also knew immediately why Butch had called him. His cousin knew that one of the Karchovskis' legitimate enterprises was their ship repair facilities in Brooklyn. The twins, Zak and

Giancarlo, along with their mother, Marlene, had once toured the facility with him and Vladimir. The boys had been sent home with replicas of the tractor tugboats *Natasha* and *Natalie*, used in real life to maneuver large ships from the harbor into the dockyards.

"If the attack comes from some big ship, I don't think the police have anything big enough to deal with it on the scene," Butch had said.

Fifteen minutes after Butch's first call, Karchovski and a small army of his "soldiers" were armed and gathered at the docks where *Natasha* and the *Natalie* were tied up. He'd gathered them and the crews of the tugboats and explained the situation and what he intended to do.

"This will be extremely dangerous," he'd said. *"I expect that some, maybe all, could die. But if we do nothing, many innocent lives will be lost."* He'd looked from one man's face to the next. Many of the men, or their fathers, had served with him in the Soviet army in Afghanistan, others he'd smuggled into the United States and given jobs. *"But I am not ordering anyone to risk his life. Many of you, like me, are not even citizens of this country. To most, we are criminals and have no chance of ever becoming citizens. But I know you . . . I know you are good men . . . many of you have families of your own and this is not your fight, so I will understand if you stay. No one will lose his job, or my affection, if he chooses to stay behind. However, if you wish to fight with me, then we must leave now. There is not a moment more to waste."*

Never in all his years of military service had Karchovski been prouder than when every man filed aboard the tugboats. They had already pulled away from the docks and were approaching the Manhattan Bridge when he received the second call from his cousin. The threat was real . . . a cargo ship called the *Ibn Jubair*; its crew was armed with automatic weapons and handheld missiles, and there was reason to believe that it might be filled with liquefied natural gas.

"Is that all?" Karchovski teased his cousin. He laughed. *"I thought you might want to arm them with some nuclear warheads and give them a few helicopters as well."*

Up ahead in the growing darkness, Karchovski saw helicopters, but they belonged to the NYPD and were shining spotlights on the cargo ship. One flew around the port side of the ship and narrowly avoided a missile that continued on into the city, where a moment later a thin pillar of smoke rose. After that the helicopters remained on the starboard side of the *Ibn Jubair*—firing at the ship while dodging return fire, obviously no more capable of stopping the ship than the small police craft that darted back and forth.

Karchovski looked around. His men were piling large hawser ropes and whatever other material they could find into bunkers. On the stern of each boat, he'd left his lieutenants—both men who had served with him in Soviet special forces—to prepare boarding parties.

A radio he held in his hand crackled on. "The ship is turning toward Manhattan," the tug captain said. "It may be trying to run aground."

"Then we must do whatever it takes to prevent that," Karchovski said.

"We need to get there in time to turn her from the Manhattan side," the captain replied. "Even then she's going to have momentum and mass on her side. It will be a tough fight."

"I'm sure you will win it," Karchovski said.

"We can try. But you might want to come inside the wheelhouse, where it will be a little safer . . . that is, if you're not too busy standing on the bow of my ship playing Admiral Negobatov at the Battle of Tsushima."

"Didn't we lose that one?" Karchovski asked with a laugh.

"*Da*. It was a disaster. The Japanese kicked our asses."

Karchovski smiled. Russian humor was always so deliciously dark.

Kane cackled as he watched the *Ibn Jubair* begin a long, slow turn toward Manhattan Island as the police helicopters and patrol boats skittered about, unable to do much more than shine their spotlights on the ship. Red tracers arced through the air from the police boats and were returned in even greater numbers from the enemy. Occasionally, there'd be the sudden bright streak of a rocket-propelled grenade or a missile followed by the flash of an explosion.

Kane had laughed uproariously when a missile went past the helicopter and struck one of the buildings across from Battery Park. A small fuel fire on the water marked where a helicopter had gone down in the initial clash, and two police boats burned merrily. "This is even more fun than I thought," he said, standing up and clapping his hands.

He leaned over again to look through the telescope, but the smirk on his face disappeared when he swung the telescope back toward the Brooklyn Bridge and saw the tugboats. And more important, the armed men on board the boats.

"What the hell!" he exclaimed. He thought he'd planned for every contingency. *Where did Karp come up with those boats on such short notice?* Reaching into his pants pocket, he tapped his foot impatiently, waiting for Lucy's cell phone to turn on. When it did, he called . . . *his nemesis*. The unbidden word made him shudder.

"What's the matter, Kane? Didn't expect the cavalry to arrive so soon?" Karp said grimly.

"Fuck you, Karp!" Kane snarled. "You call off those tugboats, or I'm going to rape and kill your daughter while you listen. Here, I'm going to put her cell on speakerphone so I can use both hands."

The cell phone was quiet and Kane began to smile again until Karp spoke. "Lucy, if you can hear me, I love you."

"I love you, too, Dad, do the right thing! I'll be okay!"

"No, she won't, Karp," Kane screamed. "She's going to suffer. Now, fucking tell those tugboats to turn around!"

"Can't do it, Kane," Karp said. "But I swear to you that when this is over, if you're still alive, I am going to spend every moment of the rest of my life coming after you. I will hunt you down, and I will choke the life out of you with my own hands."

"A little vigilante, isn't that, Mr. Law and Order? What about my Miranda warnings, and all my other constitutional rights?" Kane mocked.

Kane looked at the *Ibn Jubair*, lit up in the spotlights of the helicopters, and then back at the tugboats. "You're too late, anyway,

Karp," he snarled. "But I'm still going to rape and kill this bitch, just so that her suffering is the last thing you'll hear before you die."

Setting the cell phone down on a desk, Kane walked over to Lucy, grabbed her by the hair, and threw her to the floor. She struggled, but with her wrists and ankles bound there wasn't much she could do as he began to undo the belt of his pants.

"I feel sorry for you, Kane," Lucy said. "It's really a demon that's making you do this."

Kane stopped for a moment, then laughed and undid his zipper. "Well, too bad there's no swine around. Then you could perform an exorcism and the demon would jump into the body of a pig and go drown in the East River."

"I'm afraid it's not going to go that easy on you," Lucy replied. "St. Teresa says the Avenging Angel is on his way."

Kane laughed. "What avenging angel? Your dad's about to be turned into a crispy critter. Isn't that right, Karp!"

"I mean David Grale," Lucy replied.

At the mention of the name, Kane's smile faltered. His eyes blazed as he dropped his pants. "I don't believe in angels." He stepped toward Lucy, but suddenly she rolled onto her back and kicked up with her feet, catching him in the testicles.

The blow dropped Kane to his hands and knees. Gasping, with spittle flying from his mouth, he stood slowly back on his feet and pulled his knife from its sheath. "I'll fuck you when you're dead, bitch!" he bellowed as his eyes rolled insanely.

"Andy! Help me!" Lucy screamed.

"That little son of a bitch isn't helping anyone. . . ." Kane couldn't finish his sentence as he doubled over, as though he'd been struck again, and dropped the knife. "Nooooo!" he screamed.

"Andy. He's going to hurt me," Lucy yelled.

"I won't let him," Andy replied. "He wasn't in charge of me. I still warned your dad."

"Yes, you did, and you were a good boy. Now it's your turn to be the strong one, Andy."

Kane's hideous face twisted again. Blood surged wildly through the veins in his ruined skin as his eyes bugged out of their ruined sockets. He turned to Abu and snarled. "Shoot, you fucking idiot!"

"Stop it," Abu yelled, stepping between them and pointing the gun down at Lucy.

"Don't shoot her," Andy yelled. "Shoot me!"

Fear contorting his face, Abu pointed the gun back at Kane.

"For God's sake, you moron, shoot the fucking witch," Kane yelled.

Abu stared at Kane and nodded. He turned toward Lucy and raised the gun. A grunt escaped his lips and his mouth made little motions like a fish's. He dropped to his knees, the gun clattering away, and then fell forward onto his face, Kane's knife buried in one of his kidneys.

"I'm sorry. I didn't want to hurt anybody," Andy apologized.

"It's okay, Andy," Lucy said. "You did it to protect a friend. Now untie me, please."

Andy leaned over the twitching body of Abu and pulled the knife out. Abu suddenly shook his head violently and made a noise like a man stepping into a cold shower.

Lucy had managed to sit up and saw that the man with the knife in front of her no longer acted like a ten-year-old boy. Instead, he was a middle-aged, and very angry, sociopath. "Now you're going to die, bitch."

Kane paused as he heard Karp's voice on the speakerphone. "Got it, Espey?"

Stalking over to the phone, Kane sneered. "Got what, Karp? I'm about to gut your daughter like a pig. So what have you got?"

"You, Kane, just you."

Suddenly, there was a loud explosion from the front of the house followed by the sound of gunshots and shouts of "Federal agents, drop your weapons." More gunfire erupted.

Howling with rage, Kane turned to kill Lucy only to see that she had almost reached Abu's gun. The hunter was about to become the hunted. He dodged out of the room just as a bullet crashed into the wall behind his head.

When it became clear to Abdullah that the tugs would intercept him before he could get as far as the Brooklyn Bridge, he'd changed plans to run aground as far up the island as he could get. Looking at the map, he thought maybe as far as the South Street Seaport Museum and Circle Line boat tour docks.

Now he was willing to settle for the Battery Maritime Building in front of One New York Plaza. The captain had swung the *Ibn Jubair* in a wide turn and had the ship running straight for the land, where Abdullah could see the lights from the cars on the FDR Drive, while off to his right the Brooklyn Bridge still smoldered. He imagined thousands of people in the glass towers in front of him watching the approaching ship, not knowing the horror they faced. *It will still be a glorious end!*

Two police helicopters still buzzed around like hornets while the police patrol boats kept making valiant but ineffectual runs at the ship as his men continued to drive them off. The only real obstacles now were breaking away from the path they'd taken along the shoreline and running at an angle toward the *Ibn Jubair*.

Already tracers were flying between the tugboats and the ship. His men seemed to be running out of rocket grenades and missiles as they fired them more judiciously to keep the helicopters and boats at bay.

"They're going to reach us before we hit land," the captain said.

"Go as fast as you can and turn into them," Abdullah said. "Run them over."

"I'll try, but they're more maneuverable and probably will avoid a direct blow."

Abdullah turned to one of his men. "Go tell the others to concentrate their fire on the tugboats. They must buy us more time."

As he watched, a rocket grenade screamed away from the ship's bow and struck one of the tugboats. But it hit the upturned prow a glancing blow and exploded without seeming to cause any damage.

In the meantime, the men on the tugboats were pouring a withering fire at the ship. Being higher out of the water, especially in the wheelhouses, the shooters in the tugboats were much more effective than those of the Harbor Patrol. His men were taking more casualties and having to keep their heads down between shooting a few rounds themselves. He ducked as a stream of bullets crashed through the window of the bridge.

Abdullah heard a strange sound and turned to see the captain sitting on the floor holding his throat. Then the man's hands dropped; half of his throat had been shot away.

As God wills, Abdullah thought. *We don't need a captain anymore.*

The shooting from the deck intensified as the two tugboats approached. Some of his men ran outside the bridge and began shooting down as first one and then the other tug slammed in at oblique angles. Abdullah fought to keep his feet. He looked down below, where men from the ship and men on the tugboats blasted away at one another from nearly point-blank range.

As the tug closest to the bow revved its engines and strained against the *Ibn Jubair,* the other suddenly turned to bring itself sideways to the ship. "They're boarding!" one of his men outside the bridge shouted. The man lifted his rifle to shoot, but his head disappeared in a fine red mist. Then a man outside the door was struck in the chest by a round that nearly cut him in two from the side.

Heavy round, Abdullah thought as he ducked. *A sniper on the bridge?* "More power, more power!" he screamed.

"This is all she has," shouted the helmsman, who kept trying to turn the wheel against the pressure of the tugboats.

Mindful of the sniper, Abdullah kept the bulkhead between him and the Brooklyn Bridge as he stood. The gleaming One New York Plaza tower rose before him, beckoning him, to intertwine its fate with his. The ship was still moving forward, but slowly, inexorably, the tugs were winning the battle.

It was clear that the *Ibn Jubair* might come within yards of the Maritime Building, but it would not strike the shore hard enough to rupture the hull. There was only one thing left to do. But there wasn't much time. Shooting from the rear of the ship meant that the boarding party from the second tug had fought their way onto the *Ibn Jubair*.

The men on the deck in front of him still kept the helicopters at bay, though there were more now and they were bathing the ship in bright light, and prevented any men from the first tug from coming aboard. But it was a matter of time before they ran out of ammunition or were picked off.

Abdullah pulled his handgun from its holster and grabbed a grenade launcher. "Keep us as close to that building as you can," he said, pointing at One New York Plaza. Then he turned to Stupenagel, who had taken cover beneath a steel shelf. He pointed the gun at her. "Get up."

When they got to the door to go out, he put the gun against her back. "Just so you know, there is a sniper on that bridge; if you hesitate, he'll kill you as soon as me," he said. "But if you try to get away, I will shoot you. Now run."

The two darted through the door and had just ducked into a covered stairwell down to the deck when a bullet clanged off the steel above their heads. "That's your friends. Perhaps they think you're Ajmaani," he said with a laugh.

"As long as they shoot you, too, I'll be happy knowing there's a special place for you in hell."

Abdullah pressed the gun to her head again. "Tonight, I dine with the Prophet and all the mujahedeen who fought for Allah before me. Now go down and out onto the deck. But be careful. You have men with guns trying to shoot you."

As they reached the deck, Abdullah saw a young man with an assault rifle who appeared to be in shock. "You, come with me," he said, slapping the boy.

Numbly, the boy nodded and started to move out when a bullet caught him in the back, striking his spine and dropping him like gelatin to the deck. "Your friend the sniper," Abdullah said as they ducked behind a metal shed. "I want you between him and me. Falter once, and I will shoot you first."

"So gallant," Stupenagel said. "But I guess hiding behind women is pretty par for the course."

Abdullah shook his head and smiled. "You know, Ariadne, I cannot wait until I no longer have to hear your voice."

"Feeling's mutual, bub. Want to tell me where we're going? It's kind of hard to move around with my wrists tied."

Abdullah looked around the shed. "I need to get to the middle," he said. He didn't feel it necessary to explain that he wanted to reach the valves that had been modified to dock with the tanker and allow the *Ibn Jubair* to transport LNG. If he could release the valves without getting shot, he might still be able to ignite the ship by firing the grenade into the tanks.

He stuck the gun in her ribs. "Let's go."

"I got two bad guys trying to work their way forward," Blanchett said to Karp. "One's a woman. I think she might be Malovo. And the other one could be Omar Abdullah. I only saw him briefly."

Blanchett kept the crosshairs of his scope on the spot where he'd last seen the two duck after he shot the second man. His first attempts to help Karchovski's men in the tugboats had been off. It was a long shot at a moving target, but the toughest part had been judging the rise and fall of the vessel. He had to time it along with all the other variables. But he was getting the hang of it and had hit several men—concentrating on those he saw with grenade launchers or handheld missiles, as well as two who'd been shooting downward at the tugboats from the ship's bridge.

The man and woman suddenly darted from their hiding place. Blanchett squeezed a shot off but knew that it would miss. Before he could chamber another round, the woman, a blond, and the man ran forward again and hid. "They're pretty determined to get wherever they're going."

Karp looked through his binoculars at the ship going forward from where he, too, had last seen the pair. He was trying to keep his mind off the last sounds he'd heard from Lucy's cell phone—an explosion, shots fired, shouts, and a horrible scream before the phone went dead. *Nothing you can do. Help Ned.* He came to a group of valves partly obscured by several metal boxes in the middle of the deck, which he presumed led to whatever was beneath.

"I'll bet they want to get to those valves," Karp said. "If they can release the gas that way, they might still ignite it. I'd hate to see what it will do to those buildings and whoever's in them."

Ned patiently watched through the scope, his finger poised on the trigger. He followed the rise of the ship with his crosshairs on the spot where he thought the terrorists would have to appear if the valves were their destination. He saw movement and began to pull the trigger as a blond head appeared.

"Oh shit, it's that reporter, Ariadne!" he exclaimed.

"What? Who? Who did you say?" asked Gilbert Murrow, who'd been standing behind them and now moved to the railing.

"Abdullah is using her as a shield," Ned replied. "He's at the valves. I think he's trying to turn them. He has a gun on her, but I can't get a clear shot."

"You're going to have to take the shot, Ned," Karp said.

"I'd have to kill her first," Blanchett replied, his voice strained.

"No, please," Murrow pleaded.

"You can't let him open that valve," Karp shouted.

Murrow fainted at the moment Blanchett pulled the trigger.

On board the *Ibn Jubair*, Ariadne Stupenagel crouched in front of Abdullah. *Let's see,* she thought, *if they think I'm Malovo, they're going to keep trying to shoot me. The shooter fires when the ship gets to its high point.*

She waited for the ship to rise and at the moment before it would drop again, she fell to the deck. Something buzzed over her head like a giant bee. She looked over to the side and saw that the bee had stung her former lover and that he was no longer among the living. *God, I promise, if you just let me get home to my Murry, I'll never have sex with bad men again.*

She was still thinking about her next move when two men suddenly appeared, pointing weapons at her. "Oh, come on," she said. "I'm tired of getting shot at."

"Then maybe you'll want to get up and come with us," one of the men said. He pressed a microphone attached to his black sweater. "Officer Tomaso reporting in. We have one female hostile. The midsection is secure."

"Who are you calling hostile, sweetie," Stupenagel said. "I'm about the friendliest girl you ever met. I was a hostage, not one of the bad guys."

The other officer laughed. "She's got you there, Tomaso."

"Yeah, yeah, Baines," Tomaso replied. "Sorry, ma'am, but I'm going to have to cuff you until the sarge says otherwise."

"Handcuffs? Why, I hardly know you," she replied. "Oh, before

I forget. There are a couple of federal agents holed up somewhere on the ship. They're the ones who stopped these jokers from torching lower Manhattan. You might want to tell your guys not to shoot them, or for that matter to get too close, or they might get shot."

As Tomaso relayed the information about Jojola and Tran to his superior officer, Baines checked on Abdullah. "Man," he said with disgust, "a .50 cal sure makes a mess."

Stupenagel glanced over and then shrugged. "He's not the first man to lose his head over me."

When Kane disappeared, Lucy put down the gun and used his knife to cut the ropes binding her feet and wrists. She stood up at the same moment two men in black commando gear entered the room.

"Put the knife down," one of them commanded, training his gun on her while his partner cleared the rest of the room.

Lucy dropped the knife, but the men continued to stand there with their weapons trained on her, as if not quite sure about the danger represented by a good-looking, completely naked young woman. "Uh, you guys want to quit staring and find me something to wear?" she said.

"I think I can help." A tall, gray-eyed man entered the room, removing his suit coat and holding it out for her as he averted his eyes.

"Thanks, Uncle Espey." Lucy smiled. "You'd think those two guys had never seen a naked girl before."

"We don't have time for girls," Jaxon said, toeing the body of Abu. "I take it Kane's gone."

"Yeah. But I have a feeling he won't get far."

Jaxon looked puzzled. "You know something I don't?"

"Maybe. In the meantime, can I borrow your cell phone?" she said, holding hers up. "Mine just ran out of charge and I want to tell my dad that I'm all right."

"You just did," Jaxon said with a smile. "He says to tell you he loves you. And so does Ned."

Lucy pulled the suit coat closer and leaned on Jaxon as he put his arm around her to escort her to safety. "Well, then," she said, "I guess all is right with the world."

Several blocks away, a man in a black fedora and dark cape hobbled quickly along the Brooklyn Heights Promenade. He glanced up and saw the long, dark limo parked in the lot at the end of the section he was on. The driver blinked the headlights.

Kane had planned his escape thinking he would never need it. After he narrowly avoided getting shot by Lucy, he'd hopped in an elevator that took him down two floors to a secret room where he donned the hat and cape. Using a key, he'd opened a door that he had made that led into the sewer system that ran beneath Brooklyn Heights. It was filthy, and a home for huge rats that he feared and detested. But with the help of a flashlight, he'd gone along until finding a second door—an access door for utility workers from the boardwalk of the Promenade.

The limo driver had been told to wait at the parking lot, which would have been shielded from the blast of the ship. Just in case escape was necessary, the driver was to wait there until called to the house to take Kane and his entourage, as well as Lucy, to a private airfield on Long Island. *Ah well,* Kane thought as he approached the car. *Live to fight another day*.

The driver, a tall man who fit his uniform poorly, got out and ran around the car to open the door for him.

"God, you stink," Kane complained as he started to get in the car.

"I'll try to bathe more often in the future, sir," the man replied. "In the meantime, I think you might like to know that 'thou has fulfilled the judgment of the wicked: judgment and justice take hold on thee'. . . . That's Job 36:17, friend."

"What?" Kane scowled. "Who are you?" He turned the flashlight on the face of the driver. "You! But you're dead!"

"No," Treacher said. "But I suspect you are." With that, he grabbed Kane and propelled him into the back of the limousine.

Kane fell forward on his face. He started to push himself up, but was shoved back down by a booted foot on his neck.

"Hello, Kane," David Grale, who was seated in the back, said, leaning forward so that his enemy could see his face. He folded Karp's note that he'd received from Dirty Warren an hour earlier. "Brooklyn Heights," it read.

"I've been waiting to have this conversation for a long, long time. I hope you like rats."

Treacher closed the door and smiled, hearing the muffled scream from within.

39

Leonard stood in front of the jurors, wagged a finger at them, and shook his head. "The very brevity of the prosecution case should give you pause. Is it because the truth is so succinct, or is it, because as we have proved, the People don't have a case and know it?"

As the defense lawyer spoke, Maplethorpe, who was dressed in a black silk suit with a plum-colored silk tie, dabbed at his eyes with a plum-colored handkerchief while his followers wept behind him. Occasionally a sob would escape a spectator, which Rosenmayer dealt with by stern looks rather than interrupting Leonard's summation to scold them.

Karp kept his face expressionless as Leonard paced back and forth in front of the jury, a finger held high and pointing upward like some sort of Pentecostal preacher. For two hours, the defense attorney had cajoled, harangued, and pleaded as he essentially repeated everything his expert witnesses had said, and then began attacking the prosecution's case.

"They created a scenario and then stuck with it no matter what," he said. "It's easy for the district attorney, a man who must run for reelection every four years and must make himself look 'tough on crime' and willing to take even 'wealthy' citizens to task, to dismiss the testimony of the expert witnesses who appeared before you. But there is a reason our justice system makes specific provisions for the use of qualified, intelligent professionals to shed light on subjects with which we may not be familiar or have not had the time to research ourselves. We are all busy people who can't be expected to be knowledgeable about injury biomechanics or revenge suicide syndrome or bipolar disorder. So we have to rely on people who have devoted their entire lives to understanding these issues so that we can make intelligent, informed decisions."

Leonard then began on the prosecution witnesses and didn't cease for two very long hours. Finally, Leonard looked from one juror's face to the next with tears in his eyes. "Maybe Gail Perez didn't originally intend to kill herself in Mr. Maplethorpe's apartment. Perhap there was no RSS, no revenge motive, for her actions, though I would urge you not to discount Dr. Braunschweiger's testimony, because she is at the cutting edge of this school of thought. After all, most of the greatest minds of Europe thought the world was flat until 1492. So perhaps Gail Perez intended to leave—had even gathered up her purse, straightened her clothing, fixed her makeup—when she opened a drawer on that end table out of curiosity and found the gun. Thus her decision to use it at that moment was more one of opportunity than plan."

Leonard hung his head and stopped pacing. He stood quietly and then glanced sideways at his client. "And unfortunately, it was my client's carelessness regarding the proper storage of a firearm that presented this terrible opportunity. But that's something he will have to live with for the rest of his life."

"I'm so sorry," Maplethorpe sobbed just loud enough to be heard, and then blew his nose.

Leonard gave his client a sad smile. "Yes, my client is sorry, as he may have said that night to Mr. Gianneschi. He is sorry that he mistook a young woman's interest in him as one of mutual attraction. He is sorry that his fiduciary and creative responsibilities to his financial backers, as well as the actors, directors, and stagehands whose livelihoods depend on his decisions, force him to decide who achieves their dream . . . and who does not."

Another sob escaped Maplethorpe. "I'm sorry, I'm so sorry," he said, looking at the judge.

Leonard raised his finger to his lips. "We know, Mr. Maplethorpe," he said, and then turned to the jurors. "And that's why the only just verdict you can return with is one of not guilty. Let's not compound this horrible tragedy with another. Not guilty, ladies and gentlemen." He slammed his fist down on the jury rail and exclaimed, "My . . . client . . . is . . . *not* . . . guilty."

Rosenmayer waited until it was clear that Leonard was finished, then announced, "We'll take a thirty-minute break. Then we'll return for the People's summation."

Most everyone left the courtroom, including Katz, but Karp remained in his seat, absently rolling his young colleague's apple around on the table. The trial of F. Lloyd Maplethorpe had been postponed for a week following the terrorist attack on the Brooklyn Bridge.

Although the terrorists were stopped before achieving their ultimate aim, it had come with a high price. Forty-three people had been killed outright or later died from injuries caused by the truck bombs that had exploded on either end of the bridge. But it could have been worse. A school bus loaded with teenagers from W.E.B. Dubois Academic High School in Brooklyn, on their way to a basketball game against Manhattan's Xavier High School, had narrowly escaped. Some of the teens had reported seeing a terrorist looking at them before the bomb exploded.

In all, twenty-nine terrorists, including the two truck drivers, had died, including mastermind Omar Abdullah, and another four had been wounded and captured, thanks, the press reported, to joint efforts by the NYPD, federal agents, and "heroic members of the Russian community of Brighton Beach who worked for a Brooklyn ship repair facility and took it upon themselves to act."

Karp knew that thirteen of Ivgeny Karchovski's men had died in the assault. And when the shooting was over, they'd used the tugs to haul the *Ibn Jubair* out of the danger area despite continued risk to themselves should the ship explode.

Although some of Ivgeny's men had disappeared back into the community, others were located and brought to the center of the Brooklyn Bridge and presented citations for heroism by the mayor. There had also been press reports that some of the men, perhaps the tugboat captains, as representatives of their crews, would receive the Presidential Medal of Freedom, the nation's highest civilian award for heroism. When it was learned that some of the men may have been in the country illegally, one of the U.S. senators from New York had introduced legislation to put them on the fast track to citizenship.

When Karp called to thank Ivgeny Karchovski, who had been wounded slightly in the arm storming aboard the *Ibn Jubair*, he'd raised the possibility that his cousin might achieve U.S. citizenship. But Karchovski dismissed it. "Maybe someday if it could be done quietly—not with all the publicity that this is getting now. You and I know that the gratitude for what my men did will fade, and someone in the media would run a story about how I am a leader of a so-called crime family. It could even come back to damage you. So let's not tarnish this moment. If my men can reap some reward, then I am satisfied. . . . I do have one favor to ask of you personally. But I understand if it is too much."

"I don't think it would be possible for you to ask too much," Karp replied.

Karchovski hesitated and Karp thought his voice sounded a little huskier when he replied. "I appreciate that you did not hesitate or preface your reply," he said. "Anyway, my father, your great-uncle, Vladimir, is not getting any younger, and he would like to spend Chanukah with family, and I am a poor excuse for holiday cheer. But do you think, perhaps, that you might find a way for your family and ours to share the holiday, just a little bit, and fulfill the old man's dream?"

Karp smiled. "I'm sure something can be arranged."

Of course, the best story had been written by Ariadne Stupenagel, whose "Aboard the *Ibn Jubair*" was already being talked about as a sure Pulitzer bet. Murrow had also confided to Karp that several publishers were engaged in a bidding war for the rights to a book-length version. "They're also realizing that Ariadne has had a rather interesting life. So we're trying to negotiate a multibook deal that would include her memoirs, *and* we've been contacted by certain folks in Hollywood about a film possibility."

"We're negotiating?" Karp had said with a raised eyebrow. "Are you adding the title 'superagent' to your list of many credits?"

Murrow blushed. "I'm only advising," he stammered. "I won't let it interfere with my—"

Karp interrupted, "Gilbert, I hope the two of you make a bundle. Don't ever tell her I said so because it will ruin our relationship, but Ariadne deserves a Medal of Freedom. And I don't just have her word for it."

Indeed, Karp was referring to Jojola and Tran, who after fighting off the terrorists had been lucky not to get shot by the police. After Jaxon had convinced everyone not to shoot them, they'd emerged arguing over who got more terrorists. There were nine bodies and each claimed five. However, they'd stopped bickering long enough to report Stupenagel's heroics both on the dock in Trinidad and then aboard the ship.

On Saturday, Murrow and Stupenagel joined Jaxon, Lucy, Ned, Jojola, and Tran for a quiet dinner at the Karp-Ciampi loft. As they all sat around discussing the events, Ariadne looked at Blanchett and asked, "I've just got to know something. Right before Omar was shot, I dropped to the ground. What I want to know is when you took that shot, was I already out of the way, or were you trying to shoot me to get at Omar?"

But Blanchett just looked at her and smiled. "Do you really want to know?"

Stupenagel bit her lip, then shook her head. "No. Maybe I don't."

To her credit, Stupenagel had agreed with Jaxon's request that she not name Jojola and Tran in her stories. Instead, she referred to them as Dick and Billy, two federal agents from an unnamed agency. And while she did not know the full connection to Andrew Kane, Dean Newbury, and the Sons of Man, she agreed not to mention them on the condition that when indictments started coming down, she'd be the first to know and be free of the embargo.

Which may happen sooner rather than later, Karp thought. The morning after the attack, V. T. Newbury, accompanied by Jaxon, as a representative of the federal government, as well as Clay Fulton and two uniformed police officers, entered the offices of Newbury, Newbury and White and arrested Dean Newbury.

As he'd later related to Karp, V.T. waited for Jaxon to inform his uncle of the numerous federal charges against him, including multiple murder charges and conspiracy to commit terrorism. Then Jaxon stepped aside for V.T. to inform his uncle that regardless of all the federal crimes, "the first charge you will face, and the only one that will matter, you son of a bitch, will be in New York Supreme Court for the murder of your brother—my dad—Vincent Newbury."

When Dean Newbury scoffed and said they'd never prove the charges, V.T. had produced a recording of his uncle's meeting with Andrew Kane. *"I killed my own brother, didn't I?"*

"How did you get that?" Dean Newbury demanded, though visibly shaken.

V.T. had reminded him of the remote control car he'd been playing with one day. And then explained how he'd attached a remote-activated transmitter to the car. "I'd wait for the security guys to sweep the offices, then I'd run that little baby right down the air-conditioning shaft that runs above the Sons of Man meeting room . . . oh yes, we're very aware of the Sons of Man. Before the security guys showed up again, I'd run it back to my office and remove the transmitter. It didn't yield much until that night with you and Kane, but I think that alone was worth the $49.99 I spent on the car."

"It will never hold up in court," Dean Newbury scoffed.

"Oh, did I forget to tell you?" V.T. replied. "I got an eavesdropping warrant, signed by emeritus federal judge Frank Plaut. And that's not all, your former chef, the guy who dumped the digitalis in my dad's dinner, and Assistant Medical Examiner Kip Bergendorf, who identified your chauffeur as the man who paid him to falsify the autopsy, have all agreed to testify against you."

"You don't know who you're dealing with," Dean Newbury snarled.

V.T. shrugged and smiled at Jaxon. "Not all of them, not yet. But how will they feel about you letting your nephew into the henhouse? I believe Andrew Kane warned you about that. But here's the deal, you cooperate with Agent Jaxon here, enter the U.S. Marshal's Witness Protection Program, and help identify, prosecute, and convict any members of the Sons of Man who have broken state or federal laws, and I'll put off sending you to Attica for my dad's murder. Hell, that could eat up years, and you're no spring chicken. You'll probably be dead before you have to take your first shower with some big hairy biker named Bubba."

Dean Newbury licked his thin purple lips and made a deal. And from what Karp had gathered so far, Jaxon and his team had already been able to move on some of the information before it could be destroyed. Congressman Denton Crawford had also been arrested and was said to be cooperating.

"Unfortunately, we've got to be careful with this," Jaxon had told him. "Some of these people are very highly placed, and we're talking about murder and treason here . . . all capital offenses. This could really shake the country and we need to move deliberately but with sensitivity as well."

It reminded Karp that there was unfinished business. Nadya Malovo was not found on the *Ibn Jubair*, and the prisoners admitted that a blond terrorist they knew as Ajmaani had been removed from the ship by a U.S. Coast Guard vessel. The next morning, that vessel was located miles farther into the Atlantic Ocean than it should have been, and all the members of its crew were either dead from gunshot or knife wounds, or missing and presumed lost at sea. The blond prisoner was not on board, and the ship's boarding craft was missing.

Even more alarming at first, Andrew Kane had once again slipped through the fingers of law enforcement. However, on Sunday night, Lucy and Marlene had gone out for a walk with Gilgamesh. They'd returned bearing brownies from the Housing Works Bookstore and the news that Kane "is in good hands."

When Karp relayed that story to Jaxon, the agent had sighed and said, "*Would someone please get the word to David Grale that when he's through playing with Kane, we'd love to talk to him. We did find al-Sistani on the deck, trussed up like a turkey for the barbecue, and he's been quite cooperative, but Kane would be even better."*

As he lay in bed that same night with Marlene, Karp had finally let his guard down and mourned the lives that were lost. "I was too slow with the riddles," he lamented.

Marlene kissed him gently and noted, "Even Superman can't save everyone. Imagine what today would be like—how many thousands of lives might have been lost—if you didn't do what you did."

Ned and Lucy had left for New Mexico the next day, accompanied by Marlene. *"Lucy's still not talking much about what happened to her, and I want to be there for her and Ned if it comes boiling out,"* she'd said. *"Besides, we have a wedding to plan."*

That evening, Karp was meeting with Jaxon for drinks at Bleecker Street Bar when the subject of Lucy came up. "I don't suppose you no longer need her and Ned," Karp said. "And they can go back to their little house on the prairie to live happily ever after."

Jaxon had looked at him for a long moment before smiling slightly. "For a time, perhaps, while the rest of us try to dismantle the Sons of Man." Then he frowned. "And if she wants to leave the agency, I won't try to talk her out of it. She just went through hell, but she believes in what she's doing. The world has changed, Butch, people of good conscience can't sit on the sidelines anymore and let others take all the risks for their freedom and security. Whether it's the heroics of people like Ivgeny and his men, or the New York firefighters and police officers who rushed into the World Trade Center buildings, or a district attorney seeking justice one evil man at a time, we're all in this together."

One evil man at a time, Karp repeated to himself as he looked over at Maplethorpe, who'd just walked back into the courtroom. The spectators filed in quickly afterward, as did Katz, accompanied by Carmina Salinas, Tina Perez, and Alejandro Garcia, who took seats behind the prosecution table.

When Katz took his seat next to him, Karp picked up the apple. "Mind if I borrow this?" he asked.

"Hey, bring your own healthy snacks," Kenny Katz replied. "Have you seen how expensive fruit is these days?"

"I promise to give it back to you in just a few minutes without a single bite out of it."

"Okay, then, but I'll be watching." Katz laughed.

Rosenmayer entered the courtroom and quickly asked for the jury to be brought back in. He then turned to the prosecution table. "Are you ready to present your summation, Mr. Karp?"

"I am, Your Honor," Karp replied, standing and walking until he faced the jurors so that they could all see his face clearly. He held up the apple, turning it this way and that as though inspecting it.

"Ladies and gentlemen of the jury," he began, "I have before you a simple red apple. Nothing fancy, just an apple. Put it in a crate full of oranges and shake the bag around, maybe toss in a lime or a lemon, and it may be more difficult to see, but it is still just an apple. And none of us need a lot of people to tell us that it is an apple. We know what it is from personal experience. We held one in our hands. And I assume we've all tasted one at some point in our lives. We know beyond a reasonable doubt that if it looks like an apple, and tastes like an apple . . . it is an apple."

Karp placed the fruit on the ledge in front of the jury. "The truth is a lot like that apple. You can put the truth in a bag full of lies and it's still the truth. You can call as many psychologists as you want, or experts in injury biomechanics and the Italian language, but the truth is still just the truth. But what the defense hopes is that if they pile the lies high enough, and present unnecessary and meaningless expert testimony, the defense hopes that the bogus testimony will hide the truth. This is something I call the Big Lie."

Karp strolled over toward the defense table, where Leonard sat with a smile plastered to his face, but Maplethorpe cowered down as though he thought he might get hit.

"What is the Big Lie?" Karp asked. "Well, it's a lie built upon the foundation of so many other lies that reasonable people such as yourselves look at what you're being told and it's so outrageous, so outside the bounds of common sense, much less common decency, that we start to think that well, maybe there's some truth to it. And why? Well, we reason, why would Mr. Leonard go to such trouble and say such outlandish things if at least some of it wasn't true?"

Karp turned back to the jury. "I'll tell you why. It's because he only has oranges. There's not a single apple in all those words either he or his expert witnesses had to say pertaining to the death of Gail Perez."

Karp paused. "The Big Lie is nothing new," he said. "It's been with us a long time and has been used in many ways. Historical revisionists are particularly good at it. For instance, there are those like the president of Iran who tell the world that the Holocaust never happened . . . that the extermination of six million Jews, and six million other people, was a hoax perpetrated on the world to garner sympathy. Even reasonable people, if they hear that sort of nonsense often enough, there's a tendency to say, 'Well, maybe there's something to it. Maybe it was exaggerated. Or Israeli propaganda.' In the meantime, the Big Lie allows people like the Iranian president to disguise the truth—that he heads a government that sponsors terrorism and keeps its own people under the boot of theocratic oppression. The Big Lie is used today by Islamic terrorists to justify the murder of thousands of innocent men, women, and children by claiming that such acts are retributive justice for a hundred years, no, thousands of years if you go back to the Crusades, of crimes committed against Muslims. And even reasonable people wonder if there's some truth to it if they're willing to go to such lengths. But the only truth is that these people who believe that they can achieve their ends through murder and intimidation, they laugh at how we buy their lies."

Karp looked at the faces of the jurors. Good people. He had not cared if they were liberal or conservative. White, black, or Asian. Just good, thoughtful, practical taxpayers.

"The worst part about the Big Lie is that it doesn't just hide the truth," Karp continued. "It tries to portray perpetrators as victims, and victims as perpetrators and sometimes even scapegoats. It goes something like this: 'The Jews deserved it. The West has forced Muslims to murder.' But if we dump the crate over and kick away the oranges, we'll find our apple among them."

Karp knew that the jurors would be thinking of the recent events, and he gave them time to make the connections. "By the same token, Mr. Leonard and his highly paid expert witnesses have conspired to try to hide the apple with all these little psychobabble, high-tech oranges in order to create the Big Lie and attempt to portray the perpetrator of this crime, Mr. Maplethorpe, as the victim, and the victim, Gail Perez, as the perpetrator. And the injustice of that alone should make you want to cry out that enough is enough."

Karp walked over to the defense table again and stood looking at Maplethorpe. He shook his head. "A few minutes ago, this man sobbed, 'I'm sorry. I'm sorry,' and his attorney tried to portray him as the victim of Miss Perez. They hope that such displays and accusations will generate sympathy. But before you shed any tears for the defendant, let's not forget who deserves those tears and who does not."

Pointing to where she sat in the courtroom, Karp identified Tina Perez as one of those people. "Let's not forget who lost her sister and then had to listen to some defense attorney portray the deceased as a woman who prostituted herself to get a job. And let's not forget the disingenuous revelation of Tina's private medical records in order to paint her as a mentally unstable individual, and the attempt to make a linkage to her sister also being a mentally unstable individual, for which there is no evidence."

Karp looked over at Carmina. "And if we shed any tears, let them be also for Carmina Salinas. She didn't have to testify in this case. She was under no obligation, except a moral one, and no one paid her to render an opinion. She didn't have to take the stand and allow that same defense attorney to paint her in the same reprehensible light as he'd done with Gail Perez."

Karp turned back to the jury, moving up to the ledge that separated him from them. "We in this business call this the slut defense, which is a common factor in the defense's Big Lie when there is a young woman involved who has been sexually assaulted. Every woman in this courtroom, or for that matter in this city, this state, this country, knows that if she is sexually assaulted by a man and takes the stand against him, the defense will make every attempt to demonstrate that it was her fault. It might not be as blatant as it once was . . . they've got to be careful about accusing a woman of wearing her skirt too short or visiting the wrong bar and thus 'deserving what she gets.' But they still imply it every chance they get. So, of course, Carmina sold her body to Mr. Cowsill to get a part in his play, and for some reason hung around another two years. And of course, the defense argues, a beautiful young woman like Carmina was willing to do the same thing with that man"—he pointed to Maplethorpe—"for a better role. She's just a slut, a whore . . . she and Gail Perez deserved what happened to them."

Karp rapped the knuckles of his right hand on the jury ledge. "It's all part of the Big Lie, folks. But let's examine this using our common sense and see if we can't cut through the smoke. We have Carmina Salinas, a young woman just starting her career in the theater. She has the best role of her life thus far in Mr. Maplethorpe's current production. Yet, if she testifies against him and he gets convicted, it's likely this play will fold and she'll be out of work. And what's more, she'll be the woman who kissed and told and didn't get what she wanted, so she got even. And her chances of landing another job go right down the drain with Mr. Maplethorpe. . . . I want you to think about the tears that have been shed in this courtroom during this trial. Which do you believe were real? The theatrical sobbing of the defendant, or the tears Carmina Salinas wept when she talked about how this was the end of her dreams? She had nothing to gain and everything to lose by testifying here. Yet, the defense would have you believe that she's the one who's lying."

Karp pointed over to the defense table. "And they'd have you believe that Hilario Gianneschi is some pathological liar, too. But let's apply our common sense here as well. If Gianneschi wanted to avoid being detected as an illegal alien, he could have told the police that Mr. Maplethorpe didn't say anything to him. Or when asked to report to the First Precinct for more questions, he could have run and set up again in some other city. And let me leave you with this. On the morning he was to testify, Mr. Gianneschi was mysteriously reported to the INS and apprehended. But instead of calling an immigration lawyer, he called my office to let us know what had happened. He has no deal with us; he's going to have to go before a judge for a deportation hearing, and his dream of living in America may also be over. But he sat on that stand and let the defense attorney call him a criminal and a liar because as he said, it was the right thing to do."

Karp walked over to the prosecution table, picked up the photograph of Gail Perez performing in *Annie Get Your Gun*, and displayed it to the entire jury. "And last but not least, let us not forget to shed our tears for the deceased. We know she agreed to go to dinner with Mr. Maplethorpe, presumably to discuss a role in his play. That's what she told her sister. I don't know if she thought he might want to have sex with her, but there's no evidence that she allowed that to happen. I'd remind you of the autopsy findings discussed by Detective Cardamone that showed she had not had vaginal sex or oral sex in the hours before she died. So if she didn't sell her body for a role in a play, where does the defense find the nerve to label her a whore, and a vindictive whore to boot? Well, because part of the Big Lie requires them to make her the perpetrator, with poor Mr. Maplethorpe her victim."

Karp took a deep breath and let it out. "Let's compare what you heard from Hilario Gianneschi, Tina Perez, and Carmina Salinas to the expert testimony. What did you hear from the experts? A bunch of theories and opinions. You had computer-generated cartoons that change depending on what the computer is fed. But every single defense witness who appeared on that stand admitted that they did not have a single shred of evidence, not an apple in the bunch, to support the Big Lie that Gail Perez was a troubled young woman who sold her body for a job and then killed herself when it didn't work out. Instead, they made it all up, or spoke in generalities about theories and books that had nothing to do with the facts of this case. Together they created, ladies and gentlemen, a Big Lie."

Karp strolled from one end of the jury box to the other. "I can't tell you all the details of what happened in Mr. Maplethorpe's apartment that night. There's only one person in this courtroom who knows, and he's sitting over there at the defense table. But that doesn't mean we don't know who killed Miss Perez."

Pointing to the apple, Karp said, "Let's examine the evidence, the actual facts that we do have. We know that Mr. Maplethorpe called Hilario Gianneschi and asked him to come to his apartment. We know that when Mr. Gianneschi asked if he should summon an ambulance, the defendant shrieked 'No!' . . . Again, what does our common sense tell us? If someone found a gun in your house and shot themselves, wouldn't you call an ambulance or the police? Or if a witness asked if you wanted them to call, would you have shrieked 'No, don't do it!' When you begin to deliberate, ask yourselves, why would someone do that?"

Waiting a moment to let it sink in, Karp continued. "Ladies and gentlemen, you don't need me to tell you who killed Gail Perez. You don't need expert witnesses to throw a bunch of oranges at you and tell you that they're apples. The person who told you who killed Gail Perez is sitting right there at the defense table. And what did he say?"

Karp held up one finger. "'I've been bad.'" He held up another finger. "'Please, tell her I didn't mean to do it.'" And a third. "'I think I killed her.'" He dropped his hand. "There was no misinterpretation, no telling authorities what they wanted to hear by Mr. Gianneschi. It was a confession by the defendant, Maplethorpe."

Karp picked up the apple from the ledge and waited for the jurors to digest what he'd said. When he saw that every eye was on him, waiting for him to deliver the final blow, he nodded and pointed at Maplethorpe, who sank down in his chair.

"I don't have to tell you who killed Gail Perez, because the defendant already did. Take him at his word and don't let him make her a victim twice: once by taking her life, depriving her sister and friends of the beauty of her smile and the warmth of her companionship, and twice by besmirching her character. When you deliberate you will find the apple in that crate of oranges and return to this courtroom with the only just verdict. In this case, good conscience commands, common sense dictates, justice cries out for a verdict of murder. Thank you."

Returning to his seat, he handed the apple back to Kenny Katz. "Here's your snack, Counselor," he whispered. "See if you can put it to better use."

"Are you kidding?" Katz said under his breath. "I was just wondering if it's possible to have an apple bronzed."

EPILOGUE

SNOW BEGAN TO FALL AS THE SMALL GROUP OF MOURNERS, gathered around the grave at the St. Joseph of Carmel Catholic Cemetery in Queens, began to break up and go their separate ways. It was just a few days before Christmas and Stewart Reed's mother and a few friends watched as he was laid to rest for a second time, next to his father and plots reserved for his mother and sister, who'd written to Karp from Iraq saying, "It's nice to get a reminder of what my troops and I are fighting for."

Stewbie's mom had burst into tears when she saw Karp arrive. But as she explained with a hug, they were tears of gratitude and joy. Her son would rest in ground consecrated by the Roman Catholic Church, as his death was no longer considered a suicide.

The Reed case had officially been ruled a homicide. Swanburg's autopsy findings had been spot-on and were basically rubber-stamped by the chief medical examiner. All that remained was bringing to justice one of the men—the other was dead—who'd conspired to murder Reed.

Karp looked at his watch. Right about then, Kenny Katz would be representing the People at the arraignment of F. Lloyd Maplethorpe for the murder of Reed and attempted murder of Carmina Salinas.

It was a slam-dunk case. Former assistant medical examiner

Kip Bergendorf was singing like a canary. And a key discovered by Fulton in Gregor Capuchin's apartment had fit a safety deposit box at a bank in the Bronx. The box yielded a small vial of what proved to be a deadly neurotoxin and a tape recorder with two conversations between the killer and one F. Lloyd Maplethorpe. Apparently, the Russian either didn't trust Maplethorpe or, as Fulton suspected, was into blackmail as well as murder for hire.

The jury had deliberated for less than three hours. When they returned with a guilty verdict, Maplethorpe had fainted, causing his supporters to begin shrieking hysterically.

As soon as Maplethorpe was revived and order restored, Rosenmayer thanked the jurors and released them from their duty. The judge then remanded the defendant pending sentence and added, *"Is there anything else before we adjourn?"*

Karp nodded to Kenny Katz, who rose and announced that Maplethorpe was being charged for murder and attempted murder. The producer fainted again, and those of his followers who remained simply sank into their seats and moaned.

As Leonard left the courtroom, the press asked him if he'd be representing Maplethorpe in the new case. *"Hell, no,"* he'd exclaimed with a laugh. *"I'm going home to Montana to lick my wounds. My client has struck me with a pitcher of water and stabbed me with a pen. I'm afraid I might not survive another round of this. I need a rest."*

At last, Karp found something to agree with Leonard about. He was looking forward to a rest as well. After the funeral, he and the twins were heading to the airport to fly to New Mexico, where the family would spend the Christmas holiday.

Fortunately, Zak and Giancarlo were back on best-friends status. Zak's help in solving the riddles had given him a much-needed confidence boost. He'd even told his brother it was okay if he went to the Winter Dance with Elisa Robyn. However, the girl had apparently grown tired of the twins' squabbling and decided to go with Joey Simon instead.

"I can't believe she'd rather go with that weasel-faced nerd than you," Zak had commiserated.

"Unbelievable," Giancarlo agreed.

When he heard that Ned's future in-laws were coming for the holidays, the president of the Taos Chamber of Commerce, who was also the owner of the luxurious Kit Carson Taos Inn, arranged for the Karp family to stay in the presidential suite. The boys were looking forward to learning to snowboard at the Taos Ski Resort. But Karp planned to avoid the slopes, sit by the fire, read a good book, and maybe chase Marlene around a bit in the privacy of their suite. He and Marlene were also looking forward to long conversations and celebrating Christmas and Chanukah as a family, with the added pleasure of Vladimir and Ivgeny Karchovski for company.

As Karp walked away from the grave, his cell phone rang. He happened to look up as he pulled it out of his pocket and saw Alejandro and Carmina watching him from across the snow-covered ground. He'd been surprised to see them at the funeral. *"I just felt a closeness to him and wanted to pay my respects,"* she'd said. Now she buried her head in Alejandro's chest as Karp answered his phone.

"Yeah, Kenny, what's up?"

F. Lloyd Maplethorpe was just another number in the New York penal system as he shuffled along in a line with other prisoners making their way across the Bridge of Sighs, a raised walkway that connected the Tombs to the Criminal Courts Building. The bridge had been nicknamed for the millions of prisoners who had passed over and sighed at what was often their last glimpse for a while at the world beyond their cells.

Maplethorpe's line came to a stop to allow prisoners coming the other way to file out onto the bridge. Like maggots, dark thoughts crawled around in his brain as his cuffed hands jerked against the belly chain to which they were attached. The memory of alcoholic parents who'd fought constantly, and of when his mother left one cold winter night, how she'd pushed him away.

"Look, Mommy, I'm a cowboy."

"Get away from me, you little freak."

And a more recent memory, one with the face of Gail Perez pleading for her life.

"Stop it, what are you doing? I want to leave."

"No one leaves me, whore!"

"Put that gun away. Please don't!"

"Suck on this, bitch!"

Maplethorpe giggled as the two lines of men began to pass each other. Suddenly, a man from the opposite line attacked a prisoner six men back from Maplethorpe. As detention officers jumped in to break them up, other prisoners crowded around to watch.

Wanting to get as far as he could from the fray, Maplethorpe turned and tried to walk but found his way blocked by a large Hispanic man. The man looked down at him and said, "I have a message for you from the Inca Boyz."

Maplethorpe felt three hard blows to the right side of his belly. He looked down and saw a growing dark patch in his gray jumpsuit; something warm and wet was flowing down his leg. When he looked back up, the man was gone and a space had opened up around him.

He fell to the hard floor and lay there as men shouted. A pair of shiny black shoes and the pant leg of a guard's uniform entered his field of vision, which began to dim. *They're all leaving me,* he thought. *Nobody leaves me.* And then he was gone.

At the cemetery, Karp flipped his cell phone closed. He hesitated to look up. He didn't want to see Alejandro's eyes and reveal the truth about what Katz had just told him.

Still, he had to look. But Alejandro and Carmina were walking away as snow continued to fall.